SACRIFICIAL MAGIC

Stacia Kane was born in Illinois, raised in St. Louis MO, and lived in South Florida for a dozen years before moving to the UK with her British husband and two daughters. She is the author of the paranormal romance *Personal Demons*, and *The Downside Ghosts* is her first urban fantasy series.

Visit her authorized website at www.staciakane.net

Also by Stacia Kane

STACIA KANE

SACRIFICIAL MAGIC

Book Four of the Downside Ghosts

HARPER
Voyager

HarperVoyager
An imprint of HarperCollins*Publishers*
77–85 Fulham Palace Road,
Hammersmith, London W6 8JB

www.harpercollins.co.uk

This paperback edition 2012
1

First published in Great Britain by
HarperCollins*Publishers* 2012

A catalogue record for this book is
available from the British Library

ISBN: 978 0 00 743311 7

Printed and bound in Great Britain by
Clays Ltd, St Ives plc

MIX
Paper from
responsible sources
FSC **FSC™ C007454**
www.fsc.org

FSC™ is a non-profit international organisation established
to promote the responsible management of the world's forests.
Products carrying the FSC label are independently certified
to assure consumers that they come from forests that are managed
to meet the social, economic and ecological needs of present
and future generations, and other controlled sources.

Find out more about HarperCollins and the environment at
www.harpercollins.co.uk/green

To the real
Chelsea Mueller,
with thanks

Chapter One

Only the bravest fight the dead.
—Grand Elder Thomas, speech to graduating students, 2007

Had the roof over her head not been a broken mess, shredded insulation and pieces of tile dangling like the rotting innards of the living thing it had once been, she wouldn't be getting hit on the head with cold droplets of water at odd, annoying intervals.

That would have made her happier. Or at least not quite as unhappy. Nothing could have made her *happy* at that moment, when she was about to wander down a dark hall where a ghost lurked and hopefully manage to freeze it before it sliced off her head or stabbed her or whatever the hell else it planned to do. The odds of a ghost in this corpse of a building not having a weapon were—well, hell, there were no odds at all. Only the dumbest ghost on the planet wouldn't have found some sort of weapon in this ramshackle palace of destruction, where her boots sloshed through a good two inches of foul water, broken glass, metal shards, pulped books, and who the fuck knew what else.

"Think it's in there, Chess?" Riley Martin, a brand-new Debunker, pointed toward the mouth of the hallway ahead. In there the ceiling had apparently maintained its integrity; the hall was only shadows, a dark tunnel straight to the grave. Or rather the Crematorium, and the City of Eternity. None of which really sounded like a fun way to end her evening.

But neither did leaving the ghost here to kill other people, or telling the Church she'd decided to fuck off to the bar instead of doing her job. "Probably. No, don't turn your light on yet. Try not to if you can help it. Let's go stand right inside until our eyes adjust, okay?"

Riley nodded. Chess followed him, neither of them bothering to keep their movements quiet. If they could somehow attract the spirit, draw it out, that would be easier and safer. The last thing either of them wanted to do was to walk into some kind of ambush.

Fucking Lamaru. Fucking Arthur Maguinness-Beldarel shithead. If they hadn't played their stupid power games and set a bunch of ghosts free the month before, she wouldn't be out here doing something that technically wasn't her job but that every Church employee capable of doing it had to do at least one night a week when they weren't otherwise engaged or on a case.

Which Chess wasn't. Damn it.

They stopped in the shadows; the almost imperceptible breeze hadn't penetrated there at all, so the horrible ammoniac stench, full of mold and worse, assaulted her nose the second they entered the hall. Her eyes stung.

But more than that, a warm tingling sensation began crawling up her arms and across her chest as her magical tattoos reacted to the presence of a spirit. A ghost was definitely nearby. She looked at Riley. "Are you feeling it?"

"I— I don't know. My skin feels kind of funny." What little of his face she could make out didn't look happy.

"You get used to it."

A flash of light down the hall, so fast she only saw it out of the corner of her eye. But it had definitely been light, and it had definitely been the bluish light of a ghost.

Riley's breath caught. This was the time that, if she was a normal sort of person, she'd be able to say something reassuring and at the same time cool, the kind of thing that would make Riley feel brave but not patronized. And then they'd both sort of smile and head off down the hall to Banish that ghost.

But she was not that kind of person, and the last thing she had any idea how to do was reassure Riley and make him feel good about himself. Cliché was probably about the best she could do.

"You'll be fine," was the one she gave him, and to her surprise it seemed to work. "Come on."

Every step they took, every slow step through the soup of bacteria and rot sucking at her boots brought them closer to that faint death-glow. She'd mixed some graveyard dirt and asafetida earlier, stuck it in a bag in her pocket; now she reached inside and grabbed a small handful. Ready.

They moved a few steps in silence broken only by the occasional *plonk* of water dripping from the ceiling behind them. Something rattled. Chess spun around to look but saw nothing.

Ghosts weren't the only things that might hang out in abandoned buildings at night. They weren't in Downside, no, but they weren't exactly in the nicest area, either. This building, which had once housed offices of some kind and a warehouse, stood just a few streets into Cross Town, a whole city block of condemned cement with a ten-foot chain-link fence around it.

A chain-link fence with holes in it. She wondered how many neighborhood kids had made this their weekend hangout until two nights before, when one of them met a gruesome death just inside the front doors.

Another tiny glimpse of light.

"It is a ghost, right?" Riley whispered. "I mean, I feel

like there's a ghost here, but could that be something else?"

"It could be anything else. But it's probably a ghost, yeah."

The comforting weight of her knife sat in her pocket. Debunkers weren't supposed to be armed. Fuck that. She'd rather take her chances with Church discipline than with anyone or anything she might come across in a place like this.

She probably wouldn't need the knife anyway. Damn it, the kid's nervousness was making her twitch, and as much as she sympathized with him she really didn't need that at the moment. It had been a good two hours since she'd taken her pills, and while she still had time—she wasn't worried—places like this didn't help her keep calm. All that filth, all those germs, soaking into the bottoms of her jeans, brushing against her skin, her hair, invading her lungs. People caught diseases from places like this, especially after a rain.

Or they got their throats sliced open by ghosts armed with rusted shards of metal or whatever the fuck else. She edged her way down the hall, her back pressed against that gross excuse for a wall just because she couldn't really see well enough to walk down the center. The glow got stronger with every step. Her fist clenched around the dirt.

Another *plonk*. Another rattle. Something like a whisper, that could have been a voice or the sound of a makeshift blade leaving its sheath of soaked pulp or crumbled cement. The glow from a doorway another ten feet or so down the hall.

In its reflection, Riley's face looked even paler. The only thing keeping hers from looking the same— assuming it didn't, which she was just going to go ahead and assume—was the fact that she was still just high enough to be not quite as scared as she should be. And the fact that she was an absolute fucking expert at lying to herself.

But with every step closer to that glowing doorway, that ability drew just a tiny bit farther away from her.

Whatever. Wasn't like she could just turn around and run. So she took one last deep breath and spun around the doorframe with her arm ready to throw the dirt at the first dead thing that moved.

And found herself staring at three teenagers, who were obviously very alive, and who obviously thought they'd done something very clever, and who should have been thanking the gods who didn't exist that Riley was there too because if he hadn't been she would have been *very* tempted to beat the shit out of them with the nearest heavy object.

"What are you doing here?" Riley asked, but it was obvious from the stunned looks on their faces. Whoever they'd been expecting to walk through that door, it wasn't two Church employees.

One of them glanced at the other two, and cleared his throat when they didn't speak up. Fucking cowards. "We, uh, we thought you were some friends of ours."

Damn it, why were her tattoos still tingling, if a ghost wasn't in this room? This didn't feel right, not at all. She needed to get those little bastards out of there as quickly as possible. "You need to leave, okay? Time to go."

"We've been in here for like an hour," the kid replied. The flashlight he'd hidden under his dark-blue jacket still glowed, made him glow. That's where that bluish light had come from, she guessed, but nothing about these kids should have been setting off the alarms in her tattoos. Something else was around, waiting. "We haven't seen anything."

"Oh, right. That must mean nothing is here. This is

such a small building." She stepped sideways from the door; Riley, she was pleased to see, had already taken a step back into the hall. "Go on, get out of here."

"But we can help you," the first guy started.

Started, but didn't get to finish. Because before the last word hit the air, the ghosts—who'd clearly been waiting for just this sort of noisy fun—slipped through the walls. Four of them.

And thanks to the debris and shit on the floor, including what appeared to be a damned cigarette lighter sitting on top of a backpack tucked against one of the drier sections of wall, they were ghosts with weapons.

Chess started to throw her dirt, put as much power behind it as she could, but missed as the teenagers freaked out and started running. One of them knocked her against the wall; another bounced off her and tumbled back. The third . . . the third had a face half obscured by blood, presumably from the chunk of concrete the ghost beside it was readying for another swing.

The kids screamed. Riley yelled something. Chess fought the rising tides of fear and irritation and grabbed another handful of dirt.

Go for the concrete-wielding ghost first, because if it smacked that kid again there'd be a nice layer of brains added to the general slime and mess on the floor. She managed to freeze that one, glanced around to see Riley doing the same with another.

That left two. Two ghosts and three teenagers who really should have fucking known better crowded into that small space. There was barely room to move in there, much less do anything else, and two of the ghosts were still mobile.

Flames erupted in the corner of her vision. That backpack had apparently been filled with papers—of course it was, they were high school kids—and one of the ghosts had set the whole thing alight. It threw the flaming sack at her.

She ducked, and slipped in the vile sludge covering the floor. Eeew. Cold water—and who knew what else, probably blood and urine and vomit—soaked her jeans.

Worse, while she'd been distracted, the other moving ghost had found a length of pipe and used it to try to pop off one of the teenagers' heads like a ball off a tee.

At least that's what she assumed had happened. The flashlight in the one guy's jacket had gone out, or been smashed. The unearthly, hideous glow of the four spirits provided the room's only illumination, giving everything the unreal look of a nightmare.

Another garbled yell from Riley. She barely heard him over the sound of her breath in her ears and the shouts of the teens. One of them slipped just as she had. The ghost raised its pipe.

Graveyard dirt still in her fist. She threw it, threw her power, too. The ghost froze and dropped the pipe; it clattered on the kid's back, knocked him down into the floor sewage.

Riley had managed to freeze the fourth ghost. Not that it mattered that much. They wouldn't stay frozen forever; ten minutes tops. Riley and Chess needed to get passports on the things, and they needed to get a salt circle down as fast as possible—that would be fun, in the wet sludge.

And they needed to get those motherfucking kids out of there before the scent of their blood, the taste of their terror in the air, attracted more dead. Who knew how many there might be in the area? She and Riley had been told to expect two at the most, and here there were four. Like a deadly double-score bonus on the world's worst game show.

Well, hey, at least she got to win something, right?

"Riley, get them out of here." She managed to stand,

cringing at the feel of her nasty wet jeans touching her skin, and started digging through her bag for her salt. "I'll try to get a circle down."

"I don't think I can," Riley said.

"What?" Had some of the salt spilled when she fell? She'd thought she packed more.

"I don't think I can."

How could he not shoo a couple of injured kids out of the building? They were probably desperate to leave anyway. She looked up at him, annoyed, but what she saw changed the annoyance to the sort of oh-fuck-no feeling she was all too familiar with.

He stood against the wall, his face pale, his body still, staring at the ghosts with fear-wide eyes. "I don't think I can, Chess. I'm sorry, but I—look at what they did, look at those kids."

"Yeah, but Riley, they're frozen now, right? They can't move. Let's just—I'll lay the circle and you start the ritual, okay? Or you lay the salt. The sooner we start, the sooner we can get out of here, right?"

He shook his head. "I can't get close to them."

"You got close to them in training." In another minute or two the first ghost was going to shake off the power holding it—him—and start moving again. She needed to at least get him marked, and now. "Remember training? You can do this, you can."

"That was different. That was in class, with the Elders and everybody. I can't . . . I can't . . ."

Choice time. Keep trying to coddle Riley and hope to get him to de-stun, or ignore him and Banish four ghosts by herself, with her lone psychopomp, which would probably require two separate callings.

The teenagers—aside from the one with the broken nose, who huddled against the wall moaning—watched with interest. That, at least, wasn't a tough decision. "Get your friends and get the hell out of here. *Now!*"

"But, we want to watch you—"

Her sigh passed through every inch of her body before it finally came out. "Get. The hell. Out of here. Or I will make sure you all get a nice long afternoon in the stocks next Holy Day."

Finally, something she said produced some kind of result. They left, brushing past her as they walked out the door. They'd probably stand just outside listening, and the knowledge pissed her off, but it would take too much time to lecture them any more.

"Riley. Are you going to help me?"

He shook his head. Great.

Another bone-sucking sigh, and she popped the cap off her Ectoplasmarker. At least her psychopomp could be counted on to behave the way it was supposed to.

Chapter Two

Teach your children from a young age to be careful in their choice of friendships. Unwise acquaintances can have unforeseen consequences.
—*Families and Truth,* a Church pamphlet by Elder Barrett

And it had, thankfully, but the whole thing—including driving that pussy Riley back to the Church, filing her report, and giving Elder Griffin a quick rundown of Riley's freakout—took way longer than she'd thought, which pissed her off again. One of the benefits of taking a newbie along was supposed to be sticking them with the paperwork. Just her luck to get the one who couldn't handle it.

That wasn't fair of her, but she wasn't in the mood to be fair. Especially not when the effects of her pills were starting to wear off, leaving her ragged around the edges and even antsier than she would ordinarily be. She grabbed her pillbox from her bag, shook four Cepts into her palm, and downed them with a slug of water before heading for the shower. Rushing through her shower, really, and everything that came after.

That quick, tickly, lifting sensation in her stomach—that feeling that never got old, that feeling she would give her soul for and pretty much had—intensified when she finally got to Trickster's bar about an hour and a half after leaving the Church. Later than she wanted, but still she had made it, and given the whole quadruple-ghost fun, the result could have been a lot different.

Red assaulted her eyes when she stepped into the building, like walking into a bordello in hell—if hell existed, which it didn't. Or rather, no one else thought it did. For them the City of Eternity, where everyone's souls lived on after death, was a peaceful loving place, a quiet rest several hundred feet below the surface of the earth. Only Chess thought of it as hell, as punishment, cold and unrelenting and miserable. Life sucked, yes, but the City was worse.

Then again, sometimes life could be okay. Terrible stood in his usual spot against the back wall, talking to a couple of guys whose names she didn't remember. They all looked the same to her, to be honest, or maybe it was simply that she never really bothered to look at them. Their faces didn't interest her. Nothing they said interested her, not when she could be talking to Terrible instead.

Seeing him was like being hit in the chest. Like something exploding inside her, a quick ravenous fire that made her shiver. So bright and so hot it still amazed her that no one else seemed to notice it, that every eye in the place didn't turn to her while she went incandescent.

But they didn't—which was a good thing, since spontaneous human combustion would probably raise an eyebrow even there. No one seemed to notice at all. They were all too busy drinking dollar beers, listening to X's "Johnny Hit and Run Paulene," and talking or arguing or trying to pick each other up. Spiky heads, heads bald or slick with pomade, like bizarre flowers strewn in a humid half-dead meadow, swaying in a stale-beer breeze. None of them turned to her.

Excellent. She didn't want to be noticed. She never did, but especially not just then.

She shoved a couple of bucks at the bartender for her own beer and a tip and pushed her way through the field of oblivion-hunters until she reached him, stopping about a foot away, careful to not quite meet his eyes.

He did the same. "Hey, Chess. You right?"

She shrugged. Sipped her beer. "Right up. What time do they go on?"

"Ain't for certain. Ten minutes maybe, fifteen? Thought you was comin earlier."

"I was. My trainee lost it, I had to handle it all myself."

"Handle what?"

She gave him a quick rundown, her mind only half on her words. The rest was examining him, his black hair slicked back with pomade, the width of his shoulders, his height. His face, the face she'd once thought ugly with its crooked, repeatedly broken nose, its scars, its heavy brow and thick muttonchop sideburns. The kind of face people ran away from because the only place it looked like it belonged was behind a loaded weapon. Hell, it made his body look like a loaded weapon. Which it was. And that's all people saw.

People were shitbags, with their easy smiles and their cold eyes and brutal hearts. She knew that better than anyone. Knew, too, that the face she looked at wasn't ugly, that it was strong and it was Terrible's. That meant it was hers to look at as much as she wanted, and that made something she thought might be genuine happiness ride higher in her chest.

"Telling on getting shit done," he said, "Bump got an ask for you. Whyn't you come on out back, lemme give you the knowledge."

She shifted on her feet, glanced at the other guys still standing there, waiting to be included in the conversation. "Can't it wait?"

"Could, aye, but might as well give it you now."

The song ended; she nodded in the second or two of

silence before the next one started. "Yeah, okay then. But let's make it fast. I don't want to miss the band."

He shrugged. "Neither me. Longer you stand here, longer us take gettin back in, aye?"

She cocked an eyebrow at him, still careful not to look him in the eye, and headed down the hall that led to the bathrooms and the back door. Technically it wasn't a back door. Technically it was an emergency exit. But the alarm wires had been ripped from the wall years before, and even if they hadn't been it wouldn't have mattered. Fire trucks didn't respond to calls from Downside in general; one too many false alarms that ended in muggings and murders had stopped that particular service, and there was little worth saving there anyway.

Terrible pushed it open for her. She ducked under his arm and stepped into the alley, the soft squelch of still-wet dead leaves and garbage under her shoes reminding her for one unpleasant second of the earlier fun in the construction swamp. She couldn't decide which one smelled better, but neither was pleasant.

But while the building had been full of people and ghosts, the alley was empty. Not even any light from the tenement windows behind occupied the space; only the dull glow of the gibbous moon overhead showed her that no living beings—no human ones, at least—waited there.

Terrible obviously noticed that, too. The sound of the exit door slamming back into its frame hit her ears at the same time his body slammed her against the back wall, farther into the shadows where no one could see him kiss her long and hard.

Had she thought seeing him made her insides explode? She'd been wrong. *This* was an explosion. This was better than anything else; sometimes she thought it was even better than her pills. At his touch something inside her that had been tense and twisted and black finally relaxed. At his touch something inside her that was constantly terrified found a little security.

Security Chess hoped and hoped would last, despite the nagging voice in the back of her mind that insisted it couldn't, it wouldn't, she didn't deserve it, and she should just give up on the very idea.

Fuck that stupid voice. She wrapped her arms around his neck, pushed her hands down the collar of his shirt to feel his bare skin warm against hers. He was always warm. His palms left shivering trails of heat from her face to her throat, blazed up her thighs and ribcage, over her breasts.

Finally he pulled away enough to meet her eyes. That jolt of electricity, the one she'd been so careful not to feel inside the bar, hit her. Her cheeks tightened, her mouth curved into a grin she couldn't stop. "I was afraid I wasn't going to make it at all."

"Aye, me too. Glad you did. Feelin like I ain't seen you in weeks."

"It's been three days."

"Feels longer. We all clear now?"

She nodded. The past week had been the first time in her life she wished she wasn't what she was, wasn't a witch, didn't have extra power in her blood that meant anyone coming in intimate contact with it would be affected by it; wished the Binding effect of that contact wasn't part of the marriage ceremony and so meant a commitment she didn't think either of them was ready to make.

If she wasn't a witch it wouldn't matter. Marriages were bound by blood and magic combined, not one or the other, so they required the Church's assistance. But magic was *in* her blood, and that meant spending six days burning with frustration.

His eyebrows rose; his hands wandered with more

purpose. "You ain't really wanna stay here, aye? Whyn't we head on out now instead?"

"I thought you wanted to see the band," she teased.

"Changed my thought. Let's us go. Back my place, aye?" He was smiling, that smile she'd always loved, while his hands distracted her and his body warmed her through her clothes. Summer drew closer every day, and the temperatures reflected that, but it seemed like she was always cold when he wasn't around. "C'mon."

"My place is closer."

"Aye." He leaned in to bite her neck; she shivered. "But mine's got thicker walls, dig, an I plan on makin you scream a few times afore we get to sleeping."

It took her a minute to draw enough breath to speak, through a throat suddenly too tight for anything but a gasp. "I thought we decided we wanted to actually get out tonight, though."

"And done it. Now us can go back in."

"I don't know," she managed to say. It was becoming more difficult to talk, especially since he'd started sucking gently on her neck, making her dizzy.

"Think on this one, then, Chessiebomb. Nobody seein us right here, aye?" His nimble fingers popped the top button of her jeans. "Then we still out."

"No way." She giggled and swatted at his hands. "Last time I got a splinter—"

The sound of his phone ringing, a loud jangly sort of ring, cut her off.

"Ignore it," she suggested, but she knew he couldn't. They both knew he couldn't. Midnight was practically the start of a working day in Downside, yes, but she doubted anyone who'd be calling him at that hour would have good news.

She was right. Within seconds of answering the phone his face darkened; darkened and took on that look she'd only seen a few times before, that lowered-brow-narrowed-eyes look of absolute rage. The kind of look that would be the last thing the person who caused it would ever see. His fingers tightened on her waist.

"Aye," he said. "Get em—aye. On my way."

Her heart sank. Looked like they weren't going back to anybody's place, to anybody's bed. At least not for a long time.

His phone snapped shut. "Pipe room's burnin."

"What?"

He was already walking up the alley, back toward the street, holding her hand in an almost painful grip. "Fuckin Slobag, 'swhat. Pipe room up Sixtieth, green one. On fire."

She didn't want to say "What?" again, but she couldn't help it. She couldn't seem to get any other words into her head. A pipe room burning? All those people, even on a weeknight. All that Dream, waiting to be smoked, waiting to send those people into a soft golden fog. Gone. *"What?"*

He didn't answer. She had to trot to keep up as he pulled her along, dropping her hand just before they emerged from the alley. She almost wished he wouldn't, wished they hadn't decided to keep everything secret. Certainly she could have used more physical contact at that moment. With every step the awful picture in her mind grew clearer: burning bodies in a pit of flames, exploding glass, storerooms full of Dream knobs, their smoke wasted. She wrapped her arms around herself to still the shakes.

Terrible's car, a black 1969 BT Chevelle, waited for them in the circle of pale yellow cast by one of the few working streetlights. "Waited" being the operative word. To Chess, the car always seemed ready to leap from its resting place, ready to start mowing down pedestrians just because it could.

But it didn't. It stayed silent and still while Terrible

opened the door for her, closed it behind her, and got in on the driver's side.

On their way to the fire, to the— Wait. "The one on Sixtieth? Didn't you say nobody's in that one, Bump's doing something else with it?"

"Aye." The car plowed away from the curb in a squeal of rubber. "Were thinkin on makin it storing rooms, dig, gettin other shit done there too. Figured on setting a new room a block up."

"So no one died." The tightness in her chest eased a bit.

"Naw. Least not what Bernam say. Maybe one or two in there, ain't can say certain. But nobody ought, leastaways."

"Good."

He glanced at her, swinging the heavy car right, north on Sixtieth. "Aye, cepting, how Slobag knew nobody in there?"

"If the room's closed—"

"Ain't hardly nobody got that knowledge, though. Nobody been told. Just let em know tonight, first night it shut down."

"Maybe he didn't know. Maybe he didn't care who he killed."

Terrible snorted. "Still a fuck of a chance."

She sat for a few seconds watching his profile before finally resting a hesitant hand on his thigh, not sure it was welcome. Not sure if she should say anything. Anger still hovered around him, filled the car and tried to find a way into her body. She felt it like icy fingers sliding over her skin.

Not much she could do when he was in that kind of mood, at least not in the car on the way to check the wreckage.

Not to mention . . . he hadn't said anything. She didn't

know if he was thinking it, if he'd thought of it. But he probably had.

If Slobag had some sort of inside information about Bump's operations, he had to be getting that information from somewhere. And there she was, the one person Terrible knew for a fact had been in Slobag's pocket; or to put it more bluntly, Terrible knew she'd been in Slobag's son's bed, for months. Knew she still talked to him.

How long before she became a suspect?

Chapter Three

Because they had no unified rule, they had no peace. Peace in the world can only be found through the Church, just as peace of the soul can only be found through the Church.
—*A History of the Old Government, 1620–1800,*
from the Introduction by the Grand Elder

The last vestiges of the cheer she'd managed to find at Trickster's evaporated. It wouldn't be long. He'd think of it. He'd wonder.

And she couldn't blame him. What was she supposed to do, get all pissed and indignant because he didn't trust her? Why the hell should he trust her? He'd trusted her before and she'd paid him back by fucking his enemy. He'd be stupid not to wonder about her now.

That sucked. But it was true.

Their destination wasn't difficult to spot. The Chevelle growled up Sixtieth, chasing the orange glow of the flames ahead. A fire indeed. The building had simply disappeared. In its place a set of half walls created a bowl of fire, surrounded by curious onlookers standing too close even though it was spring. A few of them held out sticks with various animal parts on the ends; free fire shouldn't be wasted.

Chunks of cement littered the pavement, more and more of them as the Chevelle approached the scene, until finally Terrible had to park because there were too many of them to avoid. Broken glass sparkled under their feet.

Against the angry flames, Bump's profile stood like a

pimp-shaped inkspot, his hat brim ostentatiously wide, his cape moving in the breeze. Even at a distance she could see how pissed he was, just from the way he held his shoulders.

The closer they got the more obvious his anger got. He glowered at the fire, glowered at Terrible, glowered at her. "You finding they, Terrible, yay? Fuckin make they dead."

It wasn't much of a greeting, but she supposed it could be excused under the circumstances. Hell, even if they weren't standing in front of what was probably half a million dollars or so on fire, it could be excused; it would have to be excused. No matter who she slept with, no matter who she still couldn't believe she was lucky enough to sleep with, the fact was that at its base her relationship—such as it was—with Bump entailed the biggest power imbalance possible. She was a junkie. He was her dealer.

In other words, he got to say whatever he wanted to her, do whatever he wanted to her, treat her like less than nothing, and she got to take it without resistance if she wanted to keep getting her pills. Which she did.

He glanced at her now. "Ay, Ladybird. Ain't fuckin supposing you witchy skills fuckin find they done it."

She shook her head. "Sorry" sat on the tip of her tongue; she swallowed it. "Not the sort of thing I can do, no."

"But you got them fuckin snooping skills, yay? Do you findin out things, on you fuckin cases or what-the-fuck them is you doin."

Shit. Usually the problem she had with people knowing her job was that they thought she could wave her hand and make things disappear or whatever; now she had Bump obviously thinking she was some sort of Sherlock Holmes or something and could just pop in and find out who—of the hundreds, even thousands, of possible suspects—had spied, had set this up.

If she had a choice . . . well, she'd probably still say yes, because this affected Terrible's life, and that made it something she needed to do. But she didn't have a choice anyway.

"I'll try." She shifted her weight, hoped she didn't look as uncomfortable as she felt. "But really, I don't know any of the people involved, so I don't really see what I can do."

"Aw, nay, ain't you fuckin count youself short. Got them fuckin brains hidin in you head, yay? You use em for Bump. Use em for Terrible, yay? Got the thinkin you catch this one straightup fast, yay, fuckin straightup. What fuckin happening if them get Terrible afore you fuckin get the finding? Thinkin you ain't fuckin liking that."

No, she certainly wasn't fucking liking that. Did he not realize that was why she'd agreed to help out?

She'd known it was a mistake to tell Bump what was happening between them, what had happened. Being right usually felt a lot better than it did at that moment. This night was just going from shitty to shittier, wasn't it?

"I'll do whatever I can."

Bump gave her a slow, fluid sort of nod, the kind that told her he'd known all along that she would do it, and how he'd get her to do it. Damn him. He wasn't stupid; no one got to be lord of the streets west of Forty-third— almost all of Downside—without being smart, tough, and fast, and of course utterly ruthless. Bump was all of those, with a greasy layer of sleaze smoothed on top like rancid frosting covering a moldy cake.

He leaned back on his gold-tipped cane, crossed one ankle in its furry boot over the other. Somehow even standing on the street across from a burning building he managed to look as if he was lounging around his horrendous living room, perfectly relaxed, lord of his tacky pornography empire.

"Nobody in, aye?" Terrible asked. He stepped closer to her; just half a step, really, nothing anyone would notice, but she did, and it helped.

"Nay, ain't none people in there, when it fuckin go. Only our fuckin supplies, yay? Fuckin only half got out, fore it blowin the fuck up." He leered at her. "Too fuckin bad, yay? Got less smoke now, price goin up, Bump gots the guessing on. 'Course, could be you ain't gotta get the fuckin raise, you helping Bump out, get what we needing done up, yay?"

She didn't answer him. Would not. He didn't deserve an answer.

Instead, she watched the fire, watched Terrible's profile silhouetted by it and the way it cast changing golden light on everything. Downside looked almost wholesome with the flames dancing in their enormous makeshift firecan; the delicate changing light softened the sharp edges, bleached out the blood and needles and filth, the passed-out bodies and pockmarked walls and broken streets. The fire smoothed it all over, made it look almost normal.

Funny, she'd never noticed that before. But then she'd never paid this much attention to a fire before, at least not one she wasn't inside. Burning buildings were as common an occurrence in Downside as muggings and beatings; they no longer attracted much attention, save from scavengers looking for something to snatch from the wreckage.

After the fire finally died they'd swarm, looking for every scrap of metal, every piece of furniture, every smoke-damaged pipe. And of course, any lumps of Dream that might have survived. The thought pinched her heart. She could use a visit to the pipes just then. It would be nice to forget Bump's beady eyes, his dismissal of her, the confidence with which he used her.

But that was the price she paid, and she knew that. So she squared her shoulders. "You don't have any idea who could have told? Who knew the place would be empty?"

"Terrible an meself, coursen. An a some they others. They needed for fuckin clearin up, dig, movin fuckin furniture. Movin them fuckin Dream out, yay. They Bump gots fuckin trust for."

"So who could they have told?"

Bump shrugged. "Ain't shoulda given none the fuckin tell, yay? Bump's business Bump's own fuckin business. Ain't for nobody givin out."

"Well, clearly someone you trust isn't really someone you should be trusting," she said without thinking, and regretted it when Terrible glanced at her. He did it fast, just a quick cut of his eyes in her direction and then away again, but she saw it. She felt it.

It was starting already. She wished she could say she was surprised, wished she hadn't been waiting for it, expecting it the way she expected rain from black clouds overhead. Nothing in the world was permanent, especially not happiness.

She'd always known that. She just wished life would stop proving her right.

Chapter Four

That thought, and the feeling of doom it created in the pit of her stomach, burning a hole into her soul, stayed with her as she walked into Elder Griffin's office the next morning. Most cases were given out on Wednesdays, and she could use a new case. Sure, she'd made a good chunk of cash on her last one—and almost been killed a few times to earn it—but after a new car, couch, and some clothes, a weekend at the pipes and another in a hotel in Northside with Terrible, her bank account still looked good, but not as good as she would have liked.

Besides, seeing Elder Griffin made her feel better, as much as she could. And she could use it. She'd ended up home in her own bed, alone, because Terrible and Bump had things to talk about, things to do, people to beat down—so she assumed—and he didn't know how long it would be. She'd left her kitchen light on hoping he'd come over when he was done, but he hadn't. He'd texted around six to say he was just going back to his place because it was closer. She really, really wanted to believe that.

It grew so exhausting waiting for the other shoe to drop that she wondered if she wasn't trying to make it fall already. Sometimes, even, she almost wanted to tell him to just end it and get it over with. But she couldn't. Just the thought of it . . . No. She couldn't.

Elder Griffin stood up to answer her quiet knock, to greet her as she pushed the already unlatched door open and slipped inside. "Good morrow, Cesaria. How fare thee?"

She dipped into a quick, automatic curtsy. "Very well, sir. How are you?"

He smiled, his blue eyes kind. And happy. He looked . . . yeah, happy. Not happy like he usually looked. Extra happy. "Excellent, my dear. Come, sit down."

She followed him back to his broad, shiny wood desk, situated right in front of the window covered with sheers. Through that gauzy, barely-there fabric the side lawn of the building glowed with the green of early spring while the trees showed off their new leaves. Everything new. Everything except her. She hated spring.

She sat in the leather chair opposite, some of her tension—the tension even four Cepts hadn't managed to chase completely away—fading. It would never totally disappear, no matter what she did or what she took. But it faded a little. Just the sight of the room, the skulls on the shelves, the jars full of herbs and potions, the television mounted high on the wall behind her with the sound muted, felt safe. The way the building felt safe. The first place that had ever been a home to her, the place where her entire life changed.

"I'm pleased you've come," he said, folding his hands on the desk. "I have a few things to discuss with thee, if I may. My trust in you and your discretion is absolute, my dear, which is why I chose you."

Uh-oh. "Chose me for what?"

"A sensitive case. And . . . a sensitive issue I'd like to discuss with you."

Double uh-oh. "Elder Griffin, I really appreciate it, but I don't think I'm ready to be Bound again. It's—"

"Oh, no, no. I apologize. I surely did not mean to make you think 'twould be so strict. No, I merely wanted to discuss something with you of a more—a more personal nature."

Her brow furrowed. What personal issues could he possibly have to discuss with her? Sure, he liked her. She knew that. Knew she was probably his favorite out of all the Debunkers he worked with. Certainly he'd always been her staunchest supporter.

But they never talked about personal things. Not like that. "Is everything okay, sir?"

"Oh, of course, of course. All is perfectly well." He gave her a quick smile, then looked down at his hands, the smile fading. "I am certain you know the Grand Elder has decided to step down."

"Yes. I'm sorry to hear it." Actually she couldn't give a fuck. She'd never particularly liked the Grand Elder, always found him far too hale-n-hearty and far too little actual thinking-n-caring. But even she had to admit that his reasons for leaving were sad: the Lamaru—an anti-Church terrorist organization—had murdered his daughter and sent one of their own people in with the strongest glamour anyone had ever seen. Strong enough to make the girl look just like his child.

And she'd fooled him. Chess suspected that was what did it—not just that his daughter was dead, but that he'd spent a week with her killer, taking her to dinner, chatting with her in his office, touching her, hugging her. And he hadn't known.

Hell, if he hadn't stepped down, Chess would have put decent odds on him being asked to. Not that she knew for sure he hadn't been. But she kept that thought to herself.

"As am I. But his resignation leaves a spot open,

which in turn leaves more spots open. There might be one for me, methinks."

"You want a promotion?" A trickle of cold she hadn't expected slid down her back, into her heart.

She'd lose him. On top of everything else she felt slipping away, everything pouring through her fingers no matter how tightly she tried to grasp them, Elder Griffin wanted to leave her.

Intellectually she knew it wasn't about her. Intellect didn't slow her panicky pulse.

"I am considering it, yes. I do enjoy my position. I enjoy working with you—all of you." His eyes lingered on her face just long enough to make her feel the emphasis on "you." Just long enough to make her feel special. And just long enough for her to start mourning the loss of that feeling.

"But I would also enjoy moving up. Perhaps to a position with a larger responsibility. And a higher income."

She gave him the best smile she could; her face felt like plastic. "Sure, of course. That makes sense."

He sighed. "I hoped you would think so, I very much hoped. I do not know how much support there would be for me in that endeavor. Many Elders are interested, of course. But I do not think of putting my name in to be the Grand Elder. I would never presume. I simply thought, perhaps a Resident Elder, or a High Elder . . . perhaps a Master in the schools."

"I think you'd be great at any of those," she managed. He would be, too.

"Thank you. You see, Cesaria, part of the process is to give the Elder Triumvirate the name of at least one departmental employee over whom I have direct authority, so they can question you and make sure I am effective in my position, that I uphold the Truth and the laws— I am sure thou knowst the sort of thing of which I speak.

"Certainly of all the Debunkers your record is the

most impressive, but I would also hope . . . I believe that—I have always believed in your skills, Cesaria, and I believe you have always trusted me, and mine. Your recommendation would be . . . meaningful to me."

He cleared his throat. Before she could respond— before she could even think of a response—he continued. "You see, I have another person to concern myself with these days. I have . . . met someone, and we plan to be married."

"Wow, that's— Congratulations." This just kept getting better, didn't it. Well, no, that wasn't fair. She was happy for him, she honestly was. How the hell could she not be? She wasn't *that* selfish.

She'd just never thought of him as being a man with a personal life. A *romance* life. She couldn't picture him out on the town, having a few drinks and meeting people, or home with street clothes on instead of his Church suit and stockings, with sneakers or something instead of his formal buckle shoes. Elder Griffin Casual was just not an image she could conjure, no matter how hard she tried. She might as well try to picture him in a clown suit.

His blush showed faintly through the light everyday white powder he wore. "Perhaps you'll meet him? Methinks he would very much like that. Of course I would."

"Yeah. Um, of course, I'd love to."

"Excellent." His eyes caught hers again, held them. "I am glad you feel that way, Cesaria. I admit the thought of working in a different department, of not seeing all of you, is rather painful to me."

So don't go, she wanted to say, but she couldn't. Not when he looked so happy, so excited about what his future might hold. That was the way normal people felt when they were trying to move up, when they'd found someone to love who loved them back. Not the way

Chess felt, like she was trying to stem an arterial bleed with her fingertip.

But then, normal people didn't start their relationships by fucking people over, and normal people weren't convinced that at any moment the person they were with was going to realize how completely worthless they were and run away as fast as they could. Normal people didn't *deserve* to have the person they were with run away as fast as they could. So that might make a difference.

"My hope is that you will still feel free to visit me. Assuming I am promoted, which of course is not guaranteed."

"Of course you will be. And, um, yes, I'd love to visit you."

"Excellent," he said again. He cleared his throat, sat up straighter in his chair. Chess could practically see an imaginary dial on his back turning from PERSONAL to BUSINESS.

"I have a case for you." He opened a drawer in his desk, pulled out a slim manila folder. Yes! Awesome, she could totally use a case. A real one, not chasing air for Bump.

A case would leave her less time for that, but she'd still have enough. Wasn't like she was the only one looking for the rat, either. Bump and Terrible would probably suss him out within a day or so, and they could all move on. She hoped.

"The decision was made this morning to give the case to you, and I concur with that decision. You know I have always had the deepest belief in your abilities, and your discretion."

"I know." Yeah, he had. And now she'd get some different Elder, who didn't know her, didn't care. He'd probably hate her; he'd see through her to the filth inside, and he'd know everything, and he'd hate her for it.

"Good. This case was previously given to Aros Burnett." He looked up at her gasp, the tiny sound she tried not to utter but which slipped out before she could stop it. "Yes. Aros found it . . . particularly difficult, and he gave it up. Gave up his post in Triumph City as well, as I see you remember."

Her neck practically creaked as she nodded. Of course she remembered. The halls had barely stopped buzzing about it; it had only been eight or nine days.

"Aros was unable to give us a satisfactory solution. You'll see his notes in the file. They become rather— jumbled, near the end, I'm afraid. But we feel strongly that you will be able to bring us an answer. We have seen the Fact and Truth of your skill many times. I look forward to seeing your resolution."

"Thanks." The file hovered in his hand, just over his desk; she took it and started to open it. "Where is it?"

"Well. That is another reason you were chosen, in truth. 'Tis not too far from your residence. You are familiar with Mercy Lewis Second School? In Downside, on—"

"Twenty-second," she finished for him, barely noticing her own rudeness as she cut him off. Barely noticing anything except that address, staring at her from the original report in the file. Twenty-second and Foster.

Right in the middle of Slobag's territory.

Chapter Five

[
The dead invaded the schools, hiding in the shadows inside
to turn the students into soldiers of death themselves.
—*The Book of Truth*, Origins, Article 57
]

The parking lot outside Mercy Lewis Second School
hardly looked like a parking lot at all. If not for the four
or five battered cars parked at odd angles among the
gravel and weeds, Chess would have thought it was just
a vacant lot like any other.

Four or five battered cars, and one sleek shiny coupe,
gunmetal gray, the same color as Chess's new car, although hers wasn't as stylish. Or as expensive. As unob-
trusively as possible she wandered over to where the car
sat, pretending to be interested in the view on the other
side of the rusty, torn chain-link fence, and committed the license plate number to her temporary memory.
She'd write it down as soon as she got inside.

Despite everything else—and really, given its location
and the fire the night before, this case couldn't have been
worse for her—her spirits lifted as she headed up the
cracked concrete path to the large front doors. Working again. Something else to focus on, something she
could actually do something about, something with actual procedures to follow and clues she was trained to
understand. That felt good.

Mercy Lewis Second School—formerly an embassy

for some South Pacific country, she thought—was clearly a product of that phase of architecture that had believed bland was better. It just . . . sat there, dull and brown, staring out at the dirty streets and crumbling buildings with an air of resignation. Whatever had happened to it, whatever changed in the world, it would remain, glowering at them all, suffering the crowds of teenagers abusing it every day.

It could join the damn club. She made her way to the graffiti-covered entrance, pulled open a heavy door that gave a loud shriek of protest. Great. Well, good to know, anyway. When and if she came back at night with her Hand, this was not the entrance to use. She made a note—writing down the license number of the too-expensive car in the lot while she was at it so she could let it drop from her memory—and followed the faded signs to the office down the hall.

The itching started when she'd made it about halfway down. Not withdrawals—not even possible, she'd dosed up right before she got out of the car—but something worse, something that told her three Cepts wasn't going to be enough and made her wish she'd washed them down with a couple of shots, too.

Second school. Any school. She couldn't say the worst memories of her life came from schools—far, far from it—but the ones she did have weren't fucking good, that was for sure. The memories she had of when she'd gone; when she'd been *forced* to go. All of her foster parents made her, because if her attendance dropped they wouldn't get paid anymore, but none of them gave a shit if she actually learned anything, and her teachers hadn't either.

Those voices still echoed with every step she took. Just the air in the building, that particular chalkboard-antiseptic-dust-and-despair smell of school, reminded her where she was, made her remember how it felt and how much she'd hated it. The cold metal lockers lining the walls watched her, considered her, as her boots clicked on the polished concrete floors. She didn't care what they thought, or what anyone she was about to meet thought, but she still felt that invisible cloud of judgment that seemed to hover near the ceiling of every school, ready to descend on anyone unlucky enough to walk beneath it.

Whatever. She'd never gone to this school, and it wasn't her prison now. She was an adult, she was a fucking Churchwitch, and someone in this school was trying to scare people and scam some money out of the Church. So she would catch them. It was as simple as that, and she knew it and believed it as strongly and purely as she knew Facts were Truth.

Although . . . who would get the money, if the Church ended up paying a settlement? The Church owned the school, of course, and ran it, at least ostensibly. The Church wouldn't pay a settlement to itself. So . . . another note in her pad. *Who profits?*

The classroom doors she passed were closed. Through the narrow windows in each of them she caught glimpses of chalkboards and teaching Goodys standing before them, the occasional slice of backs bent over desks. Boredom and sadness seeped through the walls.

Finally she reached the end of the hall, another closed door. ADMINISTRATION was written on it in peeling black letters, with "Fuck the" scratched into the glass above it. Heh. Without knocking she pushed it open, got a good visual snapshot of three women standing around chatting before they stopped to look at her.

The one behind the desk, an enormous woman—she had to be close to six feet tall, and solidly built—with thin, frizzy brownish hair hanging limp from the top of her head, gave her the sort of disapproving smile Chess thought people with minor authority must practice in front of mirrors. Inexpertly applied red lipstick made her mouth look like a wound. "Can I help you, Miss?"

The other two stepped away from the desk, almost in a flanking motion. Had they been Downside kids and not school ladies Chess would have thought they were getting ready to jump her. Then again, maybe they were. Just not physically.

"I'm Cesaria Putnam." She didn't offer her hand. "From the Church. I've come about your haunting."

A moment of silence, as if none of them knew what to say. What the hell? They had to be aware of the procedure, they'd had another Debunker out there already. Then one of the women outside the desk, petite with red hair and a horrible baggy plaid dress, gave her a tentative smile. "Of course, yes. Please come in and sit down. Can we get you anything? Coffee, tea?"

"No thanks." Like she'd ever drink anything a subject gave her, at least in a situation like this. She did sit down, though, on the dingy couch that sank too far beneath her, so her ass hung lower than her knees. Getting out of that would be fun.

The third woman just looked at her, an odd sort of smile on her face. As if she knew something Chess didn't and was waiting for Chess to figure it out, or she was waiting for Chess to speak so she could belittle her. A smug look. Chess didn't like it, and she didn't think she liked the woman, although something in the way she stood, the tilt of her head and that smirk, reminded Chess for some absurd reason of Lex.

Yes, the woman was Asian, but that certainly wasn't it. She didn't know what it was. She'd seen other men who had some sort of Lex-like quality about them, but never a woman. Oh well. There was a first time for everything. Women could be smug bastards, too.

Then the woman shifted, and the resemblance disappeared, leaving just an attractive woman with straight, shiny dark hair in a casual knot at the base of her neck. Compared to the other two she looked especially gorgeous, in her black pencil skirt and loose white Oxford shirt with the sleeves rolled up.

"We weren't sure we would get someone else," she said, one graceful elbow propped on the counter. "Aros left so abruptly, and we haven't heard anything since."

Chess grabbed her notepad. "He told you he wouldn't be back?"

The women smiled at each other, as though Chess had just said something adorably naïve. Bitches.

"We got that impression," Horrible Plaid said, "when he screamed at us all that he was never stepping foot in this place again, broke a window, and ran off in the middle of the day."

Damn. What exactly had he encountered?

She didn't know Aros; he'd been a recent transfer. So she had no idea how tough he was, or what kinds of cases he'd handled wherever it was he'd come from. She made a quick note to ask Elder Griffin about it, and pushed the tiny flash of sadness out of her head.

"He never seemed comfortable here," Big Frizzy—the name plate on the edge of the desk read LAURIE BARR— said. Or rather, deigned to say. She still looked at Chess as if Chess was something rotten that had melded with the refrigerator shelf. Whatever.

"Do you have any idea why that might be?"

"Working with youth isn't for everyone."

"Yes, but, did he seem to have any particular troubles?" It really wasn't her business; it really wasn't part of the case. But she couldn't help being curious, and who knew. Maybe there was something there. If someone had been harassing him, that might be a good lead.

Or it might not. Anti-Church sentiment wasn't too widespread in Downside—most people there didn't give a fuck about the Church, either pro or con, save being suspicious or getting the hell out of her way when they saw her ink—but on this side of town, that changed. That could very well account for the Asian woman's smirks, too. People whose religion had centered on ancestor worship didn't tend to appreciate the government that told them they weren't allowed to do that anymore, not without paying a hefty fee and going through the Church itself.

This just kept getting better and better. As if it wasn't shitty enough working a case that would put her in more contact with the wrong side of town, and how that would look—she was not looking forward to Terrible's reaction when he found out where she'd be spending large chunks of her time—it was in an area where she'd be even more unwelcome than usual.

"He just seemed nervous," the Asian woman replied. None of them had volunteered their names yet. How polite of them. "He seemed to particularly dislike Vernal Sze and his friends. I believe he was afraid of them."

"Did he have reason to be?"

She shrugged. "I don't think so. They like to look tough, but they're really not. They just haven't been shown enough examples of proper behavior."

Laurie gave an eye-roll so elaborate Chess almost expected her head to topple off. Horrible Plaid noticed—or rather, noticed Chess noticing—and said, "Beulah is our Community Liaison. She's not a teacher."

Chess waited, but none of them explained what that meant or why it mattered. Okay. "And what does that entail?"

The Asian woman—Beulah—smiled that smug smile again, her eyes focused tight on Chess's face. What the fuck? Those Significant Looks were starting to creep her out. "I'm actually here on a volunteer basis several days a week, working with students and helping to foster a better relationship between the school administration and the community."

Chess had never heard of such a thing. She supposed it made sense, given that most school administrators were Church employees—most of them were Elders, actually—and that might be tense in this area. She couldn't see it being such a huge deal that they needed community outreach, but what the fuck did she know? Her pretty much sole experience with anyone on this side of town was Lex, and he didn't care about anything enough to get angry about it.

"Who handles that?" she asked. "I mean, is there a charity set up that you work for, or . . . ?"

"I'm paid out of school overflow funds," Beulah said. "Whatever the school manages to raise through donations or other outside sources, beyond their annual budget, gets put into a separate account. That's divided among several programs, and mine is the largest one. So technically I am a school employee, but I administer my own program."

Must be nice, Chess thought. Laurie seemed to agree; she watched Beulah with a look of such open hostility that Chess almost expected her to start hitting her.

Something to think about later, because hadn't Beulah just given her a very important piece of information? So any extra cash in the school coffers went to Beulah— well, Beulah and whoever ran these other programs. She'd need to see those records. Aros hadn't included those, or even mentioned them, in his file.

But for now . . . she stood up. "Maybe one of you could take me around? And if you could show me where entities have been seen, or anyone experienced anything unusual, that would be great."

Chapter Six

Death simply means the opportunity to live on in eternity. And that is Fact, which makes it Truth.

—*The Church and You,* a pamphlet by Elder Barrett

Horrible Plaid's name—surprise!—wasn't Horrible Plaid. It was Monica—Monica Freeman—and she was the secretary to Master Elder Conrad, the school's headmaster. She told Chess this with self-deprecating pride, as though she expected Chess to be impressed but wanted to seem like she didn't, as though she thought it was silly to expect it.

Which of course it was. Chess tried not to mistrust the woman—mistrust all of them—on general principles, but she couldn't help it. Even if she hadn't been there investigating a possible haunting she would have mistrusted them. They might claim to be Church—at least the Elders did, and the teaching Goodys did—but they weren't, not really. They didn't give a fuck about any of the students, about anyone but themselves.

"In here is the theater." Monica leaned against the thick door, its wood stained a horrible orangey color. Who the hell had picked that color? Almost every school she'd ever seen had it, and it looked awful in every one of them. "The first sighting was in here."

Now they were getting somewhere. "Okay. Can we go in? And you can tell me what happened?"

"No one's been in here since then."

Chess raised her eyebrows. Okay. Monica didn't seem to understand direct questions. "Can we go in, and you can tell me what happened?"

"I can unlock it." Beulah pulled a set of keys from somewhere. Where she had room to hide them in that skirt Chess had no idea, although she had to admit the skirt was gorgeous. Either "community outreach" paid awfully well, or Beulah had a sugar daddy. Or simply lived beyond her means. Checking her financials would probably be a good idea.

Monica moved out of Beulah's way a little too fast, as if she was afraid Beulah would mow her down. Funny. They'd all seemed perfectly friendly when Chess walked into the office.

The door opened with a creak right out of a horror film. For fuck's sake, was the school budget really so tight they couldn't afford a can of fucking WD-40? Chess had never seen a building so creaky in her life. Another note to make.

Through the open door she saw only darkness; the air breathing out at her smelled stale and felt cold against her skin. An air conditioner still hummed somewhere inside.

"No one's been in here? Why? And for how long?"

Monica answered, standing right behind her. "It's been about three weeks, I guess. Well, Aros might have been in here without telling us, but three weeks since any of us have been inside."

If Aros had entered the theater without even bothering to lubricate that hinge, then something was seriously wrong with the man. Oh well. "Because of the haunting?"

"Of course." Beulah pushed past both of them. For a moment her head and lower body disappeared, her white blouse just a faint glow in the gloom, before something slammed like metal against metal and the lights came on.

Not that it made much difference. Shadows still lurked along the walls and between the rows of seats, which rose stadium-style from the sunken stage at the front to a small booth in the center at the back. It wasn't a large room, really, but then it wasn't a large school. Maybe a hundred seats, a hundred and fifty? Drama didn't seem to be a popular activity at Mercy Lewis. It hadn't been at any school Chess had ever attended.

Beulah walked toward the stage, her slim figure appearing and reappearing between the rows like a lion through tall grass. "A few students were in here after school, about three weeks ago."

"Where they shouldn't have been," Monica muttered.

"They were hanging out on the stage," Beulah continued, ignoring Monica. Ignoring, too, Monica's next snide interruption, which was the word "Drinking."

Beulah glared at Monica. "Talking. According to Vernal."

"This is the person you mentioned before? The one Aros was afraid of?" Chess asked.

"Yes. Good memory. Anyway. They were in here *talking*, Vernal and three of his friends, when the ghost appeared. They said it came through the curtains there"—she pointed to the right—"and started moving along that wall. Then it apparently noticed them and came toward them, which is when they ran."

"Did it follow them out of the theater? What did it look like, did they say?"

"It didn't follow them," Monica said. "And they said it looked like Lucy McShane."

Chess looked at her blankly. It was always so cool when people expected her to know things there was no possible way she could know. Of course she was familiar with all of the famous ghosts and hauntings; the special team that still lived in the Tower of London, for example, just to contain them all. Edward DeWitt, the ghost of a murder victim who was so hell-bent on revenge it took them four weeks to track him down and Banish him. And of course the Fallow Creek Five, and the suburb they'd turned into a literal ghost town back in 2007.

But nowhere on that list, and it was quite an extensive list, did anyone named Lucy McShane appear.

Either Beulah saw her blank look and sympathized, or Beulah saw her blank look and patronized. Whatever her motive, at least she told the fucking story. "She was a suicide from just after this building was converted into a school, maybe 1999, 2000? According to the story, she was in the school play and fell in love with the director. He seduced her, and then when she got pregnant he dumped her. So she flung herself from the lighting platform up there."

Chess glanced up. Above her head a rack of lights hung in a gentle arc, white cone-shaped fixtures aimed at the stage. "She jumped off of that? How would she get up there?"

"There's a catwalk," Monica said. "Want to go up and look?"

Ugh, not really. Chess wasn't afraid of heights, but the thought of depending on the rickety-looking metal walkway she could just make out near the ceiling didn't appeal. But it was her job, so . . . "Yeah, sure."

The theater looked smaller from up there. So did Monica and Beulah, both of whom had used their skirts as an excuse for why they couldn't accompany her. Not that she cared. Without them watching her quite so closely she could be more thorough.

They couldn't watch her closely if they tried, in fact. When she stopped and looked down at them, the floor almost seemed to spin so far below. A girl had jumped from that catwalk, thrown herself from it. Had her body cracked open on the seats down there, on the edge of the orchestra pit? Had she died instantly? How must it have felt for her, watching the ground come at her, knowing that she'd done it, she'd really taken that final step and it was really over, it would end and she wouldn't have to feel it anymore, it—

Chess blinked. Her fingers convulsed on the railing. What the fuck had she been doing? Leaning over that rail, the empty space beyond. Not a good thing to do. She didn't want to die, not that day. Work. That's what she needed to be doing.

She'd grabbed a couple of small video cameras from the Church supply before she left, but she hadn't expected she'd get the chance to use them. She grabbed one from her bag and affixed it to the light strip, so the stage filled the tiny screen. Good. It would start recording if it detected movement.

The catwalk stretched from the tiny booth at the back of the room all the way to where she now crouched, where the light strip hung from the ceiling. From that point it branched off; another walkway ran perpendicular to it, from one side of the room to the other. On her left it dead-ended at the wall. On her right . . . On her right it seemed to turn left again at the wall and head back, behind the curtain. An odd arrangement.

"Hey, why does the catwalk cross the stage over there?"

"What?" From Chess's position Monica looked like a blob of shrieking plaid. Beulah had, of course, settled into one of the chairs, where she lounged as if she was about to light up a smoke and crack a beer. Or, not a beer; she didn't appear to be much of a beer type. A wine spritzer or something equally girly.

"The catwalk," Chess said. "Why does it cross the stage?"

"Oh. Not sure, really. I've heard that it's a leftover from when this was a meeting room for dignitaries, or maybe it was built because they needed it for effects for some play."

Weird. "Where does it go? Does it hit the back wall?"

"Um, I think so."

Wow, she was helpful. Sure, she was an administrative assistant, but it still seemed to Chess that Monica might have some knowledge of the oddities of the building.

It didn't matter. Whether or not she knew what it was for, she'd have to walk it all the way. So she arranged her bag more securely on her shoulder and started moving, her thighs aching from the peculiar squat-walk she was forced to use.

The catwalk rattled beneath her, which was just what she needed, but it seemed steady enough. After a moment or two she found a sort of rhythm, even, with one hand on the rail and the other on the floor to help keep her steady. In no time, it seemed, she reached the wall, made the left, and kept going.

Over the curtain, which seemed unusual, but then how else could it go, right? Right. Dust coated the top of the curtain so thick the color of the fabric was no longer visible; Chess only knew it was red because she'd seen it from the floor.

Backstage—well, it looked like every backstage Chess had ever seen. No, she'd never been in any school plays or anything—the very idea was ridiculous—but backstage areas were dark and private, the perfect place to skip class and get high or steal a few naked minutes with whomever she'd felt like giving the privilege to that particular day.

Tall canvas-and-wood flats rested against the wall; old desks and a battered sofa and other odds and ends of furniture braced them up. Boxes of costumes, boxes of props, general dust, and detritus littered the floor. Typical.

What wasn't typical was the faint odd smell in the air, and what her adjusting eyes could see was a stub of candle and a small tray on the floor.

Shit. She grabbed her camera and snapped a couple of pictures, but what she really needed to do was get down there and look. And she needed to do it without bringing either of the women with her; she didn't want her discovery of the candle and tray—if they were even related, and not just left behind by some kids who came here to make out or whatever—to be noted. Never let them know you've seen anything of interest: one of the first rules of Debunking. That went double for this case, when one Debunker had already been driven away and the potential suspects numbered in the hundreds.

So she'd have to go back to the booth where the catwalk started and get backstage alone. The alone part wasn't a worry; she had the authority to tell them both to fuck off back to their offices, and she had no problem doing so. But the turning around . . .

The catwalk narrowed here, and the way it jiggled beneath her as she started to turn made her muscles tense. Had it been that jiggly when she'd first climbed up? It hadn't seemed so but—maybe it was just the way she was moving.

So, move differently, right? Her feet shifted slowly, her thighs aching, as she gripped the rails harder. Boots were not the best choice for this sort of thing; she would have liked more mobility in her ankles. If she'd known tightrope walking—or, okay, catwalk walking—would be on the menu, she would have worn her Chucks.

But she hadn't, and she focused on keeping the damn metal from bouncing beneath her feet. It seemed to be bouncing no matter what, though, and no sooner had the thought registered in her mind than another one did, one much darker and more unpleasant, which was that it was bouncing like that because someone was bouncing it.

Even the dim light in the theater was enough to show her that no one stood at the far end, and she was close enough to the back wall—only fifteen feet or so away—to see that no one stood there, either. What the fuck?

She'd shoved her small flashlight into her pocket. Its beam made a pale spot over the plates and bolts connecting the walk to the back wall.

One of the bolts was moving. Someone at some point had scraped off some of the dull patina on the metal, leaving a naked streak that shone bright silver; it caught the flashlight's beam, spinning in ever-faster circles as she watched.

"Miss?" Monica's voice, tinged with panic, flew up from the floor below. "Are you okay? The walk is shaking."

Yeah, no shit. Not just the walk, and not just the bolt. Wires connected the catwalk posts to the ceiling. One wire released with a horrible *boing,* the kind of sound that was practically an announcement that she was about to die.

The bolt dropped. The catwalk jerked crazily to one side. And Chess, who'd been standing there staring like some kind of fucking moron, started running.

So what if she fell, right? She was going to fall anyway. Maybe running she had a shot at falling closer to the floor. Monica and Beulah's shouts and screams or meows or whatever the hell useless noises they made just barely hit her ears above the sound of her feet pounding on metal, slipping as the catwalk twisted.

She had just enough time to think that of all the ways she'd ever pictured herself dying, tumbling fifty feet and breaking her back on a fucking chair in a fucking school was one she'd never considered before, when the other side of the walk gave way with a snap that should have been a lot louder, a lot more dramatic, than it was.

She threw herself forward, already bracing herself for the fall. Already picturing the City, already terrified, already furious that she finally had something real in her life besides work and the Church, someone real, some reason for living that wouldn't disappear after she'd ingested it, when the metal beneath her slipped with an awful groaning sound. The far end broke the curtain rod, knocked it down with a crash, and hit the floor.

Her face hit the walkway itself, the metal grid biting her cheek and slamming her chest hard enough to make her momentarily picture her breasts—what there was of them—exploding like smashed balloons. The air in her chest left in a gasp, and she lay there, fifteen feet or so off the ground, on the catwalk that had now become a ramp.

So much for the impending death. Not that she was sorry or anything, but really. That was it?

Monica and Beulah milled around below; in her dizzied mind it appeared at first there were several of each of them before her vision snapped back into place. For a second she thought Beulah was smiling.

Chapter Seven

When questions arise, the Church is the first place to which one should turn. Always.
—*The Church and You,* a pamphlet by Elder Barrett

When she blinked the image disappeared, and there was Beulah, with a look of concern that was either real or a pretty good approximation. And as Chess's fingers loosened on the metal, she realized her own lips were curved into a grin. Now that she was alive, really alive and not likely to stop being so, adrenaline or relief or whatever the fuck it was coursed through her like the first rush of a line of crushed Nips. As if all at once she'd floated a couple of feet into the air and every nerve ending shivered in pure delight.

Except the ones in her chest and cheek, which still felt like someone had hit them with a hammer. But it didn't matter so much.

She hauled herself up from the catwalk—catramp?— and picked her careful way down, ending up on the stage, where her joy evaporated. Where quite a bit of her joy evaporated, anyway.

Yes. A candle, and a tray filled with ashes and the charred ends of herbs. Right there where Beulah and Monica could see them.

And they did. Both of them had hurried to meet her, and both of them saw the items at the same time. Neither of them mentioned them. Could be they knew the things existed. Could be they just didn't think they were important. Either way, they both now knew something had been there, that something had happened, and she still had the presence of mind to be irked about that.

Especially since that unscheduled journey to the floor hadn't been an accident. She'd watched the damn bolts come unscrewed, for fuck's sake.

She cut off their worried interrogations. "What's on the other side of that wall?"

They blinked. Monica started to stammer something, but Beulah cut her off. "Two floors. On the bottom is a science classroom, I believe. The top is the drama room." Then, anticipating the question before Chess could utter it, "The stairs are there, at the far end backstage."

Chess wasted a few seconds she really couldn't afford navigating the fabric and steel now littering the stage floor. Whoever had decided to send her on a ride wouldn't be in the classroom back there anymore, she knew that. But maybe there'd be someplace nearby they would hide. She flung open the stairway door, flew up the stairs in the darkness to the top, where another door barred her way. Another locked door. Fuck!

Beulah almost hit her from behind. "Is it locked?"

"No, I'm standing here for fun," Chess snapped, but Monica had already tottered up the stairs, jingling a bunch of keys in her hand. At least Chess assumed it was keys. It was either keys, a very jingly weapon, or, what the hell, a bizarre S&M toy, Chess didn't know and didn't really care as long as it could open that door. Picking the lock would waste even more time.

Not that it mattered. Anyone in that room already knew they were coming.

She'd dropped her flashlight but had a cheap plastic lighter in her pocket; she flicked it on, and Monica found the right key and opened the door.

Empty.

Well, not empty. It was a classroom. It had classroom things inside it. But it was empty of people, and people were what Chess needed. Her heart would have sunk if she hadn't been expecting to find no one there, and if she wasn't still buzzing from adrenaline.

The adrenaline gave her extra speed to cross the room. That door wasn't locked. It hit the wall with an echoing bang when she flung it open, when she flung herself into the hall and found nothing but silence. More emptiness. Of course.

Beulah might be a bitch—well, okay, to be fair, Chess couldn't yet say that with absolute certainty, just with a lot of it—but she wasn't stupid. She started opening doors down the right side of the hall, peering into each room, leaving them open so that Chess could look into them as she opened the doors on the left.

"Where else could they be? Where could they have gone?"

Beulah shook her head. "Anywhere. The stairs at either end lead to the science hall and the cafeteria. From there they could keep going into the rest of the school, or out to the parking lot. There's some sort of activity going on in the gym right now, they could slip in there and we'd never know it."

Fuck! It was about what she'd expected, but fuck! anyway.

The adrenaline started to fade, leaving her hands shaky and her chest and head aching. She could take care of that, but . . . Damn it. She pressed her palm to her forehead for a second, took a deep breath, and headed back into the drama classroom. The odds of her finding anything useful in there were slim to none, but she'd look anyway. At least she could make a note that she'd looked, that she'd—

How had they known?

She hadn't called before heading out, hadn't told anyone at Mercy Lewis to expect her. Nor, to her knowledge, had anyone at the Church, although of course she'd have to double-check that.

She hadn't spoken to anyone when she arrived except Beulah, Monica, and Laurie. Hadn't seen anyone, and although technically anyone could have seen *her* when she arrived, nothing about her—her scuffed and dusty boots, her black jeans, the faded blue polo she wore over a black long-sleeved T-shirt, or her black-dyed Bettie Page haircut—screamed "Church employee." Quite the opposite, in fact; she'd deliberately worn street clothes.

So how had anyone known who she was, to sabotage the catwalk while she was on it? How had someone not only known who she was, but made it into the drama room in time to start fucking with the bolts? Not to mention the wires.

That suggested a planned attack. More than one person.

Had it even been aimed at her at all? And if not, what the hell was the point?

She grabbed her notebook to scribble all of that down while it was fresh. Especially because now that the shakes and flashbacks were starting—she could feel the way her hand gripped the pen too tightly—and she knew she'd be alone for, oh, four or five hours at least, she planned to head home, crack her pillbox, and try to forget it all as quickly as possible.

Someone had tried to kill her. Or at least, given the way the catwalk had hit the stage fairly harmlessly, to scare the fuck out of her. Whether they knew she was Church or not, someone had just fucked with her in a particularly unpleasant way. A particularly unpleasant way that wasn't already on her list of things she took drugs to forget, anyway.

Unless, of course, someone had made some calls. Both Monica and Beulah had made bathroom or office stops before they headed to the theater, so either of them could have picked up the phone. Laurie could have done so after they left the administration area. Shit. Four hours on the case, two of them spent doing research at Church, and she'd already survived a murder attempt. That didn't bode well.

But it boded better than what she saw on the wall, what she found on the wrench lying on the floor nearby. Just two little smears of it. Two little smears of what she hoped was Vaseline or some similar substance, but which the knowledge she'd gotten from her Church training and the knowledge she'd gotten from a lifetime of having everything go wrong every damn time told her was something much worse.

Ectoplasm.

After all of that—after inspecting the roof above the theater and finding nothing at all, after finally getting out of the building she was already beginning to hate on more than just general principles—the last thing she expected to see was Lex, leaning against her new car, smoking a cigarette and grinning at her like she had dirty words written on her forehead and he wasn't about to tell her.

"Hey there, Tulip. Ain't usual seeing you this side of town, aye?"

"What are you doing here?" They shared one of those awkward kiss-hug-or-what moments, ending up kissing on the cheek. Odd, that. She and Lex had never really been cheek-kissers, but since they weren't kissing anywhere else these days she guessed it was the thing to do.

Especially since it gave her another few seconds to figure out how to react to his presence there in general. As far as she knew, Lex didn't spend a lot of time hanging around schools; why would he? He'd gone to one, she assumed, but his business didn't involve spending time there.

Or again, so she assumed. For all she knew one of the teachers had a habit bigger than hers, or part-timed as a hooker and Lex was there to pick her up for her shift. The possibilities were endless; someone could be a fence, someone could have—

Information. Uh-huh. "How did you know I was here?"

His grin widened. "Glad to see me?"

"Surprised." But she smiled. Of course she was glad to see him; she usually was. "Who told you I was here?"

"Why anybody gotta give me the knowledge? Could be I just makin a drive-by, see them new wheels you got and gave you the stop, me. That so hard to believe?"

"Kind of, yeah."

The spring sunlight hit the black spikes of his hair and made them shine; he tilted his head and the light spilled across his face. Sometimes she forgot how handsome he was. But then, it was easy to forget things like that when it didn't matter. "Been hearing crazy shit on this place. Figured on givin it a check-out, I did, then look who shows up. Got any knowledge what's on the happening in there?"

"Even if I did, I wouldn't tell you."

"Ain't expect any else. An what's the happening with that face you got? Ain't run into that Boil again, I don't think."

Shit. How bad did her face look? She hadn't checked.

But she smiled at the reference. "It was Doyle, and no, I just fell down."

"Must have fell hard."

"Yeah, I did."

His fingers stroked her sore cheekbone, light and delicate and warm. She fought the tiny shiver threatening to rise and risked a glance at his face, but his gaze focused on her cheek. "Ain't a safe place," he murmured.

Chess swallowed. The sun still shone, the air was still clear and fresh with the smell of blooming spring, but something had changed. No more breeze; everything seemed to stop and wait, including her own breath, damn it.

Nothing like that had happened the last couple of times she'd seen him. If it was even happening, which how would she know? The only men she'd ever spent more than a single night with were Lex and Terrible—one of whom she used to touch all the time because they were generally together for that purpose, and one of whom she'd almost never touched until they started touching in private. Maybe friends did that sort of thing all the time. He was only touching her cheek, inspecting it. It wasn't like he'd started playing with her breasts or something.

Then it ended, as suddenly as it had begun. A gust of wind chased away the stillness, chased away the expression on his face so thoroughly she wondered if she really had imagined it. "You leaving?"

She nodded.

"Got time, maybe you wanna come back mine for a few?"

No. The answer should have been no, especially after that weird little moment. But then . . . aside from one night of wandering around and the night in Graveyard Twenty-three she'd tried her damnedest to forget, she'd never really been outside his bedroom on this side of town. He might have some information that would help her. Hell, he might have some information about the explosion at Bump's pipe room, although she didn't much expect he'd be willing to say a word to her about that.

And she kind of missed hanging out with him, if she were honest with herself, which she generally tried not to be. And nothing had happened in that moment, and nothing would. She knew that. "What have you got in mind?"

"Nothing good, Tulip." Then, seeing her eyebrows rise, "But nothing you gotta worry youself on, neither. C'mon. Getting twitchy standin here, aye?"

Oh, what the hell. "You drive."

His room hadn't changed. The house hadn't changed. Only the looks given her by the various guards or enforcers or whoever they were had, from bland acceptance to subtle suspicion.

And she'd changed, it seemed. At least a bit. In the car, chatting, all had been well, but when the door closed behind her it occurred to her how long it had been since she'd been there. And what had happened the last time she'd been there. Happened several times and again in the morning, if memory served, which it did.

Another awkward moment when she started walking toward the bed, remembered, and turned back to the couch against the wall. Lex already sat there, lighting a cigarette, flipping a switch behind him so the Jam started playing in the background. King of his room-castle, just like one day he'd be king of his side of town.

"So what's up?" The question sounded lame even to her, but she couldn't think of anything else to say. The bed with its plain blue blanket and sheets loomed larger and larger in her vision.

"Church sent you that school? Thinkin on it being for real? The spooks, meaning."

"Too early to tell." Not totally a lie. She'd taken the wrench, scraped the ectoplasm off the walls and into inert plastic containers to be tested. It felt like ectoplasm, sure, but that could be faked. People had faked more conclusive evidence than that. Hell, for all she knew it was some new hair gel or something. Way too early to start convincing herself that that bonus wouldn't be hers.

"Aye? Some fucked-up place, that one. Ain't envy you wanderin around there at night."

"Who says I wander around there at night?"

He gave a short, low laugh. "Aw, c'mon now, Tulip. You forgetting, I been along with you on a few of them cases you get. Know the drill, I do."

"Maybe this one is different."

"Aye, and maybe it ain't. Only thing I gots to say is be careful. Ain't a good place, there."

"Why?" She pulled out her own cigarette, lit it up to give her something to look at. Not sure how much credence she should give anything he said to her, if she should even listen, but at the same time listening hard.

Yes, sure, things were different now. But while she couldn't say Lex had never lied to her—of course he'd lied to her, and she'd lied to him—she couldn't see any reason for him to lie to her about a case.

Then again, she'd never had a case on his side of town before.

"Just ain't safe. All kinds of shit in there, them teachers and all."

"How do you know this?"

He looked at her with his head tilted. "It matter?"

"No. I just wonder what you know."

"Ain't know much. Hear tell on they being the sort sell them mamas it get they what they wanting, if you dig."

She blew out smoke, shifted in her seat to face him better. "How does that make them different from anyone else?"

"Guessing it ain't. Only most people ain't big crowds like they. Could get up a fuck of a double-cross, be what they wanting to do."

Chess looked at him without speaking, let the minute

drag on long enough to have made anyone else feel uncomfortable. Lex didn't, of course, because Lex never did, but his expression went from bland to curious before she spoke. "Is that what you came there today to tell me?"

"Nay, just came by check the place out, I did."

"But why? And why today? And how did you know that was my car, you've only seen it like once before."

He smiled, slowly, letting the change of expression itself waste time. "Aye, somebody gave me the tell you was there. Came by give you a hello. That a bad thing?"

What wasn't he telling her?

And how much did it matter?

She pushed it all into the back of her head for later. He wouldn't tell her if she asked outright anyway. Better to move around the question and see if anything else came out later. "So I guess I'll be spending a bit more time on your side of town for a while."

Lex stood up and headed for the mini-fridge he kept against the wall. Without asking he pulled a couple of beers out, opened them both, and handed her one. "Guessing you will."

His amused expression told Chess he knew very well what she was getting to. Damn it. But not a surprise. "And I guess I won't be the only person who lives on my side but spends a lot of time here."

The couch sank when he plunked himself down, close enough that his hand almost touched her thigh. "Aw, Tulip, figured you come up with a better try-on than that. You know I ain't givin you that knowledge anyroad."

"Yeah, but I had to try."

"Aye, guessing you did." He laughed. "An now you done it."

"But someone did tell you. About the pipe room." That was pushing it, she knew. Sure, he'd laugh at her attempts to find out who the snitch was, which one of the people Bump and Terrible trusted had given Slobag the let's-go on blowing up that pipe room. But he wouldn't laugh for long. Especially now that her attempts to feel him out for information were no longer followed by her allowing him to perform his own feel-outs on her.

Sure enough, his eyes narrowed a little. "Maybe them did. Maybe not. Maybe somebody's luck were just running right up. Thought you and me weren't having the troubles on this one."

And there it was. The iron door slamming shut. "I'm not trying to cause trouble. I just— Never mind."

Yeah, she could probably tell him why it mattered so much to her. But so what? Their friendship seemed to be persisting despite the fact that they kept their clothes on when they met these days, but that didn't mean he'd actually go out of his way for her. Her life wasn't in danger, just her— Well, okay, it *was* her life, but not in a way Lex would care about.

Not to mention she just didn't want to. She didn't want to admit to him that she felt as though a big red pointing finger of suspicion hung right over her head, and that everyone saw it. Including the man Lex probably knew she'd essentially dumped him for.

It was her problem, and she'd deal with it.

Because dealing with personal problems was so fucking high on her list of skills.

Chapter Eight

You might not think it's true, but it is: Everyone is capable
of some magic, no matter how small. Everyone can change
things in their lives. Even you.
—*You Can Do This! A Guide for Beginners*,
by Molly Brooks-Cahill

Lex dropped her back at her car a couple of hours later,
pleasantly cotton-wrapped from the Pandas he'd given
her and ready—mostly—to head home. Lurid orange
streaked the sky above her, above the Mercy Lewis
school; the building stood against it like a lurking
shadow, cold and unreal.

Or maybe she was just high.

She didn't think so, though. Well, yes she did, of
course she was fucking high. But she suspected the sunset was really that gorgeous, the lone cherry tree beside
the school blooming pale pink, the evening chill about
to set in but not enough to make her cold in her long
sleeves.

Lex had just driven away when she heard the sound, a
clanging, crashing noise behind the building. At least she
assumed it came from behind the building; the spring air
still held enough crispness for sound to carry well.

Probably just a custodian emptying the trash. Or a
Cooking Goody doing who the hell knew what to the
food. Or a ball hitting a steel fencepost, or any number
of things.

But it could be someone who liked to play with metal,

maybe someone who hadn't known a person would be on the catwalk and decided to go ahead and bring it down? It wouldn't bring in a lot of cash, but not a lot was usually enough, especially in Downside. You could bolt things down to keep people from stealing them, sure, but they'd just get a wrench.

Her boots slid through the grass, jewel green at her feet, as she walked around to the side of the building. Not tiptoeing or sneaking, no. Just walking. With care.

Voices floated toward her, and another clank, clearer than the last one. Female voices, murmuring and giggling. It didn't reassure her. Women could be just as dangerous as men; life had certainly taught her that.

These weren't really women, of course. They were girls, high school girls. So focused on the small firedish before them, the pocket-sized floral book next to the little portable stang they'd set up—they were fucking serious—that they didn't even notice Chess rounding the corner of the building and approaching them until she was close enough to hear their individual breath. Her shadow fell over their altar, and they froze.

For a moment they all just stood there—or in the case of the girls, knelt there—looking at each other. What was Chess supposed to do? Magic certainly wasn't illegal. Quite the opposite. Citizens were encouraged to try their own spells, though the girls were being more elaborate than most. Even if magic had been illegal, Chess's authority only covered one or two very specific crimes.

And even if it didn't, the bottom line was that she just didn't care enough to bust them. Especially not when she was there to investigate their possible haunting; the last thing she wanted to do was set herself up as a horribly strict authority figure. She needed them to talk to her.

Finally one of the girls—her bleached-blond hair made a striking contrast with the warm, pale golden color of her skin—spoke, rather bitchily. "You needing something?"

Right. Her arms and chest were covered; the girls had no idea who she was. "Just wondering what you're doing. I was about to get in the car and heard you, and thought it might be related to the haunting I'm here to investigate."

"You the new Churchwitch, then? The new Debunker, or whatany you're called?"

Chess nodded. "Do you know anything about it, have you seen anything?"

Bleached Blonde shook her head, but her friend—oh, such a typical best-friend type, a little chunkier, a little less pretty, a little more desperate—spoke up. "I ain't— we ain't—but Vernal did."

"Vernal Sze?" The one Beulah had mentioned as a good kid who needed a place to hang out, and Monica had acted as if he was one step down from a serial killer.

The boy who'd apparently scared Aros.

The girl nodded. "Saw in the theater, and in the gym on the later."

In the gym, too? No one had mentioned a sighting anywhere but the theater.

Of course, it was possible they just hadn't gotten to it yet. Aros's notes were as bad as Elder Griffin had implied; after the first couple of pages they degenerated into scribbles and random words like "turtle" and "butler." Who knew what information he'd gathered?

And he'd disappeared, so she couldn't even ask him.

"Vernal told you about it?"

The girls glanced at each other, like they needed to check before they answered. Hmm.

"Aye," said the bleached blonde. The challenging look in her eye grew deeper, stronger; an edge crept into her voice. "Gave the story to lots of people. Sayin it's proof the Church ain't doing them job."

Chess would not rise to the bait. Wouldn't remind them that they were only alive because the Church was doing its fucking job, and that the general statistic in the District of one ghost-related death per 350,000 people was further proof. If the Church wasn't doing its job, no one would be alive.

But no, she wouldn't say it. Wouldn't, wouldn't, wouldn't. Instead she just shrugged, let the girl see the comment didn't bother her. "Do you believe him, that he saw a ghost?"

Another pause. Another glance. "Aye. Vernal ain't give us the lie, not on a tale like that."

"Besides, he ain't the only one seen it," her friend said. "Were like four of em in the theater, I recall, they all seen."

If that meant anything at all in cases like this one, Chess would be glad to have that information. As it was, who the fuck cared? So a bunch of kids lied for each other. Yeah, that was really trustworthy confirmation.

They could all be telling the truth, of course, but lying was probably the better guess. "Do you know who the others were? And maybe what they were doing in there that day?" The tray and candle behind the curtain crept back into her head. Had Vernal and his pals been doing something they shouldn't have been doing in that theater? Not just drinking, as Monica had said, but magic? Summonings, even?

It shouldn't have been possible. If they had the kind of power required to do that sort of magic, the Church would have found them, and they'd be in school there.

Unless, of course, being from this part of town they'd refused. But even then— She forced herself to stop the mind-wander she was about to take when Bleached Blonde opened her mouth again.

"One of them Goodys should be able give you the

knowledge. Ask them." Her mouth turned down. "In the middle of something, we are. An wanna get it finished up."

Little bitch. "Right. What are you doing? Memory spells for studying, or a glamour or something?"

No answer. She crouched down herself, bracing one hand on the ground so the weight of her bag didn't make her tip over. Maybe they were doing a love spell or something equally embarrassing, and that's why they didn't want to say?

No. Whatever they were doing, it was not a love spell. Wasn't any kind of spell anyone should have been doing outside of the Church, and she would have known that even if the girls hadn't leapt up, snatched the book, and run when she saw the Herb Paris berries in the firedish.

Half an hour later she closed her front door behind her with a sigh, grabbed a bottle of water from the fridge, and headed for the two-week-old couch. Pretty cool not to have to dodge broken springs when she sat down anymore, yeah, but . . . That old couch had been one of the first things she'd bought when she moved into the cozy one-bedroom apartment in what used to be a Catholic church. One of the first things she'd ever bought for herself that was permanent, bought for the first real home she'd ever had outside the Church.

But then, she probably could have held on to it longer if she and Terrible hadn't broken it one night, so she guessed that was a pretty fair trade-off. Blood rushed to her face at the memory; her face, and other places, too. He wouldn't be there for at least another hour or so.

Which she supposed was fine—or, not fine, it sucked. For the tenth or twentieth time she considered calling him, just to hear his voice. Just to see what he was doing, to know from the way he answered the phone that he was happy she'd called him, that he wished he was with her.

But he was probably busy, and she'd be interrupting him. He'd get annoyed, and she'd look clingy and pitiful. It would be like admitting she needed—no, not admitting, there was nothing to admit. It would be like *saying* that she needed to have him around, and if she did that he'd be turned off.

How the hell was it that she'd always been so comfortable with him before, but as soon as she'd realized she was in love with him, as soon as she told him that . . . she was nervous all the time?

So she didn't press the button on her phone. Instead she pulled out her case file to look over while she waited, and hoped that when he got to her place he wouldn't be in a worse mood over the fire at the pipe room. Had that really been only the night before? It felt like years had passed.

The girls had been playing with Herb Paris berries, and whatever that book was that they'd snatched from the base of the stang when they ran.

Could have been some sort of love spell, sure. Herb Paris berries were very versatile.

But Herb Paris berries were also used in casting the Evil Eye—among other things—and something told her the girls were a bit more the Evil-Eye-or-other-things type. Perhaps it was the fact that they took off so damn fast. Chess didn't buy the old "innocent people have no reason to run" line—the only people she'd ever known who did were naïve, stupid, or just plain assholes—but given the shit attitude both girls had given her before she discovered their little firedish crime, she suspected "innocent" wasn't a word that would describe either of them. It wasn't a word that described anyone in Downside, really. Certainly not her.

Anyway. The girls and their spell were probably irrelevant. The ectoplasm . . . that was relevant. The fact that Aros's notes degenerated further and further into utter nonsense with every page—alarmingly quickly, in fact— was relevant. Had the ghosts made him crazy? Someone doing some sort of illegal magic? Had the stress of the case snapped a spring in his brain? Or was he just fucking insane, and it had finally come out?

What would really help would be a conversation with Aros himself. Too bad nobody seemed to know where he was. He'd dumped off his notes with Elder Griffin, thrown his fit at the school, and took off.

If they hadn't cleared his cabin on the Church grounds, she might be able to get some information from looking through it. She also needed to know if he had family anywhere, people he might have gone to. That should be in his employee file, but perhaps she could find some of his friends or whatever through the cabin.

The sound of an engine rumble outside—the rumble of a particular engine—drew her from her ruminations. Her heart gave a cheerful leap; most of her other body parts started tingling in anticipation. And there was that damned grin again.

That was so dangerous. So fucking dangerous. And every day that went by only made it worse, only made it harder to face the inevitable moment when he'd decide he'd had enough of her, when he'd get tired of her body and realize who she really was. That he didn't trust her and never could.

Every day that went by was another day gone. Another day closer to the end.

She popped into the bathroom to give her hair a quick brush, give her face a bit more makeup. She had to tell him where her case was. She had to tell him she'd gone to Lex's place. Had to tell him right away. Not just because he might find out himself, but because that was the right thing to do, and she wanted to do that.

She threw three more Cepts into her mouth, washed them down just as his key turned in the lock and the wards on the door slipped open around him.

His presence filled the room. He seemed to vibrate when she looked at him. Of course that could be her nerves, but she didn't think so. It wasn't the first time it had happened.

She stood up, waited at the juncture of kitchen and living room, trying not to grin like a lovesick lunatic. Trying to be casual. Trying to gauge his mood. "Hi."

His eyes sparked hard behind their darkness as he crossed the kitchen floor, not speaking. Too much energy moved in the air around him, and when he stood right in front of her—close enough to make her tilt her head all the way back—and reached out to touch her cheek she knew what it was. He'd had quite a day, she guessed; violence clung to him like black oil.

Violence and a wild sort of intoxication from that violence, to be more exact. Whatever it was inside him that made him so good at his job, that made him the most feared man in Downside, had been riding him for hours from the looks of it, the feel of it. Now there was nothing else to hit, and that energy, that almost feral whatever-it-was . . . wanted to find some other satisfaction. Something or someone else to overpower, something or someone else to subdue, to defeat, to conquer.

She knew he'd never think of it that way. He probably wasn't even aware of it, that dark bloodthirsty excitement lurking behind his eyes, surrounding him like a vicious cloud. His work—fighting in general—didn't always do that to him, not that she'd seen, but when it did . . . Her heart jumped into her throat, then fell straight into her pelvis and stayed there, beating like a hummingbird's wings.

"The fuck happened here? It hurting?"

"Oh, I just . . ." She bit her lip. "I got a new case today. And no, it doesn't hurt, not really."

"Aye? Ain't so much?"

"Yeah, it looks worse than it—"

Definitely violence. Even if she hadn't known from his energy she would have known from the way he kissed her, the way he fisted her hair tight at the nape of her neck, the firm possessiveness of his hand on her bottom as he yanked her up against him, bending her backward. Rough and eager, and that energy infected her, too, made her grab his shoulders, wrap her leg around his.

She bit his tongue just hard enough to hurt a little, her head already swimming. His gasp shot a thrill straight down her spine, shot her temperature up what had to be ten degrees or so, because she was sweating even before he slid his hand between her legs from behind and it was her turn to gasp. A gasp more like—almost embarrassingly so—a whimper. A week was too long, way too fucking long. A minute was too long, it was all too long when he was every fast panting breath she took, when the smell and taste and sight of him blotted out everything else in the world.

She already had one leg around him; she wanted to add the other one, to climb up him and let him take her wherever he wanted to go.

Which he did anyway. Instead of her climbing him, he grabbed her hips, hustled her the few steps into the living room until the backs of her thighs hit the arm of the couch. She drifted over it slowly, controlled by his hold on her.

She needed to tell him. She needed to tell him right away. Now, as he helped her slide up on the couch so he could cover her with his body. Now, before they actually had sex. If they had sex before she told him, it would look as though she'd been trying to hide it from him, as though she'd known he'd be mad and wanted to make sure she got laid first. Or as though she hoped that after, he'd be in such a good mood and so relaxed that he wouldn't care. It would look like manipulation.

But fuck, she didn't want to say anything or do anything that might make him stop. Not when his mouth left hers to play with her neck, sucking on it, biting it. Not when she could feel the energy around him changing, that savagery that told her what he'd been doing all day turning into something else, something just as primitive. Just as dangerous. Her heart pounded and wouldn't stop; desperation choked her.

She ran her palms down his back over his shirt, then up under it over his chest to feel his skin, the thick hair and the scar on the left side, over his heart. The heart beating fast against her hand, almost as fast as hers. The heart that kept beating because of that scar, because of what she'd done.

What she was so glad she'd done. Because if she hadn't done it he wouldn't be alive, wouldn't be there with his hands hot on her back, unfastening her bra beneath her shirt, then sliding around to her front. She wouldn't be shivering harder and arching her back into those hands, reaching up to grab his hair thick between her fingers.

She swallowed; hard to do with her breath coming so fast in her throat. She couldn't get enough air to speak louder than a husky whisper, didn't want to break the kiss long enough to speak at all. But she had to. "I wanted to tell you something."

In response he lifted the hems of her two shirts together. It almost hurt to have to take her hands off him so he could tug both of them over her head, catching her open bra on the way; the second her arms were free she grabbed him again, feeling as if it had been months and not barely an eyeblink. And every fearful alarm in her brain warned her about that, and she couldn't ignore it but neither could she help it.

She wanted to continue, to tell him what she had to tell him; instead she put her mouth to much better purpose, tasting the skin of his throat salty from sweat. And while she was pulling the collar of his shirt out of her way she might as well start undoing the buttons, get it off him so he could take off the shirt underneath and she could feel his skin against hers. Her insides buzzed; she felt shivery and hot, like her body was made of liquid just about to hit the boiling point.

Or maybe just *at* the boiling point. His lips traveled over her collarbone and farther down to tease her nipples in turn, to pull them into the hot cavern of his mouth, and what had been a whimper turned into something even more than that. More like begging, and his eyes flashed satisfaction at her when he glanced up. Pleasure at his victory.

It felt like years instead of a week since he'd touched her, since she'd gotten to feel his weight on hers, his lips on her body; they'd decided it was better not to start anything they couldn't finish.

She had to tell him. Had to, but the words wouldn't come out. Not when every cell in her body threatened to explode, not when her body acted on its own accord from wanting his so fucking bad and she knew he felt the same.

She tilted her pelvis up so the ridge of his erection pressed against her through their jeans. Another gasp from him, a mumble of something that sounded like her name but the roaring of her blood made it too hard to hear.

Her thoughts were starting to disappear, to focus less on actual thinking and more on instincts and sensations, especially when he popped open the button of her jeans, tugged the zipper down, and hooked his fingers under the waistband and her panties. She lifted her hips so he could pull them down, his gaze fixed on her bare skin being revealed.

The words burbled up in her chest, flew out of her mouth before she could stop them. Before she even realized she'd thought them. "I hung out at Lex's place for a while today."

Pause. Long pause. His head dropped, hanging loose from his neck. His hands stopped moving and left her hips to sink into the couch cushion beneath them. Oh, shit. Even for her—and her track record of saying the right thing, or of not saying the wrong thing, was pretty abysmal—that was bad.

"Aye?"

Just one word, but that one word felt like a slap, so distant, so . . . so impersonal. Fuck. He wouldn't even look at her; he sat up, ran his hand through his hair and rubbed the back of his neck with his gaze focused somewhere off in the distance. She'd known he wouldn't react well—how could he—but she hadn't expected him to be this cold.

Kind of a stupid expectation on her part. Particularly stupid given the mood he was in when he arrived. Sure, Lex's name had come up before, but she hadn't spent "a while" with him since the battle in the City of Eternity. And Terrible had been there then. She certainly hadn't been to Lex's place since then; hadn't been there in a couple of months, actually, since two nights before Terrible caught them in the graveyard. Hadn't really been alone with Lex.

Not to mention that having this conversation—any conversation—was obviously not what he'd wanted to do. Especially not when that had been their first chance in a week, and he was so cranked up that her skin felt ready to burst into flame just from his energy touching it.

"My case, my new one? It's on Twenty-second, the

Mercy Lewis school." It felt rather odd to be discussing work while she lay on the couch naked from the waist up; part of her wanted to grab her shirts or at least her bra, but she didn't want to sit up, either. If she did that she'd be admitting this was going to be a real talk, a long serious one, not a quick interruption. "He showed up as I was about to leave. I guess someone told him a Churchwitch was there and he wanted to see who it was."

Actually, that wasn't right, was it? Someone had told him *she* was there, specifically. Or they'd described her and he knew who it was. Maybe she shouldn't mention that, since she wasn't certain.

"An lucky chances, turns up bein you."

"Terrible . . ."

His bowling shirt lay in a careless heap on the floor; the heavy muscles under his skin moved as he dug around in it—shit, she could watch that all day, even through her fear—pulled out two cigarettes, and handed her one.

When he flipped the wheel on his black steel lighter the six-inch flame cast shadows on the walls, on his face; sunset had darkened the room to thick dusk.

"I didn't ask for the case. They just— Elder Griffin gave it to me, because Aros, the guy who had it before me? He took off and Elder Griffin thought I'd be able to handle it."

Still no response; still he didn't look at her. Shit.

Her shirts draped over the arm of the couch where he'd tossed them. It took her a second to flip them right-side-out together; then she pulled them over her head, tugged them down, wished she'd kept her damn mouth shut.

"It's not like I can say no. This is— Damn it, I can't help where they assign me, and I shouldn't have to—"

"They tell you head back his place after?"

She folded her arms over her chest, hugging herself. "No. But I thought maybe I could find something out, maybe I could find out who the spy was, how they knew the pipe room was empty last night."

The silence changed a little, thawed a little. "Get anything?"

"No. He wouldn't talk to me about it. At all. I asked as soon as we got to his bedroom, but—" Fuck. Oh, motherfuck, what was wrong with her? She'd almost been off the hook, or at least on her way to it, why had she just said that? Why had she said it that way? Damn it. "Nothing happened or anything, okay? Nothing."

"Stayed a while, though, aye?"

"I just— I almost died on that fucking catwalk—I was on a catwalk and it fell, that's how I hurt my cheek— and I didn't feel like being alone and I knew you were busy, and he was there."

"Oh, I dig. Hey, maybe you give me the number that dame Cassie, the one wore your face? Next time aught happens to me, I give her a ring-up for company. No worries, aye?"

"He's my friend, okay, that's all, and you know that, you know I still talk to him. You said—"

The ringing of his phone interrupted her, loud and annoying. Terrible shot her a this-isn't-over glare and checked the phone, then answered it. More bad news, probably. The only people she could see him taking calls from at that moment were Bump or Felice, the mother of the daughter he had in another part of Triumph City. No one except Bump and Chess knew about Katie; Katie didn't know Terrible was her father. And Terrible wanted to keep it that way. "Aye."

His face paled, so pale her heart skipped a beat before the dull red flush of anger started creeping up his neck. "Aye, what— Aw, fuck. Aye."

What should she do? Should she touch him? Or would

that just piss him off more? What the hell did people in relationships do when shit happened, when the other person was probably regretting being there to begin with and wondering how they could have ever thought they actually wanted to be?

"Coming." He snapped the phone shut, scooping up his long-sleeved shirt in the same movement and slipping it on. Even in the midst of everything Chess felt a pang of regret seeing his chest disappear; not just because it was his or the fact that she liked to look at it so much— which she did—but because of what its disappearance meant. He had to leave, probably right away, while something awful and painful and all her fault crouched between them like a troll under a bridge.

And he might not be able to come back that night. Hell, he probably didn't *want* to come back. Ever. Fuck!

"Get yon shoes on." His voice was flat; he didn't look up from buttoning his bowling shirt.

"Why, what—"

"Found a body. Corner man, name of Bag-end Eddie. Just find him in the pipe room, half-burned, dig. Gotta get us up there."

The fact that he wanted her to go with him should have made her feel better. And she had to admit it did. But not much.

Why did he want her to go? Sure, maybe he wanted to finish their "discussion," but he was going to look at a dead body. Surely he didn't think she should be forced to look, too? Looking at dead bodies wasn't really very high on her Things-Chess-Enjoys list. And yeah, her total knowledge on what people in relationships did might fill a shot glass—especially if she used extra-large letters to write SEX—but something told her "looking at dead bodies" wasn't a generally accepted togetherness-type activity, either.

Of course, not going might look— Oh, fuck this.

"Um, I'm fine to go with you, but . . . do you actually want me along? I mean—"

The look on his face cut her off, grim and dark. "Bump say me bring you. Ain't just killed. Say got magic shit all around. Somethin you oughta see."

Chapter Nine

The presence of dark or evil magics should be reported immediately. That is your duty as a citizen.
— *The Church and You,* a pamphlet by Elder Barrett

They'd almost hit Brewster before Terrible finally spoke again, his voice a low rumble over Black Sabbath on the Chevelle's stereo. "Ain't like you seein him."

"I know." Relief flooded her chest; at least she hoped it was time for relief. "I'm sorry. I just, I thought maybe I could find something out. And yeah . . . I was kind of shaken up, and having some company sounded good."

"Aye, guessin it did." Something in his tone made her narrow her eyes, inspect him more closely. He almost sounded . . . upset? Pissed off? Hurt? She couldn't tell for sure, but he definitely didn't sound the way he usually did.

But then there was no reason for him to, was there.

They rode on in silence for another minute; he hooked a right onto Brewster. She'd been this far north before—of course she had, the day before during the fire—but only once or twice before that. If they kept going, eventually they'd be as far up as the Crematorium, and the Nightsedge Market she'd been to once with Lex.

Terrible made a sound next to her, a sort of half-laugh. "What a time you choose to gimme the tell."

More relief. "I didn't want you to think I was hiding it from you or being sneaky or something."

He didn't say more; she knew he probably had more to say, but she hoped when he did he'd say it like that, and they could talk about it, and she wouldn't have to sit there with terror icy in her stomach because she'd fucked everything up—again—and the minute hand on their relationship's internal clock had just moved a tick closer to midnight.

The very thought made her already chilled skin colder. She grabbed her pillbox and water bottle from her bag and took two more Cepts, hoping they might warm her; the three she'd taken when he'd arrived at her place had hit, but not enough. She needed to get rid of that cold inside her, that frozen-solid knot of fear and guilt she couldn't stand, didn't want to feel anymore. Five was pushing it, she knew, but what-the-fuck-ever.

If she was lucky they'd kick in before they got to the body, and that would be a help, too.

Why did she even bother thinking what might happen if she was lucky? The only luck she'd ever had in her life pulled the Chevelle up to the curb and threw it into neutral, and she seemed hell-bent on fucking that one up for herself no matter how hard she tried not to.

Spring had come and the cherry trees were in bloom, but the nights still held the remainder of the dead winter, and the breeze, heavy with the acrid resinous scent of charred wood, cut through her clothes when Terrible opened her door. Good thing she'd put her bra back on, but she should have remembered her cardigan.

Candlelight danced in a few windows, making the buildings look like carved Festival pumpkins with horrible greedy eyes. The burned-out shell of the pipe room, destroyed walls supporting nothing, sat there in silence. Dull moonlight revealed the ruin beautiful in its destruction, dignified in death. Chess shivered.

Bump's unmistakable drawl rode the wind to where she and Terrible stood. The anger in his voice didn't ease the feeling of foreboding.

Nor did the open doorways on the street, tall lean shadows like upended coffins. Anything could be hiding in those openings, in the alleys and empty spaces. She was glad of Terrible's arm touching hers as they walked, grateful for the knife she knew he could grab instantly if necessary.

Details on the dead building grew sharper as they neared it; well, of course they did. Black streaks above the glassless windows, the fire's signature. Ashes collected in the cracks on the street, covering the sidewalk, obscuring the garbage piled everywhere. A stray cat ran by, its fur smudged with soot. And over it all that silence, that odd intrusive silence. Even Bump's voice, droning on, didn't break that silence. It only made it clearer and stronger. His voice was an insult to it, one it paid no attention to. Bump would be gone soon. The silence would stay.

The horrible creosote smell of smoke burned her throat, stung her eyes. It was so heavy, thick enough to make her want to gag; it made her desperate for even the air around the Slaughterhouse.

But she couldn't head over there, couldn't go anywhere at all. Instead she stayed at Terrible's side, walked through the crumbling archway that had once been the door and into the short dark hallway just inside.

To her right was the bar, the chairs and charred countertop now exposed to the city-gray night sky, the floor littered with chunks of metal and wood, scraps of black-edged rags, broken glass. To her left a wall covered with curled strips of wallpaper, its pattern indistinguishable. How old was that building? How long had it stood there?

Once it had been someone's home. It had survived

Haunted Week. It had seen thousands of people over the years it had been a pipe room. And now . . . it was destroyed, thanks to Slobag and his attempts to wrest territory away from Bump. It had outlived its purpose. It had nothing more to give except perhaps a few bricks that would always bear the imprint of its death.

She reached out, touched the wall with one tentative finger. The building was finished, but at least it knew that. At least it didn't have to wait and wonder anymore. She blinked, fast. Her eyes were damp.

Terrible's hand found the back of her neck. Blindly she turned in his direction, hit his broad solid chest with her forehead and wrapped her arms around him tight. After a second, his closed around her, his lips brushed her hair.

It didn't last long. Ten seconds, maybe. Fifteen. But warmth spread through her anyway; it could have been her Cepts kicking in, but she didn't think so. And those seconds chased some of the darkness's threat away, so she could move again. She curled her index finger in his belt loop and let him lead her across the wreckage-strewn bar and through a short hallway.

Narrow streams of light spilled from cracks around a door at the far end of what had been the actual pipe room, lessening the gloom and revealing the blackened skeletons of couches and pipes. The place should have been hopping, filled with Dreamers . . . she could have lounged on one of the couches herself and left all of her worries behind for a few hours, and wouldn't that be the most welcome fucking thing in the world right about then.

Instead she stood in a charred death-pit about to go look at an apparently mutilated body, absorb the images of it. How typical.

Something else hid there beneath the horror of sudden, violent death. Magic. Not that she expected anything else; from what Terrible had said, she expected exactly that. But it wasn't . . . wasn't right. It felt muted, distorted somehow. Like a spell that had been done there years before and simply never cleaned up. It didn't feel *fresh,* and it didn't feel like horrible death, either. That could have been the fire, of course. It fucked with magic, changed the energy. So it probably was the fire. She just couldn't be certain.

Terrible reached for the door. She let go of him as he pushed it open—"pushed" being the operative word, since it was just a slab of wood blocking the room and not a proper door—revealing something that made her wish she'd kept holding on to him.

Bump, standing against the wall beside them, gave them an annoyed glance as they walked in. "Bout fuckin time you get your fuckin show-up on, yay? Ain't hardly fuckin dig standin round this shit." He gestured toward the scene with a wave of his hand. "Had me a fuckin meal before the fuckin call finding me, almost fuckin emptied up me again."

Agreeing with Bump wasn't something Chess usually did, but in this instance she agreed wholeheartedly. The sight before her was horrifying.

Bag-end Eddie had been . . . crucified. Not in a standing position, no, but it was clear from the position of his charred body. Crucified on the cement and burned, the flames turning his corpse into an overcooked bone-in roast spread-eagled on the floor like Leonardo da Vinci's Vitruvian Man. Unburned flesh remained on his face and chest, and in strips down the centers of his thighs.

His eyes, wide open in horror, stared at the dull moon above through the hole in the roof.

"What you think, Ladybird? I fuckin saying, looking fuckin witchy to me, yay? An ain't fuckin wrong, do I? Bump never gets the fuckin wrong side." He looked so smug, as if the gruesome death in front of them all only mattered as a way to prove his intellectual superiority again.

Or like it had taken a fucking genius to figure out there was magic involved in this. Like the body arranged carefully on the floor, the precise lines of soot she picked out around him, were some sort of obscure clue to the presence of witchcraft and not a blinking sign.

"No," she managed. She should have taken three more Cepts instead of two. She should have brought a kesh or a bottle of vodka. As it was she'd have to settle for water. "No, you're not wrong."

"Yay, see?" Bump turned to the man beside him, grinning. The man's face was a horrible shade of pasty, as if he'd covered himself in glue and let it dry. She'd always wondered what that would actually look like, if it would be shiny or not, but then she was just trying to distract herself so she wouldn't have to look again at what had once been a living person.

Distraction was good. So was delay. All those *D* words, especially "drugs." Another Cept would make six, and why the hell not. She dry-swallowed it while she was reaching into her bag to pull out a pair of latex gloves and her small camera. What else might she need . . . She'd have to get a closer look to know.

A closer look. Great.

Within reach of where she stood were Eddie's feet. Just beyond those were the soot lines she'd noticed, dark lines, as though the cement itself had burned.

But the energy still didn't feel right. Didn't feel like death magic. It definitely didn't feel like any kind of spell she was aware of that needed a murder to help power it. Those were— Wait.

"His—his face, the top of him, isn't burned." She looked at Bump and the pasty guy. "Why is part of him burned?"

Bump's lips went thin; he stared at her for a long moment. "Had we a fuckin fire, Ladybird, ain't you was fuckin here on the last—"

"Gee, really? No shit. Why is his body burned everywhere except on top? He's burned from the ground up but the—his skin is still there, on his nose and forehead and chin."

Pause, while they all inspected the body. Ha! Look at her, actually noticing something that might be important. She gritted her teeth to keep from smiling. Six was definitely her magic number after the food she'd forced herself to eat earlier. Or it could be the five finally really hitting, in which case six would be too much. She was too high to worry or care. If blessings were legal, that would certainly be one.

But smiling around a corpse wasn't really appropriate, so she managed not to, concentrating again on standing still so her high flowed through her body in a smooth arc, making her feel like she was floating. Like maybe things were okay after all. Like maybe *she* was okay after all.

"Fuckin metal all on, yay," Bump said. Oddly festive sparks of light danced on the walls as he waved his beringed hand; Chess followed it to see a slab of sheet metal—what had once been the reinforcement of the floor above, she guessed, which had probably been some kind of processing room—leaned up against the wall. "Got he on the fuckin find neathen it."

"It fell on his body?"

"Ain't it what I fuckin saying?"

Whatever.

So the metal slab had fallen on the body, and on the symbol. And had kept the parts touching it from burning. That had to mean something. What did that mean?

"The fire was here before the metal fell. I mean, look. Look at the lines. He was on fire, the fire started on the floor. Or, maybe it didn't start here, but the floor was on fire when the metal fell. So the spell, whatever it was—it was burning already. Was there carpet here?"

"Naw," Terrible said. "All cement."

She looked at the blackened lines again. "Maybe they used lighter fluid to mark the spell? So they could burn it after. Burn the spell, change it with fire."

Terrible shifted his feet. "So you ain't can get a feel on who done it, aye? Causen that energy's all fucked up from burnin."

"Right." Her smile refused to be denied for that one; she felt it spread across her face. That felt good. Almost as good as seeing color rise up his neck, the way it always did when he was right about something and she told him so.

With effort she kept herself from trotting up to him for a kiss. Not really the time. Not when things might have been smoothed over between them—mostly—but she still had to worry about who had told Slobag about this building being empty. Not when some pasty-faced guy she didn't know stood there, and no one was supposed to know about them.

And especially not when they stood in a roomful of horrible magic. It might not have felt like that at the moment, but somehow she didn't think the spell had been done to make bunnies happy or something.

That foreboding feeling, that certainty, grew stronger as she walked around the lines, trying to somehow separate what she saw on the floor like so much burned or rotten meat from the living, breathing person it had once been. Had been only the day before, apparently. And the pattern emerging didn't really make it any better.

She looked up; all three of the men were looking back at her expectantly. No pressure or anything.

"It's a *hafuran*," she said.

Bump raised one lazy eyebrow. "The fuck that one is?"

"It's a kind of sigil. Not a sigil, but a design, a symbol."

"Thinking I coulda fucking guessed on that me own fuckin self, yay?"

"This is a Church symbol, though. It's . . ." She stepped sideways, both to get farther away from the symbol and to get closer to Terrible, before she pulled the collar of her polo open, pulled aside the crewneck of the long-sleeve shirt she wore underneath it. "See? I have one here."

Actually she had two, but the one just below her collarbone was the easiest for her to show at that moment; the other was on her opposite biceps, and no way was she pulling her arm out of her sleeve and lifting the shirt up to show that one.

Terrible folded his arms and inspected it, just as if he hadn't seen it dozens of times already, hadn't kissed it, caressed it. Her skin warmed under his gaze and she started talking again to distract herself. "It builds energy, is all. We all get them because it—well, we get a lot of different sigils and runes and symbols and stuff, but this one is an all-around power enhancer. Whatever we do, the *hafuran* makes it stronger."

Bump leaned over to peer at her skin too closely; he smelled like kesh smoke and one of those sleazy colognes that promised to make men instantly attractive but actually just made them smell like men who wore sleazy cologne. She didn't say anything, didn't look at him. Whatever. He couldn't see down her shirt, he was just being a dick. Their relationship was imbalanced, yes, and Terrible worked for him, yes, but one thing she never had to worry about anymore was that Bump would try to touch her in places she didn't want him to touch. Which was pretty much anywhere.

"Be one of you fuckin Church things, then, this be the fuckin Church doing it? Killing Eddie, meaning."

"No!" Was he crazy? "No. It's a Church symbol, yeah, but it's not like we're the only ones who can use it. Anyone can use it, it could be anyone."

She couldn't tell whether he believed her, but he let it go. "So what they there givin the fuckin try an make stronger? Why them fuckin doin this to Eddie?"

She moved on to Pasty. He didn't know about Terrible, obviously, because he stood way too close.

"Ain't thinking I see good enough." He reached out to grab her. Pervert.

Pervert whose face grew even paler—she hadn't thought that was possible—when Terrible grabbed him by the hair and slammed him back against the wall.

A moment of silence; Pasty's momentary glare turned into acquiescence, a silent gaze at the floor. Fucking right it did. What was he going to do, fight Terrible? Ha. She would say she'd like to see that, but enough death lurked in that room as it was. Pride rose in her chest. Maybe that was mean of her, but she couldn't help it. She couldn't wait to get him home, either.

Bump cleared his throat, interrupting the images beginning to form in her head, part memory, part fantasy. He'd asked a question and she guessed he wanted her to answer, not stand there like a dope staring at Terrible.

So she blinked, hard. "I don't know. Obviously—well, not obviously, but I assume—they used the *hafuran* to make whatever ritual they did stronger. And whatever the ritual was probably wasn't a very good one. Most clean magic doesn't require a murder to get it going."

"Be one of them death curses?"

"I don't know. It doesn't really feel like anything at all, because of the fire. But I don't think so."

She started walking around it, inspecting the floor as

closely as she could. Maybe they'd done something to alter the *hafuran,* to make it do something else?

She pulled on a latex glove and grabbed a roughly rectangular chunk of wood. More lines might have been preserved under the burned body, and she sure as fuck wasn't going to touch it—or anything that came in contact with it—with her bare hands.

"Lemme get that one." Terrible was halfway across the room already; she barely managed to get her hand up in time, to get her mouth open. "No, don't. I . . . you don't know where the lines are, I don't want them to shift. I'm fine, I'm okay."

Bullshit. The lines wouldn't shift. What she didn't want was for him to step into something like that when she didn't know what the sigil on his chest might have done to him. The month before, he'd touched a toad fetish—a dead toad stuffed with horrible magic, used to create a glamour—and passed out; granted, it was a hideous fetish and had made even her physically ill, and granted, the energy she felt right now was weak and not particularly negative, but still.

He knew it, too. His eyes caught hers, and in them she saw the knowledge, the frustration of it. Oh well. Better frustrated and alive. As much as it sucked, keeping him alive and safe was worth any amount of gross.

And it was gross. In a couple of places the body didn't want to move; it'd . . . melted, sort of, into the cement, and when those parts finally did shift, it was with a horrible squelching sound that turned her stomach.

But she saw enough to convince her their murderous friend probably hadn't added any extra runes or anything to the *hafuran*. It was still a possibility, of course, but she didn't think it was the case.

Trying to figure out what the hell they'd been trying to do without feeling anything from it was like being half-blind; missing some of the information she usually got as a matter of course. It made her feel awkward, unbalanced, even under her still-damn-good high. Hell, that high was the only thing that allowed her to even move the body without being sick; she could retreat into it, force herself not to really see what she was doing, not to really think about it.

And to photograph it. Through the lens she noticed a few more things, still visible despite the char: *hafuran*s carved into the skin of his hand and a piece of his chest. *Hafuran*s scattered around, more of them in darker burn-lines on the cement beneath the body.

Well, maybe "scattered around" wasn't exactly right. "Carefully placed" described it better. "Completely fucking disgusting" described it best of all, but that didn't really give her any clues, except that the person who had done this was probably, well, completely fucking disgusting.

But then, anyone was capable of any manner of atrocities if they wanted something bad enough. People could justify anything to themselves if they wanted it bad enough. No one was immune to that.

Not even her. Maybe especially not her.

So what did her new fucking disgusting friend want? And wasn't she just thrilled that she got to try to figure it out?

"Gots us an even fuckin bigger bad needs fuckin chattering on," Bump said. He lit a cigarette slowly, waiting until they were all giving him their full attention before continuing to speak. "Ain't come on this by fuckin accidentals, yay? Gots me a fuckin tip on it, got the knowledge fuckin gave to us."

Terrible waited. Pasty waited. Chess couldn't. She couldn't because she thought she knew what he was going to say, what he had to be going to say; she was sure the others did, too, but she didn't think it made them feel as sick as it did her. "Who gave it to you?"

He raised his eyebrows. "Crankshot fuckin gave it on the earlier. Hear Slobag fuckin givin the chatter on he fuckin witch him find heself. How's that fuckin sound, Ladybird? Slobag gone and gotten heself a witch."

Chapter Ten

The hordes of ethereal killers were terrifying and unstoppable, and the citizenry quailed at their approach.
—*The Book of Truth,* Origins, Article 39

She'd hoped that when she woke up Terrible would be in bed next to her. She'd slept so fucking hard she probably wouldn't have noticed if he'd come in and started jumping up and down on the bed, and he'd sneaked in to surprise her before, so the hope was there. But no.

She couldn't think about that. Not when she got up, not when she checked her phone and found the text he sent around four—not even that fucking late—saying he was staying at Bump's. Which wasn't that damn far from hers. Why would he want to sleep in that museum of gynecological art when he could sleep with her?

Slobag had a witch. Slobag had someone doing magic for him. Slobag knew about things Terrible had told Chess, and now Slobag's witch was doing rituals inside buildings Terrible told her were empty during a time she'd been off working and had been late to meet Terrible, and she knew he'd put that together in his head just as fast as she had, maybe faster.

And he knew she'd been hanging out with Lex the day before. Slobag's son Lex.

And he hadn't come home with her, hadn't come in to sleep with her.

Another thing she didn't want to think about; way too many reasons for that particular decision flew into her head.

What she needed to think about was work. What she needed to think about was finding Vernal Sze and his friends and getting them to talk to her. No, she didn't need to *think* about it, she needed to *do* it. Right away.

She left her new car in the gravel-strewn lot at the side of the building and started for the front doors of the Mercy Lewis school.

But today the walkway wasn't empty. Students— she assumed they were students, they carried books— stood in straggly clumps outside, talking or smoking furtive cigarettes, listening to the Circle Jerks. Their eyes stripped her bare as she walked past; their conversations died when she got close enough to hear their words. It wasn't just paranoia from the couple of Nips she'd popped to help her wake up after sleeping so hard, either. Their suspicion and aggression felt like pebbles against her skin, stinging where they hit.

The front door opened with the expected screech, though not as loud against the music playing as it had been in the previous afternoon's silence. For a second she almost missed that silence. No one had been staring at her then.

Down the hall past the empty classrooms—apparently Mercy Lewis had a late lunch period, since it was just past one—to the office, where she was greeted by . . . a whole fucking crowd of people.

Frizzy—Laurie—was there, as were Monica and, smirking in the back in a gorgeous charcoal-gray suit, Beulah. She was the only one smiling. The others just glared—at each other, at the walls, at the various doors to small offices within the main Administration area, and especially at Chess.

"Here's Miss Putnam now," Beulah said. She unfolded her arms and straightened from her elegant lean. "I'm sure she'll be happy to answer your questions."

Bitch. She'd barely finished the last word before they all started talking at once. Because it was totally easy for her to make out individual comments from that, right? How stupid were these people?

Asking that question wouldn't win Chess any friends. And the worst part was that she actually needed them to be—well, not friends, but at least sort of friendly, because there were too damn many of them and she had nothing to go on in the case.

So she stood against the door, waiting for the inevitable moment when someone would finally drown the others out.

The drowner emerged rather more quickly than she would have expected: a man, not tall but solid, with thinning hair and a broad face. "When is the Church going to do something about this? Students are afraid to come to school."

"It's been three weeks," a woman—heavy, officious, sneering—interrupted. "If you people actually cared about us, you'd have done something by now."

Another voice, she didn't see whose. "The Church doesn't care. They've never cared."

"They care about our money," said another, and as if that were some sort of switch, the yelling started again.

But they weren't yelling at each other. They were yelling at her, looking right at her with their eyes narrowed and their faces reddening. She pressed herself against the door and shifted her weight, getting ready to duck from the angry voices and their condemnation, to brace herself for the fists and use her own, when she realized what she was doing. Getting freaked out? By these people? Who the fuck were they, anyway? A bunch of officious assholes who thought she owed them something. Fuck that, and fuck them.

So she straightened her back, raised her eyebrows, and just looked at them. Waiting. Sure enough, the shouts turned into speech, into grumbles, and finally into the embarrassed silence of someone who's just vented their rage and discovered that the subject of that rage doesn't give a shit.

Which she didn't. Well, she did, of course she did, but not about them. Or their self-righteous desire to play victims.

She gave them another minute in the silence. "Who are you all, again?"

Balding-and-Stocky glowered at her. "We're concerned parties."

"And what is your concern? Do you work here? You have kids here? What?"

The small crowd was suddenly full of shifty eyes. Uh-huh. "I'm Wen Li. I'm chairman of the Student Association."

"What is that?"

"We help mediate between students in trouble and the school administration."

A woman—helmet hair, glasses—piped up, "I'm co-chair. Martha Li."

Yes. They looked perfect for each other.

The introduction game made its circle around the room; every single damn one of them was chair or head of some committee or project or something. Which meant, if her memory served and what she'd learned the day before was correct, that every single damn one of them stood to bank some cash if the haunting turned out to be real. Which made them and their anger about as believable and sincere as a declaration of pure and faithful love from Bump.

After they'd finished she gave them another minute of silence. "And have any of you actually seen or experienced anything here?"

She didn't expect anyone to speak. She was right. No one did.

"Fine. If anyone has information that might help me, let me know. I really am here to help, and believe me, I want this situation settled just as much as you do. Okay? But if you'll excuse me, I do have some work to do today."

She pushed herself through the crowd—well, not pushed, they stepped out of her way—and handed Laurie the list she'd made earlier. "I need to speak to these students individually, and I need an empty room to do it in."

"Those students have a right to have an adult with them while they're being questioned," Wen said.

She wanted to roll her eyes, but refrained. "No, actually. They don't."

"They're—"

"They're not suspected of any crime, I'm not the Squad, and they're over fifteen."

Laurie scanned the list. "Room 122 will be empty in forty-five minutes. You can use that one. It's down the hall, at the other end of the building."

Damn, who would have thought Laurie—who still looked just as sour and disapproving as she had the day before—would be helpful? But then, with a roomful of people, none of whom she appeared to like, why wouldn't she be? "Thank you."

Beulah still watched her. Well, good. She could quit smirking and do something for Chess, since she obviously had nothing else to do. And since she had keys. And since the crowd apparently looked to her, for whatever the hell reason. "Beulah, will you come with me, please?"

Chapter Eleven

The wreckage of the catwalk still stretched across the theater, a dead steel monster staring at her when she stepped into the room. Beulah brushed past her to hit the lights. Brighter this time. Interesting. And worth mentioning. "There are overheads?"

"Yes, why?" Beulah did innocent very well. "Oh. Sorry, I just didn't think to turn them on yesterday."

"Uh-huh."

Beulah followed her farther into the room. "They're farther along on the— You can't think I deliberately left it dark in here."

"Can't I?" Hell, why not just say it outright? Wasn't like Beulah thought they were becoming friends or something. Wasn't like Chess cared if she thought that, either. The only reason Beulah was there was to open the door and turn on the lights, and to get her out of the office.

"You can believe anything you want to believe. That doesn't make it true."

"Wow, you're so wise." Chess walked down the aisle, ducking under the catwalk, toward the stage. Checking the camera she'd tied to the catwalk the previous day would be useless; all it could have filmed was a small section of floor, and since it was motion-activated she seriously doubted it would have caught anything.

But there was plenty of work she could still do in the theater.

"Are you trying to be unpleasant, or are you just like this all the time?"

Chess didn't even glance back. "But gee, you've been so nice to me."

Beulah muttered something; Chess didn't hear it well enough to know if it was in English or Cantonese, and she didn't care. All she cared about was searching that backstage area. Alone. She'd wanted Beulah to let her in, wondered if she would say anything about the others; since she hadn't, and since the theater was open, she'd served her purpose. "You can go now."

"Oh, am I being dismissed?"

"Do you plan to keep sniping at me? It's not my fault you have an issue with the Church."

"Who says it's got anything to do with the Church?" The amusement in Beulah's voice made Chess turn around. "Maybe I just don't like you personally."

"I guess I'll have to live with that pain," Chess replied, turning back to the stage. It wasn't until the sound of the door closing echoed in the empty room that she realized Beulah had left. And that she herself was smiling. Weird. But oh well.

A set of short black-painted steps led from the floor at the bottom of the rows of seats up to the stage; off to the left a small orchestra pit hid quiet and empty. Chess ignored that for the moment.

Dust hit her nose when she walked across the curtain now crumpled on the stage, sending her into a brief sneezing fit. Ugh. And she couldn't even have a cigarette to settle it down; the staff at— Wait a minute. Yes, she could. She could do anything she wanted to. What were they going to do, fire her?

And while she was at it she could grab another couple of Cepts from her pillbox.

The overheads revealed a floor covered in dusty footprints; the faint scent of kesh smoke hung in the air, but whether that was recent or from the curtains or, hell, from her cardigan, she had no idea.

She walked around some boxes and a stack of wooden platforms of varying heights, looking for something, anything. Any evidence of ritual magic.

The odds of her finding any were about as good as her odds of getting Terrible and Lex to have a pajama party together. If she'd been able to look the day before . . . But she hadn't, and that left them plenty of time to clean up. For all she knew, the minute she'd left the office they'd had an alert raised.

Sometimes, for just a second, it bothered her to be so suspicious of everyone. Then she remembered she was dealing with people, and that people were capable of every sick fucking thing she'd ever experienced or imagined and a whole lot of other shit that even she hadn't, and that feeling disappeared.

Something creaked on the other side of the curtain.

She stopped, one foot half off the floor ready to take her next step. Her body buzzed. Was that a ghost, or nerves?

It didn't feel totally like a ghost. It didn't itch as much as ghosts did. But her skin tingled and crawled an alarm, the kind that told her someone was doing something with magic or ghosts, something they shouldn't be doing. The kind that told her she wasn't alone anymore, that made her feel as though a target stood out clear and bright on her head and someone had their finger on a trigger.

For a long, aching minute she stood there without

moving, until the sound of the creak began to blur in her memory and she couldn't be sure she'd actually heard it. Fuck. Her cigarette fell to the dusty stage and she ground it out with her toe.

The silence waited. Breathed around her.

Her muscles ached. This was bullshit. She'd count to five, and then she'd get back to work. One . . . two . . . three . . .

The movement came at four. A tiny blur in the corner of her eye, so fast she couldn't catch it. Fuck!

Her skin tingled worse. Something wasn't right. That felt like a ghost, but it also felt like magic. A witch doing ghost-magic? Shit, after Maguinness she really didn't want to deal with that again.

Too bad it wasn't up to her. There was a ghost, and there was magic, period. A summoned ghost, maybe, or a ghost working with a mate. Double fuck.

She pulled her knife out of her pocket and snapped it open, used her left hand to grab a handful of asafetida and graveyard dirt. Let them fucking come. She was ready.

What she wasn't ready for was the fast *whoosh* of something flying through the air, or the heavy sharp weight slamming into the back of her skull. The dirt and her knife flew from her hands; the floor flew up to greet her. Painfully.

She barely had a chance to realize what had happened before everything went dark.

It was still dark when she opened her eyes, and her head felt like someone had jammed nails into it.

Not that the rest of her was any more comfortable. She felt stiff and *smushed* somehow. What the—

She was in a box. She was trapped.

Holy shit. Oh holy shit holy shit holy shit. Trapped, trapped in that tiny space that made her heart pound and her lungs feel cracked and unable to work properly. For a long horrible minute she lay there panting, struggling to move, to make her head stop spinning, before she managed to get herself under control. So she was trapped. That didn't mean she was dead or something. She could get out of this. She would get out of it.

The top side of the box—of the trunk, rough wood dry against her fingers—was an arm's length above her head, enough for her to sit up if she was careful. That was the first thing she needed to do. Sitting meant control, sitting meant not cringing on the floor like a little girl trying to hide behind the water heater or in the crawlspace under the house.

Hiding like a little girl who got found anyway, no matter where she tried to hide.

She swallowed the memories, swallowed the rising panic. She was sitting, she would get out of this.

A barely detectable seam under her fingertips told her where the lid was. The trunk apparently sat on its side, with the lock at the top. Great. The floor would keep the hinges from opening. If she wanted to get out, she'd need to flip it onto its bottom first. That would be fun.

I'm trapped, I'm trapped, I'm trapped—

No. Fuck that. Sitting up had given her legs some room; not a lot, not enough, but some. At least her heels weren't pressing into her ass anymore.

Her tattoos weren't tingling.

Her tattoos weren't tingling, so the ghost or the witch or whatever wasn't around anymore. That was good news, at least, right?

Oh, yeah, that made it totally better to be trapped in a trunk in the school theater that— Shit, that no one had entered in three weeks or so because everyone avoided it like it would dye their skin green.

So much for hoping someone would come along and let her out.

And— Shit again. That seam, the seam she could barely feel. How airtight was that? How much air did she have, *how much fucking air did she have?*

She pressed her face against the wood, against the seam, in a futile attempt to feel if air could get through. No. Or if it could, she didn't feel it.

Pushing on the lid didn't do anything, either.

Time to flip it.

That at least gave her something to do with her panic. She turned it into energy, throwing herself to the left as hard as she could.

The trunk might not actually be airtight, but it sure as fuck felt like it was, like the air around her was getting too hot, too thin. Her head hurt worse with every second, and that wasn't withdrawals. That was fear, biting into the back of her neck and tearing, slicing at her with icy talons. She'd never liked close spaces—who the hell would, after being shoved into them so many times, left there the way she'd been—but they didn't upset her usually; she'd been able to get past it. Her job demanded she get past it.

That's what pills were for, too, right? She could— She didn't have her bag. Of course not. Her bag with her pick case. That would have come in way too handy, wouldn't it?

She slammed herself against the left side of the trunk with all the strength she could muster, finding a rhythm. The trunk started to rock. She pushed harder, barely hearing the booming sound of her body hitting the wood, barely aware of the choking half sobs escaping her throat. How much air did she have, she was trapped, they were never going to let her out, never, never—

The trunk flipped. Stars exploded in the blackness before her eyes, so bright it hurt. Or maybe it was just the impact that hurt, because that was sure as fuck not pleasant, either.

It took her a couple of minutes to unwedge herself enough to set her feet and bottom on the floor again. She gave the trunk lid a shove. Nothing. Of course.

How solid was the wood? She scooted herself farther down onto her back, pressed the soles of her feet against the lid. One slow, solid push, or a bunch of fast ones?

Fast. She couldn't stand to do anything else, not when she thought for sure her air would run out any second or her heart would explode from panic.

The wood caved the tiniest bit under her feet. Nowhere near enough. Fuck, that wood was solid. Of course. It was important that a fucking stage prop for a fucking school play or something would be built airtight and strong enough to survive a fucking explosion.

Another kick. Another. Another. How long had she been in there? How long had she been unconscious? Ten minutes? Three hours?

Her legs started burning. It made her madder. Made her kick harder. This was bullshit, she was not going to suffocate or starve or what-the-fuck-ever in this box. She had things outside that place, she had Terrible, and she was not going to die when things were weird between them.

Or any other fucking time, either.

Strength she didn't know she had pulsed through her limbs, and she used it. The wood started to creak. More. Harder. The sounds coming from her mouth weren't choking little noises now, they were louder, screams, unstoppable and sharp in the tiny space.

One last kick, one last scream, and the lid flew open. Air blew over her, cold on her sweaty brow, so fresh it made her dizzy.

She was free. She'd gotten out, she was free. She felt like she'd just run a marathon that ended with plummeting down a flight of stairs, but she was free.

Her legs shook as she stood up. Even the dim light

in the theater hurt her eyes; white spots expanded and exploded in front of them, expanded and exploded.

"Are you okay?"

The voice made her stumble, almost falling over the back of the trunk. What the fuck, what— She squeezed her eyes shut, opened them again, and saw Beulah.

"Are you okay? What were you doing in there?"

Beulah stood halfway down the aisle. Halfway down. In the theater. How long had she been there? Had she— Someone had slammed a pole or a slab of wood or whatever it was into the back of Chess's head, a heavy one. That didn't take a lot of strength to do. It wouldn't have taken much strength to shove her into the trunk, either, especially not with an accomplice.

Chess ran her fingers through her sweaty bangs. "What are you doing here?"

"I came to see if you were hungry, actually, and I heard you screaming. What were you doing in there?"

Like she was going to tell. Sure, it would totally be cool to let Beulah know she'd gotten jumped and locked in a trunk. Didn't make her look like an idiot at all. "Investigating."

"Uh-huh." Beulah sat down, held up a plastic tray and cup. "Here, I brought you these."

Eating or drinking something Beulah offered her didn't seem like the best idea. But her water bottle was almost empty and her throat felt like someone had set sawdust on fire and shoved it down there, so . . .

She took the cup, downed the contents in one long swallow, and almost spit them back up. "Ugh, what the fuck is that?"

"Green tea. It's unsweetened, it's good for you. Cleans the blood, gets rid of impurities."

For fuck's sake. She didn't spend most of her income on drugs so she could have clean fucking blood. And that green tea tasted like swampwater and death.

Beulah obviously saw the look on her face—Chess wasn't making any effort to hide it—and continued. "You should really start taking care of yourself. You'd feel much better."

"I feel fine." At least she did until she opened that plastic container. The smell assaulted her, that horrible sodium smell, damp meat and soggy pale fries, old pasta with sauce dried into crustiness. Institution food. Food she'd find in Dumpsters behind the school because no one gave her money to buy any. She gagged, swallowed hard the saliva flooding her mouth, and snapped the lid back shut so fast she gave herself a cut with the sharp plastic edge.

"Sorry," Beulah said. "I know the food from there is gross, but it's really not great anywhere around here, and I didn't know what you'd like, so . . ."

"It's fine." She needed a smoke. She needed her pills. Needed them like she needed . . . well, needed them like she needed her fucking pills, and that was an awful lot, more than anything. Beulah's presence annoyed her, an itch she couldn't scratch; why wouldn't the woman go away so she could take her pills? She closed her eyes, wished as hard as she could that Beulah would just leave.

"So why were you in that trunk?"

That didn't sound like leaving, damn it. Chess opened her eyes to see Beulah watching her with an intensity that made her want to squirm. She didn't, and she wouldn't, but she wanted to. "What do you mean, why?"

"I mean why? Did you see something? A ghost?"

"No."

"Then why—"

"Why nothing. I was looking in it. The lid fell. I got out. No big deal."

Beulah nodded toward the trunk—the wreckage of the trunk, the hole in the center of the lid a ragged exit wound. "You just destroyed it? Are you going to replace it?"

Beulah deserved a punch in the face. "I have the authority to destroy, take, or use anything I want."

"Yes. And you do exercise that, don't you?"

"What the hell is your problem with me? Seriously. You don't know me, or anything about me. Is there some reason why you keep acting like I spit on your baby or something?"

A flash of surprise on Beulah's face, and then there was that damned look of amusement again. "You're right," she said after a pause. "I'm not being very nice."

"Were you like this with Aros?"

Beulah tilted her head. Thinking. "No. Aros wasn't as cold as you are. I mean, he seemed very nervous all the time. Like he thought someone was going to start yelling at him. He talked very quietly and he didn't ask a lot of questions. He probably would have peed himself if he'd walked into that crowd in the office earlier."

"The ambush you set up for me, you mean?"

Beulah smiled, a broad, genuine smile. "I didn't set it up. I just didn't do anything to discourage it."

Beulah certainly did seem to have an awful lot of authority in the school for someone who wasn't an administrator. Hell, she wasn't even technically a school employee.

So why did she have the keys to all the locks in the building? Why would she talk about the pissy party that had greeted Chess as if her encouragement or discouragement would make a difference?

"Why?"

"I guess I wanted to see what you were really made of. As a person, I mean."

Right. So Chess was apparently some sort of experiment for Beulah now. Okay, well, good to know. She didn't trust the other woman anyway, but now she knew really not to trust her. The last thing she wanted to do was hang around near someone whose idea of a good time was to set up mind games for others to navigate, so they could sit back and laugh at them.

Her phone beeped at her. A text from Terrible, a reminder to let him know when she left Mercy Lewis. He must have just woken up, and— Shit. It was five after two.

She stood up, fast enough to give herself a headrush. Her stomach gave an unpleasant lurch, too, and she really, really wanted to get some pills into it as fast as possible. "I have to go. I have to talk to those kids."

Beulah's delicate eyebrows rose. "You think they'll talk to you?"

"Not really." She slung her bag over her shoulder. "But who knows?"

Chapter Twelve

Yeah, they didn't want to talk to her. The first one Laurie brought her was Maia Song. Or, as Chess knew her, Bleached Blonde. Didn't matter, because she wouldn't say a word.

The nausea started right before Maia left, the dark hollow feeling in her gut. So quiet at first she barely noticed it, thought it was frustration from Maia's zipped lips. But no. It grew, kept growing, until Chess realized she was sweating, sitting behind the teacher's desk staring at her notepad blurry in front of her.

She was going to be sick.

That tea . . . Was it the tea? Had that shit even been tea?

Whatever it had been, the taste of it, the sour-bitter dankness of it, flooded her mouth again. A hideous reminder that she'd actually put that shit into her body. That was where the nausea came from. The tea—assuming it had been tea—seemed to coat her tongue, throbbing there, waves of it stronger and stronger.

Fuck, that was so disgusting.

She had a few minutes before her next interview—hell, she had all day if she wanted it, and who the fuck cared, they weren't going to talk to her anyway—and she'd be damned if she was going to spend another minute with that flavor, worse than crunching up Cepts with her teeth, worse than the metallic, gritty feeling of her teeth during a speed comedown. She always kept a folding travel toothbrush in her bag; brushing in a public restroom didn't exactly appeal, but if she didn't get the essence of slime out of her mouth she was going to puke, and that would be even worse.

Her feet echoed in the empty hall as she half ran down it looking for the bathroom. Where the fuck was it? Hadn't it been down— Yes!

The bathroom was grimy, coated like all school bathrooms with a thin, sticky film of estrogen and teenage angst. Chess didn't need either touching her. She felt queasy enough already; the building was depressing enough.

Having Mrs. Li walk in while she brushed her teeth at the sink didn't help. The woman looked at her with shocked disapproval, as if Chess was giving herself a full-on intimate wax instead of just brushing her teeth.

Ha, that was one thing she didn't have to do anymore, not after Terrible admitted he liked it better when she didn't, and now that she wasn't sleeping with anyone else.

Not that that helped her at the moment, as she stood over the sink drooling foam while Mrs. Li's cold eyes, beady behind thick glasses, stared her up and down. "What are you doing?"

What the fuck did it look like she was doing? Chess didn't answer, just started cleaning the toothbrush. Rinsing and spitting while being stared at really didn't appeal—she hated having anyone watch her brush her teeth—but neither did she want to stand there with a mouth full of toothpaste, either.

She finished up, trying to ignore Mrs. Li. Not easy

when the hair on her arms and the back of her neck stood on end. Not magic, just creepiness; Mrs. Li was creepy. Who stood and stared at someone while they brushed their teeth?

"I know what you're doing."

Oh, for . . . "I don't think it's too hard to figure out. Toothbrush, sink, toothpaste—"

"Not that. I know what you're trying to do to us. Undermine us. Get control of this school back to the Church. Get rid of us." Her painted-on eyebrows drew together. "Get rid of *me*."

Chess sighed, tossed the paper towel she'd used to dry her face into the trash can. "Mrs. Li, I'm not trying to get rid of anyone. I'm just trying to find out if there's a ghost, that's all."

"A ghost. Incredible. Almost twenty-five years since she died and that slut's still causing problems here."

"I don't have any— What?"

Sometimes people grew more attractive the better you got to know them; Terrible again. Mrs. Li was not one of those people. With every passing second she looked more and more like one of those crazy-haired troll dolls vendors in the Market sometimes sold for a dollar. "You heard me. She was a slut. Slept with everyone. Made them fall in love with her."

"Made them?"

Mrs. Li sneered. "Love spells. The kind of thing you people do. The kind of thing you people brought into the world."

"The Church didn't create magic, they just used it. To save humanity, remember?"

"Not the kinds of spells Lucy did. Ruining boys, making them obsessed with her, writing about her, pages and pages, and did she care? No. She didn't even know who that baby's father was, not really." The woman's eyes started to glaze over. Chess's stomach fluttered.

Lucy? The name rang a distant chime somewhere in Chess's memory. Lucy . . . Beulah had mentioned the name, right?

Yes. Lucy. Lucy McShane. The theater suicide from twenty years or so before, the ghost the kids thought they saw—said they saw. Well, damn. This could be good, and the more Mrs. Li lost herself, the more she'd let slip.

"She slept with all of them, everybody knew it. And she said it was his, but—"

The bathroom door opened. Fuck! That could have been—almost definitely *had* been—important information. But the way Mrs. Li's face flushed when she saw Monica, the way her gaze hit the floor and she scuttled into one of the stalls, told Chess there was no point asking questions, then or ever. Mrs. Li wouldn't open up like that again.

Monica watched Mrs. Li close the door of the stall, gave Chess a smile and a shrug, a friendly eye-roll. "How are you? How are your interviews going? Good, I hope."

"Fine so far, yeah."

"Great. Do you want me to get Vernal Sze now or . . . ?"

One last glance at the shut stall door. "Um, yeah, thanks."

Monica wasn't done with her, though. She followed Chess out of the bathroom, waited until they were about halfway down the hall before she spoke again. "Having fun with Mrs. Li? She's awful, isn't she?"

"I wouldn't say that," Chess replied, even though she totally would. But what was she going to do, admit that to Monica? Hell, no.

"I guess you haven't spent enough time with her yet. She's always in the office, hovering around, watching all of us like a hawk. She's convinced that every woman in the world is after that husband of hers. If we so much as say hello to him she looks like she wants to kill us."

"Really." Mildly interesting.

"It's especially bad because she insists on being involved in everything, so she's always here, and he's always here, and—it just makes things very uncomfortable. I mean, really, it's not like Wen Li is some sort of lothario, with a girl in every room." She laughed at the thought, and Chess felt an unwilling smile spread across her own face.

They reached the front doors of the school. One of them stood open to the warm breeze; through it Chess saw more kids, standing around, sitting on the steps or the greening crabgrass.

"There's Vernal." Monica pointed. "The blond one, see him?"

Vernal Sze stood maybe a couple of inches taller than herself—he was definitely under six feet—but stocky, with a short-sides-long-front retro skater boy haircut bleached blond on top. Rubber bracelets covered his right wrist, a silver watch covered his left, and he wore skinny black jeans and a snug black T-shirt.

She checked the back of his left hand. Clean. Not one of Slobag's, then, at least not fully initiated or dedicated or whatever they called it.

"I guess I'll see you later, then." Monica gave her a smile, a quick wave, and trotted off down the hall. Her outfit that day was even worse than the day before, wide orange and purple stripes like something puked up by a barber pole.

Chess pushed through the doors, through the crowd outside it to Vernal's side. "Come talk to me, Vernal. I have some questions for you."

"Ain't talkin shit with you," he mumbled. His eyes looked everywhere but at her.

She'd bought a small bag of pretzel sticks and a Coke

from the vending machine earlier. Vernal shook his head when she offered him a pretzel—she figured he would—but she needed to get something into her stomach. "So you can listen to me. Come on."

He followed her toward a cherry tree at the edge of the makeshift parking lot, still with the same sullen expression. He didn't speak again, and she was too busy chewing to talk. But someone from the crowd had something to say. "Vernal! Have fun with the *yee mm lui*!"

Laughter followed this comment; Vernal didn't laugh. Neither did Chess. She'd heard that phrase a few times that morning already, and it wasn't one she'd picked up from Lex. Which meant it probably didn't have anything to do with sex. "What did that mean?"

He shook his head.

"You're going to have to talk to me at some point, Vernal. You might as well do it now."

Shrug. For fuck's sake.

"So you've seen two ghosts? Or was it one ghost in two places? Do you have any idea why they might be after you or attracted to you?"

That was a thought, actually. Vernal couldn't have the power to be a witch. If he did, he would have been discovered through the tests every child in the world took in their fifteenth year.

But then . . . Terrible had never been tested. He didn't have a name; well, he had a few, on different forged identification cards and licenses, but legally, according to the Church, he didn't exist. He probably had a birth certificate somewhere—he'd been born before Haunted Week—but without knowing his name, birth date, or who his parents had been, how was he supposed to find it?

The point was, he hadn't been tested. "Vernal, when you were fifteen did you undergo Church testing?"

He eyed her, the suspicion in his gaze so hard she could almost feel it physically. "Aye. Ain't everyone?"

So much for that theory. "Tell me about the ghosts."

"Ain't telling you shit."

They'd reached the tree, its pale blossoms delicate and almost unbearably pretty against the bright blue sky. Just as she'd hoped, the ground was dry and the shade perfect to sit in. That she did, and after an awkward half minute or so Vernal sat down, too. Not next to her, of course, or even particularly close to her. But not too far.

"I really don't want to keep you here all day," she said when he'd gotten himself settled and she'd grabbed her notebook and pen.

"Ain't that just like a Churchie, wanna throw around the power. Ain't ascared of you fuckin Church."

"I didn't think you would be." The breeze blew a lock of her hair over her face; she tucked it back behind her ear, flicked it over her shoulder. Crunched another pretzel stick. "I'm not trying to scare you. What I'm trying to do is just get you to tell me about the ghosts you've seen. Why don't—"

A car pulled into the lot beside her, blasting the Damned out of its open windows. Not just any car, either. Lex's car. What the hell was he doing there? Hadn't he gotten her in enough trouble?

But then, he didn't actually know he'd gotten her into trouble, though she was sure he could guess. For that matter, he didn't necessarily know for sure that she and Terrible were together. She thought he knew, he most likely knew, but she'd never actually come out and said it.

Probably because knowing him, that would only make him try harder to get her into his bed again. Nobody liked to lose, but Lex enjoyed winning a bit too much.

"Give me a minute," she told Vernal, and stood up. "Just think about it. I really could use that information."

She probably wasn't supposed to smoke there, but what the hell. The kids were. She tugged one out, lit it up as she waited for Lex to come talk to her. Which he did, wandering across the gravel lot toward the tree as if he was just out for a stroll, enjoying the lovely weather. "Hey, Tulip. What's on the happening?"

"Why are you here again?"

"What's that for? Still mean, you is. Ain't I can just come check you, see how you do?"

She took another drag off her smoke, more to waste time than anything else. "You can check anything you want. I'm just not sure why you want to."

He shrugged. "My side of town, dig. Shit like this going down, I wanna see the tale is."

"Did you come here when Aros was here, and check on him?"

"Ain't knew him."

Vernal was watching them both very closely, she noticed. So was the crowd of students gathered outside the front doors; didn't they ever go to their fucking classes? "So you're checking on me, but not on him."

"Came to check he were here, aye. Just ain't got him chatterin much."

"What did he say?" Shit, she'd left her notebook by the tree. Didn't matter, though. Lex probably wouldn't appreciate her writing down what he said.

"Say ain't sure be a ghost. Say none talking to he neither. Say you Church ain't trust him, sendin he out here. Like they wanting he dead, he say."

"What? That's crazy."

Another shrug. "What he say. Ain't my words."

"Sure. Well, look, I'm trying to interview somebody here—that kid there, by the tree—and it's Church business. You can't sit there with me while I talk to him, and I don't know how long I'll be, so you might as well go."

He grinned. "Aw, nay, thinking I gots meself all kinda shit could be doin here, me. You get on your business, I get on mine, aye? Maybe after we get some food in us."

"I have to go to the Church after that. And what do you have to do here that's going to keep you all busy?"

"Just business, aye? You give me the wait when you done, before you get your drive on for that Church."

Her cigarette was little more than filter between her fingers; she dropped it, gave it a slap with the toe of her shoe to crush it out. "Hey, really quick. I need a translation."

"Aye? What you hearing?"

"It's not really important, I don't think, but . . . *Yee mm lui*. What does it mean?"

He burst out laughing; the sound of it scraped at her, irritating like poison ivy. She folded her arms and waited until the laughter finally settled into deep breaths. It couldn't be that fucking funny, whatever it was. "They callin you that?"

"What does it mean?"

"Saying you a snitch, they are. Think you playin the greasy-tongue, ain't trusting you."

"And that amuses you?"

"Gotta get my kicks somehows," he said, still grinning. "But guessing that ain't make it easy get you job done."

"No, it doesn't."

He glanced at Vernal, still watching them; glanced at the crowd of students, larger than it had been. She felt those eyes on her, on both of them, felt their curiosity and the way they pretended they had none. "Mayhap I give you some help."

"I think I can manage—"

Holy shit. She didn't know how to react, what to do,

because he kissed her. Hard. His left hand squeezed her hip; his right clasped her neck and kept her from pulling away.

And before she had time to think, she was kissing him back.

Chapter Thirteen

Involvement with others is a way to serve Truth, but Truth always comes first.

—*The Book of Truth*, Laws, Article 1056

She'd always liked kissing Lex. Always liked doing anything that *involved* kissing Lex; he was awfully damn good at all of those activities. It wasn't as good as kissing Terrible, but it certainly didn't suck. Somehow her own hand was on his shoulder and her other hand touched his neck, slid up into his hair, and it felt so familiar she could almost ignore the burning throb of guilt in her chest.

She didn't, though. It only lasted a few seconds, really; she took her hand off his shoulder almost as fast as it had landed and started to pull back, anticipating a struggle.

But Lex let her go, though both his hands rested on her hips. His voice had that soft tone to it, the one she hadn't heard in a couple of months. "How's that for some helping?"

She glanced back at the crowd of kids, just in time to see a few of them close their mouths and turn away, to see heads duck together in whispered consultations. "Is that what that was supposed to be?"

He shook his head. "You give it the try-on now. See iffen you get some words out of em."

He was probably right. If they all thought she was somehow connected to Slobag, then . . . yeah, they'd probably talk to her.

Nice. They wouldn't respect or talk to her because of her abilities or talents, because of the place she'd earned in the Church through hard work and nearly getting herself killed several times over. But let Lex kiss her, let it look like she was with him, and suddenly their mouths opened. No respect for herself or her power; respect because she fucked someone powerful.

Well, what the hell did she expect? Hadn't she known pretty much all of her life that her only real value came from what hid between her legs? She'd been told it often enough.

And the one person who truly cared about her for more than that, for more than just what he could get out of her and what she could do for him, the one person to whom she was more than a commodity to be traded or discarded . . . well, she'd just fucking betrayed him again, hadn't she, the instant she responded to Lex. A few seconds or a few minutes, what did it matter. Betrayal was betrayal.

Shame settled so thick over her she thought she might collapse under the weight; she'd done it again. What the fuck was wrong with her?

She loved him, and she'd hurt him, and she couldn't seem to stop; couldn't stop taking her own happiness, throwing it on the floor, and jumping up and down on it until it shattered.

Lex's finger caught her chin, lifted it. Softness still touched his voice; she couldn't quite read the look in his eyes. "Just business, ain't needing to give nobody the tell, aye? Just giving you the help, me."

Yeah. Just hide it, don't ever tell. That would make it all okay. If only. "And that was the only way you could think of to help me out?"

He grinned and became the old Lex again, the one she was used to, jaunty and a bit arrogant. "Nay, but surely were the most fun."

"Yeah, I'm glad you enjoyed it."

"And you did. Ain't try the pretend game with me, Tulip. Got experience with you, I do."

Fuck. She had to get out of there, get away from him, immediately. He was right, and she knew he was right and he knew she knew it, and she couldn't stand there and see that knowledge on his face and feel it heavy in her heart another second. "I have to get back to work."

"Aye, sure you do. Gimme the wait here, aye? When you done? Or maybe I wait for you."

"Do I have a choice?"

"Always got a choice," he said, and planted a kiss on her forehead. She opened her mouth to reply, but he'd already turned and started walking toward the school building, glancing back to give her a casual wave.

Bastard.

"Were the same ghost in the gym as the theater, aye," Vernal told her. They sat in an available office in the Administration section; after the kiss she didn't want to stay outside. Couldn't stay outside, where they could all see her. Their gazes burned holes in her back.

But Lex had been right. Vernal had started chattering the second she closed the awful orange door behind her, and had hardly stopped since. Twenty minutes of solid talk; damn that kid could ramble. She wondered how often in his life someone older than him had actually listened to what he had to say for that long a period of time, for any period of time.

But then, Beulah probably did. She'd seemed awfully defensive of him.

"You're sure it was the same one?"

"Aye. Got a good look, I did. Thought it looked like

that dame, the one offed sheself back in the when. But I ain't got that solid, dig me, causen I ain't seen no good images of she."

Right. She'd wanted to look Lucy McShane's photos up anyway, hadn't she? She scribbled that down, adding it to the list of things she needed to look up when she got to Church. *Without* hanging around to spend more time with Lex first. He'd done enough damage for one day. For a week, actually. Hell, for a whole fucking lifetime.

"But definitely a female, and definitely the same ghost?"

"Aye."

Chess leaned back in the chair behind the desk, a cheap one with a blue fabric seat and a plastic oval to support her back. The whole office was low-budget, from the threadbare rust-colored carpet to the scratched, paint-peeled metal filing cabinets with a couple of broken handles, to the desk so flimsy she was surprised it didn't bend under the stack of papers sitting on it; it looked like something a six-year-old would put together. Whoever worked in there must not be high on the administrative totem pole at all. "But you said the ghost in the gym came from the bleachers, right? And in the theater it came from the curtains?"

He nodded. Immediately after sitting down he'd plucked a rubber band from a little dish on the desk, and he twirled it between his fingers and around them, the movements almost hypnotic.

But not quite. "And it was daylight outside. Just after school? Or still during school?" Then, at the look on his face, she added, "I don't care if you were skipping class, that's nobody's business and I'm not obligated to tell anybody anything."

"Were skippin. Theater's a cool spot for it, got its own ins an outs, big an quiet an all. Gives the privacy, it do."

"What were you doing on that day, the theater day,

I mean? Just hanging out? One of the administrators thinks you were drinking; not that it matters."

"Had we a couple," he said. Flick, stretch, twist, went the rubber band. "Ain't got aught else to do, not here. They always tryna set we up them activities an shit, sayin keep us off them streets. Bullshit. I ain't joinin. Ain't even join Miss Beulah's."

"What was Beulah's activity?"

He shrugged. "Some spuddle on positive changin, an makin shit happen, dig? *Dame* shit. Maia an Jia played she game. I ain't."

Maia and Jia had been outside with Herb Paris berries and a firedish. Did Beulah know about that?

"They all gots them groups," Vernal continued, apparently not noticing her distraction or her raised eyebrows. "Mr. Li tryna get us all joinin too, do some camp-out shit or outdoors or whatany. Wants us playin along, like him our father."

She scribbled that down, although she was fairly confident it was useless information. So some second-school busybodies thought they should have more influence over the kids? They felt that desperate need to be popular and liked, they'd never grown up more than that? Ugh. Chubby polo-shirt boy-men. She could practically see them, with their too-jovial smiles and slightly off-color jokes, carefully calculated to make them seem cool without being dirty or rude.

Ridiculous. Grow the fuck up. Any adult who spent a lot of time trying to win the confidence or affection of teenagers through community spirit activity bullshit was a moron, and an immature moron to boot. For that matter, anyone who spent time trying to win anyone's confidence or affection, whether through those stupid activities or whatever else, was an immature moron.

Giving a fuck what other people thought was a road

straight to misery and pain; an obsession of the weak. To believe otherwise was to live in a fairy tale.

"Can you think of anything else that might help me out? Anything else you noticed? Maybe you overheard someone talking about this and you didn't make the connection at the time?"

He grinned. "Aw, now, you testing me for snitchin? I ain't pull that. You give Lex that one, I ain't no teller."

Fuck. "No, it's not—"

He stood up. "I ain't hear nothin, nay, but iffen I done, and were one of us, I ain't gonna blow-back. Dig?"

One of us? Great. That was just what she needed. Sure it might be useful in the short term, but it wasn't going to help in general.

She didn't even want to think about being known as Slobag's Churchwitch on this side of town.

If she wasn't already.

Holy shit, she could be. Bump had said Slobag had a witch; *she* knew it wasn't her, but . . . did Terrible? Did he think maybe she was doing it, that she'd killed Bag-end Eddie, that she'd— No, he couldn't. He couldn't think she'd actually do that, could he? Ritual murder? Was that why he hadn't come back to her place to sleep?

Slobag's witch was something she could ask Lex about. He very well might not tell her—probably wouldn't— but she could ask. The thought calmed her down a bit, as much as anything could.

"Yeah, I got it." She tore off a half sheet of paper from her notepad and hunted in her bag for her pen, which had apparently slipped out of its loop. Shit.

Rather than dig around for it, she opened the top desk drawer, which gave a burbly squeal as the tracks stuck. At least it held a pen. Even better, the pen had ink. She scribbled her cell phone number down and held it out to him. "Call me if you think of anything, please. Or if you hear something. It's not snitching, it's helping everyone out, okay?"

"Aye, sure." He winked, took the paper from her hand. "Helpin out."

"We'd really appreciate it." Meaning herself and the Church, but she knew Vernal would think she meant herself, Lex, and Slobag. Well, hey, it wasn't her fault if he made an assumption. Maybe that was sleazy, but she didn't have much choice.

It wasn't until he finally left the cramped office and closed the door behind him that she looked back into the drawer. A few sheets of red construction paper, some loose glitter, maps of campgrounds and parks. Crap, but not typical desk crap. Someone apparently did some art projects in there, or— Damn. Someone did other things in there, too, it seemed. Three condoms hid under one of the maps. Interesting.

And gross. What was this cheap-ass desk, this half-broken chair, used for? Ugh. Good thing she had some hand sanitizer; she used it liberally, spraying everything in sight. Including her hands. For the third or fourth time in the last hour.

The drawer made that broken sound again when she began pushing it shut, but over that she caught a rattle of some kind. A rolling rattle, like beads or marbles.

Maybe it was. Maybe it was something else.

A quiet jab of a button locked the door. Best not to be interrupted. Normally she'd wait until night, when she could come in with her Hand if she needed it and look at her leisure, but when opportunity struck . . .

Not beads. Not marbles. Two Herb Paris berries.

Well, fuck. What the hell was going on at that school? And who used that office?

Chapter Fourteen

It is not a surprise that the Church was so quickly able to take over and fix the Old Government's destroyed systems, because the Church's power comes from magic and Truth, and from righteousness.

—*Rise to Power: How the Church Made the World*

Beulah sat behind her desk—a much nicer desk than the one Chess had just dug around in, with a smooth, polished wood top and a leather blotter in the center—in a pose so casually graceful it looked planned. Once again Chess found herself thinking that something about the woman seemed familiar, some sort of— She blinked, and it was gone. And what did it matter, anyway?

"Hey," she said. "I was wondering, who uses that office? The one on the other side of the administration area here, the small one with the filing cabinets?"

"Which one?"

It was such fun when people stalled. Beulah was pretty good at it, and at looking innocent while she did it, but Chess wasn't falling for it. "The one right there. You can see the door. It has filing cabinets. Monica told me I could use it to interview students."

"I thought you were going to be in 122."

"I was. Then they needed the room back."

"Your interviews take a long time, don't they. That's not a very efficient system. Perhaps the Church ought to rethink the way they handle things." Her eyebrows rose. "Or, of course, the way their employees handle things."

Chess tensed her jaw to keep from laughing. "Perhaps the school ought to reconsider who they give administrative offices to, when those people are so unaware of their surroundings."

To her surprise, Beulah giggled. A genuine giggle, a pretty one that softened the air around them. "That's a storeroom, mostly, but it's also used as an office on occasion. Wen uses it, Martha uses it—you met them, the Lis, remember? They're supplementals, like me. Sometimes Otto Pao uses it; Monica; teachers or students who need a quiet place to work . . . all sorts of people."

"Students are allowed into a file room?"

"The cabinets are locked. And I'm sure you have no idea what this is like, but a lot of these kids don't have a quiet place to study. They can't do homework at home. They don't have electricity or heat—"

"I live in Downside." Beulah's words sent a wave—a small wave, but a wave nonetheless—of shameful memory from her gut to her head. Yeah, sure, she had no idea what it was like to not have any privacy or safety or quiet in what was supposed to be her home. No idea how it felt to be excited to go to school even though it sucked because it meant she actually got to focus on something kids were supposed to focus on, how it felt to know no one was going to hit her or make her do things she didn't want to do while she was there, to hate weekends because she had nowhere to hide.

School had never been safe like the Church. But it had been better than some of the homes-cum-prisons she'd grown up in.

Beulah didn't even blink at that information; somehow Chess thought she already knew. Probably knew exactly where Chess lived. "Then you understand how it can be for them. Part of my job is to facilitate their learning, to build a sense of self and community spirit and a respect for tradition and history."

That struck a little chord in the back of Chess's mind. "Church tradition and history?"

"Of course. Church tradition and history." Beulah's smile was as fake as a red plastic plant. "Our children should definitely be proud to live under the Church's thumb—I mean, guidance and protection."

"I certainly hope they are proud," Chess replied, forcing what she hoped was a natural-looking smile onto her face. Fuck Beulah. "After all, the Church is what keeps all of us alive."

"Of course it is. It's not like ghosts weren't always vicious and attacked people, right? It's not like it was a very unusual event that suddenly brought them up and made them want to kill. It's not like that's a suspicious thing to have happened, or like anyone would have had a motive to do that."

Great. Beulah bought into conspiracy theories. What was next, UFOs? Drugs in the drinking water? Too bad that one wasn't true. Save her some money.

But it wasn't. "You're right. It's not. And they'd never appeared in such numbers before. For all we know, they were plotting and planning their revenge on the living for years."

"Right." It was said a little too slowly, the vowel sound drawn out, pulled just to the cliff edge of sarcasm but not quite tipping over and falling into the valley of rude.

Irritation like wiggling fingers inside her chest. "So lots of people use that office, correct?"

"Yes. It's a catch-all."

"Would you happen to know who's used it in the last couple of weeks?"

"I don't keep track, Chess. And I'm not here every day, either. You should ask Monica about it."

"Sure, I will. Thanks."

Beulah said something, probably some sort of sarcastic version of "You're welcome" or "See you later." Then again, it was so mumbled Chess wouldn't have been surprised to learn it was actually "Go fuck yourself."

And she certainly did feel fucked at the moment. Two days of investigating and all she'd found was a bit of illegal magic, some probable ectoplasm, a falling catwalk, and the inside of a trunk.

The catwalk hadn't been an accident. Neither had the trunk. But the point was that she'd spent five or six hours in that damned place and hadn't learned anything of use, except that people on this side of town didn't think much of the Church. Wow, that was news. She might as well cut herself her bonus check with that inside information. Chess Putnam, Ace Detective.

The filing cabinets were indeed locked. Good thing she had picks.

With the door securely shut behind her she put those to use. Even easier than she'd imagined; the locks on those things might as well have been made of foam.

Student files. Her heart jumped in her chest, then fell again when she saw the dates. BT student files, from Before Truth, before the Church. Some from the year or two after Haunted Week.

Actually . . .

The BT files seemed to have come from whatever schools students attended before they switched to Mercy Lewis. And those from right after Haunted Week, from the very beginning of the building's reestablishment as a school . . . those could be useful indeed.

Her fingers skipped over the tabs, looking for *Mc*. McElroy, McMasters, McNabb . . . McShane, Lucy. Excellent. She yanked the file from its spot, flipped it open, ready to at least get some kind of lead.

Except the folder was empty. Not a single slip of paper, not a list of grades, not a picture—did they put pictures in student files?—or a class schedule or anything else. Certainly not any information about the girl's death, suicide or not, and nothing about any kind of ghost or haunting rumors.

Nothing at all. Odd, that. Chess had a very distinct memory of a third-grade teacher finding a note she'd written about another kid in class and telling her it was going to be put into her Permanent Record, so everyone at any other school she attended, and the Church hierarchy itself, would see it and know what a horrible person she was.

Her hands didn't seem quite under her control as she stuffed the folder back into place. She glanced at the clock, hoping enough time had passed that taking more pills would work, that she'd actually feel them.

She would. Awesome. Her supply was getting a bit low, but she grabbed three and shoved them into her mouth. Her water bottle lay tangled in a bunch of other shit in the bottom of her bag. Of course. She dry-swallowed the Cepts, grimacing at the bitterness somehow sticky in her mouth, then finally tugged the bottle free to wash them down. She could really use another Coke or something.

What she could *really* use was some speed, but given that she'd already felt something ghostlike in the theater that day, she couldn't have any. Coke was the next best thing.

The file put away, the cabinet relocked and the door *un*locked, she headed for the soda machine at the other end of the Administration room, opening the small pouch she used to hold change. Two dollars for a Coke. Almost as bad as the prices in the Market.

A hint of movement behind her. She turned, expecting to see Beulah standing there with her irksome smile, but it wasn't Beulah. It was Wen Li, and the look on his face told her he wasn't pleased to be anywhere near her.

Chapter Fifteen

People will seek to hide even the most innocuous of secrets.
But they also seek to hide the important ones.
—*Debunking: A Practical Guide,* by Elder Morgenstern

He gave her the barest possible nod, more of a twitch
than an actual greeting. Oh, he was an asshole. And she
was in just the kind of annoyed mood to want to pro-
voke him.

"Mr. Li, how lovely to see you again." She smiled her
biggest, fakest smile and turned to face him, still holding
her money in her hand.

He glanced at it, then up at the slot on the machine.
"Miss Putnam."

"I was wondering if you had some time to talk? I have
some questions for you."

"I'm afraid I don't at the moment, no."

"Are you sure? It's really important."

"No. I'm sorry, but I'm terribly busy." Again his gaze
traveled from the money to the machine, the machine to
the money. Was he sweating? He certainly didn't seem
normal, but then how would she know? She had no idea
what was normal for him.

But he did seem . . . He reminded her of a speedfreak
riding a comedown: the darting eyes, the fidgeting—he
flicked his fingers across the bills in his other hand over
and over—the shifting of his weight from foot to foot

and the tightness of his pose, like he itched everywhere but couldn't scratch.

She doubted he was actually a speedfreak. If he was, he wouldn't be so husky. But something was obviously making him nervous, and it most likely had something to do with her.

"Oh? What are you doing?" Annoying people wasn't something she usually got off on, but she had to admit it was kind of fun when the subject showed their irritation so obviously.

Not to mention when they were such pretentious, self-important pricks.

"I don't feel comfortable discussing that, frankly."

"Should I ask Monica what you're doing?"

Another twitch. Hmm. What did that mean? "What? Why would you do that?"

She was quite thirsty, too, but this was too interesting to stop. "Is there some reason I shouldn't?"

"No, of course not." His tone indicated that the very idea was ridiculous; he laced it with so much scorn it practically soaked her skin. Obviously fake.

"Are you sure? I wouldn't want to make you uncomfortable or anything. I'm sure she'll tell me what you're doing. She has access to your schedule, right? She always knows where you are?"

"I'd really like to get my drink now."

"Oh, of course." Her first dollar slipped neatly into the slot. Next came the change. "Oops!"

Heh. While she pretended to hunt around on the floor for her quarter—it had fallen right by her foot—she got a good look at his expression—and the fact that beneath his cheap shiny trousers, his leg shook slightly. Interesting.

Just as he seemed ready to explode she "found" her change. "See? Here. I'm sorry. I didn't mean to keep you from whatever you're about to do. What is that again?"

"I have a meeting with some of the young men in my Outdoorsman group. We're doing some volunteer work this weekend."

The mention of volunteer work might have made Chess feel a little bit bad for dogging him like that, except she was fairly certain he was one of those people who volunteered so people would think he was wonderful and charitable and all that shit, rather than out of a genuine desire to help others.

All of those fucking goody-two-shoes "I care so much" people were such liars. They'd certainly never cared about *her*.

Thinking of it made her stab the button on the machine hard enough to cause pain. "What kind of volunteer work?"

Their eyes met. She let every bit of I-can-stand-here-all-day show in hers, every bit of semi-bored amusement. Hey, her pills were starting to work; that slow, smooth warmth spreading from her stomach outward. She really could stand there all day. She could do anything she wanted, at least at that particular moment.

His eyes widened, then focused down. "We're helping to clean and repaint an abandoned building to turn into a community center."

"Oh? Where?"

He raised his wrist practically to his nose to check his watch, peered at her over the top of it. Yeah. His time was so important blah blah blah. She didn't move. Didn't change expression.

"It's two blocks from here. Twentieth and Grant."

She stepped aside so he could get his Coke. "And that's when?"

"Saturday."

It didn't surprise her. But she let a hint of that emotion slip into her voice anyway. "On Holy Day? Don't you think those boys would be better served by going to Church?"

His Coke tumbled into the bin at the bottom of the machine with a clunk. "I think they're better served doing something for their own community, instead of one that tries to alienate them from it."

When he bent down to retrieve the can she had to fight the urge to plant her shoe right into his saggy ass. Sure, Mr. Li was entitled to feel however he wanted to. And she'd told herself before she walked into Mercy Lewis for the first time that she wouldn't start any trouble over the Church. But she couldn't help herself.

"I'd think you'd want them at Church, because you want a better future for them."

"I think their future is with their people."

"I think you're not giving them a choice."

He glared at her. "May I go now?"

"Who's stopping you?"

He gave her one last glare while he clutched his Coke like a scepter, then started to push past her. She stepped out of his way. Even if he didn't repulse her physically—which he did—some vague part of her mind was convinced he would rub asshole all over her.

He left the Administration area; if he was aware of her narrow-eyed stare at his back he didn't show it. Shithead. And a shithead she couldn't do anything to or argue with any more vehemently than she just had, at least not until this case was tied up. When that happened, though . . .

The Coke helped with her cottonmouth, but unfortunately it didn't make any clues or information suddenly appear. Pity. The walk back to the temporary office felt a bit like walking into a trap; she wouldn't be able to get out of this case, and she wasn't learning anything, and while she hated to admit it, she was a little freaked out when she started thinking about it. Teams of ghosts working together to bring down catwalks and trap her inside trunks—though, granted, she didn't know for sure that either of those had actually been ghosts, and she sure as hell hoped they hadn't been—and grumpy "community leaders" and sullen kids . . .

It felt like living her school years all over again. Except this time she couldn't just skip out and talk back, because she actually needed these shitty people to give her information.

She loved her job. Just not right then.

Standing around the school looking at nonexistent files wasn't going to help, either. She'd head to the Church, do some research, maybe come back later. That might help. In fact, there *was* something that would make her feel better. She closed the office door and hit a button on her phone. He answered on the second ring.

"Hey, Chess. You right?"

See? Just hearing him speak, low and gravelly and so fucking sexy, made her smile, despite that mean little voice in her chest telling her not to get too comfortable.

She ignored that voice. But she paid attention to the one telling her not to sound too needy. "Yeah, I just— What are you doing later?"

"Takin you to bed."

It took her a second to reply; she was too busy reminding herself to breathe. "You think so, huh?"

"Aye."

She gave a big fake sigh. "I suppose I can make time for that."

His short laugh made her smile widen even more. "Where you at? Church or you place?"

"I'm still at the school, actually; I'm just about to leave. But I thought I'd come back tonight. I want to look at some other stuff. Want to come with me?"

"Aye."

"Okay, good." Sure enough, the knot in her chest had

eased. It was amazing how that worked. "I'm heading for Church now, so I'll probably be home in a couple of hours. Are you okay? What are you doing?"

Pause. "Later on that, aye?"

Please let that mean he'd found something. Maybe something that would keep her from having to spend too much time chasing down Bag-end Eddie's killer. She'd managed to almost forget about that, what with being trapped and being sick and being annoyed. Lucky her. Sort of.

"No problem," she said. "I'll see you in a few hours, then, okay? Just come over when you're done."

He agreed and hung up, leaving her feeling better for having talked to him and worse for being reminded of her new ritual-murdering friend.

Better or worse, though, time to finally leave the teenage prison and actually learn something at Church. She slung her bag back onto her shoulder, switched off the lights in the office, and headed out into the hall.

Only to practically run headfirst into Jia Zhang.

Fuck. Just the person she wanted to see—well, one of them anyway—at just the time when she least wanted to see her. Despite the steady soothe of her pills, she itched to escape. The building itself, with its smells of chalk and cafeteria food and crushed hopes and misery, made her skin crawl. Being there was like being inside the belly of some hideous beast digesting her bit by slow bit.

Jia's shiny face flushed as she picked up her books. "Ain't you got the lookin where you walk?"

Yes, it was just like being back in school. "Let me help you."

"Nay! Ain't needin the help." Jia snatched the book Chess had been about to pick up and clutched it to her chest, but not before Chess saw the title. Not before Chess realized that her desire to talk to the girl had been spot-on.

Being right was some comfort, but not much. Especially not when the girl had somehow gotten hold of a copy of the *Vocaran Phasmaterius*.

The guide for ghost summoners.

"Hey, what—"

Jia punched her. Hard. Chess's left eye exploded in pain; she stumbled back, tears running down her cheek to blur her vision, agony radiating dark blue around her head while red spots flashed before her eyes. "What the fuck—"

Footsteps loud on the tile and the horrible sharp squeal of the door. Jia was running away, running outside. Chess could see her just fine if she closed her left eye.

Which she did. Chasing the girl probably wasn't the best idea, all things considered. It sure wouldn't endear her further to anyone at Mercy Lewis. But the little bitch had punched her. Case or no case, her snippy ass was hitting the ground.

The door had almost closed again when Chess hit it, dangling her bag by the strap like a sock-and-lock. She'd use it that way, too, if she had to. Her eye screamed at her and felt like it was about to fall out of her skull.

Through her good right eye she caught sight of Jia running across the field behind the school. Shit. If she made it to one of those streets back there, she was gone. No way could Chess catch her in that neighborhood. Hell, almost no way Chess could expect to walk out of that neighborhood alive and intact.

All the more reason to haul as much ass as she could. Damn it, on top of everything else this was wasting her high; all that adrenaline would totally fuck with it. Jia had more than just a punch to answer for, even if Chess couldn't tell her that.

Her throat burned from sucking the cool dry air hard and fast into her tight lungs. Her suddenly too-small lungs; maybe her heart was pounding so hard it had squeezed them almost shut.

But she was gaining on Jia. The girl was hindered by carrying a stack of books—one book in particular, of course. And Chess was taller by a few inches.

Jia's back grew larger and larger, she was close, she was almost there, she—

One last desperate leap forward. Her chest slammed into Jia's back, knocked her down; Jia's weight crushed Chess's arms into the dead grass, and a cloud of musty-smelling dust rose to sting Chess's eyes further, to tickle her nose.

"Lemme go! Lemme the fuck go, you ain't got—"

"Shut up." Those lessons Terrible had given her came in handy at the oddest times, didn't they? She pressed her palms down on Jia's upper arms, shifted position so she straddled the small of Jia's back.

Doing this to a kid—no matter what that kid had done to her—didn't feel good, but what the hell else was she supposed to do? She needed to know where that book came from.

"Give me the book, Jia."

"Ainno what you talking—"

"Give me the book or I'll call the Squad, and you can spend a couple days in the stocks for assaulting a Church employee." She really didn't want to do that, damn it. Bad enough to tackle the girl; a crowd of interested onlookers had already gathered, far enough away that they couldn't hear what was being said, but close enough to see what happened, that was for damn sure.

"Go 'head, I ain't ascared of—"

An idea. A sleazy idea, but an idea nonetheless, and what choice did she have? "Give me the book or I call Lex and tell him you refuse to help. How does that sound?"

Silence. Fuck yeah, she had her. "Hand it over, Jia."

She lessened the pressure on Jia's back just enough for the girl to get her arm out from beneath her and give Chess the slim purple volume.

Chess took it. Energy slunk up her arm. Not strong— whoever had owned this book, whoever had used it enough to put their energy into it, hadn't been very powerful. Chess didn't even think the owner had been a witch.

But the book definitely had energy. "Where did you get this?"

"Found it."

Should she threaten her again? Threatening the girl felt so gross, despite the throbbing ache in her eye and the complete disappearance of her buzz. Fuck. Punishing Jia wasn't the problem. Threatening her with Lex was the problem; that was the gross part. "Where did you find it."

"Ainno."

Damn it. Chess opened her mouth, to ask again or to come up with a different tack, but the front cover of the book fell open, and she saw the name written on the inside of the cover in fading blue ink.

Chelsea Mueller.

Chapter Sixteen

Being tested is nothing to worry about. Better to worry when you are not tested.
—*Careers in the Church: A Guide for Teens*, by Praxis Turpin

Chelsea Mueller was not a Church employee. Not in Triumph City, not in the District, not in any of the neighboring districts or states. In fact, Chelsea Mueller was not a Church employee anywhere in the world.

She'd almost made the cut, though. Chess opened her notebook to a fresh page, set it on the Church library table before her, and started scribbling. She'd earned a 6.5 on the energy push test, 6.7 on the energy identification test . . . it was the same for all of them, scores between six and seven. Shit, poor Chelsea, she'd missed it by less than a point.

And she'd been tested in 2001 at the then newly opened Mercy Lewis Second School. Good thing the test scores were stored separately in Triumph City because of space limitations, so they were available; Chess couldn't find any other information on the girl anywhere.

So was Chelsea still in the neighborhood? Was she still in Downside, was she still alive? No way to tell. Jia had pled ignorance of who she was so steadfastly, even when faced with what one of the other students called in passing "Slobag's witch"—how interesting was that?—that Chess actually believed her.

Jia also insisted she'd found the book in the field. Chess didn't believe that for a second. Interesting, though, that Jia would lie about it even to someone she thought was that important. Which meant whoever had given her the book was even more important, at least to her. Hmm.

Where the hell was that Chelsea Mueller file, though? And how fucking suspicious was that?

But then, it might not be at all. If Chelsea did have some sort of connection to her case, it was possible Aros had taken the file. Files weren't supposed to leave the building, but just like the place files nobody ever remembered to update, nobody hesitated to take a citizen file if they needed it. Especially not when they lived on-grounds and could have the files back within five minutes.

He must have taken Lucy McShane's file as well. All Chess could find was Lucy's listing in the mainframe, with her dates of birth and death and a single scanned photo of a dark-haired girl with a pretty smile. Sad. But not particularly useful.

Elder Griffin might have more for her, though, or might be able to give her more information on Aros and his investigation. Being new, Aros might have reported more regularly than the rest of them did.

But if Elder Griffin knew more, wouldn't he have told her?

Of course he would have. She'd just have to ask him the next day, when he was in his office. He could help her find the files, too. Yes. The next day, she'd get some answers.

So she hoped, anyway. Which meant she could focus on a more immediate problem: figuring out a way to tell Terrible about Lex and the kiss in a way that wouldn't make him hate her and kill Lex.

Oh, and speaking of Terrible, Lex, and grisly death . . .

She gathered up her notes, shoved them into her bag, and crossed the library to the Restricted Room.

Goody Glass gave her a dirty look as she approached the Goody desk to request access. What else was new. She gave the Goody her best innocent simper. "Good morrow, Goody Glass. Can you open the door for me, please? I need to do some research."

"Thou mutters, Miss Putnam. Speak up."

Like she couldn't hear. She'd hear Chess if Chess ran to the other end of the room, covered her mouth with her hands, and whispered "Fuck you," but she couldn't hear Chess standing four feet away from her.

Chess repeated her question at exactly the same volume, but dipped into a proper curtsy as she did so. That was probably the miserable bitch's problem anyway.

It was. Goody Glass glared at her for a minute—probably trying to find something else to criticize her for—and the door behind Chess buzzed. Part of the new security system, the electronic locks.

The Restricted Room smelled like ancient paper and creaky leather, like knowledge.

As always the smell comforted her. It was safe. It smelled like those nights when she was in training, when she finally started to realize nobody was going to hurt her there, nobody would even touch her, and she could stay up as late as she wanted and read. She'd spent hours in there then, with the door locked behind her, curled up in the corner reading everything she could, studying as hard as she could so they wouldn't kick her out.

The sigil ritual books were kept on the right, near the cheerful golden Buddha who always made her smile. That day was no different, even in the mood she was in.

Spirits Unbound. The Power of Death. Overcoming Death. Necromagic. Death Magic: Theory and Practice. Death Made Manifest. And a battered gray volume with its spine worn to threads and supplemented by packing tape, which proved, when she pulled it from the shelf, to be titled simply *Death*.

Shit, they all sounded likely, didn't they? She grabbed the first three and *Death* from the top shelf; she'd just go left to right across each one.

She was going to be there all fucking night. Hopefully it would be worth it.

Not all night, but late enough, and Terrible wasn't waiting in her bed for her. He wasn't in her apartment at all, actually.

Which sucked. And was a bit of a relief. How the fuck was she going to tell him? What was she going to say, how the fuck could she possibly say it in such a way that he wouldn't explode?

She wanted him there so bad. And she wished so bad he wouldn't come, so she could have more time to think.

At least she had a half-full pillbox—ha, was it half-full or half-empty?—to help her calm down.

She took four Cepts, added a Panda to help her dip a bit lower. The Nips, sweet little red pills like cinnamon candy, smiled up at her. It'd be so good to pop a couple of those, wake herself up a bit, get her mind buzzing.

Too bad they messed with her ability to detect ghosts, and given where she planned to go that night, that wasn't a good idea. And considering who she was going with . . . a bump would probably be fine, but too much and she might as well not bother trying to have sex at all. She'd only end up wide awake by herself, totally frustrated and chain-smoking until she came down enough to get some sleep.

So speed was out. Luckily she had everything else, though, to take away the sting.

She had to tell him right away. Shit, it felt like a fucking semi-instant replay of the night before.

And just as it had the night before, her heart leapt

when the sound of the Chevelle's engine finally drifted into her apartment not long after midnight, leapt higher when it cut off. If he would just understand, not be mad at her . . . trust her. It was too much to ask, but she didn't really have a choice, did she?

At least one thing went her way. Her pills started to hit as she watched him walk across the straggly patch of grass gone to seed and cement pebbles by the side of her building up to the front steps. She closed her eyes, let that slow smooth . . . *delight,* was the only way to describe it, really . . . wind its glorious way from her stomach up through her chest, settling soft white peace over the ragged edges of her nerves. Murders and magic and ghosts and above it all the memory of Lex grabbing her, the memory that made her feel like she was going to throw those pills right back up . . . all of it faded just a bit, just enough to let her take a breath.

She waited, looking out the window, watching a hooker pick up a trick and one of Bump's corner men make a sale. A typical night, the streets alive with degeneracy. Sometimes she loved Downside.

His key scraped in the lock, and he was there, his heavy footsteps getting closer until finally she did turn, forcing a smile.

He smiled, too. Was it her imagination or was there something . . . something off, in his eyes? Something that didn't seem right, like he was pretending to look at her the way he usually did but really he was thinking something else.

Somehow she found her voice. "Hey. How'd your day go?"

He shrugged. "You?"

"Okay." Were her legs shaking? It felt like they were shaking. Maybe she'd better sit down.

The couch seemed so far away. Funny. Before all of this she'd never even have imagined she could despise herself more than she already did, make herself even sicker over her stupid weaknesses. Especially the stupid weakness that had made her think she could actually handle this whole relationship thing.

Well, fine. Enough with the weakness and the fear and the waiting for the ass-dumping axe to fall. If it was going to happen, let it just fucking happen.

"Hey, I, um, I need to tell you something."

"Aye?" He sat down next to her. Her fingernails dug into her palms to keep herself from reaching out to touch him.

Instead, she stood up again. Her legs now seemed to be shaking with energy. Too much energy, like she'd just sucked back a dozen lines, like she could walk ten miles and still be ready to race around some more. Her stomach danced from nerves and drugs, floating right below her head.

Fuck this. Fuck Lex, and fuck her guilt and feeling shitty and being scared. She started again. "Okay. I have to tell you something."

"So tell." Was that impatience in his voice? He still sat on the couch, watching her pace with his hands on his thighs.

"So, my case. It's— Well, you know where it is. And I couldn't get anyone to talk to me. So I mentioned to Lex that I couldn't get them to talk to me, and he . . . he kissed me in front of all of them. To help me out. With the case."

He didn't move. Fine. She was going to kill Lex for getting her into this, she really was.

"So that's what happened, and it didn't mean anything and I didn't want to do it but it happened. Nobody would talk to me until he did that and then they did, and it's a big case and I need it. And I'm sorry."

She paused for a second. Didn't take a chance looking at him again. Looking at him might break the simmering froth of anger she'd built up, and she wasn't done talking yet, and if she got the rest of it out fast enough she could probably keep that froth going.

"So if you want to dump me now or whatever, just do it, okay, because it's—it's making me feel sick and I don't want to have to think about it anymore."

The silence grated on her; it was too loud, like the air was beating against her eardrums. Like her fear was beating against everything else, thrumming in her chest and head. Would he just fucking say something? Her high and her panic were just about equal at the moment, but if it went on too much longer panic would totally win, and once she lost that righteous anger she'd be fucked.

He cleared his throat. "Wondered if you was gonna tell me."

"What?"

"Wondered on it, dig. Iffen you'd tell me or tryin hide it."

What the fuck? She'd been panicking and freaking out and he already knew?

Oh, right, except that wasn't actually good news. Righteous anger at Lex was one thing. Letting that righteous anger convince her that she had nothing to worry about was another. "You knew about it? How did you find out about it, so fast?"

"It matter?"

"No, no, I just wondered, is all." If he knew, maybe the fact that she'd told him would be a point in her favor. Maybe it would mean he'd believe her, he'd trust her—well, he wasn't going to trust her, probably, but maybe she'd get some kind of reprieve.

Of course, maybe he'd think that she'd told him hoping that would be his response, so he'd trust her even less, because— Oh, whatever.

He shrugged. "Ain't important. But aye. Heard on it."

Of course he knew, though. He might not have heard rumors about Lex sharing his bed—privately—with a Churchwitch on occasion, no, but he certainly would hear about Lex playing hide-the-tongue with a Church-witch in the middle of the day, in the middle of a crowd of gossipy teenagers.

"So . . . are you mad at me?"

He shrugged. "Ain't happy."

"Yeah, but . . . do you believe me? I mean, are you . . . leaving."

"Don't know what I should be doin."

But he hadn't left. He hadn't gotten up and left, and he hadn't raised his voice, and maybe that was a good sign, right? She was just high enough to think maybe it was. Just high enough to think maybe she could change the subject and sweep all of it into the past.

Not that she'd ever forget, or he would. She knew better than anybody that some things could never be forgotten. Some wounds never stopped hurting. But maybe in a relationship it was different? People in relationships forgave each other, right?

She sucked in a breath and sat down next to him. Her throat felt like plaster; a drink would probably be a good idea. If she could manage to swallow anything, anyway. "Don't let him do this. Please."

He looked at her. Waiting.

"Lex. Don't let him do this. I mean, I don't know if he knows about you and me, but I know he kissed me just to fuck with me. Not in that way, you know what I mean. Just because he thinks it's funny."

"Chess—"

"No. He just grabbed me and I didn't know what to do. I needed to get them to talk to me and I didn't feel like I could shove him away or something and alien-ate them more, and I hate that. But I really hate that he's managing to—to make you mad, or whatever, even though he's not even here, and he has nothing to do with us."

He shook his head. "Trustin you . . . Ain't makin it easy, aye?"

"I know. I'm sorry. But I'm trying to be honest. I'm not hiding things from you. I don't want to hide things from you again." She reached out a tentative hand, took it as a good sign when he didn't yank his arm away.

He turned his face to her, opened his mouth to speak, but she didn't let him. Couldn't let him. She needed to kiss him; she'd never thought she'd *need* something like that, but she did. Especially at that moment, when she felt like one wrong step would sever the thin cord of their relationship forever.

So she leaned forward and took his face in her hands. His muttonchops tickled her palms as she pressed her lips against his, willing him to respond. Please let him respond. She couldn't speak above a whisper; all her hopes and fears had clogged her throat, and it was still so hard, so scary, to say the words anyway. Like sticking her hand into a trap. "I love you, okay? I love you."

His hand reached up to touch her hair; relief washed down her body.

"Aye." He pulled back. It hadn't gone on for very long, no, and she wasn't stupid enough to think he'd completely forgotten or forgiven or whatever it was people did in that situation. But he was there, and he wasn't looking at her with anger or contempt. So that was a good thing, right?

She waited to see if he'd say anything else. He didn't. Should she explain again, apologize again? What the hell was she supposed to do? Something told her grabbing him and taking him to bed, or ripping off her clothes, or something along those lines, was not the thing to do at that moment.

So. From the kiss to the murder. "Um, I have some

other stuff I have to tell you about, too. I did some research today, on death spells. Spells like that one, to create energy from death? Those sometimes catch fire."

He nodded, looked at her. The first time he'd looked her in the eyes since she'd told him. "So Slobag's witch maybe does the job, already got the knowledge the pipe room's gonna burn? Starts up the fire that way, dig."

"Right. Um, you're sure it was Slobag's witch?"

"Know Slobag's got heself a witch, dig, for a certain. Don't know iffen he witch the one killed Eddie." He shook his head. "Ain't can see how some other witch might have got the knowledge on the room bein empty, though, aye? Only were shut down that day."

Right. And didn't she look better and better as a suspect. She got up and grabbed herself a bottle of water from the fridge. It was hard sitting there next to him and not touching him. Hard not climbing into his lap or pulling him on top of her; even if she hadn't been thirsty she would have gotten up just to distract herself. "Any luck finding the spy? You sounded like you might have some news, on the phone."

"Naw, not much." Was that true?

When she turned around, he'd stood up. "Why we ain't head over yon school now, aye? Thinkin be good getting out of here."

Chapter Seventeen

A well-managed home is always ready to receive guests.
—*Mrs. Increase's Advice for Ladies,* by Mrs. Increase

"And you ain't had a chance ask Lex on this witch."

"No," Chess said. They were in her new car, the engine purring under the hood and the Vibrators drifting at low volume from the speakers. The streetlights had that curious vivid brightness they seemed to take on when the weather warmed up; no longer tiny pinpoints like sparks shrunken by cold, but fuzzy halos.

And the streets teemed with people, even at this hour. One in the morning was practically midafternoon in Downside, especially on a night as warm as this one. It almost made Chess wish they could stop the car, get out, go for a walk.

Or even better, sit up on her roof with a twelve of cold beer and her portable disc player on low.

Instead they were on their way back to what she was rapidly coming to think of as her prison. Funny, that was just how she'd felt about school the first time. Except then, of course, she could get out of it.

"When I was talking to that girl at school someone mentioned Slobag's witch, they thought it was me because—because they thought I was with Lex." Fuck fuck fuck, she had to say that, didn't she. "So whoever it is, it's not really public information. At least I don't think so."

"Kinda fucked up, him keeping it secret. Ain't can see why him would."

Unfortunately, she could think of a few reasons why Lex would keep that secret, from the obvious one sitting next to her to the possibility that Slobag planned to use magic to help him take over Downside, which would put her right up against the wall, wouldn't it? If someone started using magic against Bump, she knew exactly where he'd turn. And if someone started using magic against Terrible nobody would have to turn to her at all, because no way was she going to stand back if that happened.

And she knew from the tone of his voice that he knew those reasons just as well as she did.

What other reasons was he thinking of, though? Other reasons why Slobag—why Lex—might keep the identity of his witch hidden? Like because Slobag's witch and Bump's witch were one and the same?

The silence sat heavy between them.

"I'll keep trying to find out," she said finally, before asking again, "Um, did you find out anything? Anything more, I mean."

She slowed for the red light, didn't stop. Too many kids on the street corner with their hats pulled down and their collars pulled up, hiding their faces. Red lights in Downside were always a gamble, but playing odds like those was just stupid. They'd back off when they saw Terrible, sure, but why bother?

Pause. "Got some people work both sides, if you dig. Gave me the tell on—on what happen with you. Gave me the tell on Slobag getting heself some plans, big ones. Only don't got any knowledge what them are. An nobody hear more on he witch."

She wanted to ask if that meant maybe the rumors

about Slobag having a witch were exaggerated, then. Or if maybe Slobag's plans and Slobag's witch weren't quite as related as they could be.

But to ask . . . it might make it look like she was trying to cover something up, to obscure her own guilt. Damn it. Something just didn't feel right, she couldn't help it. "How did Eddie end up in the pipe room?"

His head tilted, his eyebrow rose. Right.

"I mean, why him? Do you know why he ended up being the one?"

He paused, a slow heavy pause she didn't like. Was he trying to decide how much to tell her? How much he trusted her to know? "Lived on the border streets, he did. Figured him got snatched offen em."

"So just random, then." Right. *Bullshit* ran down her spine, down into her chest to squeeze her heart.

His mouth opened, then shut as she turned the wheel again. The dark hulk of the Mercy Lewis school loomed before them, a dead beast abandoned to the elements. She switched off the headlights and half drove, half coasted around to the back, merging into the shadows like being sucked into a pool of thick dark water. And about as comfortable.

Being there with Terrible helped. At least she wouldn't be all alone in the building if something decided to lock her in a janitor's closet or slam her over the head with whatever.

But much as she hated to admit it, Terrible brought along his own set of problems. Like the fact that if anybody saw him they might very well try to kill him. Or someone could call Slobag and then Slobag would try to kill him. And that would be her fault.

Which made it kind of selfish and shitty of her to bring him with her, but she couldn't help it. She was nervous—the empty school at night wasn't like someone's house while they slept—and she felt like she hadn't seen him in days, which frankly sucked, and after everything that had happened . . . she just wanted him there. Even feeling his caution slick on her skin, she wanted him there.

Her car rattled and bumped its way over every rock and patch of uneven ground, banging Terrible's head on the ceiling once. "Shoulda brung my car."

"No, we shouldn't have, and you know why we didn't."

He sighed. Heavily. " 'Stoo small."

"Every car is too small for you." Her smile felt good.

"Mine ain't."

She slid the car up to the theater door and shoved it into gear, set the brake. "Come on."

She'd already turned the interior light off—she did that as soon as she bought the thing; when the light came on inside the car at night it made her too visible, made whatever lurked outside it too *in*visible—and the moon was just a blur in the cloud-covered sky. The air smelled like rain. Shit. That pitiful field of dirt next to the school would turn into a mudpit, and she'd be stuck right in the middle of it.

With a man who probably had an awfully generous price on his head. Not even counting what he was worth to her.

It wasn't raining yet, though. And what was she going to do, take him home and then come back? No. So she should shut up about it.

To aid that, she grabbed a couple of Cepts along with her flashlight, lube syringe, and pick kit. Her water bottle was almost empty; she used the last of it to chase the pills, then set to work on the lock.

Set to work on the cheap, barely effective lock. Interesting. Security at Mercy Lewis didn't appear to be too tight, which opened up a shitload of other possibilities for her case.

"Anybody get in here, aye?" Terrible pulled the door back for her, waited for her to walk in before following. "All them locks so shitty?"

"I don't know about all of the locks, but that one sure was."

"Somebody faking a ghost in here, could be just tryin give them kids the scare."

"Let's hope not. It's hard enough to find out who's responsible inside the school, much less outside."

She took his hand as they started through the maze of scenery flats, past the destroyed top of the trunk that had almost been her coffin. She shuddered, started to speed her pace, then stopped.

When she'd escaped that thing she'd broken the lock off, sent pieces of wood everywhere. Now the floor was clear: no lock, no wood, not even a few scattered splinters.

So somebody had been in there since she escaped, and tidied up. So what?

So nobody was supposed to be in there.

"Chess? You right?"

"Huh? Oh, yeah, right up. Sorry. Just . . . thinking about something."

Darkness hid his expression from her, but she knew what it would be. That half-patient, half-curious look, waiting to see if she'd tell him more and not wanting to ask.

She didn't want to tell him. He already knew enough of her stupid problems and weaknesses; he didn't need to hear about The Time Chess Got Trapped in the Trunk, too.

But he also didn't trust her, did he? So she settled for "I was here earlier and it was messy. There was stuff all over. Now it's cleaned up."

"Somebody been in here."

"Right."

Together they walked up the aisle to the lighting booth in the back, where Terrible boosted her up so she could attach a camera above it to face the stage. Just in case. "Okay, done."

He turned her so she slid down him rather than being set down, so her chest pressed against his when her feet hit the floor. His hands stayed on her hips. A shiver of excitement bloomed in her stomach, and lower, when their eyes met.

She ran her fingers up over his shoulder, up the back of his neck. Her voice came out huskier than she'd expected. "Hey. I'm glad you came with me."

"Aye?"

"Yeah." She urged his head down with her fingers, strained on tiptoe to kiss him. "I— And we'll figure this out, who the spy is. I know we will."

Mentioning it—the elephant in the room, the scarlet letter on her chest—might not have been the smartest thing, but she couldn't help it. She wanted to talk to him about it. She wanted to reassure him. Wanted to make him feel safe, the way his arms around her waist made her feel, the way her chest pressed against his made her feel.

So she kissed him again, this time feeling him relax a bit against her, then more, playing off her enthusiastic response until her head started to swim. His hands slid up under the hem of her shirt to the small of her back and stayed there, warm and solid, and her own hands found places under his collar, in his hair. The booth had a little ledge in it . . . A week was way too long.

Terrible must have thought the same thing. Without breaking the kiss he lifted her, propped her on the ledge.

She started to smile, then stopped because she needed her mouth for something else. His belt buckle made a faint clank when she pulled it open, barely audible over the sound of her breath loud in her ears as she tugged open the button fly of his jeans, felt him do the same to hers.

For a second she thought of saying something, thanking him for believing her—if he did, which she guessed he was at least willing to give her the benefit of the doubt and wasn't that way the fuck more than she deserved— telling him how much she'd missed him all day, how more than being glad he was there, she was *grateful* he was there. The words formed in her mind, on her tongue.

She shoved them back. No. She couldn't bring those fears into it, couldn't start talking and thinking and, especially, making him think, not then.

This was the one time she didn't worry about how long she had, how he really felt, what she was going to do to fuck it all up.

This was the one time she felt totally safe, totally comfortable, when his body pressed against hers like she could melt into him. When she could run her hands over his chest, up and down his back, farther down to pull him even closer so they both gasped.

But the words in her head were a reminder, one she didn't need. A reminder that she *was* failing, that she *was* fucking up, that it wasn't a question of *when* she would spoil everything but of *how long* he would put up with the way she was spoiling everything. They made her feel as if she was standing on a railing above the city, balancing there with nothing to hold on to, and if she lost her balance she'd fall off.

And she'd never stop falling.

It was pitiful and wrong to feel that way, but then, when had she ever not been pitiful and wrong?

She didn't want to think about that, didn't want to ruin a moment she'd been waiting for—craving—for the last seven days. Instead, she slipped her fingertips under the waistband of his boxers, brushing against his skin. The sound he made, a small quiet kind of sigh, sent a roar of happiness, of something oddly like triumph, through her.

Behind his back she started toeing off her shoes. Or her *shoe;* the right one flipped off, the left one didn't. Fuck it. That was enough. More than enough, especially when his lips caressed her collarbone, his hands slid up her shirt, and his thumbs passed over her nipples so sparks shot from them through the rest of her body. Particularly all points south. She tingled everywhere, all up and down her arms and across her shoulders and chest, her skin too warm and begging to be stroked, almost crawling in its eagerness to reach his hands—

Shit.

She pulled back so fast she banged the back of her head against the window of the booth. "Fuck!"

"Aye, just—"

"No." She twisted away from him with her heart still pounding, and clumped a few one-shoe-off-one-shoe-on steps to peer out the door of the booth. "Fucking magic. Someone's doing magic in here."

"Aw, shit. You must joke."

She glanced over her shoulder to see him bracing himself on his fists on the counter, glaring at her with his jeans hanging open and his belt buckle dangling. Well, no, not glaring at her, glaring at the empty space just beyond her. "I wish."

Fury. Absolute fury. Not just at the interrupted moment—could she get a fucking break already?—but because someone else was there when no one was supposed to be. Because the thickness of what she felt, the particular itchy darkness of it, made her sure that whatever that someone was doing wasn't pleasant. At the very least they were probably summoning a ghost, and wouldn't that fucking suck.

"Got all yon herbs an all?" The heat from his skin

caressed her when he walked up behind her; she had to fight herself not to turn around and get right back to where they'd been. Only the tons of sharp steel all over the floor of the theater kept her from it. That wreckage was like a one-stop shop for weapons, and the last thing she wanted was to be sneaked up on and killed in the middle of *that*.

A flash of pale light caught her eye, to the left. Another. The theater doors hung open; when the hell had that happened? Was it while they were in the booth, or were they open before? Shit, she hadn't even looked, not that she could remember. Those doors were supposed to be closed—and locked.

Of course, ghosts were perfectly capable of turning locks and opening doors. So were witches. So was anyone, for that matter, but she wasn't feeling the way she felt because a couple of kids had sneaked into the building to graffiti the Master Elder's office or booby-trap a friend's locker. Nothing but magic, nothing but ghosts, did that to her.

Her tattoos itched and stung like sunburn, and that glimpse of bluish-white hadn't been a flashlight. She ducked back into the booth, tugged on her other shoe while trying to slow her breath. Damn it damn it damn it damn it.

And her water bottle was empty, and there was no fucking way she was going to get anything done with all that frustrated heat coursing through her. She had a couple of Pandas in her pillbox. They didn't always help much but maybe they would this time. *Something* better help this time, or she'd explode.

She dry-swallowed them while she shouldered her bag. Terrible had closed his jeans, refastened his belt. His hair still tufted a bit in the back, and a couple more buttons of his shirt were undone than had been before—she didn't even remember doing that.

"Sorry," she said.

He shrugged. "Better us catch em up afore them get the sneak-up, aye?"

"Yeah, but it still sucks."

"Aye."

She slid out of the booth and headed for the atrium beyond the theater. Handling a witch wouldn't be too difficult, not with Terrible there. Unless the witch also carried a gun or something, chances were the two of them would be able to take him or her—both male and female energies seemed to be in there, but that could be to do with the gender of the summoned ghost—down. Banishing a ghost would be pretty easy, too. She had her psychopomp in her bag, had everything else she'd need.

Finding it to Banish? Finding its summoner? That was the hard part. And hooray for her, she got to do that next.

Chapter Eighteen

Do not think the dead do not see you. They do. Do not think the dead do not wish you to join them. They do, above all else.

—*The Book of Truth*, Veraxis, Article 78

They headed through the atrium without touching, down the hall to the left where Chess had seen the flash of white. Her tattoos still tingled. She glanced at Terrible; he looked fine in the half-light seeping in through the windows, but she asked anyway: "You okay?"

"Aye."

"You sure? Because—"

"I'm right, Chess, no worryin, aye?"

Sure. She wouldn't worry. After all, he was only more vulnerable to possession because of the sigil she'd carved into his chest two months or so before, right? So there was absolutely no reason to worry about him when in the presence of ghosts or magic.

Somehow she doubted he'd appreciate it if she expressed her concerns, though, so she didn't. In silence they hit the landing and descended the stairway. No light entered there at all, not even the faint moonlight. She had to clutch the railing and feel her way.

About halfway down, right after they'd turned and started on the next flight, she saw it. The open doorway at the foot, and the faint glow emanating from it.

She fisted some asafetida and graveyard dirt, ready

to throw. Beside her a faint sliding noise, metal against metal; Terrible pulling out the iron knife she'd given him, she imagined, since iron was the only metal that had any effect on a ghost.

They separated, hugging opposite walls and creeping down with their eyes pinned on the doorway. The glow didn't change, didn't fade or increase, almost as if the ghost was standing still just beyond the door. As if it waited for them. Which it very well might be, and wasn't that a happy thought.

With every step down more of the room grew visible; more of the ghost grew visible, until she could see that it stood not moving, watching the stairwell. Pipes or some kind of bludgeons hung from its hands. Shit.

Nothing else to do, really, right? She started to run, leaping down the final four stairs and speeding toward the ghost—a female, she thought—as fast as she could, her bag bouncing and clinking.

Terrible was faster. He was just about to slice at the ghost when it disappeared.

Fuck! They didn't usually do that, crazy as it sounded; their arrogance and anger distracted them, and they never expected anyone to have iron, much less the asafetida she held.

Luckily the weapons the now-hidden ghost had carried couldn't disappear with it. They lay there on the floor. As she tried to focus on the ghost's energy she saw Terrible pick them up, a couple of random silvery strips of metal.

Focusing was easier said than done. Energy filled the room, but worse, it still filled her. Her pulse raced from running and fear, but it had never fully stopped after the interrupted scene in the booth.

It got worse when Terrible pressed his back to hers. Her tattoos still burned and itched, uncomfortable and prickly, but where the ghost was she had no idea. All she knew was that the hair on the back of her neck stood on end and she had goosebumps, and at any second the ghost might appear, snatch up a weapon, and kill her, kill either or both of them, before she had a chance to react.

Around them, the room—an enormous room, she thought it was the cafeteria—waited, hushed in the darkness. She felt eyes out there, hundreds of them, maybe thousands. Bugs and rats and who knew what else. People, of course; the magic felt too strong to be old. Anyone could be hiding in those shadows.

Did the magic feel familiar, too? The energy? Now that she stood there, despite her nerves and everything else, she thought maybe it did. But why? Where had she felt it before, and when?

Not the time to focus on that, not when the ghost or the witch or both could be only a step away with sharp weapons at the ready. Chess took a deep breath. The air carried the sharp, stale smell of institution food: plastic cheese and reheated leftovers damp under red heatlamps. It reminded her of the Corey Youth Home where she'd spent a few months before the Church took her, turned her stomach like the tea Beulah had given her earlier, that afternoon that felt like it had taken place years before.

The ghost appeared. At the far end of the room, too far away for them to reach it.

"It sposed to do that? Hide, 'stead of fightin?" The words, barely more than a whisper, slid over her skin; his back moved against hers with the rhythm of his breath.

"No. I've never seen one—"

The ghost blinked into existence, closer this time. Shit! Still too far away for them to have a chance in hell of reaching it before it disappeared again, but close enough to worry her just that tiny bit more. She cocked her arm, ready to throw the dirt and asafetida at the next thing that moved.

Unless, of course, that thing was thirty feet away. What the fuck? It wasn't heading for them. Barely even looked at them. It headed to its left, still flickering in and out like a dying lightbulb.

Terrible and Chess started creeping along together, following it. If she could get close enough while it wasn't paying attention, she could freeze it. Then she could Banish it and be done.

It had almost reached the wall; she didn't know what lay on the other side, if it was more building or if it was patchy vacant lot, but she did know there wasn't another exit along that wall, at least not one she could see.

They sped up. The closer they got, the more the ghost came into focus. Long dark hair—it wasn't really dark, of course, but it had that particular way of absorbing light that indicated dark hair, they'd been taught that early in Church training—and a tight top that ended above the curve of her waist. Below her waist a hint of jeans, fading at her thighs until all she had at the bottom were pale columns like stilts. Fuck. Chess had an awfully good idea what she would see when that ghost turned around.

It knew they were there. It had to know they were coming for it. They'd already tried once. So why wasn't it fighting them? She'd never seen a ghost back down from a fight, much less try to escape. Sure, not all of them were killers, just about ninety-nine percent of them; hell, some of them were still violent but liked to fuck with people first, passing through them and rattling chains and moving things, like disembodied stereotypes.

Somehow, though, she didn't think this ghost was one of those, either. It just . . . didn't care about them.

Or it didn't until she got closer to it. Then it spun around to face her. She caught a glimpse of its face, lips twisting in sudden rage, eyes black holes stretching in its face, before it produced a metal bar and slammed her arm with it.

Ow, fuck! It felt like the veins under her skin had exploded, like they'd somehow popped. Hot pain like rings of reddish flame radiated from it, racing up her arm to invade her entire body.

Of course it hit her right arm. The dirt and herbs fell from her hand.

Terrible had started moving the second the ghost did. The iron dagger slashed through it like a toothpick through custard, leaving a smeary trail across its midsection.

The ghost raised the pipe again—it was a plumbing pipe of some kind, a joint hooked down at the end—and brought it around sidearm. The rage on her face turned to fury and her eyes started stretching down her cheeks, her teeth gritted, so the image of the skeleton her body would have been could be seen superimposed on top of it; Chess could make out the details, the flaky bits of skin and sinew hanging from the moldy bones. What the hell? Why was that happening?

The pipe whistled down, fast enough for her eyes to lose it. She knew where it landed, though. The same spot on her arm. "Ow! What the fuck—"

Terrible slashed at the ghost again, leaving another trail. It was starting to lose its form, to widen and soften at the edges. Its energy brushed against her, ice cold, the air around her stronger and more malicious.

The ghost swung at her again, missed, and finally noticed Terrible when he brought the dagger down into its arm. It dropped the pipe but caught it with its other hand; it slammed the pipe against his left thigh and started to run, a horrible jerky run.

Where that thing got the power to run she didn't know, but it did, heading straight for the staircase.

Chess and Terrible followed. Chess managed to fill her hand with more asafetida and dirt, hoping she wouldn't have to do it again. She was almost out.

Terrible ducked behind her, grabbed her and started pulling her along. He ran much faster than she did. They started gaining on the ghost.

It turned and flung the pipe. At Chess. She managed to duck out of the way, but as she did she caught sight of a pile of metal there in the stairwell. Fuck, how long had that ghost been gathering weapons? Was that why it had been in—in the theater, damn it. It had been in the theater, with all that metal.

Sure enough, bits of the catwalk started flying at her. Terrible stood in front of her—she tried to push him out of the way but it was like trying to push a fucking mountain—and blocked the ones he could, shoving her head down with his hand when he had to duck.

Grisly triumph spread across the ghost's face when Chess peered out from behind him. Both of the ghost's hands were bristling with weapons. Both of them kept moving, throwing things. Metal thudded to the floor, clanged against the railings, echoed in the empty darkness.

Terrible pushed her down, ducked again. Her hair stirred; whatever it was, it had passed not far from her bowed head. It was aiming for her again.

Aiming, but not approaching. It must have known what she carried, that if it got too close she could end the miserable game it was playing.

Enough of this shit. She jumped out from behind Terrible, flung the handful of herbs and dirt at the ghost.

And missed.

Fuck! Fuck fuck fuck. The ghost's smile grew even more triumphant. Terrible's dagger brushed against its head, creating a smudge. It stepped back, threw a piece of grate—and disappeared.

They stood there, watching the air where it had been. Its weapons had fallen; Terrible ducked forward to grab them up, crossed the doorway to stand in the corner where the stockpile was. Or rather, where it had been. Hardly anything littered the floor there. No wonder the ghost had finally run.

Chess's arms and chest under her ink still felt as if someone had given them a sandpaper massage, but less than they had just a minute before. No longer screaming, as though her skin was trying to jump off her body and hide. The magic was gone; whatever spell had been working was finished. The energy faded like the sound of a passing train receding in the distance.

"She still here?" His voice quiet again, calming her.

"I don't think so. It's fading. The spell, I mean, the magic. And if someone summoned her, then yeah, she might disappear when the spell ends. It depends on how strong the witch is, you know?"

They started walking back to the stairway. "Summoning ghosts . . . that's not easy to do, and it requires a lot of energy."

"Shit."

"Exactly."

They rounded the final corner, back into the wide expanse of the cafeteria. "So now what? You gotta know who summoned it, or just its name? The ghost name, meaning."

"I already know." She didn't even bother trying to keep the bitterness out of her voice. Damn it. "Her name is Lucy McShane. She was a student here when the school first opened. She killed herself in the theater."

They started toward the stairwell, picking up pipes and scraps of twisted catwalk as they went to return it to the theater. The last thing Chess wanted to do was leave evidence that someone had been in the school that night.

"How'd she do it?"

"Threw herself off this," she said, waving a piece of steel. "The catwalk in the theater."

He shook his head. "Fuckin drop, aye?"

"Far enough, yeah." She thought about it, that vertiginous second looking down at the floor so far below. "Far enough."

He plucked off most of her metal pile as they hit the stairs, added it to his own. She was glad, too, even though his hand brushed against her breast when he did and sent another sharp stab of desire through her, so hard it almost hurt.

They started up the stairs in silence.

"Good thing you ain't done it," he said. Casually, like it didn't matter. "Glad you ain't, meaning." His gaze focused on the landing, looking straight ahead. Not at her. Giving her privacy.

She hesitated. No point in asking how he knew she'd thought of it when she was younger, before she'd joined the Church. There had been days when suicide was all she could think about, when it was a secret dream she'd clutched to herself, the ultimate escape. And the only reason she'd never done it was that if she failed, she'd be in even bigger trouble.

It didn't surprise her that he knew that, either. He would. She kept her voice just as casual. "Did you ever think about it?"

"Naw." Now he did glance at her, fast but enough that she saw it, felt it. "Weren't me I wanted dead. Only all them others, aye?"

"Do you still?"

He shrugged. "Don't give a fuck neitherway, most of em."

A window at the landing showed her a glimpse of the empty field outside as they rounded it and started up the next level. It looked dead out there, cold and still under the mottled sky. She wanted to point it out to him, to say something about it. She wished their arms weren't full so she could touch him.

He cleared his throat. "We get this dropped off, get us home, aye? Ain't likin the thought some other witch in here. Feels like bein watched."

Relief. "We probably should, yeah, and come back tomorrow night."

"This give you the help? The knowledge somebody doin magic there, callin the ghost. Make a difference?"

"Yeah, but—shit. It just sucks, is all. I won't get a full bonus on this one. When ghosts are summoned the Church doesn't have to pay a settlement, but it's not an actual Debunking, either."

His eyes fastened on her, waiting for her to continue. When she didn't, he said, "Ain't needing the lashers, aye? Causen I got—"

"No, no, I'm fine, I have money, I just . . . it's depressing to lose, you know? I don't like it."

He smiled, and even in the middle of her misery, in the furious tangle of her mind, she was able to see it, feel it all the way down to her toes. "Oh, aye? Never would guess that one."

Her smile couldn't compete with his, but hey, at least she was able to make the attempt. "Yeah, I guess that's not really a secret, is it?"

"Ain't to me."

Her arms ached. "Let's drop this stuff off now, huh?"

They passed into the theater, headed across the back to the booth and then down the stairs toward the stage. Damn it. What a fucking night, what a fucking waste. She'd managed to set up one camera, discover she wouldn't earn her full bonus, and get injured. Whoopee. She could have spent the last two hours in bed with Terrible, bursting into flame again and again. Feeling secure for the first time in days.

"Got any thought why she? That ghost, meaning. Still around causen she kill herself, or aught else?"

She thought about it for a second, setting her metal down—finally—by the catwalk's wreckage. Oh, that felt good. She flexed her hands, turned her wrists to try to wake her skin back up. "It could be any reason, really. The spell felt like two people, but I think one of them was her. Lucy. So it was a man doing the summoning, at least I think so. And whoever he is, I guess he wanted her."

A clatter of metal as he dropped his pile. "That why the ghost ain't come after us at the start? Like we wasn't even there, aye?"

"Probably. That implies a really close relationship between the summoner and the ghost, you know? Like a Binding or something. Communication."

He nodded.

The stage rose a few short steps above the theater floor. She switched on her flashlight as she climbed up them, turned to give the light to him. As she did, the beam caught his face. "Hey!"

"What?"

Across the base of his neck on his left side a dark red line marked his skin, just above the tattoo there. She reached out and touched it.

"Aw, got me with a pipe, 'sall. Don't even hurt."

Sure it didn't. He could lie all he wanted but that had to fucking hurt; being hit in the neck wasn't fun, as she knew from experience.

The top few buttons of his bowling shirt were still undone, so she could pull the collar away, hook her finger into the neck of the white T-shirt he wore under it, and pull that aside, too.

"Ain't worry on it. No problem, aye?"

She'd never done this before. Never really seen it done outside of a movie or something. Certainly no one had ever done it for her, not seriously. Lex didn't count; he didn't tend to be area-specific enough.

Terrible was probably going to think she was an idiot for doing it, too, but she wanted to try it anyway. That skin looked so raw, so insulted, and it was soft and defenseless. It was her fault he'd been hurt, and he'd been hurt trying to protect her. And it seemed like . . . well, it seemed like something people did, right?

"C'mon, let's get us—"

"Us" almost echoed in the warm still air around them as she pressed her lips to the beginning of what she knew would soon be an ugly bruise. She loved his neck, especially that part, loved the way he reacted when she sucked on it. No sucking this time, of course, but the smell of his skin, that soapy-smoky-bay-rum-pomade smell, still made her tingle.

His hands warmed her even more, fingers curled tight at her waist. He swallowed. "What you doin?"

He'd probably laugh, or think she was a total dork, but she said it anyway. "I'm kissing it better."

She kept going, moving slowly from one end of the bruise-to-be toward the other, making sure she got every bit of it. Wouldn't do to miss a spot. Just the feel of him under her lips, the taste of him, made her dizzy. Overwhelmed. She could keep going, she could kiss his earlobe, down his chest—

"Chess."

"Yeah?"

His left hand curled into her hair, gathered it, and twisted it. Tugged it to pull her away. "Think it's all better now."

The words were a handful of dirt tossed onto the burgeoning fire inside her. Shit, she knew it. What a dorky fucking thing to do. "Oh. Right. Um, sorry, I just—"

His mouth on hers, the kind of insistent kiss she knew well. The kind that made her blood race through her veins until it found a good place to stop, the kind that made her clutch at him harder than she meant to.

The kind she felt sometimes when he wasn't even there, because she'd thought of him, his hands touching her head, her face, sliding over every inch of her body, and no matter where she was her stomach leapt and her muscles tightened.

Just like they were doing at that moment. He kissed her deeper, harder, as he took her hand in his and turned it, guiding it down past his belt so she could feel how hard he was. How the hell was she supposed to breathe when he did that?

The theater floor was cement. Probably not very comfortable.

"My car," she managed. Harder to talk when his fingers caressed the back of her neck. Harder to talk when his right hand slid over her bottom, yanked her tight against him, heat seeping through her shirt.

Both hands at her hips now, down to her thighs so he could pick her up and climb the remaining stairs, stopping to kiss her again when he reached the stage. The car seemed too far away, they'd never reach it, the top of her head was going to blow the hell off if—

"Well, well, well. So it *is* true."

Chess pulled away from him, fast. Lucky his reflexes were fast, too, or she would have fallen on her ass on the stage.

Right in front of Beulah, who stood next to the booth at the top of the rows of seats. Chess couldn't make out her expression, but she'd have bet money the woman was grinning.

Chapter Nineteen

The psychopomp exists solely to do its duty. It has no other thought or purpose. We would do well to emulate it.
—*Psychopomps: The Key to Church Ritual and Mystery,*
by Elder Brisson

Terrible set Chess down on her unsteady feet; they both turned to face Beulah. Out of the corner of her eye Chess saw him reach around to grab the handle of his knife under his shirts. Just in case.

It was on the tip of her tongue to tell him not to worry, but that was bullshit, wasn't it? Obviously they needed to worry. What the hell was Beulah doing there in the middle of the night?

And what the hell was "So it *is* true" supposed to mean?

Beulah hadn't spoken again, and Chess was not about to speak first. Not when she was already pretty much as powerless as she could be in this situation. She couldn't even tell Beulah to get out because her presence interfered with some made-up magic thing Chess could pretend to be doing; however much Beulah had seen, she sure as hell knew it wasn't related to the school or the investigation.

"Cat got your tongue? Or I guess it wouldn't be the cat, huh." Beulah started down the steps toward the stage, slowly, then stumbled when Chess lifted the flashlight so the beam caught her full in the face. "Ow, shit! Turn that thing off. What the hell are you trying to do, kill me?"

"Maybe."

"Oh, for fuck's sake." Beulah had reached the foot of the stairs. Terrible's arm tightened against Chess, ready to pull the knife; Chess slid her own hand into her pocket, curled her fingers around hers. She wouldn't really be able to use it but it made her feel better, like a talisman.

Beulah sighed. Damn, she was good at that. She managed to convey irritation, exhaustion, condescension, pity—all in one exhale. That took skill. "Cut it out. I'm not going to attack you."

"Why are you here?"

"Why shouldn't I be here? I work here."

"A couple of days a week."

"Sometimes more." Beulah lowered herself into one of the chairs in the first row, her legs crossed tidily at the ankle. She wore snug black jeans and a pair of shiny black ballet flats, a black V-neck sweater with just the right amount of drape. How the hell could she afford that wardrobe? Even Chess could see that shit was expensive, and the nicest item of clothing she'd ever owned was the Church ceremony dress that had cost her forty bucks.

More to the point, there was the fact that it was all black. Just the right color to blend into shadows, especially in vast dark rooms, in unfamiliar places. "What are you doing here?"

"Not what you were doing, obviously, but—"

"Come on."

"Oh, lighten up. Someone heard noises outside. They called me, and I found the side doors unlocked. You really shouldn't leave those open like that, you know."

Chess glanced at Terrible. He was still staring at Beulah—glaring at her—with the kind of intensity with which hawks tracked mice. Dislike sat in the faint downward twist of his mouth, subtle but there.

"We didn't leave that door open," she said to Beulah. "We came in through the . . ." Shit.

A pause, a long one, while she wondered whether she should tell Beulah about the magic, the other person in the building. To stall she said, "Why would they call *you* to come check out a noise? Why would you come?"

"I was afraid it was Vernal and his friends. They've done it before. I didn't want them to get busted."

"But why you?"

"Why not me? I'm not exactly a stranger around here or anything. If you didn't open those doors, who did?"

Above the flashlight's beam her face was blurry, set back in soft shadows. But her eyes glittered as she looked back and forth between them. "Ah. Someone else was here, huh? Did you— No, I guess you didn't catch them. Maybe you scared them off?"

Damn. Chess shook her head.

"No what? No, you didn't catch them, or no, you didn't scare them off?"

"Both. I guess. We didn't catch them." She was beginning to feel like an idiot standing there on the stage while Beulah sat below her, like a director holding auditions. But when she started to sit, Terrible grabbed the back of her shirt. Why wouldn't he want her to sit down?

He wasn't going to tell her right then, that was for sure.

"So were you going to look for them, or what? Oh, I guess you weren't, were you?"

"We knew they left the building. So we were going to leave, too, is all."

Beulah's gaze switched to Terrible, swept from the top of his head—pomaded strands falling over his forehead, messy from her hands—past his half-unbuttoned shirt and stretched collar, all the way to his dirty worn-down boots. "You don't talk much, do you, Terrible? I'd heard that about you."

When he didn't answer she shrugged and turned back to Chess. "Well. I guess I'll let you two get on with it. I'm tired." She stood up.

"Wait." Chess shook off Terrible's grabbing hand on her shirt again and headed down the stairs. There was one thing she could do, and she would. Beulah could say all she wanted to that some good Samaritan—ha, good Samaritans in Downside were about as common as diamonds in boxes of rat poison—had called her, but Chess didn't buy that for a second. There had to be some other reason Beulah was there, and she intended to find out what it was.

Reaching for Beulah's hand felt like a stupid thing to do, and Chess had no idea what to say as she did it, but it needed to be done. Her mind clicked and flashed until she finally came up with, "Are you going to be here tomorrow?"

Wow. That was clever.

Beulah's eyebrows rose; she looked down at their joined hands. "Are you asking me out? Holding hands is okay, but I don't kiss on the—"

"Ha-ha. Yes, Beulah, I'm dying to—"

Behind her Terrible made a sound; not a sarcastic one, more like surprise. Beulah's gaze snapped to him; her face paled for a second before she turned back. What the hell was that all about?

"I'm dying to make you mine," Chess finished. "Please. I just want to know if you'll be here tomorrow so I can ask you some more questions, that's all."

"I will be, yes." Beulah looked at their hands again, deliberately.

Chess let go. She had what she needed, anyway; Beulah's energy, the feel of it, very faint—she wasn't a witch, and didn't seem to have much talent in that direction, either—but still enough for Chess to make a judgment.

She hadn't been doing ghost magic, hadn't been around it. At least not that Chess could feel.

"Fine. See you tomorrow, then."

She and Terrible watched Beulah climb the steps, sashay behind the booth and over to the theater door. It closed behind her with a soft *clunk*.

The second it did, Terrible turned to Chess. His brows drew down; redness crept up his neck, hiding the bruise-to-be. "Why the fuck ain't you tell me she was here? She work here?"

"What?"

"You been talking to her? An you ain't said a word." Suspicion lurked behind his eyes, growing bolder by the second, almost as fast as her bruised heart started breaking into pieces.

"I don't— Why would I, she's just some community liaison person." When he didn't respond she reached out, touched his hand with her own. Her fingers were too cold, too stiff to wrap around his, and when she talked she heard the edge of panic in her voice. Too bad being ashamed of that panic, embarrassed by it—and oh, she definitely was—didn't make it go away.

"What did I do? I don't know why I would need to tell you, I'm sorry. It wasn't deliberate or anything—"

His deep-set black eyes, pools of shadow in his face, focused on her. His head tilted. "You ain't know? True thing?"

"No, I— Please tell me what I did. I didn't mean to, whatever it was I didn't mean to, okay? Tell me, please?"

Ah, yes. How much better could she make herself look? She'd failed to Banish the ghost, and now she stood there begging, with her eyes stinging and hot. Fuck.

"Ain't can believe you don't know, sleepin at—at Lex's place all you did." With a jolt of surprise that sent waves of nausea through her, she saw the hurt on his face, the confusion. This was it, this was it, she knew it was too good to last, she knew she'd fuck it up just like she always did. Just like she took anything and everything that might be good for her and trampled it beneath her irresponsible feet every chance she got.

"I'm sorry," she managed. "Whatever I did, I'm sorry."

Pause. "Callin her what? Beulah? What the fuck game she got on."

It wasn't really a question, but she tried to answer it anyway. "That's her name, I don't— That's how she was introduced to me is all . . ."

Oh, no. Oh fuck no. Oh please please please no, because the pieces snapped into place in her head and she knew what he was going to say, and her blood turned to acid. Suspicious indeed.

"She's Lex's sister, isn't she. Blue. That's her, isn't it."

He nodded. Opened his mouth to speak, but whatever he was going to say snapped off like a spent rubber band when Beulah's scream invaded the theater.

There had been worse nights than this one. This one didn't even really compete, all things considered; hell, most of her life she'd considered any night a victory if she managed to survive until morning with food in her stomach, without being beaten or used.

But not this night. Not when she still felt Terrible's distance even though he stood by her side smoking a cigarette; not when she felt Beulah's shock and grief like bristly wires jabbing her skin.

Not when the sick creep of death magic slid around her body, up her legs to wrap around her chest and squeeze, as she looked at the dead body—at what was left of the dead body—of Jia Zhang, spread-eagled within the confines of the *hafuran* painted in still-wet blood on the cracked patch of cement right outside the school's front doors. It was worse than Eddie's, in some ways; it hadn't burned, so the slices on the girl's skin, the way she'd been torn open, were still clear.

That had been the ritual being done, she guessed, the spell they'd felt. The one giving the spell caster more power. And the ghost was coincidence. Wrong a-fucking-gain.

"I can feel them this time," she told Terrible, standing close to him. Not too close, but close. If she stood *too* close she thought he'd move away, and she couldn't bear it if he did. Especially now, when even her bones felt cold despite the balmy night, and all she wanted to do was bury her face in his chest, feel his strong arms around her keeping her from falling into the abyss beneath her. She couldn't see the pit, the crack in the earth that wanted to swallow her, but she knew it was there; she walked a tightrope over it every day, every minute.

It took almost all of her strength not to throw herself at him. It took almost all of her strength not to dig into her pillbox and swallow everything she had. She couldn't take this. Too much stress, too much sadness, too much frustration . . . it would never end, and she was so fucking tired of trying to find a place to rest.

Tired of finding it—thinking she'd found it—and having it torn out from under her.

Terrible nodded. "Aye? Same as Eddie?"

"Eddie? Who is that? This happened before?" Beulah seemed to have no compunction about standing close to either of them. She circled the *hafuran* and came to a stop right between them. So helpful of her to stand there; Chess would have to remember to thank her later.

Terrible gave her a sharp glance. Right. Shit. Did Beulah already know? But—no. No, the idea that she'd deliberately come into the theater just so she could seem stunned and upset at the murder to throw them off the trail seemed a bit much, didn't it? Why wouldn't she just not show up at all?

Lex had mentioned Blue more than once, yeah, but never in connection to work. How much did she have to do with all of that?

Guess it was time to find out. Chess took a deep breath, filtered through her tight throat. "He's—he was—from our side of town. Killed the night before last, just like this."

Beulah's mouth turned down. "And you didn't tell me. Or Lex."

"Why the fuck would I tell you? Or Lex? Why do you need to know?"

"Someone's performing ritual murders in Downside and you don't think—"

"Someone performed *a* ritual murder, on *our* side of town." A ritual murder Beulah's father might already know about, but she bit that one back. She'd find out soon enough. And even if he didn't, fuck Beulah. "So no, I didn't think it was time to call in backup. Sorry. I should have known how much more skilled at this shit you and Lex are than me. Oh, but how would I have known, when you didn't even tell me who you are?"

"Don't get on your fucking attitude train with me. You should have said something and you know it. You knew I had connections in the community, you knew I could have had people watching."

"Yeah, your fucking community watchdogs were really effective when those hookers were being murdered. Very impressive how they caught the guy— Oh, no, wait. That was me."

"With help from my brother."

"Oh, bullshit. If you think he was any—"

Her gaze fell on Terrible watching them with the disinterested expression he generally wore when he was bored or trying not to react to things. She didn't know which one it was at that moment, but she knew neither of them really appealed.

Beulah seemed to come to her senses as well. After a few seconds of embarrassed silence she said, "I'm sorry, Chess. You're right, why would you have told me. Or Lex. It wasn't our territory."

"Thank you." That sounded stiff, so she softened it with, "I shouldn't have yelled, either."

Beulah smiled, a quick flash in the darkness. She turned her head toward poor Jia's mutilated body. "I guess I should call my father about her, get someone to come pick her up—"

"You can't," Chess said, but as soon as the words left her mouth she realized there was no way in hell she could call the Church and report this. Not when she hadn't reported Eddie's similar death the night before. What could she say? "Oh, yeah, well, I saw a man murdered just like this last night, but my drug dealer just took care of discarding his body somehow so we didn't have to get you involved." Sure. That would totally work, and totally not get her ass fired and thrown in jail.

If she called the Church, she would lose everything. If she didn't, she'd be giving Slobag something serious to hold over her head, something that wasn't her addiction and didn't implicate him in it. If she didn't, she'd have to handle the case by herself, and for some strange reason that thought just didn't hold much appeal for her.

Two choices, both of them shitty. Story of her life.

Chapter Twenty

Church employees sacrifice much to protect you from the threat of the dead. Your allegiance is owed to the Church for this.

—*The Book of Truth*, Laws, Article 17

Beulah stood before her, arms folded, eyebrows raised. The look on her face told Chess that the other woman knew exactly what sort of mental calculation she was doing in her head. "Well? Are you going to tell me why I can't do the only logical thing?"

Fuck. Chess couldn't quite look up, couldn't quite meet either Beulah's eyes or Terrible's. "No. You're right, that's what you should do. And— Okay, I guess we should go, huh? So your father's witch can get a look at it?"

"What?"

"Your father's witch. He has one, correct?"

Beulah's eyes narrowed. "I thought they were talking about you."

"No." Okay, that answered that one—sort of, anyway. Beulah could be lying.

Whether she was or wasn't, though, what was Chess going to do, leave this for some random maybe-witch to deal with?

She wanted to. Fuck, how she wanted to. Wipe her hands of this whole mess and head back to Terrible's place, to his big warm bed. Or hers, which wasn't quite as big but would be just as warm. Either one, she didn't care, as long as no one would interrupt them again.

She folded her arms over her chest, gritted her teeth. "Fine. I'll stay. Until he gets here, at least."

Beulah nodded, but instead of pulling out her phone, she looked at Terrible. What was that about?

Oh, right. If one more positive thing happened in this whole situation she was going to explode from the sheer joy of it all. "Beulah, can you take him home? We came in my car, so—"

"Ain't leavin you here alone."

"You can't stay, though. Not here. They'll kill you when they see you."

He snorted.

"She's right, Terrible," Beulah cut in. "Not to mention what seeing you with her will do to anyone he might bring, what they'd say. She's having a hard enough time getting any information at all."

Oh, fuck, Chess hadn't even thought of that. If they knew she wasn't actually with Lex, wasn't Slobag's witch, one of "them"—ha, they'd probably think she was cheating on Lex with Terrible. Oh, the irony. So fucking funny.

Or it would be if Beulah wasn't spot-fucking-on in saying that they'd try to kill him the minute they saw him.

She took the three steps that brought her right in front of him, put her hand on his still folded arms, and looked in his eyes, wishing violently that this hadn't happened, that none of it had happened, and she could just get in the car and go home with him, dive under the covers and stay there.

She let that wish show on her face, hoped he'd be able to see it. "They don't trust me. It'll be worse if they see you."

He shook his head. "Ain't leavin you alone."

"I— You can take my car. Take my car, and Beulah will drive me home. Right, Beulah? See, she'll drive me home. Just please, take my car and go, okay?"

"Don't trust her." He said it loud enough for Beulah to hear it. Deliberately loud enough.

Thankfully Beulah didn't respond, although she very well might have made a face or something. Chess didn't know; she refused to turn around and look. Didn't want to look, anyway, not when she could look at him instead.

"Please. I don't want anyone else to get hurt, not tonight. Especially not you. I'll be fine, you know I will."

He was going to give in. She saw it in his eyes, in the way his brow furrowed. "Ain't like it. Who the fuck knows what them might give a try on. Ain't want you here when they do."

"I don't either, but—"

"Lex and I will both be here," Beulah cut in, and Chess's heart—along with any hope she'd had that this would be resolved without making him angry—smashed to the bloody cement at her feet. She had to bring him up, didn't she?

Of course if Chess knew anything about Terrible—which she did—it was that he'd already thought of that, already seen it play out in his head. But knowing something was one thing; having it confirmed was something else entirely.

And oh, shit, was that why he didn't want to leave? He'd seemed to believe her about not knowing who Beulah was, but she knew very well how much he could hide when he wanted to. What if his wanting to stay didn't have anything to do with worrying about her? What if he was really worried about what she might be up to with Slobag, with Lex?

She didn't want to think about that, but she couldn't help thinking about it, either.

"You know Lex won't let anything happen to her. You know that."

The almost-bruise on his throat disappeared again, lost in the dark flush spreading over his skin as he glared at Beulah. Shit. Just what Chess needed. Reassurance from Beulah about how Lex would take such great care of her.

Nobody spoke for a long moment, the silence hanging between them like a crystal globe about to shatter.

"Aye." He reached up, rubbed the back of his neck, turned his head away.

"I'd rather have you here," Chess said, quietly so Beulah might not hear it. She wasn't embarrassed or anything, she just didn't think it was any of Beulah's damn business. She put her hand on his chest. "You know I would. But I'm tired, and I want to go home as soon as I can, and if you stay— You need to tell Bump anyway, right? Go let him know and everything?"

Beulah coughed. A deliberate cough. "I'd like to go home myself sometime before dawn, if that's okay with you two."

Rather than punch her, Chess handed Terrible her keys. If it made him trust her less, fine. At least he'd be alive to do it. "Have fun driving my car."

That earned her a sort of half smile, a semi-laugh. "Aye. Be all cool in it, maybe get myself one."

Relief flooded her system, in the same way and pattern as her pills; and damn, how she wanted a few of those, too.

But then, she could have them, couldn't she? Wasn't like Beulah didn't know.

Still . . . something kept her from pulling out her pillbox and chasing her troubles away enough for her to breathe. "Will you go back to my place?"

"Aye, leave yon car there. Then Bump's. You text me aught happens, dig? Anything."

"I will."

He hesitated. She waited for him to kiss her, to give her some sort of reassurance, something she could hold on to after he left. Some sign that he trusted her.

It didn't come. A nod; a short glance at Beulah. Chess watched him disappear around the corner of the building, into the shadows there, black as a murderer's heart. It was an effort to keep her feet from running to catch up with him.

Beulah's voice formed an oddly familiar background, speaking Cantonese into her phone while the grass behind the school turned briefly, shockingly red from the taillights. Chess watched the car slither through the grass, slow and smooth; watched him drive away. He was too far for her to see his face, so she didn't know if he was looking at her or not. She lifted her hand in a useless wave anyway.

"They're coming," Beulah said behind her. Like it was good news or something, instead of yet another fucking complication destroying yet another night. Like Chess wasn't probably going to sleep alone again, like her stomach hadn't landed in her shoes and decided to set up housekeeping there.

She slipped a little on the damp cement patio as she neared the body again.

She and Terrible had been inside. They'd been *making out* inside while a sorcerer killed a young girl right outside the building. Had Jia known what was coming? Had she screamed?

Would Chess even have heard her if she had? Over the sound of her own heart and her breath and the curious isolation of desire that made the entire rest of the world, everything but herself and Terrible, disappear?

Never mind that they'd been hunting, battling, and losing a ghost for part of the time. When the spell started, they'd been in the booth. If she hadn't been yanking his jeans open they might have heard sounds outside, might have been paying attention.

She knelt by the symbol, taking care not to lean over it, not to let the energy touch her yet. She'd have to touch it, yeah, but she wanted to examine it first; this one wasn't destroyed by fire.

"You know I'm not going to tell him," Beulah said, yanking Chess back from her speculation.

"What?"

"I'm not going to tell him. Terrible. About you kissing Lex today."

"Lex kissed *me*." Bitch.

Beulah waved her hand. "Whatever. The point is, I won't say anything. I won't tell him."

Chess waited for the rest of it, for the "as long as you do this or that," or "if you give me a couple of hundred bucks," or whatever.

It didn't come. So why the hell would Beulah bring it up in the first place? If she wasn't going to tell, why not just pretend she didn't see it at all?

Beulah must have seen her thoughts on her face. "I don't want you worried about that, or wondering. So you can just focus on this."

Ah, right. "Thanks for your concern."

"Don't be— I'm trying to be nice to you."

"Why? Why be nice to me? What's the point? You weren't worried about it before. Or was it just because you didn't have a use for me then? What do you need to butter me up for?"

Beulah stared at her long enough for Chess to really feel it. "You know, Lex said you could be a real bitch sometimes. And I didn't believe him, I thought it was just because he'll drive anyone crazy, but I guess I was wrong. Fuck you, Chess."

She stalked away, over to the wall of the building, and leaned against it. The white light of her phone's screen hit her face, made it glow there in the dark while she frowned and started fiddling with the buttons.

Damn. The last thing she needed was to start feeling guilty because she hadn't been nice to Lex's sister. Beulah hadn't exactly been nice to *her*, what with the office ambush and the sly grins and the snotty comments. That was pretty much the opposite of nice, in fact. Chess didn't owe her shit. Especially not niceness.

That was Truth. So why did she still feel like an asshole?

A feeling she didn't need, not compounded with the memory of her car driving away, of the look on Terrible's face when Beulah mentioned how safe it would be once Lex got there. Not when she saw headlights approach and knew Lex had arrived.

Chapter Twenty-one

Your parents know more than you think. Don't be afraid to talk to them or ask questions. That is what they're there for.
—*Teen Truth,* the Church magazine for teenagers

This was the Slobag she'd always imagined. Not the one dressed in bells and velvet when he met with Bump, but the one in soft gray trousers and a tidy button-down shirt. The only indicators of who he actually was were his hands heavy with gold and his broad-brimmed red fur hat, like a wealthy Siberian cowboy.

Did he recognize the ritual, the symbol? Had he ordered this?

But if he had, why there? Why Jia, why outside the school?

"So what's the tale, Tulip?" Lex slid his arm around her, kissed the side of her head. Great. "What we got on here?"

Okay, there was one good thing about that awful dead body. It gave her an excuse to slide away. Had he really told Beulah that she was a cold bitch sometimes?

Not really the time to ask. "It's a ritual murder, it—"

"Oh, aye? You for certain on that one?"

"Ha-ha." She gave him a dirty look, even though it wouldn't be effective in the dark, and if she held her flashlight up to her face she'd just look like a creepy idiot. Looking like a creepy idiot would be a dumb thing to do. She didn't want to alienate him or anyone else there; they'd brought two other men along with them, tall stocky men who looked quite serious about the job they were obviously hired to do.

Terrible could kick their asses, she thought, examining both with a critical eye and more than a little pride. He definitely could. Easily.

Too bad he wasn't there, which meant she'd need to be careful, didn't it? Bad idea to accuse the drug lord of murder while his men watched. Sure, Lex was her—her friend. But she somehow didn't think he'd take her side if that subject came up.

"Anyway. It's a ritual murder, a sacrifice. The symbol on the ground is called a *hafuran*. It's designed to build power."

Lex looked at it, looked at her. "A couple of them in that ink you got, aye? There, and there." He pointed at her right shoulder and her left upper arm.

If she hadn't been blushing before, she definitely was now. And if the two men Slobag brought with him hadn't already thought or known she'd slept with Lex, they definitely did now.

And Lex . . . he remembered her ink that well— remembered her naked body that well? She'd never thought he paid that much attention to those particular parts of her. They were usually busy with far more fun ones.

But then, she supposed if she thought about his, she could remember it in vivid detail, too. Just like she could remember Terrible's. That thin line of hair down his stomach—she'd never thought she'd like that, but she did, a lot—the scars and ink on his arms and side and back; she could draw those from memory, couldn't she?

Just like she could remember the way he'd looked at her the first time he saw her naked—the way he looked at her every time—the way his hands slid over her stomach, her ribcage, and farther up—"Huh? What?"

"What kinda power they tryna raise by killing people?"

Oh. Right. Dead body. What the fuck was wrong with her? "The *hafuran* is a power builder, like I said. So whatever they're doing, it's to try to make someone or something stronger."

"Ain't got any else?"

"No. Only that whatever they're trying to build their power for isn't good. Positive spells don't usually require ritual slayings."

Lex's eyebrows rose. "Aye? Wouldna guessed that one, me."

The impulse to stick out her tongue was childish, she knew, but she did it anyway, fast so the others wouldn't notice. Lex did; his grin widened.

She was grinning, too, at least until she glanced down and saw the dead body again, wondered why the hell she was there again. Unfortunately, there was something else she could do. Something she *should* do. She inched closer to the circle, concentrating on holding on to that good feeling, and held out her hand.

Power flew up her arm, raced through her body as fast as a speed-loaded spike and almost as strong. Not just death power, death energy, either. She hardly felt that at all. Instead it felt like earth energy, earth power. What the— Why? Why would a death spell feel like something else?

The thought flashed through her mind so fast she could hardly grab it, because the air left her chest in a hoarse gasp; she felt her feet move, felt her legs shake and struggle to keep her standing. Felt it like it was happening to someone else, because the only thing her conscious mind could feel was that power flooding her body, filling her, seeking . . . something. Looking for something inside her, some energy to latch on to and strengthen. Oh shit. The only real energy inside her at that moment was—

Sex. The realization hit her mind at the same time as the swirling, charging power found what it was looking for.

This time it was an entirely different sort of gasp. The kind that spoke of warm hands in the dark, a warm body close to hers, on hers, inside hers. Sweat broke out on her skin, her blood pounding through her veins and stopping, eager and tingling, below her waist. It was so hot all of a sudden, so hard to breathe, this was torture. Somewhere in the back of her mind it registered that the energy was male but she couldn't think of it, couldn't focus on it, not when her mind whirled and spun and she was afraid she was going to drown in the thick warm desire swirling through her.

She yanked her arm back, snatching it away as if from a blazing fire. Which it had been. The energy inside her lessened. Didn't disappear, but lessened, at least enough for her to be able to breathe again.

A shame it wasn't enough to stop her from feeling totally embarrassed. Sure, it might have looked like she was just focusing or even being hurt or whatever else. Probably did, to Beulah and the men.

Probably didn't, to Lex.

She couldn't look him in the eye as she wiped her damp palms on her thighs—a residual tingle ran up them just at that—and dug in her bag for a smoke. Focus. That was what she needed: focus, clear, concise thinking. What had she felt, what did it mean?

Nothing good. That was for damn sure.

"Right. Anyway. The symbol, the *hafuran,* increases the power that's there. It helps . . . helps it focus, is the best way to describe it. But in this case, it's stealing power, at least it feels like it is. Transferring it from the earth to whoever it is doing the spell. So they're using the murders to steal power. At least that's the best explanation I can come up with."

Beulah had been staring off into space, up at the sky, anywhere but at Chess. At those last words her head snapped down, though. "That's what happened on your side of town, too, right? The stealing power?"

Shit. She'd forgotten Beulah knew about that now. "Um, yeah."

"Hold it, now. What you meaning, she side of town?" Lex looked at Chess. "You got this same shit happen before?"

Was he serious? He looked serious. That didn't always mean anything when it came to Lex, but . . . he genuinely seemed perplexed.

So did Slobag, for that matter. And his musclemen, the ones who could rip her apart if they wanted to and probably didn't have any idea that would mean putting themselves at the top of Terrible's kill list. Assuming he had one, which she figured he did. What the fuck was she supposed to do?

She avoided Lex's eyes. "Yeah, a pipe room burned down two days ago, and a body just like this one—the sigil and everything—was inside it."

Slobag's eyes narrowed. "Someone broke into the wreckage? Bump doesn't keep his—"

"No." Was he kidding? "No, the ritual started the fire. Someone broke into the room before it burned, and did this. Exactly this. That's what started the fire."

Damn the poor lighting out there. The moon wasn't far from full, but the cloud-filled sky diffused the light, weakened it. She couldn't make out Slobag's expression well enough to know how much of his shock was genuine; she didn't know him well enough to know, either.

She pushed a little further. "The guy who was killed

was named Bag-end Eddie. He was mutilated, just like this."

Okay. No mistaking that response. Slobag's eyes narrowed. "He worked for me."

Her mouth opened. Thank fuck she managed to snap it shut before she spoke, but . . . what?

So Eddie had been killed on her side of town, but Eddie worked for— No, that couldn't be right. Bump and Terrible acted like Eddie worked for them. Not just acted like; Terrible had *said* Eddie was one of Bump's corner men, a street dealer.

Did they not know?

Lex glanced from her to Slobag and back again. "So who done this, then, Tulip? You got the knowledge?"

She looked at Slobag. Looked at him and took the plunge, despite her fear. "I don't know. Did that pipe room get burned by accident, or did someone order it?"

Yeah, maybe it wasn't a huge plunge. It was more cautious than that. A semi-plunge. But she wasn't fucking stupid, was she?

"I don't see what the difference is," Slobag said finally.

"It makes a difference when you think about who knew the room was empty."

"Lots of people could have known that."

"Yes, but who ordered a fire in that pipe room? What witch might have known it was empty?"

Slobag drew himself up—he was about Lex's height—and glared at her. "Do you—"

"You said the spell takes power from the earth, right?" Beulah cut in, her gaze jumping from Chess to Slobag and back again, her voice just a touch off nervous. "Does that weaken the earth's power or something?"

Shit. Chess didn't take her eyes off Slobag, but the moment was over, and she knew it. Damn it, she'd been so close, so close to having something she could give

Terrible, to having a piece of this bizarre and deadly puzzle.

She gave Slobag a final glare and turned to Beulah. Time to pretend to be calm and confident. "I'm not entirely sure. Power needs to be in balance. Throwing it off, like this does, can be kind of dangerous. Aside from just making the spell caster really, really powerful."

"Dangerous how?"

"When power goes out of balance like that, and stays that way—that's the real problem, you can take that power but you need to give it back, and this is a lot of power—it can cause problems with the barriers in the world. The veil between the worlds, the one the ghosts came through during Haunted Week. That's what we think caused it, a serious energy imbalance."

"Good," Slobag said. "So you know how to stop it."

"What? How the fuck would I know?" What the hell, she'd already practically accused him of murder. She figured a little "fuck" here and there was no big deal.

"The Church started Haunted Week. So surely you have been taught how to stop it."

For fuck's sake. This again? "The Church didn't cause Haunted Week."

The others snorted or rolled their eyes, a circle of patronization. "Aye," Slobag said. "Of course it didn't."

"Just like you didn't burn the pipe room?"

Okay, that was too far. The silence felt solid, like a heavy damp cloth over her face, making it hard to breathe.

Slobag glared at her through it. "Just get it fixed. None of us want more ghosts."

"I don't know how. I don't even think it can be done."

Nobody believed her. Not even Lex—he'd shifted closer to her, which she had to admit she appreciated—looked as if he believed her. Terrible would have. But of course he wasn't there, and no amount of lonely wishing would make him appear. "The veil repaired itself. The Church didn't do it. It doesn't— It can't stay open long, the veil I mean. It's unequal when it's open, it's an interruption."

"The world wants to be back in balance," Beulah said.

"Right. The earth's energy—that includes the veil and everything else—needs to flow. If it's interrupted like that, it can't, and all that energy backs up. It could— It's really not good. And the person doing this could steal that power, and that would be a huge problem. It *is* a huge problem, I mean, because that's what they're doing. At least that's what I think."

"So stop it." Slobag's expression had gone from disbelieving to angry to threatening.

She swallowed. Hard. Why the fuck did she keep getting involved in shit like this? Wasn't there some other witch who could handle all of the body parts and sick magic and dangerous killers? She didn't need it. She needed to be home in bed. Who knew how many nights of that she had left?

"Why can't your new witch do it?"

Silence. Not a long silence, but one she felt just the same. "He's busy."

Right. Busy. So guess who got to do the dead body cleanup? Chess. Everybody's favorite murder maid.

Of course, it didn't escape her that Slobag had referred to his witch as "he," either. Hmm.

"Waiting," Slobag said. "Sure you can find a way."

Chess looked at Lex, at Beulah. Neither of them said anything. Fuck, and double fuck. She really should have been nicer to Beulah; she had a feeling Beulah would have stood up for her if she had been. She seemed like the type.

Lex? He probably thought it was funny. At least that's what she figured until he said, "Hey, it ain't magic she

got. How she can do it iffen she ain't got the knowledge?"

"She'll think of something." Slobag's eyes never left
her face.

She felt those eyes like just-spent matches, scraping
her skin with rough black ends, burning tracks down
her back as she crossed the patio back to the circle. Punishing her for questioning him.

With every passing minute Jia's body looked worse.
Which made sense, sure, but didn't make looking at it
any more pleasant. If she hadn't had all those lovely
drugs in her system to soften the blow, she probably
would have puked. As it was she just held her breath for
a few seconds until the nausea went away, and tried her
damnedest to think of a way to neutralize that symbol.

"I guess we should take the body out of it first," she
said, more thinking aloud than actually speaking to anyone. "That should lessen some of its power."

"Go ahead."

Damn, she was high, but she couldn't be that high. He
couldn't mean that. "Me?"

"It's powerful magic, you said so. I don't want any of
mine touching it. You know the magic. So you touch it."

Yeah. She knew something else she'd like to touch just
then. Like a trigger. Or her knife. Or anything in one
of the pipe rooms, or in her apartment, or in Terrible's
place, or—hell, anywhere. She'd rather be sitting in that
foul temple of lewd that was Bump's ghastly crimson living room than standing there, about to reach into a wall
of death magic and pull out a human body.

Why couldn't she just call the Church, again?

Fuck.

They all watched her as she pushed up her sleeve and
grabbed a pair of latex gloves from her bag. She always
kept a couple in there for situations like—well, no, not
for situations like this, she didn't pack her bag anticipat-

ing the possible need to fondle dead bodies—but in case she needed to touch anything she didn't want to touch. They snapped onto her hands, tight and powdery dry. Teeth-gritting time. Jia's leg lay right at the edge of the circle; she'd grab that and start dragging.

It was just a leg. It wasn't a bomb, even if it felt like one. She reached in for it, and fear like ice water poured over her entire body.

What the fuck? Sweat formed on her forehead, rough itchy fright sweat, as her heart pounded and she snatched her hand back. "I can't."

Lex opened his mouth, but Slobag spoke first, his face almost immobile under his hat's heavy red brim. "You will."

She looked again at Lex, again at Beulah. Neither of them met her eyes. Fine. Maybe she should take more pills; it certainly seemed like one of the best ideas she'd ever had, but by the time they hit she'd be done. So she hoped.

So instead she took a deep breath, held it. Gritted her teeth again, and reached for the leg.

This time the spell found something else inside her. Fear. Not just fear. Terror. Pure thundering terror enveloping her, smothering her. The leg almost disappeared in the hazy purple mist of it, in the sudden tears blurring her eyes, as it drew closer and closer around her. Choking her.

Screams wanted to escape her throat, crammed against her tonsils, held back only because her jaw was clenched so hard it almost hurt. Would have hurt, if she'd been able to feel it; she couldn't, not really.

That should have been a good thing. It wasn't. Instead of feeling the ache in her jaw she felt walls closing around her, felt the lights go out and the door lock. Spiders on her skin, bugs on her naked body, huddled against a grimy wall in the dirt. Hiding in the same closet hoping they wouldn't find her—

Every second brought another wave of it. Brought memories she didn't ever want to revisit, thoughts she didn't want to think; memories and thoughts she'd spent years and thousands of dollars on every bit of artificial peace she could find just trying to forget.

Someone was behind her, a knife raised. She gasped and glanced around. No one there.

In front of her now. Beside her. The Dreamthief. Maguinness grinning his sharp-toothed grin, Maguinness licking her blood off his fingers. Horatio Kemp, black with ink, pointing his gun.

Pointing his gun at Terrible. Terrible falling. Terrible leaving. He hit her. He pushed her away. Her heart hammered her chest so fucking hard she thought it would explode. Not that she cared. Let it explode, make it explode if it would end this, these movies of horror that felt so real she couldn't tell anymore if they were.

Please let them not be. She was so alone there, so alone, and she had only one person in the entire world who made her feel like she wasn't, and she was losing him—maybe had already lost him—and her head was too heavy for her back and neck to hold. She fell forward, felt herself falling, and didn't give a fuck. Maybe she'd hit her head on the cement and pass out. Maybe she'd die.

The City. The City rose before her, ghosts pale and vicious in the darkness, their eyes dripping, their mouths twisted and obscene. Her entire body shook, it hurt, it hurt so fucking bad, the Lamaru stood over her, ghosts swung knives, doors locked, bodies crushed hers, Elder Griffin told her to get out, Terrible slammed the door behind him as he left for the last time.

And over it all the panic, the pure head-banging throat-drying panic, that made her want to curl into a ball and hide, bury her head in the sand, bury anything she could in the sand. She couldn't see anymore. Couldn't hear a thing but the screams in her ears, the angry voices, the sick ones laughing at their awful pleasures. Doors slammed in her ears; the sound of flesh against flesh—

Her arm burned. Not a memory burn, a real one. And with that burn, with that pain, came the end. The fear and panic stopped. Instantly.

Well, no. They didn't stop. They would never stop. But they lessened; the deep mist before her eyes lifted, and Lex's arms were strong around her, holding her up, holding her to him, yanking her away from the fire. Her throat ached, felt like she'd been gargling fiberglass. She must have screamed.

Somehow she found her legs, managed to speed along with Lex to where the others stood, to where they all watched as the *hafuran* burned.

Chapter Twenty-two

[Death magic done outside the Church is theft. It steals the life of the victim. It steals energy from darkness, and it steals authority from the Church. The last is the most serious crime.

—*Death Magic: Theory and Practice,* by Elder O'Brien]

It felt like Church magic, like twisted and bastardized Church magic. That thought refused to leave her—that thought, and the dark suspicion that blossomed inside her because of it—as the symbol outlined itself in flames, sparks dancing across the ugly lines. It singed her face, burned her soul.

Orange, then red, then a bright, painful blue, beautiful and terrifying as they rose into the night sky. Sparks flew from them, sparks and the most oppressive, intense heat she'd ever felt, worse even than when she'd been trapped in the burning Slaughterhouse the month before. Worse because this heat came from within, from her, and it turned her body into a torch. Greedy fire, taking what it could; it would destroy her with its heat, suck her into the inferno and make her another sacrifice. It pulled at her. Only Lex's hands on her arms kept her from giving it what it wanted.

Fear washed over her again, all of those vivid terrors the symbol had shown her, playing across the fire where everyone could see. Or could they?

She managed to drag her gaze away from the bright flames—now heading toward purple—and glanced at the others, panting from the pain, her mouth so dry and hot she thought she felt her tongue crack.

All of them watched the fire with expressions of frozen horror on their faces; even Lex looked worried, and not only was he completely impervious to magic, she didn't think anything in existence could actually scare him. That symbol was some powerful shit.

She turned back to it as it went to purple, then to black, deep shiny black. The pain grew worse, tearing into her organs, pulling her apart to see how she worked, like a cruel child with a spider. It raged at her, dug into her, seared her soul until all she saw was flames, all she felt was pain, she hadn't been even herself anymore—

It exploded.

Chess hit the cement with a thud that would have hurt if she hadn't been so fucking grateful that the pain inside her had finally stopped. Would have hurt, too, if she wasn't just a bit loaded. Too bad her pills didn't do much for magic-induced pain, but she couldn't have everything.

And that almost didn't matter, not at that moment when the pain had disappeared, the symbol had disappeared. That the memory never would was something she'd just have to deal with; hell, it could join the gang already in her head, the gang that poked her and slapped her and yelled at her every chance it got.

Her legs felt limp and disjointed, like stilts rather than her own body, but she managed to stand on them anyway. Before her lay the charred remains of the symbol, Jia's body like a misshapen lump of coal inside it. No longer a symbol but a scar, a black wound in the cement, crusted and bubbled like the pipe room floor. Heat still radiated from it, too, and the sharp too-dry smell of burning hung so thick in the air she tasted it.

The others stirred, moaned. Tried to rise themselves,

all of them looking like animated scarecrows, wobbling and leaning on awkward feet.

She waited until Beulah was standing. She could at least do that. But the second that woman was upright, she was ready. No discussion; Chess didn't trust the discussion to any of them. But she knew what she'd felt.

"Okay, Beulah, can you take me home now?"

Air-conditioning blasted from the dash of Beulah's car—the sleek expensive one Chess had noticed in the school parking lot. She should have guessed.

They'd been driving in silence for ten minutes or so, broken only by the Operation Ivy disc in the stereo. Discomfort grew in Chess's stomach, in her head, creeping down her arms and legs. Damn. She thought she'd be over that, that her exhaustion and the memory of pain that made her muscles feel like hot wet rags would erase it, but apparently not.

She hauled her bag up from the floor. At least there were pills. Just holding them made her feel better; swallowing them made her feel a lot better, and in fifteen minutes or so she wouldn't care about anything or anyone. She couldn't fucking wait.

But for now . . . "Hey. Um. I'm sorry. About earlier."

"Why are you sorry? Is it because you realize you acted like a cunt, or is it because of my brother?"

Chess stared at her for a second, at her smooth profile sharp against the candlelit windows and fuzzy streetlights. "Are you serious?"

"I think so, yes."

Ridiculous. Whatever impulse had led her to apologize, it was well and truly gone, and wasn't she grateful for that. She should have gone ahead and talked about Slobag's witch and the pipe room instead. "Forget it."

"I don't think it's such a bizarre question. Just because you do doesn't mean it isn't valid."

"It means I don't have to answer it."

"No, you don't. Just like I don't have to give you a ride. I could have let Lex drive you. Hell, I could have let you fucking walk. But by all means, don't worry about your apology."

For a second Chess wished she *had* let Lex drive her; the only thing that had stopped her was knowing Terrible would probably be watching, would be waiting for her. Having Lex drop her off in front of him would not be a good idea.

Too late, anyway. "Why are you like this?" she asked.

Beulah glanced at her; the light caught her face for a second, gave Chess an impression of drawn-together brows and a frown. "What the hell is that supposed to mean?"

"It means why are you like this? Are you always this big a bitch, or am I just lucky? I said something kind of shitty. Sue me. I'm sorry I didn't realize that you, a total stranger who hasn't exactly been cheering me on so far, were trying to be pally with me and not just get something out of me like the rest of your family does."

Beulah breezed the red light at Thirty-seventh and Ace. "I'm not a total stranger."

"You are."

"I'm not. You fucked my brother for months, in my house. He talked about you. I've washed your clothes, don't forget. I've seen you almost naked."

The words fell on Chess's head like cold raw eggs. Fuck. Beulah *had* seen her almost naked, at least in her underwear; that first night, the night Slobag's men kidnapped her from her building. He'd told her then that he'd had his sister Blue search her.

"Didn't know the search was that thorough," she said, not bothering to keep the bitterness out of her voice.

"Give me a break. It's not like I gave you an internal or something."

"Oh, thanks. I'm really grateful for that."

"Hey, be glad I did it and not one of the musclemen. How'd you like to have one of those guys pawing you while you were unconscious?"

The first wave of the Oozers hit her, swirled into her head and made her cheeks tingle, pulling her lips into a soft smile despite her irritation. "No, I guess I wouldn't."

"Right."

The lights outside the car windows started to streak, dazzling tails of bright yellow that grew longer and longer. Fuck, that felt good. She wanted to close her eyes, wanted to stop talking and just sit feeling it. Even better, she wanted to close her eyes and sit feeling it with Terrible, in his lap, or with her head on his chest.

Her phone beeped, and her heart skipped with relief. A reply to the text she'd sent when she got into the car; he'd be there, he'd wait. More of the darkness in her head, wrapped around her, faded away. He'd be there, she wouldn't have to be alone. Wouldn't sleep alone wishing he was with her, because he would be.

"Good news?"

"Terrible's going to meet me, he's going to be waiting. So I get to spend some time with him. We have the whole night."

"Did you always want to be with him? Even when you were with Lex?"

One problem with Oozers, especially when coupled with brain-soothing happiness: they made her lips as loose as her muscles. Well, she'd started it—she hadn't meant to, but she apparently had—so she might as well finish it, despite the mental cringe. "Um, I don't— I guess I did, yeah, but I didn't know I did, if that makes sense."

"Because you guys were just friends."

"Right."

"So what happened? Did he kiss you, or something?

Is he a good kisser? I guess he is, why would you be with him if—"

"We're not talking about this." At least she still had the presence of mind to clamp down on that particular topic. On any Terrible-related topic, honestly, but particularly on that topic. None of Beulah's business. None of anybody's business. It was hers, something secret she shared with him, and nobody was going to take that away from her, not ever. She'd kill anyone who tried.

Not to mention the sick sort of squirm in her head, sending waves of panicky irritation through her body. How much did Beulah actually know about her? Wasn't it bad enough she knew about her habit, that she knew all about Chess's relationship—such as it was—with Lex, probably right down to how often she went over there and what sort of things they did to each other? She had to discuss Terrible, too?

That was too much, way too much. Beulah wasn't her friend. Wasn't anyone she trusted. And even if she had been, she wouldn't want Beulah to know that shit about her. Once people thought they knew someone, they started expecting that someone to care what they thought or felt or said; they thought their information or instinct obligated that someone.

Chess would be damned if she was going to let Beulah feel that way about her, dig her oh-so-sensitive little hooks into Chess's skin and tug until it tore away so she could inspect Chess's soul with curious, satisfied fingers covered in blood. "Not ever."

"I was just making conversation." They turned onto Forty-seventh; Cross was only a block down. Almost home. She started scanning the side of the road, looking for the Chevelle, but didn't see it.

Then again, she could barely see any of the cars that slid so slowly past her, their edges soft in the now-sparkling world.

Beulah started talking again. Chess didn't pay attention. Where was the Chevelle?

Her own car sat on the street, quiet and peaceful, but the Chevelle wasn't there. If it hadn't been for the Oozers coating her with an artificial layer of calm, she would have panicked. As it was she just felt sick.

And Beulah kept talking, her voice an irritating tickle on Chess's neck, like a hair she couldn't find.

Until she caught something. "What?"

"What? This is it, right?"

"Yeah. What did you just say?" Her eyes wanted to roll back in her head; she floated a couple of feet above her body. Amazing.

"About Aros?"

"Yes, yeah. What—what did you say about him?"

Beulah looked at her oddly. Was she slurring her words? Not that she gave a fuck, but she still wondered.

"I asked if you'd been to Aros's apartment near the school."

"Where was it?"

"What, his apartment?"

She wanted to be sarcastic, but she was too high for it. Beautiful. "Yeah. Where was it?"

"It's behind the school, on Twenty-first. Twenty-first and Foster. You didn't know?"

That hadn't been in her case file. No dispensation to rent an apartment had been noted, no other address.

It should have been. If he'd been sleeping right near the school, he should have—would have—written it down. Even as he freaked out and broke down or whatever, she'd think he would have made some kind of note.

Not to mention, how did he manage to get an apartment down there so fast? In a part of Downside where to admit to being Church was akin to wearing a KILL ME NOW sign? The Church wasn't too popular anywhere in

Downside, but those east of Thirty-fifth made hating it a fetish.

Okay, maybe they wouldn't kill a Church employee, but they sure as fuck wouldn't rent to one. Even on her side of town she'd had to get a couple of Bump's street dealers to talk to her landlord, had to bribe him to let her in, and it had been over a year before anyone even looked her in the face.

"How'd he get it? The apartment, I mean. How—how would he get that?"

"How would I know? I never went in. He had it, was all I know."

"Is he still there, do you know? Can I see it—can you get someone to let me see it?" The question made her feel vulnerable, yeah, and maybe it was too much information to give Beulah, but she couldn't help it.

"Probably, yeah. I'll ask. And actually . . ." Beulah's face split into a grin, the kind of quiet grin that meant the grinner was up to no good. Chess didn't want to respond to that grin, but she couldn't really help it. Not when her own cheeks felt so tight and cheerful, drawing her lips into a smile that would almost hurt if she dropped it; especially not when she heard the familiar rumble of the Chevelle's engine and its headlights bathed the interior of Beulah's car in silvery white for a few seconds before shutting off. He was there. He'd come for her.

"Actually, you could ask Monica about his place. She took her student group there once, I think."

"Her plaid dress is horrible. It makes her look like a patterned pumpkin." The words sounded funny, felt funny in her mouth.

Beulah laughed, that pretty, girlish laugh that sounded odd coming from her, especially when she was so viperish in general. "Think you're high enough now?"

Was she kidding? The question was so odd, Chess stared at her for a second. "It's never enough."

A few seconds of fumbling with the door handle until it caught, while Beulah watched. "Thanks for the ride." She stepped out onto the soft dark street.

Chapter Twenty-three

When you have always lived in Truth, there is never a reason to fear.

—*The Book of Truth*, Veraxis, Article 745

For the first time in hours she could breathe, really breathe, the familiar, comforting scents of leather and smoke and pomade, that enginey smell, invading her head, sinking into her muscles. The streets slid by; the Chevelle floated through them ten feet off the ground, fifteen.

"You right, Chess? Ain't got hurt?"

"No, no. I felt the symbol's energy and then it caught fire and exploded, but I'm fine. Just fine."

He glanced at her, streetlights illuminating his face at intervals, washing over the scars, the deep-set eyes, the broken nose. She loved watching it. Loved *him*. "They get she body out first?"

"No, I started to do it, but—"

"What?" He looked so angry for a second she thought he was going to slam on the brakes, and braced herself. Well, braced herself as best she could; she didn't think she could have picked up anything heavier than a cigarette at that particular moment. "They made you—Fuck. Shoulda fuckin known."

His thigh was tense under her palm. Shit, she should have kept her mouth shut. But then what was she supposed to do, lie? "No, it, it wasn't that bad. I had my gloves, you know, it just—the spell changes according to energy, like whatever energy it finds when you touch it. It wasn't that bad, though, really."

He shook his head, his anger still filling the car. "Sure it weren't. 'Swhy you tanked up soon's you left, aye?"

She blinked. That stung. A lot. And what was she supposed to say in reply? Especially when it was true. "Are . . . are you mad at me?"

"What? Why? Naw, baby. Just ain't can believe they made you do that, is all."

Even high as she was, she could read the look on his face, and it clearly said she needed to drop the subject immediately. He wasn't mad at her, sure, but he was mad enough at Lex, and she wanted him to cheer up before they got to his place. She had definite plans for once they arrived. The kind of plans that made her temperature go up several degrees.

It was already up a bit anyway, because he was there, and, she had to admit, kind of because he was so mad. It made her feel . . . cared about. No one had ever gotten mad on her behalf like that before, or upset that she wasn't being treated the way they thought she should be. Most people in her life who'd seen her treated badly—and there were a fuck of a lot of them—had laughed or joined in. None of them clenched their fists around the steering wheel with murder in their eyes. Maybe it was wrong of her, but it made her feel good, and she couldn't help it.

Still, she didn't want to make him any madder. So instead of speaking she just sank back into her seat, watched the empty buildings go by, watched them appear in the distance then suddenly snap past, leaving streaks of black and gray behind them, until they reached his building.

The walk to his apartment took forever and no time

at all, and then she was inside behind the heavy gray steel door. She always felt so small there; the building had been some kind of multilevel warehouse and he had an entire floor, one big wide rectangular room with black metal posts set at intervals to support the steel-beam ceiling. A single wall broke the space in half on the left side, creating a kitchen and living room. A bathroom hugged the other wall.

Her shoes made a dry scuffing sound against the cement floor as she crossed to the couch, planted in the middle of a gray carpet worn thin from feet and vacuums.

But it was comfortable, and cool, and she waited for him to join her with her perma-smile in place and her stomach doing cheery swoops. The familiar room welcomed her, the old-fashioned jukebox in the corner, the bookshelf, the rarely used TV and the often used stereo. If she hadn't known whose place it was, she would have known anyway; it looked like him, smelled like him.

"So Slobag ain't seemed to got any knowledge on it?" He appeared in front of her with a beer in one hand and a bottle of water in the other, the latter of which he handed her before sitting down with his arm along the back of the couch behind her.

She always felt so awkward at this part. Should she cuddle up to him, tuck herself under that arm and kiss his neck? She never did. Better to wait for him to do it, so she knew he wanted to. Forcing herself on him wouldn't do anyone any good, least of all her.

It all seemed so easy before they started "officially" doing whatever it was they were doing. Then she knew exactly what she wanted to do, and how. Sex was simple.

But affection, this whole relationship thing . . . wasn't. It was complicated and messy and terrifying. Scarier even than almost everything she'd seen in the symbol at Mercy Lewis, and far more dangerous.

He was watching her expectantly. Had he— Oh, he'd asked her a question, hadn't he? "What?"

"Askin if Slobag seemed like he got knowledge on that magic. Iffen he say aught make you think he do."

"I don't think so, no." She took a swig of water, cool and crisp, and felt her eyes moisten. Hydration was good. He didn't look quite so blurry that way. "I can't be sure, but he seemed—I mean, he was—really pissed off when I suggested it might have been him."

Terrible rubbed his chin, smiling behind his hand. "You said on it?"

"I did. He was all— Oh, fuck, did you know Eddie worked for him? He said Eddie worked for him. He was really surprised when I said Eddie was dead."

The smile weakened. "You said on Eddie?"

"Beulah brought it up. I couldn't, I couldn't really think of a way to lie about it when she mentioned it, you know?"

She drank more water. Some of it spilled down her shirt; she giggled. Fuck, she felt good, better than she had in days. "He said his witch was busy, that's why I was there. So he definitely has one, and he really didn't like it when I sort of asked if his witch had done the ritual. Oh! And it's a man. I asked about his witch and he said 'he' was busy. So it's a man, his witch."

Terrible nodded. His arm still rested on the back of the couch; she was acutely aware of it, almost touching her hair. If she tilted her head back it *would* touch. "That magic, that the one happened when we was inside? The one you felt, meaning. That one. Same as Eddie?"

Oh, good question. Good thing she had an answer, too. "I think so. I felt the energy again before it caught fire. It was different, in the structure, I mean, but I think it was the same as with Eddie. And it was definitely what was happening while we were—the male part of it was stronger than we felt—I mean, than I felt—inside. That felt more female, but I think that was the ghost. The sigil felt almost totally male. But it's the same person. The same people. I think."

Her tongue was too big for her mouth; she could feel it hitting her teeth when she talked, feel the words forming before they wandered out. She wished she had something else to do with that tongue. "And it feels like stealing. Whatever they're doing, they're stealing. Stealing power from the earth. That's bad."

She quickly gave him the same explanation she'd given Beulah, waited in silence while he digested it. "Thinkin that why it bein done? Like maybe them Lamaru, or Maguinness?"

"No. It felt too, too clean. Maguinness was so dirty, his magic felt like, like bugs or something, but this one is bad but feels kind of, well, clean. Like the caster's not right in the head but learned magic from someone who is, if that makes sense. I guess it could be to cause another Haunted Week or something but it doesn't feel like that."

Oh, right. Speaking of which. "The energy can be other things, too. It's pure, you know? Not formed. So, it can turn into anything. Any sort of power. Does that make sense?"

"Be just power? An they holdin it just that way, till they use it an turn it into what they needing it for."

"Right. Exactly."

He shifted in his seat, but left his arm where it was. Maybe he did want her to curl up next to him? Maybe he was waiting for her to do it?

But why would he do that, especially after she'd just been spending time with Lex? She was the one who'd lied and betrayed; she was the one who'd had to beg. She was the one who'd kissed his worst enemy that very afternoon. She couldn't take his forgiveness—or forgetfulness, whichever of the two she'd been blessed with—

for granted and just assume it was okay to crawl all over him like some sort of parasitic nymphomaniac. If he turned her away . . .

"Been thinkin," he said. "Got the wonder why they done it there, dig, outside the school an all. They know you inside? Or they tryna make a point, let the body get seen? Got any thoughts?"

"I didn't even think of that." She twirled a lock of her hair in her fingers, enjoying the cool slide of it over her skin. Hoped she looked alluring doing it, because she was starting to get tired—heart-pounding horror and Oozers tended to wear a person out—and she wanted to make sure they didn't miss out again. Her body heated and squirmed below the false Oozer soothe, wanting to be touched, kissed; wanting to be pressed against his. "Yeah, it's a really good thought. Why would they do it there, and with Jia? She's a student. Was a student. The dead girl, she was a student."

"Damn. Why her, wondering."

"Oh!" She jumped in her seat. "She had the book! Jia did, earlier. She's the one I took the book from. Did I tell you about that? The book? She had the—a ghost-summoning book. I took it from her. And they summoned a ghost, Lucy McShane, right?"

"So she weren't just some dame them grabbed theyselves. Took her on purpose."

"Right. Maybe, maybe she knew them or something. Maybe, oh, shit, yeah, maybe we can find out who she knew, and that'll help, d'you think?"

He smiled and touched her hair, gentle fingers brushing it out of her face. "Aye, got a good sound to me."

That was it. She couldn't take it anymore. It was probably the wrong thing to do, yeah, but she had to try anyway, because sitting there so far apart was a slow torture she couldn't endure.

The banked fire inside her burst back into ravenous

flame when her lips touched his, when her arms wound around his neck. She'd practically jumped into his lap, his thighs beneath hers; when he responded she shifted position so she straddled him, reveling in the feel of him so close to her.

Not close enough, though. His shirt buttons stumped her numb fingers, but she managed to get one, then another, all the while keeping contact, deepening the kiss. She wanted to kiss his neck, his chest, but she couldn't bear to leave him, not even for a second. She'd been so desperate for this for so long, and the rush of getting it was so fucking sweet.

His hands rested on her thighs, squeezed them gently. She waited for him to slide them up under her shirts or in her hair or her face, the back of her neck . . . all those places he usually touched her at first, the places that made her feel special and safe.

But he didn't.

Okay, something was wrong. She shifted her hips, found no physical reason why he'd have a problem—on the contrary—but he didn't touch her, or kiss her throat or ears or collarbones.

She pulled back far enough for their eyes to meet so she could let him see how much she wanted him, once she managed to focus. Damn, she was really high.

"Let's go to bed, okay?" She ducked her head to kiss him again, but missed his mouth and had to slide over to hit it properly. "Take me to bed."

Shit, she should have known. She *had* known. Making the first move like that was a mistake. He smiled, but she didn't see anything in his eyes, or not what she wanted—needed—to see. His fingertips brushed her cheek. "Thinkin you oughta get you some sleep. Lookin worn up, aye?"

Sleep? Was he joking? "I can sleep after, I can sleep

late tomorrow. We finally have a chance, I mean, it's been a week . . ."

The words died in her throat. No. He wasn't looking at her. Wasn't picking her up to carry her to the big gray bed, or grabbing the hems of her shirts to peel them off.

"Always the morrow, aye? Got plenty of time. C'mon, tired myself, too. Let's us get you resting."

Her eyes stung. "I don't want to rest, I want to—"

"Awful late, an you havin that magic you had to handle . . . Just got the thought might be better if—"

"It wouldn't be. It won't be." Panic lurked around the edges of her voice, struggling to break through; she swallowed it, hard, so he wouldn't hear it. "I don't want to sleep, I want *you*."

"I got a fuckload to do on wakin, an so do you, ain't want you up so—"

Holy shit. As she leaned back and looked at him, really looked at him, it hit her. Like seeing pictures in her head, all the things she'd let slip past her because she was fucked up. "You don't trust me."

"What?"

"That's it, right?" She scooted off him; her feet hit the floor and she struggled for a minute to get her balance, grasped the low arm of the couch to do it. "I told you Bag-end Eddie was working for Slobag and you didn't even look surprised. You knew. Didn't you?"

He shook his head. "Aye, but—"

"You didn't tell me." Yeah, she was fucking high, but she still had a brain, and it still had memories in it. Memories from earlier, in her car. "I fucking asked you why it was Eddie, if you had any idea, and you didn't tell me. Was he a spy, or was he working for Slobag all along?"

He hesitated. Hesitated just long enough for her heart to smash itself on his cement floor. "Workin for us, dig, only spendin time on Slobag's side."

"You told me he was one of Bump's corner men. You told me that two fucking nights ago."

"An he were, only sometimes—"

"You—you lied to me. I asked and you didn't tell me, in my car, you didn't say a word."

"Aw, naw, started to say, only we got to—"

An ugly thought crawled into her mind, burrowed down deep where all the other ugliness lurked, and dug its horrible claws into her.

"This is because of Lex, right? Because he kissed me this afternoon. This is because of, of fucking Beulah or Blue or whatever the fuck, because you don't believe I didn't know who she was. You think I told them the pipe room was closed, I'm spying, and you, you're just keeping me around to watch me now—"

She couldn't see his expression clearly, but she sure as hell saw him stand up. "The fuck are you talkin? You think I—"

"Don't— I get it, I see now, okay? Just, I just want to leave, just please let me leave, let me go home. I get it, it's over, you and me, but—"

"What?"

"Fine, that's fine, whatever, we're done, just— I can't, I wasn't lying, I wasn't. I—just let me go."

Silence for a second while he took a deep breath, silence broken only by the sound of her polluted blood rushing in her ears, the silent screams in her head. Her throat ached from holding back sobs, a horrible straining cold pain that radiated into her head, down into her chest.

"Chessie. Listen, aye? Ain't pullin some—"

"Would you just fuck off? Just take me home, I want to go home."

"Chess—"

Her feet were too big; she stumbled over them as she backed up, making sure to get out of his reach. The tears, the pain, they were all still there, she didn't think they would ever leave, but anger started to sidle up to them as well and she welcomed it.

Anger at him, anger at herself for being so stupid that she believed. "You know what? Forget it. I'll call Lex. He'll come for me."

The rough edges of his voice scratched her skin; the anger in it, in him, beat against her head like a fucking slab of iron. "One fuckin time more, Chess, I—"

Her phone sat right in its little pocket, right where it was supposed to be. She snatched it, held it up. "I'm calling Lex. He'll come for me, he'll take me home. He'll spend the night, too, if I ask him. Maybe I will. You already think I'm still fucking him, right? You already blame me for it, you don't trust me anyway. So why not."

That did it, just like she'd known it would. Even through drugs and tears she saw his face darken, that flush that always gave him away covering his neck, his face. "Bettin he will. Never cared who he fucks, 'slong as it moves. Ain't give a shit you too fuckin high to see straight, just—"

"You— What, are you, are you judging me? *You?* You— Who the fuck are you to— You're judging me, and you beat people up and kill them for money."

"Fuckin stop it, that ain't—"

"What, Terrible? Ain't what? Yeah, you know, I take drugs. But you sell them. You work for a guy who fucking sells them, so who the fuck are you to say anything."

His eyes narrowed further by the second; the air around them started practically vibrating against her skin. Oh, he was pissed, getting more so with every word she said, and somewhere in the deep ugly parts of her soul—which was most of it—she was glad. "The fuck did I say? Ain't—"

"You did, you did, you—you think you're fucking better than me? Is that—"

"You even know what you sayin? You got—"

"Do I? No, Terrible, I guess I don't. I guess I'm too fucking high to know, right, just some dumb fucking junkie slut, right?"

"Fucking crazy shit you—"

"Oh, I'm crazy? Crazy dumb junkie slut and her crazy—"

"You need to quit—"

"I don't need to do shit, not for you." A chain saw revved in her head, louder and louder, clouding her thoughts and her vision. This couldn't be happening, this could not fucking be happening, he still didn't trust her and she wanted to die. "I don't need to stand here while you act like you're so much fucking better than me, you asshole. Lex doesn't judge me, doesn't pretend he cares—"

"Then why you here, you could be off fuckin Lex? Go on, Chess, give him a ring up. Want me to get gone, you can fuck him right here if you're wanting, don't gotta wait, aye?"

"Oh, no, I'm sure I can wait until I get into his car. I know it'll be worth it."

"You sure? You don't wanna go stand on the fuckin street, get ready? Maybe some other else come along first, get a warm-up in?"

"Fuck off! Just— I—you asshole, you fucking asshole, I hate you. I never want to see you again, never."

"Aye? True thing, you little bitch?"

"Yeah, it is. You think you're so fucking special, oh big Terrible, so tough, and you're just a petty fucking thug who thinks he's better than he is, you beat people up because you can't do anything else, you—"

His fist came at her so fast she almost didn't see it; some instinct threw her to the floor. When she looked up his hand was buried in the wall, a good foot and a half or so from where she'd stood. Either he'd deliberately missed her or his aim was off; she didn't think she wanted to know which.

His chest heaved, his breath like a steam engine in the cool quiet air. His apartment was so still around them, impassive, indifferent to what had just happened; she felt like she was going to die and couldn't bring herself to care, either. His apartment wasn't bothered that the silence choked her when it invaded her throat and nose, her lungs; it was a mist over her eyes.

"Thinkin you oughta go," he said finally. He pulled his hand out of the wall; she caught a glimpse of his knuckles red with blood before he shoved it into his pocket. His other hand covered his face, his mouth, then slid to the back of his neck. "Do whatany you wanting, dig. Just get gone."

"Fine. I can't wait to get out of here."

Her bag sat on the floor in front of the couch, so she had to duck around him to get it, conscious the whole time of him standing there staring at his feet. When she bent over to pick up the strap, she gagged. Fuck, she had to get out of there immediately, faster than that. Had to keep some kind of dignity, at least the kind she'd get from not throwing up on his carpet.

And she was going to throw up, no doubt about that. If only she could puke everything up, all the pain, her stupid hopes, the bullshit of his she'd swallowed whole. How could she have been so fucking stupid?

She'd been so stupid because she loved him so much, and that last thought broke her. She'd never loved anyone like that, not in her whole life—had never loved anyone at all, for that matter—and it was useless and stupid and she'd lost.

She sucked in a deep breath, trying to keep it smooth,

but it didn't work; all she managed was a series of pathetic gulping gasps, the kind that would be sobs with just a little more volume.

She ran for the door, fumbled with the locks. She was going to be sick, she knew it, she swallowed hard over and over to try to stop it.

He appeared at her side. The heat from his skin, the way he smelled, the feel of him so close to her . . . it had all been a lie, and she'd bought it, and she could never forgive herself.

Yeah, she could add it to the list, right?

He flipped the locks for her, yanked the door open. She didn't look at him. Didn't want to see him, hated having to be so close to him as she ducked out the doorway.

His door slammed shut behind her. She ran down the hall on unsteady feet, almost fell on the stairs. Wished she had fallen, and broken her stupid fucking neck on the way. Even the City would be better than this, this ache that enveloped her whole body, clouded her head.

Cool, damp night air hit her face when she stepped onto the dark empty street. It didn't help. Nothing would help, but at least she was alone. Her head hit the brick wall and she was sick, messily, shamefully sick there on the street like a fucking animal. No wonder he hated her, no wonder she disgusted him. She was disgusting.

And she couldn't breathe. Between her sob-choked throat and her stiff painful lungs, every intake of air feeling like a million tiny knives and her body trying to get rid of everything she'd eaten or drunk, every pill she'd ever taken—fat chance of that one—she couldn't get any air in at all.

At least the wall was cool against her feverish head. Her phone was still in her hand; she checked it, saw that

Lex had responded and was on his way, and thought she'd never felt so grateful to him. Well, maybe when he saved her life, but— No. No, she was definitely more grateful now.

Too bad she couldn't enjoy it. The sobs kept coming, burbling up out of her throat, ragged, broken sobs that hurt. Fuck, fuck . . . how had that happened, how could she have been so stupid, she knew how stupid it was, knew she'd end up hurt, and for what.

What the fuck had she taken that chance for, gambled her fucking heart and soul for? A chance to see Terrible naked? To spend long delirious nights in bed, shivering when he touched her, when he whispered her name in the darkness? To wake up in the morning with him beside her, to have him look at her like she was the most gorgeous thing he'd ever seen? She'd given up everything just for a chance to feel whole, to feel like she was valuable to somebody, mattered to somebody. And she wasn't, and she didn't.

No wonder he hadn't wanted anyone to know about them. It wasn't to keep her safe, it was because he was lying. Because he was using her to find out whatever he could about Lex and Slobag.

She managed to stumble along, hugging the wall, to the corner where she'd told Lex to pick her up, and huddled shivering on the cold pavement. She couldn't stop shaking. Fuck, she was a mess. Tears pouring from her eyes, her supply of tissues barely enough to keep her nose from dripping all over everything else, her throat killing her, her chest aching, her head—well, the less said about that the better.

In the distance a scream, some breaking glass. Typical night sounds. Maybe she should walk that way, maybe she could get someone to finish the job Terrible had started.

Lex could take her to the pipe room. Yes. She'd have

him drop her at the pipe room, and lay down in the thick sweet honey-smoke haze until she forgot it all, forgot everything. It sounded so good she would have given her life for it.

And maybe she had.

Headlights in the distance, getting larger. Lex. Her shoulders dropped, a tiny bit of her tension easing. He was there, he'd come for her. She owed him for that, big time. She managed to make it to his car and open the door, managed to plunk herself down on the seat and get her legs inside.

"What the fuck, Tulip? Lookin like you ain't slept in a month, an you got somebody hittin you—Terrible ain't hit you, aye? Did he—"

"No," she managed. "No, he didn't hit me. Can we not talk about it, please? Can you just take me to the pipe room by my house?"

He looked at her for a long moment; she could see herself through his eyes, rumpled and smeared, stinking and gross. "Why we ain't head back my place instead, get you some eats? Blue there, she—"

"No! No, just take me to the pipe room."

"Ain't thinking that's—"

If one more person interrupted or contradicted her she was going to pull her knife on them. "I don't give a fuck what you think. Will you take me or do I have to fucking walk?"

"I—"

"Please. Please Lex, just please take me there, I can't— I can't—I'll walk, I'll just . . ." She couldn't finish. Her throat closed completely; not even sobs could get through it, just harsh rough gasps ugly in the silence.

And it didn't matter, because after a few seconds— seconds in which she felt him watching her, hated the feeling—he put the car in gear and started driving. She dared one last look back at Terrible's building and saw the light still on in his apartment, his shadow in the center of the window; it stayed there for a second then turned away and disappeared, leaving only an empty space where it had been.

Chapter Twenty-four

Romantic relationships are important, of course. But the relationship with family is more so, and the relationship with the Church is the most important of all.
—*Raising Girls in Truth,* by Lana Hunnicutt

She awoke on the floor in her hallway, freezing cold, her neck stiff and her muscles sore. She'd— Shit, she thought she'd been in bed, hadn't she gone to . . . ? She didn't remember. Had some vague memories of being home. Had a not-vague desire to get back to sleep, or to get back to the pipe room. Too bad she needed to get up, get to work, despite the pounding in her head, loud and fast like a woodpecker nesting in there.

Maybe that wouldn't be so bad. That would kill her, right? Or at least make her unable to feel, unable to think.

It took almost a minute to realize it wasn't her head, it was someone at her door. Terrible! Her heart practically exploded from her chest, had he come for her, to talk to her, to fix everything? Had he— She jumped up, lost her balance, braced herself against the wall until her head stopped spinning. She'd slept in her clothes; her entire body felt fuzzy and dry. Covered in grime, like her soul.

The pounding didn't stop. She finally got to it, noticed with gratitude that she'd at least remembered to lock the door, and flung it open.

Beulah.

"What the fuck are you doing here?"

If Beulah noticed her confrontational tone, she didn't say anything. "You didn't come to school today. You said you were going to."

"What? I just got up, it's only—"

"Chess . . . it's almost seven o'clock. At night."

Oh. Fuck. She was supposed to go to the school; she was supposed to go to the Church, take a look at Aros's files.

Beulah held up a can of Coke. "Here. Lex said you don't really drink coffee, so I brought you this."

"Oh. Thanks." She took it, realizing she was dry as sand, and chugged some down. Her sinuses, her throat, her chest . . . every drop of moisture sucked out by smoke. Why was Beulah still standing there, why— Oh. "Um, do you want to come in? It's kind of messy, I haven't really cleaned . . ."

That was an understatement. But oh well. What did she care? That was the way disgusting slobs lived, disgusting people who couldn't even keep friends much less anything else, who said horrible things and had horrible things said to them.

Beulah brushed past her—she smelled like spices, and a little like Lex, like his house, which only made sense— and sat down on the new couch. Chess would have to get another one. She couldn't stand looking at that one anymore. Not when she remembered why she'd bought it, remembered how he'd gone with her to Cross Town to get it, where nobody knew them and they could hold hands in public. Remembered, too, how they'd tried it out when they got it home, how they'd—

She caught a glimpse of Beulah's eyes but couldn't hold them, not while she was running for the bathroom, when she knew she probably wouldn't make it.

She did, mercifully, but the next few minutes were so bad she almost wished she hadn't. She was fucking up, she was losing it, she had to get it together, *had* to. She had a job, she had people depending on her, she had a bunch of teenagers whose lives were in danger and they needed her to help them.

She'd never felt sorrier for a group of people in her life. How the hell was she supposed to help anyone? What idiot would trust her with the life of a fucking mayfly, much less actual living people? Those kids would be better served just cutting school, dropping out.

A cold damp washcloth appeared by her face, and she grabbed it, pressed it to her skin. "Thanks. I, um, I must have caught a bug or something."

"Sure," Beulah said. "That's probably it. There's always something going around."

Chess looked at her, inspected her face for signs of sarcasm or snotty superiority but saw none. That was almost worse than if she had. She didn't want to be grateful to Beulah.

"Hungry?"

Ugh, was she kidding? The only thing Chess intended to put in her stomach was her Cepts, maybe some vodka. "No."

"You sure? I could run out, get us some—"

"I'm fine." She hauled herself to her feet, flushing the toilet, wiping her face with the damp washcloth. "Look, Beulah, thanks for coming by and everything but I really, I don't want you to get sick, and I'm sure you don't want that either, right, so—"

"I'll leave soon." Beulah followed her back down the short hall into the living room. The couch sat there staring at her, filling her vision. Accusing her. It knew what she'd done, how she'd ruined everything, how stupid she'd been.

She pulled the squashy, broken-spring chair over instead, perched on the end of it. "Soon?"

"I need to let Lex know you're okay." Beulah waved

her cell phone. "He asked me to check. I'll just tell him you got a stomach bug, right?"

Fuck. Lex would know that wasn't it. But then Beulah knew that wasn't it, too, didn't she. They all knew, everybody knew. She sighed; her whole body sank into it. "Tell him whatever you want. I don't care."

Beulah looked down at the phone in her lap and started pressing buttons. Giving Chess what privacy she could, or so it seemed. "You want to tell me what happened?"

"No."

"You sure? Sometimes it—"

"Hey, I— I appreciate you coming and everything but I still have work I could do, and I want to get started on that, okay? So it would probably be better if you just go, and I'll see you tomorrow."

She glanced at the kitchen counter; perched on the end of it was her small frameless mirror, a straw. Had she been doing speed? Had she planned to? She couldn't remember. Shit, she must have been completely out of her mind to just leave that out in the open, she never did that, not ever.

Beulah watched her for a minute; the measuring directness of her gaze made Chess want to squirm. With effort she resisted.

"I don't think I should leave you alone right now."

Shit. "Oh, for fuck's sake. What are you going to do? You want to follow me to Church, stand there while I work? That'll be fun, right? Why—why are you here, why are you doing this?"

"Lex told me—"

"Yeah, well, Lex should mind his own fucking business, and you should too. Whatever happened it's my problem, right, it's my fault, it's my—it's my—"

Shit. Her eyes were stinging again, pain like a softball wedged in her throat. This had to fucking stop, she couldn't keep going like this, not when she had work to do.

She pressed the heels of her hands into her forehead, held her breath, and for once something went her way. It wouldn't last, she knew, but at least it was a respite. "I need to get to work. So you really should just get going."

"I'll go with you."

"What? You can't." Well, this was good; she wasn't even thinking about Terrible, or anything else except for how crazy Beulah was if she actually thought she was going to walk into the Church library with Chess, stand there while Chess looked through files. "I have work to do, actual work."

"I could help you."

"How the hell— I'm just going to work, so—"

"No, Chess, I really think I should go with you. I really think you should be seen with me. Don't you think that's a good idea?"

Was she still high? Maybe she was still asleep. Hell, maybe she was still in the pipe room, and this was a very elaborate Dream hallucination. She'd certainly spent enough time there to get a few of those. "What the fuck are you talking about?"

"Oh shit. You've been sleeping all day, haven't you? You do remember last night, right? Not whatever it was that did or didn't happen to you later, but Jia? The symbol, the body? Any of that ring any bells?"

"Oh shit" was right. Like Chess's stomach didn't feel hollow enough, like her body didn't feel empty enough.

And like she wasn't a shitty enough person. A young girl was dead, and it was partially Chess's fault for not catching the killer first, and she'd completely forgotten. Another kid had died because Chess wasn't smart enough, fast enough; she had another name to carve onto her soul. "I remember."

"Right. Well. I'm sure you're capable of making the connection between Jia and a set of parents, right? And those parents and other parents? And those parents with the community in general?"

Chess stared at her. Oh, no. Oh, no, things couldn't get worse, right, that couldn't happen, it wouldn't—

"Our community isn't really very fond of the Church, as I'm pretty sure you know, and they're, ah, they're a bit unhappy. Aggressively unhappy. So I kind of think— well, I think, and Lex thinks—that you really shouldn't be out places without one of us. Okay? Especially not Aros's place, which I thought you wanted to visit today. So why don't you go take a shower, and I'll drive you."

Technically the Church offices closed at six, but employees—especially second-level employees like Chess—had keys. Had the code and thumbprint to bypass the Church's security system, too, the one Elder Ramos had ordered expanded from the prisons to every Church building almost before the smoke had even cleared from the battle in the City of Eternity.

So she could enter and use the library and files any time she wanted, even with a guest. Even with a guest she didn't want. Like Beulah. The temptation to have Beulah just take her to Aros's Downside apartment and skip this was strong, but she wanted to see the file first.

Their footsteps echoed in the great empty hall, pale-blue walls dull in the dim light cast by a lone bulb in the storeroom behind the stairs. For once the sight of it, the feel of the walls around her, didn't comfort her much.

Not that there was anything left to be comforted. There was nothing left inside her at all.

"See?" she said, not bothering to hide her irritation as she started to lock the door behind them. "There was no reason for you to come here with me."

Beulah raised her eyebrows. "Whatever. You know you'll definitely need me at Aros's place."

Sure. Sure she would. Suspicion in her head, in her chest, that either Beulah just wanted to keep Chess away from the pipe room, or she wanted to get a sneak peek into some Church files.

Like that was going to happen.

She led the way to the library, though, using her flashlight to help Beulah rather than switching on the lights. Sometimes if Church employees in the cottages were up and saw lights, they'd come over to see what was happening, and she did not need to be found with a guest. It wasn't against the rules, but it was frowned upon after hours. The last thing she needed was trouble at work.

Then again, she had—through a bizarre combination of skill, dumb luck, and incredible misfortune—managed to build up a file any Debunker would envy. She could probably wander naked through the halls in the middle of the day at this point and just get her wrist slapped for it.

That made it all the more important to keep Beulah's presence hidden, though. Work was the one thing in her life she hadn't managed to completely destroy. Keeping it that way might be good.

"Sit there," she said, jerking her head at one of the tables. The main library floor, like pretty much every library Chess had ever seen, was filled with dark wooden tables, twelve of them in three rows with one more, the thirteenth, centered at the head. Shelves sunrayed from them to the walls in a loose semicircle; at the far end sat the Library Goody's desk, and behind that the glass walls and locked door of the Restricted Room.

Chess wouldn't be needing that room that night, luckily. Entering it after hours hadn't held much appeal to her since the night months before when she'd almost been killed there.

But hey, nobody actually was trying to kill her at the moment, right? Maybe a couple of ghosts, sure, but that actually made a refreshing change after the last few months. No *humans* trying to kill her.

Except herself, of course, but that was hardly new.

She left Beulah sitting at the end of the table closest to the doors and headed over to Goody Glass's desk on a hunch. Sometimes files got handed to the Library Goodys to be refiled, and Goody Glass was lazy in addition to being unpleasant. Chess hadn't been able to ask before, but . . .

Yes! A few minutes of hunting found her Lucy McShane's slim little manila memorial, and just for good measure she went to the cabinets and grabbed the Mercy Lewis file again. She didn't think she'd missed anything the first time, but anything was possible.

Anything else? She wanted to see Aros's employee file, but that wouldn't be in the library; she'd have to ask Elder Griffin for that one. Assuming he'd let her see it, but she imagined he would.

And while she was back there, out of sight of Beulah, she went ahead and took a couple of Nips; speed and work didn't always mix, but reading files and taking notes didn't really count as the type of work speed interfered with. Besides, exhaustion still dulled her mind. Plus she wanted to also grab three more Cepts and toss those down her throat, because "completely numb" was really the only possible way she'd be able to get through the next few hours. In fact, another of those would be good, too.

Desk lamps stood dark on each table. Chess switched one of them on, set down her bag, grabbed her notebook. Time to get to—

Beulah's voice cut through her thoughts. "What are you doing?"

"What?"

"I asked what you're doing."

"Um . . ." Chess picked up the McShane file, waved it. "I'm working."

"Really." Beulah folded her arms, looking meaningfully at her seat at the desk closest to the door, and Chess's on the opposite side of the room.

"Yes, really. You wanted to come along, I brought you along. You don't get to sit and look at confidential information when you're here."

Big heavy sigh, like this was the worst inconvenience Beulah had ever suffered in her entire life. Of course, given whose daughter she was, that was very likely true. "Fine. Can I at least look at a book or something, or do I have to sit here staring off into space?"

"Whatever. Just don't go in the files." Most of the books were Church histories or academic texts, or books on the Old Governments, especially the American one. A smallish section of fiction and some nonfiction on various other topics, and that was pretty much it; the advanced magic and religion books sat behind glass in the Restricted Room, so Beulah couldn't get into much trouble wandering around.

Better that than trying to make conversation.

Okay. Lucy McShane. Born May 1984, died April 2001. A month away from seventeen. Shame.

A stiff, shiny piece of paper: a photograph. The same picture Chess had seen scanned into the mainframe, but bigger and clearer; innocence projected from the smiling eyes, the cheerful curved lips.

Chess didn't buy it, not one bit. She set the photo upside down on the other side of the folder with distaste. Seeing someone's photo after having seen their ghost always felt a bit like seeing them after having seen them naked, only naked of both skin and clothes.

After all, wasn't everyone a lot like a ghost, under the skin? Angry, vicious, vengeful? Thirsty for the pain and blood of others, for anything they could get, desperate to make themselves fat on their own superiority?

Church theory was that ghosts killed out of envy, because they hated the living simply for being alive, because they wanted to steal that life for themselves and would never give up trying no matter how many times they failed.

Chess agreed. But she also wondered—wondered a lot—if it wasn't simply that without the pressure of society, with nothing to lose, the cruelty and viciousness of the dead were simply the cruelty and viciousness of the living permitted finally to surface.

Ghosts were what living humans would be if they thought they could get away with it.

Lucy McShane had been a Triumph City baby, born in Northside. Since the file indicated Lucy had lost both of her parents, had gone to live with an aunt and a cousin, they'd probably been part of the Relocation program the Church ran in those first years while they reorganized.

Downside had been wealthy once; the kind of wealth people were stupid enough to think equaled protection. Chess had always imagined they'd gathered together there behind their thick walls of privilege, *Masque of the Red Death*-like, and instead of a mysterious guest in bloody robes had found a gathering of ancestral dead waiting for them in that dark room at midnight.

That left large homes empty, large homes the Church could fill with people who no longer had homes or were afraid to go back to the isolation or memories of the ones they had. In time, people who could afford to left and bought their own places; those who couldn't stayed in an area where the property values dropped by the minute, and where enterprising men like Bump and Slobag found plenty of privacy and room to expand their empires.

Didn't matter. Downside was what it was, and it was home, no matter how alone she was in— She shook her head. No. She had work to focus on.

Work, the thing that didn't send stabs of shrieking pain like cold silver knives right into her heart, or make her want to slam her head into a wall until she passed out just to stop the ache.

Or to take more pills, which luckily might not be necessary since her stomach was just beginning to warm with the ones she'd taken at the file cabinet.

The file didn't mention where— Okay. Lucy McShane's aunt had died. Her cousin, Chelsea Mueller, had left Triumph City entirely about ten years before.

Chelsea Mueller.

Lucy McShane's cousin. Lucy's cousin who'd owned a book on ghost summoning and who'd missed Church training by less than a point.

Lucy McShane's cousin whose copy of that ghost-summoning book had been tainted with energy, and that energy had been what Chess felt the night before. She'd thought it was Lucy's—well, some of it had been—but of course, they were related, their energy might very well have been similar.

Chelsea Mueller had been summoning her cousin's ghost.

Well, wasn't that interesting. Damn! So where was Chelsea? Was she in Downside? Well, yeah, duh, of course she was in Downside—but where? Her side of town, Lex's side of town? Did she live by the pipe room, or the school, or . . . ?

Both victims had been from Lex's side of town, at least to some degree. Even—even Terrible had said Eddie lived on the border streets. And Jia . . . Well, Jia had had Chelsea's book. Jia must have somehow known Chelsea, had some contact with her.

She could just ask Beulah. Beulah was right there. But

no. This was rather important information, confidential information, which meant it should be sought with care, when the time was right. Especially since if Jia had somehow come in contact with Chelsea at the school, asking Beulah outright might tip her off that it mattered, and she might mention it to who knew who else.

So she made a note—not that she'd forget—and went back to the file. Lucy's suicide, yes, a few very unpleasant black-and-white photographs that Chess flipped image-down the second she realized what they were. Looking at them made her think of the catwalk, and the talk she'd had with Terrible. Back when he'd been glad she was alive, when he'd known without having to be told that she'd thought of suicide every day of her life and accepted that knowledge the way he accepted everything about her.

Or the way she'd thought he had, anyway.

Before the thoughts could dig too deep, she forced them away. Work, this was work, and it needed to be done. She jotted down the drawer number of Lucy's grave supplies. Those would have to wait until morning. A summoned ghost required special Banishing, yeah, but it was nothing she couldn't handle. She could at least do that right.

She flipped through more pages. An autopsy had been done on Lucy, and she had indeed been pregnant. They'd done a DNA analysis on the— Hmm. Okay, that she could ask about.

"Beulah?"

"Yeah?" Movement in one of the aisles; Beulah appeared at the end, holding a thick white book. "What?"

"Didn't you tell me—or Monica, or somebody told me—that Lucy McShane got pregnant by her drama teacher?"

"Um . . . I think so. I don't know the story very well, but I think that's what she said, yeah. Why?"

Chess glanced at the file again. "They— No reason."

"Oh, come on. I know you have to be all confidential and everything but you know, maybe I could actually help you, since I know the school and the neighborhood and you don't. I've lived there my whole life."

"Do you remember when this happened?"

"Kind of, yeah. I was only little, of course, but I kind of remember them talking about it. It was a big deal, you know?"

"Yeah, I guess it would be." She looked at the file again. "This says they tested the teacher's DNA, and Lucy McShane's baby wasn't his."

Chapter Twenty-five

> The Church saw what was happening and rose from their obscurity, they rose from their own quiet, and they began to work.
>
> —*The Book of Truth,* Origins, Article 114

"Really?"

Beulah rounded the tables, her slim form weaving through the patches of light cast by the windows along the outside wall until she reached Chess's side. Chess glanced down at the file, scanned it to see if that sheet contained anything Beulah shouldn't see—but oh, hell, who the fuck cared? It didn't matter. Lucy McShane's death was Fact and Truth, and it wasn't being investigated anyway. This was just background. Chelsea's name was on it, sure, but not in any way that connected her to anything.

So she just pointed at the pertinent line. "See?"

That spicy smell again, that almost-Lex smell, as Beulah leaned over. Her slim hand rested on Chess's shoulder.

"Where does— Oh. Okay. Is that important?"

Chess shrugged, which had the added benefit of getting Beulah to move her hand. When was the last time anyone other than Terrible or Lex had touched her? Kind of odd, really. How often did people touch each other? Was that normal, to just touch someone like that?

Didn't matter. "It's not important, really. I mean, it

doesn't make a difference to me, as far as the case goes. It's just odd, that she supposedly killed herself because she was pregnant by this teacher but she wasn't."

"So she was sleeping with somebody else, too."

"Maybe." Duh. "I mean, yeah, obviously."

"Maybe she just thought it was the teacher's? Maybe Monica just heard it wrong."

And Mrs. Li had said Lucy didn't know who the baby's father was, that Lucy was a "slut." Interesting. She'd have to try to get another chat with Mrs. Li.

She flipped the page. "Oh well. Like I said, I don't care why she did it or who was involved or anything. I just need to get her grave supplies so I can Banish her, really."

"So it's a definite haunting."

Shit. She hadn't—well, what the fuck ever. Wasn't like Beulah wouldn't find out anyway. "Yeah. I saw her last night."

"Lucy McShane's ghost."

"Yes."

"But you didn't Banish her or send her away or whatever it is you do."

Chess sighed. "No, I didn't. She kind of caught me off guard."

She waited, tense, for some sort of snide comment about how exactly Chess had been distracted; thankfully it didn't come. Instead Beulah grabbed the other file. "What's this? The school's file?"

Chess grabbed it back. "Yes. And it's none of your business."

"You are really fucking touchy, aren't you? Again. My side of town. Maybe I can help."

"Funnily enough, I've managed to solve lots of cases in parts of town where I don't live without help from random local residents. So thanks, but no."

Beulah didn't answer. Chess glanced at her and

found her staring at the open page of the McShane file. "What?"

Okay, that could not be a good smile. That smile, the one spreading across Beulah's face, could only be described as smug. "Oh, really?"

Shit. "What."

A slim finger rose into the air, planted itself right down on the page in front of Chess. "Look at the address."

Chess did. "What? What's the— Oh." Little wheels in her head spun; double-time, in fact, because the speed was starting to kick in. "That's the building, right? The one Aros rented an apartment in?"

"Oh," Beulah said, widening her eyes, batting her lashes like Chess was a Victorian suitor, "I'm sure you would have figured that out on your own, though, right?"

Being wrong sucked.

Well, not wrong, exactly. She would have put two and two together when she got to the building—of course, Beulah wouldn't have known that, but still. She had to admit it was nice to have it pointed out to her, and especially nice to know she already had an arrangement to visit the place, thanks to Beulah.

She also had to admit that checking the place out after dark, as she was doing at that moment, was better than having to come back during daylight, because Beulah hadn't been lying when she said Chess wasn't exactly popular in that part of Downside.

Standing on Twenty-first with Lex on one side, his arm around her, and Beulah on the other, she could almost ignore the stares of the small group of people on the opposite side of the street. They didn't glare at her, not outright, but they watched her, very carefully, and their anger blew in sharp gusts across the empty pavement. She didn't need either Lex or Beulah to tell her that only their presence kept her from getting attacked, and thankfully neither of them did.

She wasn't scared. But she didn't want to stand on the street, either.

And she didn't have to, or at least she wouldn't have to once the owner of the building showed up. Hopefully that would be any minute.

Lex lit up a smoke, leaned against the wall. "Ain't feelin like spending my whole night here, aye? Gots places I could be, me."

"I'm sure Lena's going to be free later," Beulah said.

Chess blinked, turned her head in time to intercept the glare Lex shot Beulah's way. "Lena?"

He shrugged. "Ain't like you still around, aye?"

"Ain't like you weren't seeing other people even when I was." Somewhere deep inside her something twinged, a rather uncomfortable little pinch she didn't like one bit.

That was a feeling, and those were what she absolutely, positively did not want. She dug in her bag for her pillbox, ready to open it the second she got inside; what had she taken? Three or four Cepts, three Nips to wake up? It had been an hour and a half or so, she could take more. And if she couldn't she didn't really give a fuck. What was going to happen, she'd pass out? Oh, yeah, that would suck. Unconsciousness was just so undesirable right about then.

Lex looked as if he wanted to say something else, but he was stopped by the arrival of what could only be the building's owner, a female sack of bones with pure white helmet hair and fingernails so long and shiny that Chess thought for a second the woman was some sort of clawed mutant.

She raised one of those taloned hands; from the index finger dangled two keys on a tarnished ring. She didn't say a word.

"Thank you, Mrs. Pai." Beulah plucked the ring off the woman's finger and inserted one of the keys in the lock to open the front door.

Mrs. Pai didn't reply. Instead she glared at Chess, cloudy white eyes like crystal balls set deep in her wrinkled face. Chess forced herself to meet the stare; when she did, Mrs. Pai started to giggle. The charm necklace she wore—tiny bones and gold lightning bolts—glittered with the movement.

Chess's hand tightened on her knife. This woman looked like she'd left sanity behind her a good ten or fifteen years before, and Chess could see those shiny sharp nails impaling her with scary ease.

Either Lex thought the same or he was just in a hurry to rush off to see that Lena person, because he practically shoved Chess through the building's doorway and into the dim hall.

The stereotypical naked lightbulb fizzed at them from the center of the ceiling; a warped door to the left leaked the scent of boiling cabbage. Beneath it was another scent, an unpleasant one. The hairs on the back of Chess's neck rose. That was not good news, that smell. She glanced at Beulah and Lex; their expressions told her they noticed it, too—their expressions, and the way Lex's hand moved under his jean jacket.

The staircase creaked beneath their feet. Halfway up, the bare bulb's glow became so weak as to be useless, and Chess switched on her flashlight instead. The scent didn't grow stronger. Hopefully it was a memory of death, and not evidence of it.

"It's number three." Beulah fiddled with the key ring. "That one, I guess."

Lex snorted. "Aye, with the three on it? Ain't let em say you ain't sharp, Blue."

Beulah opened her mouth, but Chess stopped her with an upraised hand. "Hold on."

If her flashlight had had new batteries, she might have missed it, but as it was the light was just oblique enough for Chess to catch the scratches in the door, almost camouflaged by the general ruin of the wood and paint.

"Witchy shit, aye?" Lex leaned in. "Kinda like on you door, Tulip."

"Yeah. Kind of." Except it wasn't, not really. Chess had general protective wards on her door, a few special ones she'd developed thanks to her Church education.

The wards Aros—it had to be Aros, she couldn't imagine who else might have done it—had carved into his door were much, much darker than the ones Chess used. The Bindrune the light picked up was *kesrah,* and it was violent and bloody. Illegal.

She waved the light. "Get back, okay?"

Violent, bloody, and illegal. But not active. Or at least not energized. When her fingers brushed against it a jolt of yuck ran up her arm, like touching a wire live with evil.

But just the evil of the rune itself; highly unpleasant, but if it had ever been powered by a witch, that energy was gone. It was . . . anonymous, was the best way to put it, really.

She ran her hand over the door from the top to the bottom. If Aros—or whoever—had booby-trapped the apartment with illegal wards, setting them off would be a bad idea. Almost as bad an idea as falling in love had been.

The rest of the door felt clean. Well, not clean, but not smeared with evil like the *kesrah* rune. Just the typical yuck of any Downside building; misery and hate, greed and lust, attempts at theft spells and death spells and any other magical vice the human mind could come up with, and the human mind was in general a pretty sick fucking place, as she well knew.

"Okay." She held her hand out for the key. Beulah

placed it in her palm. It slipped into the lock, didn't stick on opening.

Something told her this was not going to be good.

She was right. The door creaked open. That smell, that foul stench of death festering in private, belched from the open doorway in a moldering cloud to cover her, to cover Lex and Beulah, and sent them all staggering back to the wall.

"Tell me that's not what I think it is," Beulah gasped. The sickness in her voice twisted Chess's stomach even more.

"It is," she managed in reply. Fuck, fuck, fuck. Something was dead in that apartment—something or some*one*—and she had to walk in and take a good look at it.

And she didn't have a handkerchief or cloth or anything. She pressed her sleeve-covered hand over her mouth and nose, waiting for the nausea to subside. Oh, fuck, that was so awful. So awful and just teeming with bacteria and sickness and germs waiting to invade her body, to marry the sickness already inside her so deep it would never leave.

Bleach might clean the apartment she was about to enter, but they didn't make bleach for people's insides. She was stuck with her own filth. She didn't need to add more.

Beulah tied a cloth around her face; Lex improvised with a sleeve, like Chess; and they stepped forward to see what new horror waited for them.

Chapter Twenty-six

Horror indeed. Chess barely saw the apartment around her, bare walls scribbled with words in black and the dried brownish-red of blood. Nonsense words; the man had seriously gone bug-fuck crazy, hadn't he? At least if someone considered scribbling "tutu," "minerals," and "dancing" in blood on walls to be bug-fuck crazy, which Chess did.

Her flashlight picked up a sofa with stuffing erupting like mushrooms from holes in the rough fabric, a pockmarked table flecked with paint, scraps of thin carpet grayish in the light's beam. On the left, a stove crusted with filth; on the right, an open doorway emitting stench like a blast furnace giving heat. The bedroom.

Lex's gun caught a ray of thin moonlight that fought its way through the grimy windows. Beulah pulled a silver dagger from somewhere; Chess followed suit and flicked the blade on her knife. Her new knife. Terrible had given it to her two weeks before. She wished she'd thought of that and brought her old one.

And it wasn't necessary anyway. As soon as they'd walked far enough to see into the room, she knew it wasn't. The only person in the room capable of injuring them was as disarmed as it was possible to be, quite literally.

Aros's naked body lay on the bed, barely recognizable. He had to have been dead at least three or four days, in that tiny apartment with the heat turned up.

At least she thought it was Aros; she'd only seen him once or twice, quick glances around the Church building. She'd been distracted, to say the least, the kind of distraction where every man looked the same save for one, their faces blurring into a haze in her mind. But she remembered darkish, longish hair such as covered the head of the corpse on the bed, and thought she remembered . . . well, she didn't remember anything else. But the apartment was in his name, and it was definitely a man's body; enough remained of it for her to be certain of that.

And she could be certain the death hadn't been pleasant. The face was . . . obliterated, was the best term she could think of for it.

Well. So much for the loose—more than loose—idea she'd had that maybe Aros was the man behind the murders, that maybe he was Slobag's new witch. She hadn't fully realized until that moment that the idea had even been there; she'd been mentally classifying Aros with Riley, really, as someone who just couldn't handle the job. But as she looked at what was left on the bed, she realized that yeah, she'd wondered. Hadn't wanted to admit it to herself—and had been too high the night before, too busy since Beulah showed up at her place—but she'd wondered. And she'd been wrong.

Aros must have found Chelsea. Must have discovered something that drove him crazy, that led to his murder.

"Ain't know why I let you get me into this shit, Tulip," Lex muttered. "Could be doin all sorts else, 'stead of here."

"Oh, come on," she managed. "What could possibly be better than this?"

He acknowledged the joke, lame as it was, with a thin smile and jerked his chin at the remains. "Gotta call you Church this one, aye?"

She nodded. At least there was that. At least this wasn't a death she needed to hide; she could report this one, and the Church could take care of it, and maybe she'd get a tidy report at the end if they thought she could use the information provided.

Seeing the body, the apartment, though, reminded her that she hadn't gone into Aros's cottage on the Church grounds, hadn't even asked yet. She supposed that could be excused, or at least understood; she hadn't planned to spend her day passed out in her hallway. But it certainly made that task more urgent, didn't it, that Aros was apparently dead. In a very grisly fashion. He hadn't done that to himself, had he?

No. She somehow doubted he'd managed to chop off both of his own arms.

How close had he gotten to Chelsea? What the fuck had happened to him?

Beulah found a window, thickly covered by black burlap, and opened it. Fresh air—what passed for fresh air in Downside, that was, which meant it stank of poverty and old grease, but thankfully not of death this far from the Slaughterhouse—began to chase a bit of the suffocating heaviness away, but not much. Not enough.

With that feeble air came light, enough for Chess to see the pills strewn everywhere. She snapped on a latex glove, bent to pick one up with a superstitious shudder.

Vapes; Vapezine. Heavy psychotropic, one she didn't have a particular interest in. Hallucinatory meds never really did it for her. The odds of a good trip just weren't good enough. But the floor in that room was littered with them, shiny hot-pink-and-white capsules all over the carpet, crushed into it like bright candy melting in the sun.

"Lookin like he spend himself some time on the other side," Lex remarked. "Strong shit there."

Chess dropped the pill she'd been inspecting. "I guess so."

"That's not all he was taking, either," Beulah said. Against the window she was a silhouette, silver-edged in the dark; she held up a couple of empty pill bottles. "He didn't buy these from us. He had a prescription. Lots of prescriptions, for all kinds of shit."

Chess looked at the labels, looked around. "How old are the scripts?"

"Recent. All of them in the last few weeks. All the same prescribing doctor, too: Pritchard, in Cross Town."

"So he was taking more than just—" Something snapped into place then, the thing that had been bothering her since the second she saw the pills on the floor. Or rather, the other thing that had been bothering her, the thing that had nothing to do with the case at all.

She needed air. "I'm, um, let's go, okay? Let's get out of here, and I'll call the Church."

"What? But shouldn't—"

No. She couldn't stand there another minute, not without a smoke, and another handful of pills, and she wasn't about to put anything into her mouth in that foul death-chamber. "I'm going to get some air, okay; I'll be right back."

She banged her knee against something as she stumbled out of the apartment, the dull circle her flashlight cast bobbing before her as if on a spring. She started to turn right to head back to the street but had the presence of mind not to go down there alone, so instead she went left and up, to the next floor and the roof access door she hoped would be there.

Her breath grew shorter with every step, panic creeping from her stomach to her head, hitting her harder and harder. That body in there, that body all alone on a bed in a room full of pills, the body of someone who'd gone on a hard run that never ended. It was hers. It was her body, her future, what her future could be. What her future would be now that she'd fucked up everything with Terrible, fucked up her entire life. Again.

The roof door—thank fuck it existed—burst open with one heavy shove; her rubbery legs carried her out onto the flat cement surface, wandering from one side to the other like a pinball while she tried to get herself under control. Dead and alone in a room full of drugs, rotting and alone with pills crushed into the carpet. Dead while nobody gave a fuck, a lonely addict's death in silence with no one to even notice. Tears poured down her cheeks and she couldn't stop them; her breath whistled in her chest. Without Terrible that's what she'd be, no one cared, no one really gave—

Wait a minute. If Aros had found Chelsea—so she assumed, and it seemed like a reasonable assumption—and if she'd killed him like that . . . how long would it be before she realized Chess was on her trail, and found a way to do the same thing to her?

Terrible hadn't called. Hadn't texted. Hadn't tried to get in touch with her at all.

Well, what the fuck was she, surprised?

No. Just sick. But what else was new.

Thankfully, this wasn't the time to brood about it. Even more thankfully, she was stuffed so full of Cepts that brooding would be almost impossible even if it had been the time. Not completely impossible, of course; she could still feel the stab there, the emptiness beneath her ribcage where everything important was supposed to be. Where it had always been empty until he came along, and which he'd left empty again when he'd torn himself away from her. It felt like death.

But she could get through it. She could and she would, because she had to.

Elder Griffin finished looking at her hastily typed report and sighed. "Oh, Aros. So disturbing, he didn't seem at all . . . well. I am sorry, Cesaria."

Chess nodded. Yeah, she was sorry, too. She was getting only part of her bonus money, and if she was going to finish every night at the pipes like she had the last two, the cash in her account wouldn't last more than another couple of months, tops. Sure, another case might come in, but it might not. She'd gone five months once; that had been the first time she'd gone into debt with Bump, two years before.

Not to mention that whole Chelsea-might-try-to-kill-her thing. And the memory of that body cold and ignored on its diseased bloody bed. And the feeling of walking blind into something big and murky and dangerous, something waiting for her with claws extended.

Elder Griffin's curtains were open; gray light from the unhappy sky flooded over his desk, made his expression hard to read. "He did ask for permission to rent the place, feeling it would help him to fit in. He said the students refused to speak to him. Did you find that a problem?"

"Kind of." She shifted in her seat. Yes, kind of, until the son of the local drug lord kissed her in front of a crowd. Then they talked.

"I suppose it matters not. When will you perform the Banishing?"

"Tonight, I think. Might as well get it over with, right? Have you heard anything about Chelsea Mueller, where she is? Any picture yet?"

He shook his head. "Her physical file should have been housed here, but as you know, it has also disappeared, along with the records in the computer. Aros seems to have deleted it. We are hoping it will be retrieved from the backups by tonight."

At least that was one thing. The Squad would go with her to make an arrest once they had a face, an address.

Elder Griffin's chair sighed as he moved. "May I ask, have you yet received the evaluation form for me?"

"Oh, um, yes. I'm going to start it this evening before I do the case paperwork, if that's okay." Shit, she'd forgotten it; well, she hadn't forgotten it. The truth was she didn't want to fill it out. She wanted to give him a negative report so he'd have to stay with her. She'd lost Terrible. She didn't want to lose him, too.

But he nodded, smiled his gentle smile, and she knew she couldn't do that. Just because she didn't deserve happiness, just because she'd ruined her only chance at it and gotten her ass dumped, didn't mean he didn't deserve it. She could help him, and she would. Chess Putnam, fairy fucking magicmother.

"Sir, do you know if Aros had some family in the area that I could talk to? Or maybe one of his training Elders in his last post?"

"He had no family, no," Elder Griffin replied, leaning back to open a drawer in his desk. From it he pulled a pale-blue file. Aros's employee record.

She took it from him, opened it while he continued to speak. "Of course he had high recommendations from the Elders in his previous office—Indianapolis, that was—and an excellent record."

"Nobody there knew he had all those prescriptions?"

Elder Griffin shook his head. "As far as we can tell, he did not. What information I've managed to get so far indicates he started on those while handling the Mercy Lewis case. I hate to say it but I am glad he removed himself. Were it discovered he was so compromised . . ."

"Right," she said, rather louder than she meant to.

"Um, so he started on the case and he was fine, and then it just went bad."

"Yes."

Thanks to Chelsea. So she assumed; so she'd put in her preliminary report.

She flipped through the pages he'd given her: more pictures of Aros's apartment, copies of notes and papers handed in by the Recovery Team who'd picked up Aros and done the crime scene work on his place. What the fuck?

Aros had notes about Jia . . . lots of notes about Jia. Well, she guessed that wasn't too big a surprise, given that Jia had somehow been involved with Chelsea and Aros had apparently discovered Chelsea.

But he also had notes about Beulah. And about Beulah's father. Along with an address Chess recognized. Their home address.

Chelsea had to be getting power from somewhere; she didn't have enough on her own. Chess had suspected it came from Aros, of course, but with Aros dead . . .

That brought her right back to Slobag. And his witch. She needed to find out who the hell that was.

Chapter Twenty-seven

Always remember the City awaits.
—*The Book of Truth*, Veraxis, Article 776

Beulah sat behind her desk; she looked up and smiled when Chess entered. "Hey, Chess. Why didn't you call me and let me know you were coming? I would have waited outside for you. Did they give you any trouble?"

"There wasn't anyone out there." Chess sat down uninvited in the cushy blue chair opposite Beulah's desk. "Besides, I didn't know if you'd be here. Aren't you only supposed to work a few days a week?"

Beulah shrugged. "Interesting stuff going on. I don't want to miss it."

"Right." She looked at Beulah, sitting there with her shining hair hanging straight down. How much did she actually know, what might she tell? Assuming Chess could trust anything Beulah did say, which she wasn't entirely sure she could. "Why do you do it, anyway? Work here. Lex doesn't have some kind of outside job."

"Lex is a boy. My father wouldn't let me take over the business even if Lex wasn't older. This is something to do, really. And I can get to know a lot of people, people who might be useful one day."

"Like me?"

Beulah smiled. "I think Lex already had you there, no pun intended."

Chess's answering smile felt stiff, like a pair of wax lips. "So you don't really have much to do with the business. Like you don't know about the day-to-day stuff."

"Some of it I do." Beulah's eyes narrowed. "Why do you ask?"

"Just curious. Speaking of you knowing people, though . . . that girl Jia. Who were her friends, do you know? What kinds of stuff did she do?"

"You already know some of her friends. Vernal, Maia, that gang. Jia wasn't . . . she wasn't as in with them, if you know what I mean? Always seemed to be on the edges a little bit." Beulah leaned back; the soft leather chair in which she sat tilted, rocked gently. "She was more serious, wanted to go to college. She did a lot of community stuff, too, with Mrs. Li and her girls' groups."

"Seems like there are a lot of groups here. Was Mrs. Li the only one whose groups Jia joined?"

"No . . . I don't know, really, but she was in a few, I think. I know she was in one of Mrs. Li's, yeah, but one of Mr. Li's, too. I didn't know her really well."

Uh-huh. "What about Aros? Did she seem to have any kind of relationship with him?"

"Not that I noticed, no. But then I wasn't paying attention. Why?"

Chess shook her head. "No reason. Oh, I wanted to ask, too, if you've ever heard the name Chelsea Mueller? It's only a side issue, really, but—"

"Isn't that the cousin? Lucy McShane's cousin? I thought her name was on that file you showed me."

Damn. Beulah had seen that, hadn't she. "Yeah, I just wondered if you've heard of her recently, like maybe Jia or someone else mentioned her."

"Hmm. Not that I can remember, but—"

A tap at Beulah's office door. It opened. Monica stood in the doorway, her cheeks almost as red as her hair. That day she wore a hideous bile-green and mustard-yellow polka-dot dress with an empire waist; she looked like the physical embodiment of a hangover.

"Oh, sorry," she said. "Sorry to interrupt. Hi, Chess. Beulah, I wonder if you have a second? I want to show you something, on my desktop."

Beulah glanced at Chess, who opened her mouth as fast as she could. "I'll be fine, you go ahead. I'll just sit and wait here, okay?"

Yes! Beulah nodded. Chess was alone in her office, and that was a very good place to be. It might not last long, but then it didn't have to, really. Being caught was bad form, but technically Chess had the right to look at every single sheet of paper in that office.

And she'd try to do exactly that.

She kept one eye on the door while she rifled through Beulah's drawers. Notes about school projects, a contest they'd be holding about ancestry—she gave that one a stronger examination. It looked innocent enough, but given Beulah's apparent views on the Church . . .

Not her department. And not a point she could press when she needed help from Beulah, either. Instead, she kept going, her fingers skipping over the tabs, until she found a file marked GIRLS' PROJECTS.

She flipped that one open. Pay dirt. Awesome. Jia's spidery little signature at the bottom of a page with a few other names; at the top were listed Mr. Li, one of the history teachers, and Monica. Repainting a home for the elderly, performing a traditional dance . . .

It wasn't a surprise to discover that Jia lived—had lived—on the same street as Aros's apartment—on that same block, in fact.

She scribbled it all down in her notebook, even though

she didn't need to. That, at least, she knew she wouldn't forget.

Beulah's voice outside the door. Chess slipped the file back into place and turned her back on the desk just as the door opened. No point trying to get back to her chair; throwing herself into it would look more suspicious than simply having gotten up to have a bit of a wander around the office.

To complete the effect she turned her head a bit. "This is a nice print, where did it come from?"

It was a landscape framed in dark-blue metal, and actually rather dull; just a handy excuse for standing where she did, not at all the sort of thing Chess would imagine Beulah liking enough to display in her office. But what did she know?

"It was here when I got the office, actually." Beulah came around behind the desk. Chess stepped away, almost stumbling in her haste.

That was when she noticed the two Styrofoam containers in Beulah's hands. Beulah raised one of them. "I didn't know if you'd be hungry, but I brought you some lunch anyway. Laurie's made a ton of food."

"And she packed it in Styrofoam?"

Beulah smiled. "No, we keep a supply of these. I just figured it would be easier than carrying it in my bare hands, you know?"

"Right. Thanks." She was hungry, surprisingly; but then, when was the last time she'd eaten? A couple of days ago, maybe? Certainly not since the argument. She'd barely been able to keep her pills down, much less actual food.

Speaking of which, she wanted to pop back into the little office for a few of those, too. She was starting to crash from her earlier dose and it wasn't pleasant.

But the food smelled good and Beulah watched her expectantly, so she unwrapped the plastic spork Beulah handed her along with the food and started to eat. It was some sort of rice dish, in a thick sauce, with flecks of beef throughout.

After the first bite her empty stomach came to life with a vengeance. Only the vague desire not to look like a total pig kept her from shoveling it in, instead just eating faster than normal. Especially since it wasn't bad at all, save the sort of awkward aftertaste, like chalk on a—

Fuck. Oh fuck, oh shit.

Beulah stared at her. Chess couldn't help noticing that Beulah had a different meal in front of her, what looked like the kind of noodles Chess bought at the Market sometimes. Made sense. "Are you okay? You look pale all of a sudden. You ate awfully fast."

Yes, and if she didn't get up and get her ass to the bathroom soon, she'd be even paler. As in *dead*. "I'm fine, I just— I have a lot to do, so I'm going to call myself done and leave you to your lunch."

"Oh, no, you should stay. Or I'll go with you, I'm not that hungry. And we can talk some more."

"I can't, I need to get going, really, I have some stuff to check in the files at Church—"

"Can't you do that later? You—"

Enough. "I can't," Chess said, slinging her bag over her shoulder. Her left hand kept a death grip on the food container; she'd need that, even though she knew it was essentially pointless. She knew what the lab would find, or at least had a damn good idea of it.

Her right hand turned the knob and flung the door open. She launched herself out of it, almost knocking into Laurie, who gave a melodramatic yelp as if Chess had pinched her ass rather than simply invaded her personal space for a few seconds.

No time for her, either. Chess managed to get out of the office before she started to run, past a couple of kids roughing up another one, past the open classrooms where the history of the Church was being taught; she caught the words "Salem witch trials" as she sped past, knew they were discussing the Church's origins.

Finally the bathroom on her right. She threw herself into it, already letting her bag fall, already reaching up to shove her finger as far down her throat as it could go. She'd never been good at this, which really irritated her. It seemed she could be sick at the drop of a dime, except when she really needed to be, and then she turned into Iron Stomach or something.

It wasn't working. How much time did she have? And what were the pills supposed to do, anyway?

It had to have been pills. That chalky, faintly bitter aftertaste couldn't be mistaken for anything else, especially not by her. Someone had dissolved some medication— Vapezine, Chess bet—in water or sauce, or opened the capsules, and mixed it with her food.

Someone who didn't eat the same thing she had. Someone who practically forced her to eat, someone who didn't want to let her leave. Someone she'd been questioning.

Someone who apparently wanted her dead, too. A heavy dose of Vapes—strong enough to leave an aftertaste in a dish as highly flavored as that one—could stop a person's heart, flood their lungs with fluid, even without adding four Cepts to the mix. And a little speed. And a Panda to keep the speed from making her too jittery.

At the very least she was going to be monumentally fucked up if she didn't manage to get rid of them, and that would be almost as bad as dying, at least if someone noticed and she ended up in the hospital. The second they did a drug test on her they'd see the levels of narcotic in her system, and game fucking over.

In desperation she scrabbled through her bag. Trying

to be sick wasn't something she normally did; usually it was the opposite, thanks to the occasional narco-nausea. So she had plenty of stuff to counteract that. But to induce vomiting . . .

To induce vomiting maybe she could just think about the fact that she was on her knees in what was essentially a public bathroom, the place bacteria went to play, and how she was like a fresh new toy for them to jump all over. How many of them did she breathe in every time she inhaled, how many of them would hide on her skin, in her hair?

Or she could remember the last time she'd been in a public bathroom before this case, five weeks or so ago, the night she'd seen Terrible at Chuck's and run away to hide in the bathroom and he hadn't let her. He'd followed her, kissed her, picked her up, and she hadn't been able to get her jeans off fast enough and she'd thought the door might break from him pounding into her so hard against it, and a crowd had formed outside and she hadn't cared and neither had he. That night when she had so much hope, that night when he'd come for her later and saved her life. The night she'd put her hands on his shoulders, looked into his eyes, and told him she loved him.

That did it. Up came the rice, up came everything else. Disgusting but necessary. Too bad that with it came the pain, the tears she'd managed to hold at bay for the last two days. She didn't know how she'd managed it—lots of chemicals, mainly—but she had, and now it was too late.

Her watch said two-thirty. Five minutes. She could give herself five minutes to sit there blubbering like a pussy, and then she'd take her pills, bump up off her hairpin, leave the stall, rinse her face with cold water, and get the hell out of the building. That sounded like an awesome plan, in fact.

"Chess?" A woman's voice, tentative and soft. Great—a witness.

Chess staggered to her feet, wiping her streaming eyes with her sleeve. Flushed the toilet again to hide the sound of her sniffles. "Yeah?"

"It's me, Monica. Are you okay?"

Chess nodded, before realizing that—duh—Monica couldn't see her. Lucky, that. She probably looked like some sort of raccoon-eyed tomato. And no faucet. "I'm fine. Why?"

"You just seemed like you were in an awful hurry, like maybe something had upset you? I know we don't know each other very well, but . . . I thought maybe I could help."

Right. Help. It would take a hell of a lot more than one frizzy-haired woman with the fashion sense of a goat to help Chess.

"No, I just . . . well, I really had to go." Chess forced a laugh. A humiliating and ridiculous excuse, but what the hell else was she supposed to say? She was in a bathroom stall, after all. She couldn't very well claim she'd had to make an important phone call.

She opened her water bottle, quickly soaked a wad of toilet paper with it, and swabbed at her eyes. That was gross, too. Public restroom toilet paper, sandpapery and rough, and quite possibly pre-gunked with all sorts of horrible infectious shit; her eyes would probably start oozing pus within twenty-four hours.

"Oh, okay." But Monica didn't leave.

Chess grabbed four more Cepts, knocked them back, and opened the stall door. Monica stood leaning against the sink, her arms folded, looking pensively at the ceiling. "You seem to be talking to Beulah a lot," she said.

Chess shrugged.

"I'm kind of surprised, really. You know how she feels about the Church."

What was her point? Chess looked at her, maybe a bit more carefully than she needed to, but nothing in Monica's eyes or demeanor indicated any sort of ulterior motive, or anything else. "Yeah, I know. It's not like it's an unusual attitude here."

"Yeah, but . . . can I be honest with you? Some people think Beulah's intentions here aren't really honorable. You know about her family, right?"

The faucet was generic, looked like every other public restroom faucet in the world. Chess pretended it fascinated her. Did Monica not know about Lex, about the kiss?

Apparently not. "Her father is a, well, a criminal. And some people—not me, but some people—think maybe she's using the students to launder money or something for him, something to do with charitable donations, I don't know. I'm not an accountant. But . . . it makes me uncomfortable, the way she's normally only here for a few hours every week and now all of a sudden she's here all day, every day."

"A few hours a week?"

Monica nodded. "Before, she'd come in at two on Mondays, Wednesdays, and Fridays, stay until school let out, and maybe an hour after, talking to parents or students or administrators, you know, settling disputes or whatever it is she does. But ever since just before the haunting started, she's been here . . . well, like I said, all the time."

Because it was interesting, Beulah had said. But how interesting could it really be? What the hell was Beulah doing there, exactly?

Not that Chess trusted Monica or believed everything she was saying, or rather implying. But she didn't trust Beulah, either, especially not after the drugs in her food. Beulah said she'd gotten it from a big batch Laurie brought in; Chess couldn't imagine it had all been dosed, so that had to be just for her.

And right after Chess had asked about Chelsea. Just like that horrible tea had come right after Chess had escaped from the trunk, and Beulah had let her into the theater that day. Had anyone else even known she was in the theater then?

"Huh," she said, because Monica seemed to expect an answer. "Well, thanks for letting me know."

"I just want to help. We all do, you know. Wen was just saying yesterday how much he hopes things get worked out soon. He hates thinking of the kids being in danger here, you know. And he's not crazy about Beulah's father trying to—well, getting the students involved in things they shouldn't be."

Duh. That reminded her. "Hey, I haven't seen Mrs. Li around. Do you know where she is?"

"She's not doing very well, not after Jia . . . you know, she and Beulah were rather close to Jia, it seemed like. I guess Beulah's told you all about that, about how she was really taking Jia under her wing. Jia and Vernal and all of those kids, they worked for her father, I guess, too."

Chess hadn't been sick quite fast enough. Monica's face blurred for a second, split in two, then snapped back into place; something was hitting her bloodstream, something she didn't deliberately put there. Shit, she needed that bump. Her tongue tingled; it was not comfortable or pleasant.

Monica glanced at her watch. "Anyway. Sorry for keeping you. I just wanted to see if you were okay, really, and let you know to be careful around Beulah. I'm sure you know that already, though."

Yeah. Chess knew that.

"And if you need anything, don't hesitate to ask me,

please. Okay? Almost everything that happens in this school passes right before my desk, so . . ."

"Thanks, Monica." Two forty-five. If Monica left now, Chess could still bump up and get out of the building before the bell rang.

Thankfully, Monica did just that. With a smile and a confident "Any time," she slipped out of the room.

Chess threw herself back into the stall, dug around for the hairpin she used; it had a little divot in the center and was slimmer than a key, so she preferred it. Hell, if she had more time she'd cut herself a line on the toilet paper dispenser, but she didn't. Not only was the bell about to ring, but her head grew fuzzier every second.

Damn that Beulah! It had to be her who'd dosed the food. Who else could it have been?

No way was Beulah really Chelsea Mueller or anything. Beulah was exactly who she said she was. But if Slobag had some sort of plan with his witch, if Chelsea and his witch were working together . . . if he and his witch had some sort of plan, maybe, to remove Chess from the picture . . .

Beulah would be perfectly placed to help with that. It could be a perfect one-two punch, couldn't it? Chelsea got what she wanted—which was apparently her cousin back—and Slobag got what he wanted, which was Chess gone. It wasn't even a very complicated sort of conspiracy or anything; all it would require would be an introduction, a frank chat about what everyone hoped to gain.

And when Aros was assigned the case, they got rid of him. Because Chess was much easier to eliminate if she was forced to spend time on this side of town, where she wasn't protected.

She sucked back three bumps, chasing them with a couple of drops of water. Much better. Her vision still wanted to go haywire but some of the clouds in her head lifted, at least the ones not forming at the idea of a bunch of people planning her death.

They lifted enough for her to hear the bathroom door sneak open. As fast as she could she wiped at her nose, resealed her baggie and tucked it back into her pillbox, licked the hairpin and put it away as well. Being caught standing in the toilet stall with a bag full of speed and a hair slide dusted white might not be too good for her.

She waited for someone to speak. No one did. Her heart started pounding, but whether that was from the kick she'd just snorted or from fear, she didn't know. Didn't necessarily want to know.

What she did know was that someone else was in that bathroom, and that someone did not want to be heard. Okay. She slid her knife out of her pocket; she'd have to click it open at the same time as she opened the door, otherwise she'd alert whomever it was that she knew they were there.

The handle of the toilet, cold and slightly damp. She shoved it down.

The sound masked her dropping her bag. Just as she'd planned, she flung open the door, clicked the button on her knife, her left hand reaching out to grab—

Beulah. Beulah, who screamed and jumped back; not a bad actress, that one. "Shit! What the fuck, Chess?"

"I'm— What are you doing?"

"I came to see if you were okay. Monica said you were in here."

For a second Chess let herself imagine going ahead and stabbing Beulah. Just sinking her knife into Beulah's arm or something—not somewhere fatal, just somewhere painful—and paying her back.

She couldn't, though. Of course she couldn't. Instead she sighed, clicked her knife back, and shoved it into her pocket. "You scared me."

"Obviously." Beulah's eyes followed the movement,

stayed on Chess's pocket like she thought the knife would jump at her on its own.

"Well, you didn't say anything, what was I supposed to think?"

"That I was swallowing the Coke I'd just drank, maybe? Sheesh. Anyway. You're fine, that's all I needed to know." She turned and swept back out of the room, shooting one more annoyed look over her shoulder before the door closed.

Yeah. Chess was sure that whether she was fine was all Beulah needed to know.

She just wasn't sure what the woman would pull to make sure she wasn't fine next time.

Chapter Twenty-eight

[
The magic of the Church is always just, always pure, and
always ready to protect you.
—*The Church and You,* a pamphlet by Elder Barrett
]

Lex waited for her in the parking lot. Fuck! Another
of Slobag's genetic leavings, when she wanted to see if
Chelsea's information had come in at the Church yet.

"Hey, Tulip." He leaned against her car, crossed his
ankles with his arms folded. "Figured I'd get some eats,
me, maybe you come along."

Ugh. "No, thanks."

"Aw, c'mon. Figure you got an owes, seein as how
they talking to you now, aye? Alls I'm wanting is company." He raised his eyebrows. "Lessin you got aught
else you wanna give me. Always happy to do me some
negotiations."

That was tempting. She could let him into her car,
drive to his place, climb into his bed with him and spend
the afternoon there. It would be so fucking good to lose
herself in something right then, and she had no doubt
she'd be able to. Lex never disappointed.

But she couldn't, and she knew it even before she
thought of what a bad idea going to Slobag's house would
be when he might have another witch there planning
her death. She couldn't because she couldn't stand the
thought of someone else, someone not Terrible, touch-

ing her, kissing her; the thought made her body grow cold even with the jittery warmth of the speed and Cepts in her system.

Letting Lex have her again, letting anyone else have her, would mean fully admitting to herself that she and Terrible were finished, that he didn't want her anymore. She wasn't ready for that. Not yet.

Lex must have seen it. "Eats still on the table, too. Come on along, I pay an all."

"Who is your father's witch? What the hell does he need a witch for?" The words slipped out, driven by drugs and irritation, but once they escaped into the air she found she was glad they had. She wanted an answer, and she and Lex had never been much for mincing words, not with each other.

"What?"

"Who is his witch, why does he need a witch?"

"Ain't got that knowledge, Tulip. Only know—after that dame's found, dig, not before—he got heself one."

She inspected him. He looked innocent enough, but then he always did. "I think he might be trying to kill me."

He raised his eyebrows. "Why the fuck he wanna do that one? Ain't liking you much, he ain't, but ain't can see him tryin that. Never gave me any say on it."

"Maybe he wouldn't."

"Ain't can say what he do and don't give me. Only know he ain't givin me any whys on what you sayin. And never gave me any on you."

"And the pipe room? Any other buildings he might be planning to blow up?"

He shrugged. Right. He didn't know much about the witch, but he sure as fuck knew about that fire. Not a surprise. "Now you comin for eats or nay? Causen I got me some hungry, lessin you want me for ought else, iffen you dig."

In spite of herself she smiled. A little. "Let me call the Church really quick first."

She was still hungry after all. And with her mind still buzzing oddly and her vision wavering just a bit, she didn't particularly want to drive, didn't particularly want to be alone.

Didn't particularly want to be with Lex, either, but she didn't have any other options, did she.

The phone in Elder Griffin's office rang four times before he picked it up, sounding a little breathless. "Cesaria," he said, cutting off her hi-how-are-yous. "Cesaria, we have a situation. With your case."

Uh-oh. "What? Did I do something—"

"Oh, no, no, my dear. But I'm afraid . . . I must tell you, the DNA test results came in today on the body from Aros's apartment."

Double uh-oh. He'd said "the body," not "Aros's body." Her stomach hollowed out.

Sure enough, he took a deep breath—audible even over the phone—and said, "The body found in that apartment was not Aros. 'Twas a man named Bill Pritchard. His DNA is on file from an arrest in his second school years, just some mild vandalism. But mild vandalism at the Mercy Lewis school."

Pritchard. Bill Pritchard. Why did that name sound familiar?

"Let me guess," she replied. "He was at school in 2000 or so, right? 2001? Right after the school opened."

"Yes. How did thou know?"

Fucking hell. Another dead body around Lucy McShane. And this one may have been directly related to her; every chance in the world existed that her ghost had killed that Bill person herself. The bright sunshine dimmed. Why was she certain she'd heard that name before? "Just a guess. It's when the suicide in my case happened, so . . . I thought they might be related."

"Ah." Pause. "Are you coming in? I know thee wanted to look at Aros's cabin, and I do believe 'tis more important now that we know he still lives."

"Yeah." She caught Lex's eye, shrugged an apology. Looked like she wouldn't be having lunch with him after all. "I'll be right there."

Every Church office in every city had its own lab. Or technically, its own labs; DNA, disease, whatever other kinds of labs there were. Chess very rarely dealt with any of them, but if she did it was usually the DNA lab. Sometimes DNA was useful in cracking Debunking cases; people left DNA in the stupidest places. They licked envelopes, they shed hairs, they left fingernail clippings that grossed her out to touch.

That day, though, she bypassed the DNA lab and headed to the door for Forensics. It opened to her tentative knock, revealing a kind-looking older man. From beneath his pale-blue lab coat peeked white stockings and buckle shoes; an Elder, then, not just a doctor. Made sense, but she knew lots of Church offices had regular doctors working in their labs.

She tucked her right foot behind her ankle, dropped a quick curtsy. "Good morrow, sir. I'm Cesaria Putnam, I'm a Debunker."

His silvery head dipped, returning her gesture. "I have heard of you, yes. How can I help you?"

He stepped back. Beyond him were rows of bodies covered in pale-blue sheets, like rafts floating down a river all facing the same direction. Beyond those were more tables, sinks and Bunsen burners and machinery she couldn't identify.

She held up the Styrofoam container. "It's rather private, sir. I believe . . . I believe this food may have been adulterated, that I was targeted by a subject of my current investigation."

The Elder's eyes widened. "Indeed? Shameful. Thou would like me to analyze the food, is that correct?"

She nodded.

He glanced at the clock on the wall, and Chess took the opportunity to peek at the small ID badge pinned to the pocket of his coat. The cards weren't necessary to access most of the building, but for the labs, the prisons . . . Gordon Lyle, the tag said. Of course—Elder Lyle. She'd heard of him. "I do believe I have time now, for something like this. Does thou care to stay here for fifteen minutes or so?"

Yes! "Of course. I thank you, sir."

She followed him to the back, through the unsettling sea of corpses. She kept expecting spirits to rise, or the bodies themselves to move. Her hand tightened on the strap of her bag, reassuring herself that she had her supplies. Seeing the row of skulls on the far wall, all psychopomps, reassured her as well. Elder Lyle didn't play around, it seemed. But then she wouldn't have expected he did.

"Please sit," he said, motioning to a stool.

Chess did, sliding it a bit farther away from the dead. "Sir, may I ask if Bill Pritchard's body is here? I was the one who found him, he's connected to my case."

"Indeed." Elder Lyle scooped some of the food from the Styrofoam, placed it in some sort of container in one of the machines. Water started pouring into it. "My, that looks like good food, too. Such a shame someone played with it."

"Yes." She sat silent for a moment, long enough to give him a chance to reply. Showing proper respect.

When he didn't speak, though, and started pushing buttons on the machine, she went ahead. "Have you happened to complete your analysis of Mr. Pritchard yet? Cause of death, I mean, or maybe if he had any drugs in his system?"

"I have." He pushed another button; the machine started to shake like a paint mixer.

"There were a lot of medications found in the apartment. I just wondered if those were in his bloodstream or not. Do you maybe have a report I can look at while I'm here, or—"

That was it. Medications. Beulah had said the prescribing physician on the pill bottles in Aros's apartment was named Pritchard.

How the fuck did he fit in, then?

"He had medication in his system, yes. A very strong dose," Elder Lyle continued, oblivious to her mental calculations. "That's what killed him, at least indirectly. His lungs were mostly full of fluid. But the damage to the body . . . quite a bit of that was self-inflicted, premortem. Drug-induced psychosis, I believe. Must have happened after the woman left."

"What med— What woman?"

The machine stopped shaking but continued to emit a low-level whirring sound, broken by an occasional beep. "The woman with whom he'd had relations shortly before his death. She must have left before the psychosis kicked in. Either that, or she was a very sick individual."

"You have her DNA? Could you get that from his— I guess that's how you knew about her being there and— everything?"

Elder Lyle gave her a wry smile. "Indeed. I did get her DNA, at least partially. Sadly, it had deteriorated so I couldn't get a full identification."

Shit. So much for that, not that she'd expected anything different. Why would something work out right?

Chelsea's energy had felt like Lucy's, though. And Lucy's DNA was on file. It wouldn't matter so much, but it would be something. "But if you had one to match it with, could you?"

"To within close probability, yes. Not completely, but very close."

They didn't speak for another minute or so. Chess inspected the rest of the room; high iron-barred windows along the far wall above the psychopomp shelves let dull afternoon light in. The morning had started sunny, but as the hours passed, the clouds had started to threaten. She didn't think the rain would wait much longer.

Just what she needed, a nice stormy afternoon to match her mood. "What drugs killed him?"

"He had a few in there." Elder Lyle reached out, hit another button. "Chiefly, though, it seems to have been vanaprestone. That would be Vapezine, which I believe from the report I was given was what you found in the apartment?"

"Was that what they were?" Hey, it never hurt to look naïve in front of an Elder, or at least, to look as if she didn't recognize most medications at ten paces.

He nodded. "They were, and . . . Oh, dear."

She knew. She knew from the look on his face, from the insistent beeping of the machine beside her, the one he'd been analyzing her food in. "Vapezine? In my food, right?"

"I'm afraid you are correct." Muted shuffling whirs came from the printer in the corner; he crossed to it, plucked a sheet off the tray along with a file that sat beside it. "I hope you have a suspect? You know who did this?"

She took both from him when he handed them to her, the report on her food—a quick scan showed her someone had upended like thirty capsules into it, fuck—and the report on the body, which she could copy down into her notes before she handed them to Elder Griffin to pass to Goody Tremmell for the main files. "Yeah," she said, giving him a quick smile of thanks. "Yeah, I'm pretty sure I do."

She was lifting her fist to knock on Elder Griffin's office door, her head spinning, when he opened it. "Cesaria! I have been waiting for you, dear. I am free at the moment, should you wish me to accompany you."

Shit. Much as she liked Elder Griffin, she really didn't want an escort just then. But what was she supposed to say? Fuck off, I feel like being alone? Sure, that would totally work.

Instead she nodded. "That would be great, I was just about to head over there."

She filled him in quickly on the latest developments as they walked, and made a mental note to find out what the relationship between Lucy and Bill Pritchard had been like, if they even knew each other at all. Wen Li said he'd grown up there, right? He wouldn't be happy to talk to her, but she bet he would. Hell, she'd make him. What was he going to do, dislike her? Boo hoo.

For that matter, what was he going to do, argue with the girl who dated—or whatever—Slobag's son? Hey, there ought to be at least some compensation for her life falling to shit around her.

They'd reached a fork in the pathway. Behind the Church building proper, the cottages had been arranged in groups, from the smallest, farthest from the building, to the largest, the residences of higher-ranking officials, closer. Chess started to turn right, to head toward the Debunker cottages, but Elder Griffin stopped her. The breeze rippled the brim of his hat; he clamped it down with his right hand. "Care you to take a short detour with me?"

Her first instinct was to say no, she didn't have time. Well, she had time, she just didn't want to spend any more of it even semi-sober. And she didn't know how long she might need to spend in Aros's cottage, while the skies above them darkened further with every second.

But he looked so hopeful, so happy, and she hadn't actually finished writing his recommendation thing, and . . . he was Elder Griffin, and she couldn't say no.

"Excellent." He smiled, pointed to the left. "Come, I'll show you—well, it's the home I'm hoping they'll give me. After the marriage ceremony. You'll be coming, won't you? I'd like all of the department to be there, of course, but—Cesaria? Are thee well?"

Shit, was she being that obvious? She blinked, fast, cleared her throat. "Yeah—yes—of course. Why wouldn't I be?"

His blue eyes tried to pierce hers; his head tilted, his mouth turned down. "Forgive me, Cesaria. You seem, well, you have seemed rather cheerful of late, but today that cheer is gone. I wonder why, and if there is any way I can help you."

To her horror—more than horror, shame—her eyes started to sting. Oh no, oh no, she couldn't do this, not there, not then. "I'm fine," she managed.

"Are thou certain? I do understand if you don't wish to discuss it, but—"

"I was, um, I was seeing someone, and now it's over, that's all." The words tumbled out, fast and monotone, before she turned away to stare down the left-hand path, hiding her face.

Something touched her shoulder. Elder Griffin's hand, light and hesitant. It rested there for a second or two, then disappeared. "I am sorry, my dear."

"Yeah, well . . . yeah." She managed to turn the choked sound her throat made into a cough. "I guess, you know, what can you do."

"I take it you did not initiate the . . . ending of the relationship."

He had to ask that, didn't he? Way to go right for the fucking jugular. "No. I didn't—we had a fight, a big fight, and it was my fault and I'm sure he never wants to talk to me again and I just—can we not talk about this? I'll be fine, sir, I swear, I just, I don't feel like talking right now."

"Certainly. Of course, dear." Silence for a minute, while they began to walk. Then he stopped. "Perhaps we shall do this another day. Come, let's go back to Aros's cabin."

"No, no, this is fine."

"Are you—"

"It's fine, show me the house you want." It wasn't fine, of course. Just knowing they were going to look at it made her feel as if someone had slit her open and started stirring her guts with a red-hot poker.

" 'Tis that one."

Chess followed his pointing finger to a modest cottage—well, not really a cottage, it had two floors, but it was still small and built like the others, with pale-blue paint and dark-blue shutters, an iron fence outside and iron bars over all of the windows. A cute house, yes. But one that still made her shudder just a little.

What was the matter with her? Why did the thought of living on-grounds make her feel so ill, why did the thought of living somewhere nice and clean make her feel so ashamed? Why did looking at that house make her want to hide?

She didn't know. She didn't think she wanted to know. And she sure as fuck didn't want Elder Griffin to know. So she smiled and nodded. "It looks great, I'm sure you'll be happy there, you and . . ."

"Keith."

"Keith."

He looked at it again. "I surely do hope so, Cesaria. I believe that when something is meant to be, it is meant to be, and I truly feel this is."

Maybe if she leaned forward a bit he'd go ahead and slice off her head for her. "I'm really glad for you."

He took her arm just long enough to start leading her back down the path toward the Debunker cottages. "But you see, Cesaria, because I believe that when something is meant to be it will be, I also feel that perhaps your fears about your own relationship are unfounded. Perhaps you should call him."

"He hasn't called me."

Her hair rose off her shoulders in the rain-scented breeze. The clouds above grew darker by the second; it was tempting to call off the search of Aros's cottage and just leave.

Chess actually enjoyed storms, as a rule, and she had some keshes at home. She could sit and watch the water hit the stained-glass window, smoke until her head left her neck, maybe listen to some Cringer or the Undertones, something cheerful.

But she couldn't ditch Elder Griffin, especially not when she knew he'd feel it was his fault for asking her about her mood. And she wanted those files. She still hoped to prove Aros had summoned Lucy, and those files might help her do it.

The path led them through a small copse of oak trees, past a few cherry trees and dogwood trees in glorious bloom. The Church grounds certainly were pretty enough.

"Perhaps he hasn't called you because he believes you're angry at him. May I ask, Cesaria, how the argument began?"

Ha. Yeah, that was a story she was not going to share. What was she supposed to say? "I got totally fucking high and wanted to have sex and he turned me down because I disgust him and he doesn't trust me because I fucked him over before?" No. No way.

Instead she said, "Hey, I really appreciate you asking and everything. But I'm pretty sure he doesn't want to see me again, I said some awful things, and it was just, it was kind of horrible. So I'm, um, I'm just going to try to move on."

"Perhaps you'd feel better if you apologize."

Was he not listening to her, or what? She bit back the sharp answer she wanted to fling at him, took a deep breath. "Maybe. Maybe I will, yeah. I'll do that if I have a chance."

He looked like he wanted to say more, but luckily they'd rounded a corner, headed past Doyle's cabin and Atticus Collins's, and Aros's sat right before them, its shutters down, its door closed against them.

It yielded to the key, though. Chess stood back to let Elder Griffin handle that; let him push the door open, straining to shift the pile of mail behind it.

She glimpsed dark furniture against a pale background before Elder Griffin stepped inside. She followed, only to almost run into him as he stood in the arched doorway—the doorless doorway—between the entry hall and the living area.

Every square inch of the walls was covered. With papers and drawings; maps and pages torn from magazines. Pentacles were everywhere, pentacles and—holy shit—a crucifix upside down between two windows. Couldn't get much more illegal than that; what the fuck was he doing with religious items?

It almost seemed unimportant, though, against everything else. Words scrawled on the walls in thick black markers, so many she could barely see the paint between them. Nonsense words like in his notes. More words in the form of newspaper headlines pinned up everywhere. Sketches of horrible screaming faces, destroyed and burning bodies.

All those drugs had more than done their job. And now the man who'd created this museum of mania was walking the streets.

Elder Griffin caught her eye. She saw the same thought in his face.

"When was the last time you saw him here? I mean, have you seen him since he left?"

"I have not." He reached out, almost touched one of the pentacles, then jerked his hand back as if it burned him; maybe it had. "But I do agree with your thinking, Cesaria. I cannot believe he left all of this behind."

"Are those active?" She nodded toward a pile of gris-gris bags on a low table. "I mean, are they powered, did he power them?"

"It seems so."

Right. Here was her chance to confirm one thing at least. She crossed the floor, placing her feet carefully— something told her not to go wandering around willy-nilly in that place—until she reached the table.

The second her hand touched the gris-gris she knew she was right, knew her hunch—okay, not a hunch, a horrible dark suspicion—was correct. She *knew* that energy, she'd felt it before in front of the Mercy Lewis school.

Aros was the killer. Aros was the one trying to steal power from the world or whatever the hell he was trying to do, heedless of what it might destroy. It was him.

And thanks to the secrecy she'd kept up until that moment, of course, she couldn't tell Elder Griffin about it. Fucking great.

Still, at least now she knew who it was, and there could be, had to be, a way to catch him for that. Maybe in the papers they'd come looking for.

His bedroom held more revelations. Pictures of Lucy McShane everywhere; photographs, probably given to him by Chelsea. Sketches and paintings.

He'd been a rather skilled artist, actually. On one wall were portraits he'd done of many people Chess knew: Monica, Beulah, Wen Li—looking particularly pouty and babyish, heh—Laurie Barr, Vernal, Jia—more than one of Jia, in fact. Several of Jia.

Including a nude.

Her already cold blood turned even colder. Had he been—had he been having an affair with the girl? How fucking sick *was* this guy, and how the fuck had he managed to get hired by the Church, stay employed with them?

But then, they let her stay, didn't they, and enough filth and sickness and slime hid behind her eyes for an army. So she guessed she couldn't judge them too harshly for that.

She could raise her eyebrows higher when she thought of Chelsea Mueller, though, and the relationship he had with her. Perhaps they weren't lovers, or maybe he'd been carrying on with both of them? Wasn't like that couldn't possibly happen. Lex had almost certainly been seeing someone else while he was seeing her—if "seeing" was really the proper term for what she'd been doing with Lex—and for all she knew . . . No. Terrible hadn't been seeing anyone else. How would he have found the time?

Not even that. He wouldn't have. She knew he wouldn't.

An itch on her cheek made her swipe at it; swiping at it made her realize tears were pouring down her face. Great. Sure, easy for Elder Griffin to say apologize, call him. Like she could do that, like she could just—sooner or later he was going to run out of forgiveness for her. Sooner or later he was going to get sick of dealing with her, was going to realize sleeping with her wasn't worth the trouble of putting up with her.

If he hadn't already, which he probably had, given what they'd fought about and that he hadn't called her.

She scrubbed at her face with her sleeve, blinked until the room came back into focus. Naked double bed, the sheets and blankets nowhere to be seen. A dresser with half the drawers hanging open, empty. A desk— Ha!

A desk with papers inside, and files. She grabbed them, lifted them from the drawer.

Her phone rang. Shit, who was calling her? She set the papers down and hunted for it, not looking away from the pages as she tried to shuffle through them. Maybe Chelsea's file would be there. Not likely, but she could still hope.

"Cesaria!" Elder Griffin's voice, shouting over the ringing of her phone. Shouting with the kind of panic she'd never heard him display, and as she started to turn toward it she realized what and why, realized it was too late.

Aros had set a trap. A trap like the rune on the door of that apartment in Downside, but this one was live, and a wave of thick black power, sharp and cruel as razor blades, roared through the small cottage. Right at her.

Chapter Twenty-nine

Chess hit the floor, knowing it wouldn't help but trying it anyway. The papers crumpled in her fist as she grabbed her bag with her other hand and ran toward the sound of Elder Griffin's voice.

With no idea what spell she faced, countering it would be difficult. And by "difficult," she meant practically fucking impossible. But the one thing she had going for her was that no matter how evil and dark Aros's magic had gotten, it still had that methodical feel, still had that *Church* feel, and Church magic was magic she knew, magic she could counter.

Not to mention that she had Elder Griffin there. He didn't have a bag full of supplies like she did, but he was an Elder, and a powerful one.

She met him just inside the living room. He stood in front of her while she dropped the papers and started yanking things from her bag. Iron filings, ajenjible, asafetida of course—not that it would be all that useful here, without a ghost, but still—goat's blood, cobwebs, dragon's blood, coffin nails, sapodilla seeds . . . damn it, what else, she could have sworn she'd just stocked up on some anti-hexing supplies at Edsel's. Okay, she had some arrowroot and vervain as well. Not much to work with.

Elder Griffin glanced down, approval in his eyes. At least she thought that's what it was. It was hard to tell, getting hard to see. Hard to breathe. The hex, the curse, whatever it was, had started draining her energy, draining her power, and with every passing second she grew weaker and it grew stronger.

Elder Griffin stumbled; it was affecting him, too. He reached out to brace himself on the desk. To her horror, Chess saw blood seeping from beneath his fingernails.

First things first. The walls wavered, the papers on them flapping and moving in the magic-stirred air. Chess grabbed a handful of iron filings, tossed them at Elder Griffin, tossed them into the air over her head. Her voice didn't want to project, but she managed to croak out a few words of power anyway.

That felt a bit better, but not enough. Aros had booby-trapped that place good.

Elder Griffin knelt beside her, started going through the items she'd laid out. His voice was barely audible over the roaring in her ears. "I touched the wall, and it—it began."

She nodded, intrigued despite her fear and anger. Not a threshold spell, then, an actual interior spell. Very difficult to do, and the sort of thing that verged on—well, that tipped over the verge of—paranoia. And spoke of a very solitary life, because the odds of a random visitor setting it off was too great, it was too hard to turn off if someone did come over.

She and Elder Griffin gathered up her supplies and walked back into the living room. With every slow careful step she felt her heart beat faster, harder. With every step she felt her legs grow weaker, until she rocked sideways and brushed her hand against the wall. Magic screamed up her arm, furious and violent; thin red lines like paper cuts appeared on her fingertips, and she braced herself for the pain.

And pain it was. The second her blood hit the air, the spell throbbed; she felt it suck at her like a vacuum cleaner.

But they were almost at the door. Chess worked the cap on the goat's blood, filled her palm with sapodilla seeds. Elder Griffin had the ajenjible and spiderwebs. Another few steps and they could do something about it, surely they could—

Smoke. The smell of smoke hit her nose at the same time that she saw the orange glow start dancing on the wall before her, saw their shadows against it. Oh, fuck, the files. Couldn't something just go fucking right? For once?

No. The hex ward had exploded into fire, burning the curtains in Aros's room, the drawings and pictures on the walls. So tired, she was so fucking tired . . .

It seemed to take hours to move a foot, back toward where she'd left the papers, and with every second the flames shot higher. Dimly over their hissing voice she heard Elder Griffin yelling; his power hit her skin, a weak echo of what it should have been but still something. She needed to be there to help, shit; she turned around and pushed through the energy again, every step an effort.

The fire spread. She put her hand on his shoulder, caught his glance and started speaking with him. "*Arkharam arkharam, parfakan parfakan, hectarosh . . .*"

The hex-rune practically glowed there on the door, especially as the fire brightened behind her. That fucking cabin was going up like a cord of dried wood in the middle of summer. But then, why wouldn't it; magical fires always spread faster, especially magical fires fed by the power of two trapped witches.

Chess set the point of the coffin nail in the center

of the rune, glanced at Elder Griffin. He nodded and chanted louder.

Weapons weren't technically permitted on Church grounds, at least not when carried by Church employees who weren't supposed to be armed, like her. Whatever. She tugged her knife—her old knife—from her pocket, used it to hammer the nail into the wood, shouting the last anti-hex words along with Elder Griffin.

The power disappeared. The fire did not. Her blood still dripped to the floor but she didn't care; the cottage would probably burn to the ground and she sure as fuck did care about that, but there wasn't much she could do.

Shouts from outside made their way through the walls. Of course—they were on Church grounds. It wasn't Downside, where a fire engine would only come if the building was something like the Slaughterhouse or the Crematorium, or maybe if it was the middle of the day. Any second, the hoses would be set up and water would start pouring on the cottage.

That would destroy pretty much everything in the place, wouldn't it?

Fuck.

As if on cue it started, thick streams of water hitting the windows, the walls, drumming against the roof. In another couple of seconds someone would bust down the door.

The fire edged so close to those files. Even as she started running, she saw she'd be too late. The sick, heavy feeling of power still sat in the air, clogging it, making her feel she was running through a cold lake. Bright flames ate the floor, ate almost a third of the files.

"Cesaria!"

She ignored him. Those files were important, Aros was a murderer and there might be something valuable in there, an address for Chelsea, something else. She threw herself forward, crashed painfully to the floor.

Her bleeding fingers gripped the burning paper, raised it to slam it against the dull carpet.

Too late.

The door of the cottage burst open; Chess glanced up in time to see a hard plume of water shooting right at her.

It hit her in the chest, pushed her back a few feet. Worse, it ripped the files from her already-slick fingers. Damn it!

The stream moved away from her. She dragged herself to her feet, took a few staggering steps in the direction the files had floated, but she knew it would be pointless. The bedroom already looked like a pool; bits of half-burned paper clung to the bed and the walls, the ink running in mottled streams.

"Cesaria!" Elder Griffin's voice again. The water stopped. Agnew Doyle burst into the cottage, followed by Dana Wright, a few other employees, Elders Ramos and Jones. With them came a blast of fresh air. She hadn't realized how smoky the cottage had gotten. Dana grabbed her, hustled her out of the building, with Doyle and Elder Griffin right behind.

She'd lost. She'd lost, she'd lost, the files were gone. Any evidence she might possibly have found was gone, destroyed by fire or water.

Yes, she knew Aros was her killer, and that was a good thing. But for some reason it didn't feel that great as she stood there staring at the wreckage of the cottage. Just . . . Damn.

Her phone had rung, hadn't it? Just before Elder Griffin set off the spell? She pulled it from her bag, took a look at the screen.

Yes. It had rung. Terrible had called her.

Her breath froze in her lungs; she couldn't seem to do anything but stare at the phone, not moving, not blinking. Somehow she managed to check her texts, found that he had indeed sent her one. "Another body. Call when."

Not exactly "I love you, I miss you, I'm sorry," but she had no right to expect anything like that, did she? No. All things considered, she was lucky she got anything at all, even though she knew the only reason she did was because Bump wanted her there.

If anyone should be sending the apologies it was her, anyway.

She glanced at Elder Griffin beside her, panting and examining his bleeding fingertips. He'd advised her to apologize, to talk to Terrible. Looked like she was going to get a chance to follow that advice after all.

Vanity. Taking the time to shower, dry her hair, and put on some makeup was pure vanity, but she couldn't help it. What was she supposed to do—go see Terrible for the first time since that horrible night looking all rumpled and sweaty? No fucking way. Bad enough that her left eye was smudged with darkness from Jia's fist two days before, that her cheek was still scratched from the catwalk and Lucy's pipe had turned her arm purple-yellow. Bad enough that the magical wounds on her fingers looked red and raw, that the fire had caught the side of her palm and turned it red as well.

So she didn't. Instead, she pulled up outside the destroyed warehouse at Sixty-fifth and Foster wearing the red top she knew was his favorite, with matching lipstick, figuring she looked about as good as possible. Wasn't saying much, but it was all she could do.

All she could do as far as her looks went, anyway. She lifted five Cepts from her pillbox, gave them a quick nose-wrinkling crunch, and washed them down with Coke. Maybe they'd slow her frantic heartbeat; maybe they'd ease the panic threatening to choke her where she sat.

They probably wouldn't. But at the very least they'd keep her from throwing herself at his feet and bursting into tears, so that was a good thing.

A little crowd stood around the body, or what she assumed was the body. Why else would a little crowd be there, right?

Right. A man, again. Burned black, carefully placed within the scorched lines of the symbol. Her skin tingled at the energy still in the air, stronger than it had been with Eddie's body, or maybe it was simply that she was attuned to it now.

Or maybe it was Terrible. She was aware of him from the second she stepped through the hole that had once been a doorway into the remains of the building. Afraid to look at him, yes, but aware of him. She smelled him, saw him out of the corner of her eye, felt him; every cell in her body cried out for him.

And she couldn't have him, and probably never would again.

She cleared her throat. Terrible's gaze sat on her; she felt it on her head, her shoulders, heavy and searing hot like molten steel. She gritted her teeth against it, against the pull toward him in her chest, and focused on the corpse. "Do we know who this is?"

"Naw. Ain't this part of town, dig." Terrible shifted on his feet, his eyes focused on the top of her head. "Gave Bernam here the tell to have a look-out when the fire stopped, figured might be another, dig. This what he found. Gave you the call-up right after."

"I was stuck at work." He didn't sound angry, or cold. Was that good? Or did he just honestly not care anymore? And how shitty a person was she, that at that moment she didn't give a fuck about the dead man or how he'd died or anything else, she just wanted his corpse and everyone else to disappear so she could talk to Terrible? Pretty shitty, right?

But she couldn't help it. Standing across from him, not knowing what he was thinking or feeling . . . every bit of energy she could spare went into not running to his side and wrapping herself around him.

The others watched her, too, not that she gave a fuck. "I know who's behind it now. But finding him—them—isn't going to be easy, and— Wait!"

They all blinked.

"Aye?"

"You said he's not from here. He's from Slo— He's from the other side?"

Nod.

Did the dead man have something to do with Aros, or Chelsea, or both? She imagined he did.

"What is this—what was this building used for, I mean?"

Pause. "Ain't much, just now. Storin stuff, dig, when we got the need."

"So why this place?" She looked around. Of course if anything had been in there it was gone now, probably destroyed—a stab of pain almost as bad as the pain of seeing Terrible, at the thought of all the drugs that might have been eaten by fire—or moved out. "I mean, why a building you're not really using? Why here?"

One of the onlookers—she'd almost forgotten there were other people there—took a half step forward, like he was expecting to be told to tuck in his shirt and fix his hair. Chess couldn't have cared less what he looked like, a slight form with brownish hair dyed green at the ends and a baggy long-sleeved black shirt over loose black vinyl pants. "Simple, ain't it? Had theyself some access to it."

"Yeah, but—"

"Aye, gettin yon meaning." Terrible still didn't look at her, not in the eyes, but her heart kicked anyway.

"Maybe them got other reasons pickin this one. Weren't even much in here, it started burning."

Excitement—well, not excitement, but a sort of eagerness, the sense of finding another Truth in her case—kicked in her head. "Like, the other night. Why take that risk to do it there, when they could do it anywhere?"

He saw where she was going, and thankfully seemed to know she meant the school, too, not the pipe room. She'd known he would; he always did. "Got me a map in the car. You thinkin maybe they got some pattern happening, aught like that?"

"It's worth a look, right?"

He nodded. If he would just look at her, even just for a second, so she could meet his gaze and show him how sorry she was . . . "You needin him for aught else, or we can get on the clearing up?"

Shit. She hadn't thought of that. Someone needed to get that body out of there, and she really didn't want it to be her.

He must have had the same thought; she caught the glance he sent her way—still not meeting her eyes—the measuring tone of it.

"No," she said. "I don't need him for anything else."

She surveyed the small gang of men: four of them including Terrible and Green Hair. One of them—one or two—would have to get the body out of the symbol, and she'd be damned if it was Terrible.

So of course it was. Before she could open her mouth to stop him, he stepped right into it.

But that sigil on his chest . . . sure e-fucking-nough, the magic in it hit him. Hit him hard, and she knew it because she felt it reverberate like he'd struck a gong with his head, because she saw his face go white and watched him stumble, watched him fall to the cement in a heap.

Chapter Thirty

To know the Truth, we must find it within ourselves. More than that, we must admit it to ourselves.
— *The Church and You,* a pamphlet by Elder Barrett

She moved before she thought about it—not that she would have done anything different if she *had* thought about it. His skin was warm against hers; fuck, it felt so good just to touch him again, even with the horrible energy of the spell around them both. It had only been a couple of days, not even, but it felt like years. It felt like she'd been spinning in the darkness alone, and now she'd finally hit the ground again.

She didn't look at him, though, afraid that if she did she'd start to cry. And with the other men there . . . not a good idea. They just stood watching with their mouths open. Fuck. "Help me with him. Help me get him out of the circle."

They obeyed; it took all three of them to lift him. Chess watched them, watched their faces, to see if any of them appeared more or less affected by the symbol. Green Hair didn't seem too bothered by it. Neither did his friend in sandals and a T-shirt with smiley faces drawn all over it in marker. Good.

Terrible's eyes opened when they got him to the other side of the lines, and he tried to stand up. She pressed him back down. Standing wasn't a good idea yet. She stayed on her knees at his side, with her left hand on his cheek, hoping he'd stay put. Hoping, because she didn't have the guts to look down at him. Her entire body shook, and that wasn't from magic.

"Get the body out of there, okay?" she managed. Her voice sounded strained and awkward to her ears. Nothing she could do about it, though. "Just put him over there, I guess. In the corner."

They obeyed. With three of them, the job took only a couple of minutes; watching them gave her the first real taste of what it might be like for someone else—for Lex or Terrible—to watch her dealing with some sort of magic. Again with the exception of Green Hair, they looked more nervous and unsettled with every passing second. Sweat formed on their brows, trickled down their necks; their mouths set in firmer and firmer lines, unhappy lines.

Guilt swarmed into her mind like locusts. That should be her. She was the witch, she was the one trained to handle that stuff, to diffuse and dispel it. She was the one who should be protecting them, helping them.

But nothing, absolutely nothing, could induce her to leave Terrible's side at that moment. Protecting people or no, she may well never have another chance to touch him, and she wasn't about to waste that one.

Even if she was still afraid to look at him, doubly so because she knew his eyes were open and he was looking at her.

They set the corpse down with a horrible *splat*. After an expectant pause Green Hair opened his mouth. "Aught else? What we doin next, you want?"

Shit. She couldn't put it off anymore, could she? She glanced down, followed the line of buttons up the front of Terrible's bowling shirt to the triangle of white T-shirt underneath it, then up his throat, over his mouth and nose until she hit his eyes and every muscle in her body tightened.

Sure, the second their eyes met he looked away. What else did she expect?

"I can't think of anything else I need them to do," she managed. "If you're wondering, I mean."

He shifted, rolled away from her and sat up, breaking the physical connection between them. Bereft of his skin her palm felt cold.

"Bernam, put him in they bag there, aye? Take he to the burnhouse."

Green Hair—Bernam, she guessed—nodded, crossed to the far corner, presumably to get a bag.

"Gettin the map," Terrible said to her. "Give me a hold-on, iffen you ain't mind."

"I don't mind. Are you okay? I know that symbol isn't very strong after it burns, but it's still pretty awful."

He shook his head. "Ain't know. Just one second were walkin to it, next were here."

Thunder rolled through the air; shit. While they'd been standing there the sky had grown even darker, the clouds almost black viewed through holes in the half-burned roof. The air around them waited for rain, that heavy expectant feeling that told her it was going to be one fuck of a storm. She thought the pressure might crush her.

The men must have felt the same way, because they bagged up the corpse in record time. "Aught else?"

Terrible shook his head.

The first raindrops hit as they left, huge drops that left dark marks on the slice of cement she saw when they opened the door. Still far apart, but she'd better get the hell out of there if she wanted to get home semi-dry.

But first . . . Shit. Shitshitshit. She bit her lip hard enough to send a shock of pain through her, caught his arm with her left hand and let go again just as quickly.

She couldn't touch him while she did it, couldn't look at him, either.

"Terrible, wait. I, I'm sorry. I didn't— I know you probably don't ever want to talk to me again and you probably don't care but I didn't do anything with Lex or anything, nothing happened. I never should have said that, what I said. I didn't mean it and I'm sorry, I'm really sorry."

Her throat ached; by the time she got to the last "sorry" she could feel the tears rising in it, had to swallow hard to try to send them back down.

He didn't respond. Fuck, she really had blown it. She'd really, completely lost him. The emptiness inside her threatened to explode.

"Um, okay, so I'll just go now, but, I wanted you to know that. I know you don't want to see me anymore and you want our, you know, whatever, to be over, but—"

"I ain't the one ended it."

"Huh?"

He looked sincere enough; well, not sincere—the word called up images of sappy teen-pop singers and men who made a habit of getting girls drunk to get them into bed—but serious. Honest. And she knew him well enough to know that was exactly what he was being. "I ain't the one ended it. Were you done that."

He stood up, brushed his palms on his jeans, pulled a cigarette out of his pocket and lit it. The six-inch flame from his lighter cut a hole in the gathering gloom, a glimpse into a brighter world she'd never be allowed to enter again.

"But . . . no, you didn't want, um, you didn't want me anymore."

He shook his head; she couldn't make out his expression, it was too dark. "Ain't what I said, neither."

"You don't trust me."

"Shit. What you wanting, Chess? Wantin go over all it again? What's this for?"

"No, I just want you to know, okay? I'm sorry. I said some things, some awful things, and I didn't mean them." Her eyes stung; she rubbed at them with fast, frustrated hands and kept going. "And if you don't want to be with me anymore because—because of everything, I understand, but I don't want you to think I meant those things. Because I didn't. I don't. I wasn't really . . . I was kind of out of it and it was so shitty of me. But I didn't mean it, any of it, and I'm so sorry."

His left hand covered the back of his neck, squeezed it while his head turned away from her. "Ain't handled myself too right, neither."

"You weren't worse than me, I was horrible."

"I weren't fucked up. Got no excuses."

"Yeah, but . . ." Where was this going, what were they saying? It felt like walking through some sort of maze, and all of the paths led to exits but only one of them was the right exit. The rain fell faster, cold drops hitting her head or her shoulder every few seconds. "Do you want to, maybe we should go somewhere else, okay? Before it starts raining too hard. And we can talk. If you want."

For a second—a second that felt like hours—she thought he was going to say no. But he nodded. "Car's outside."

She followed him to the back of the warehouse, where a steel door black with smoke sat propped open by a chunk of wood. The Chevelle waited just outside it, slick with the strengthening rain. Thunder tore the air around them, echoed off the broken cement parking lot and the warehouse exterior with its patchy, sooty aluminum siding.

Back in the Chevelle. She'd thought she might never get to sit in it again, that she might never get to reach over and unlock his door for him so he could get in without messing with the key. Almost as soon as he settled into the driver's seat the rain increased, rattling on the roof so close to their heads, smearing down the windows so the ruined building before them appeared to melt and shift.

He wiped his hand over his face, drying the rain that had fallen there. "Where you want me takin you?"

Home. Home and bed was where she wanted him to take her, but somehow she doubted that saying so was a good idea. So she shrugged. "I don't know if you're hungry, I'm not really hungry, but . . ."

"You never hungry."

"I am sometimes," she said, enjoying the feel of the smile on her lips. This was a familiar discussion, one they had a lot—one they probably wouldn't have again.

Oh, fuck this. "I'm so sorry I said that stuff. I didn't mean it. I know you don't want to—maybe we can at least still talk, be friends, you know? If you don't want more than that."

"I ain't the one ended it."

"Terrible . . . I'm not trying to be a bitch or anything here, but you kind of did, I mean, you didn't want—you didn't want me, and we had that fight and you don't trust me."

"I ain't the one don't got trust here, neither," he said. "Tryin on that one, aye. But thinkin it goes on the other way. You ain't got trust in *me*."

Her mouth fell open. What the hell was he talking about? "I trust you."

"Aye? Iffen you do, got yourself a shitty way of showin it. This whole last week you ain't givin me the listen, ain't believing me, ain't talkin, actin like you scared of me or some shit."

Of course she was scared. How could she not be, when she'd stripped herself so bare in front of him, when he'd become so fucking important to her? And how could she admit that to him when he'd been able to turn her down so easily? "So . . . what does that mean? Because—"

"What you want it to mean? I ain't can fuckin read you mind, aye? What you wanting? You just, you give me the tell what the fuck you want, Chess, ain't playin fuckin games here."

What was she supposed to say to that? How was she supposed to find the right words, when there were so many in her head and none of them felt quite right?

She didn't know. What she did know was that he looked at her then, and their eyes met and there was that electric charge, that surge of power, that feeling that he was looking into her, through her, seeing everything she was and everything she felt.

And she felt like she was looking into him, too, past the broken nose and scars and heavy brow. Like she could see all the secret things inside him, the things nobody else got to see, the things that were just for her.

Maybe she'd never get to see them again. But in that moment she could, and she wasn't going to let them go, not without a fight.

She'd tossed her bag on the floor when she got into the car, so her hands were free; she used them, reached for him, dug her fingers into his hair, and kissed him hard.

For a second she thought he wasn't going to respond, thought she'd failed, but before her heart finished falling, he did. He kissed her back just as hard, yanked her closer. Her heartbeat cranked from normal to out-of-control, so fast she thought it was keeping time with the raindrops hitting the car.

"I want *you*," she managed. The sound of the words in her voice sent fear shivering up her spine; she'd said them that night and he'd turned her away, and he might turn her away again, and she walked on a plank of those words and hoped desperately that he'd catch her when she tumbled off the end. "I want . . . I just want to be with you."

He squeezed her tighter in reply, his fingers insinuating themselves beneath her top, slightly rough on her bare skin. She pushed her hands down his collar under his shirts, tilted her head so he could bite her throat.

His back under her palms, his skin soft between the scars. Still warm, he was always so warm, and it radiated through her, found the dark frozen parts deep inside her and thawed them so she felt whole. She pulled her hands out of his shirts, found his waist and shoved them up his chest, pausing only to press her palm against him hard beneath his jeans.

His fingers inched up over her ribcage, his thumb stroking her nipple through her bra. Her gasp disappeared in the sound of the rain, the crash of thunder overhead.

She heard what he said, though. "My place, aye?"

"Yes." Her fingers shook, but she managed to undo several of his shirt buttons. The belt buckle was easier. So was the button fly of his jeans; two firm tugs took care of those so she could reach inside. "Fuck, yes."

He shifted position. His mouth didn't leave hers but she felt him moving, hunting for the ignition, felt him slide the key home and turn it. Cold air blasted into the car, smelling of rain; music blared from the speakers, Howlin' Wolf at full volume, which he turned down in almost the same movement.

The kiss grew deeper, deeper still, until she couldn't breathe. Couldn't see. When his hands left her it took every bit of strength she had not to grab them back. Instead she knelt on her seat and leaned over, started kissing his neck, letting her teeth play along. Her right palm slid over his chest, trying to be everywhere at once, feeling it rise and fall with his rapid breath.

Somehow he shoved the car into gear, backed them out of the space. Lightning cracked the sky open, an eye-searing flash in the near distance; the wipers slapped fast across the windshield.

The Chevelle roared through a puddle, sending a high white plume of water off to the right. Chess could barely see anything outside the car, just sullen sky and the dead outlines of buildings, glimpses of empty sidewalks. A rare thing, rain so hard it drove even Downsiders to find shelter, but it had. The Chevelle rolled alone down the streets.

Good thing, too, because she couldn't seem to stop kissing him, taking his face in her hands and turning it toward her, leaning across him, practically in his lap. His bowling shirt hung open, and she tugged his white T-shirt up out of the way so she could feel his bare skin.

Across his chest, down his stomach. With his jeans open her hand had room to move, and his gasp sent a fresh rush of heat coursing through her.

Chess's hand wasn't the only one moving, either. Terrible's slid over her bottom, curved around her thigh, slipped between her legs to press against her. For a second she actually thought she might pass out.

But she didn't. She couldn't. Instead she shifted, her heart pounding, and kissed a line down his stomach, pulled the waistband of his boxers out of the way and took him into her mouth.

"Fuck, Chessie." His voice so hoarse over the sound of the rain and the music, his skin salty-soapy and un-bearably soft, the thick heavy length of him solid and alive against her tongue when she started to move. She braced herself for the flashbacks, for the terror that would force her to stop, the memories that had kept her from even trying it before, but they didn't come.

And after a minute she realized they wouldn't come, that this was different. This was Terrible and she knew it was Terrible, and she loved him and she trusted him, and his hand rested so gently on her head, like an illegal blessing. She could feel him wanting to pull her hair, to tangle it in his fist; could feel him shake from wanting to move but holding himself back because he knew what this was for her and didn't want to scare her.

Everything else disappeared, shrank until the whole world was the dull roar of the rain and the Chevelle's engine, flashes of light, the darker, louder crash of thunder. And over it all Terrible, filling the world, the smell and taste of him filling her head, making her safe. Making her excited, more than she'd ever thought she could be.

The car swung to the right, halted. What . . . ? They couldn't have reached his place yet, could they?

Now his hand did fist in her hair, holding it so tight at her nape it hurt, yanking her up for another kiss. And another, his free hand busy at her waist. By the time she realized what he was doing he'd gotten her jeans halfway down her hips. "Get this shit off."

They weren't at his apartment. He'd pulled into an alley, where shadows would have been if there'd been any sunshine. But there wasn't. There was only rain, drumming loud on the car, almost drowning out their breathing.

The Chevelle was like a cave, a hot damp cave, dim and scented with leather and passion. The rain hid the buildings from her view, hid them from any curious eyes that might have caught them there, and his insistent hands pushed her jeans and panties farther down to her knees, urged her to straighten her legs, toe off her shoes so he could strip her bare and he could pull her across his thighs to sit in his lap.

Another flash of lightning, another crash of thunder, closer now. His palms running over her skin, his fingers slipping between her legs and making her want to scream. How did he know how to do that, to find the exact right spot, to barely touch it in that way that she felt all the way through her?

She'd only just managed to finish the thought when it overwhelmed her. Her voice seemed incredibly loud in the small space, drowning out even the sound of the rain. Or maybe she just couldn't hear it because she was blind and deaf, because she was floating somewhere in the air and only Terrible's hands kept her from flying into space completely.

He lifted her, turned her to straddle him. The seat was just wide enough for her legs to fit on either side of his; he rose up a few inches to push his jeans out of the way. She clutched his shoulders, let him guide her hips down until he was completely buried inside her and her voice bounced off the foggy glass again. Both of their voices. She pressed her forehead against his, paused for one long, delirious moment before she started rocking forward and backward, slowly at first and then a little faster, kissing him harder.

His hands on the sides of her face, on her neck, holding her there. "Chessie . . . shit, Chessie, I love you so bad." His teeth on her throat, biting hard, his lips soothing the spot. "So fucking much, so . . . so bad."

Fear shot from her chest to her head, spread out through her entire body. Those words changed everything, changed what they were doing, made it mean something, and that . . . Why would he do that, why would he want to do that, with her? She wasn't good at this, she didn't think it was possible for her to be good at it, didn't know what to do.

His hand found her hip, kept her rhythm steady while she panicked. He didn't seem to notice that, or if he did he ignored it, let her find her own way to process it. He pressed his lips against her chest, down the neckline of her shirt, shifted the fabric out of the way to tease her nipples with his mouth one at a time and make her cry out again.

She didn't *want* to panic. It wasn't fair that she should panic; it wasn't right, and she was suddenly angry, so fucking mad, that the man she loved was telling her he loved her, that he was trying to show her how much, and all she could feel—aside from the physical—was scared. Not of the words, she'd said the words, but of saying them there, in that situation, after she'd lost him. Scared of what that would mean. How it would mean more.

That fear coagulated in her chest, sat there like clumps of ball bearings in her lungs. He tilted her head, kissed her harder; his hips started to move beneath her and his free hand slipped down between them to touch her again. She didn't have much time, not if she wanted to respond, not if she wanted to give that back to him.

And she had to, because she knew if she didn't she'd regret it, because she was sick of being scared and he was the one person in the world she didn't have to be scared around. She had to because she wanted to know how it felt. She wanted to know just once in her life what other people—what normal people—felt.

She wanted to because he deserved it.

She had to do it soon, had to do it now, because the pressure was building and she was about to explode from it, because his breath came louder and more ragged, his eyes so dark on hers. "Chessie . . . fuck, I can't . . . can't hold up much more, Chessie please . . ."

Her hips moved faster. She clutched the headrest of the seat, used it as leverage while his hands urged her faster still.

"I love you," she blurted, a little louder, a little harsher than she meant to, but it didn't matter, because she'd done it. It didn't matter because he tightened his grip on her, and it didn't matter because she shattered over him, her voice mingling with the rain and thunder, and he didn't take away his hand or stop shifting her hips so she didn't stop bursting apart, again and again until he joined her.

Chapter Thirty-one

And this is also Fact: we are never better served than when we are served by Truth, and we are never better lived than when we live in Truth.

—*The Book of Truth,* Veraxis, Article 541

For several long minutes the only sound in the car was the storm outside and their slowing breath. She didn't want to start worrying. She wanted to feel peaceful, triumphant. He'd wanted it to mean something, and she'd been able to let it, and that was something to be proud of. She'd done something for him she'd never been able to do and she'd been fine, and that was something to be proud of, too.

And she was proud, as she sat there with her head tucked into the juncture of his neck and collarbone, with her hands on his shoulders and his arms still around her.

But the fact remained that they'd essentially broken up. Well, he said he wasn't the one who'd ended it, but she certainly hadn't, not as far as she knew.

So where they were going from there she had no idea.

He brushed her hair back from her face, kissed her cheekbone. "Ain't guessin you hungry now."

"Not really, no." Relief washed over her, sharp and crisp. "But if you want to eat I'll go with you."

Pause. "Thinkin maybe we oughta get some straight, aye? What was on the other night."

So much for relief. She pulled away from him, disengaged herself. If they were going to have the kind of discussion that ended with her feeling like the world's dumbest bitch, she'd like to at least have some pants on.

He pulled a couple of cigarettes out of his pocket, lit them up and handed her one.

"Said I ain't give a fuck what you take," he said after a minute, his gaze focused out the side window at the rain, "an I don't, true thing. Only . . . I ain't wantin take you to bed, look in yon eyes an you ain't there, dig? Might as well be on my alones, iffen that's what's on."

What? What did that have to do with trusting her? "What do my— I don't, sorry, I don't get it."

He took a deep drag off his smoke, rubbed the back of his neck, folded his arms; discomfort oozed off him and hung heavy in the air. "Knew I ain't could say it up right. Ain't . . . just wanting . . . fuck. Just forget I say aught, aye? No worryin on it."

"No, tell me what you meant. Please. I don't want to fuck everything up again."

"Aw, shit. You ain't fucked up, Chessie. Ain't you, aye?"

"But it is, I made you mad, I—"

"Ain't made me mad, neither, not causen of that. Thing is . . . Fuck. You high like that, like you was on the other night, 'slike you ain't in yon head, dig? Like— like you might could be any other dame. Only I ain't wanting any other dame. Wanting you."

"But . . . if you don't trust me . . ."

He looked at her with narrowed eyes, like he was trying to figure something out. Trying to figure *her* out. "What the fuck you think I'm wanting you for? Just wanna get my— Shit." He shook his head. "Ain't about trust, dig? Wouldn't be here iffen I ain't got trust in you, wouldn't be takin you to bed iffen I ain't trustin you."

Oh. Oh, shit. It hadn't even occurred to her before how that might make him sound, how little credit she was giving him. How little trust that sounded like *she* had in *him*.

He wasn't one of the dozens of rent-a-daddies or whatever who'd used her, who'd treated her like a toy. That was one of the reasons why she loved him, right, because he was so exactly the opposite of that, because he was safe?

It terrified her in some small weird way to think of it like that, but she had to, because it was obviously the way he needed her to think of it.

Wait, hold on. He wasn't saying she had to give up her pills, right? That wasn't what he seemed to be saying. Shit, please let that not be what he was saying, because she had no idea how she would reply to that or what she would do, and that fact, that knowledge, led her down a filthy, crooked path in her mind, one she did not want to explore.

Not an easy question to phrase, though, was it. "Um . . . so what does that mean as far as, I mean, what I take and stuff, do you mean I can't—"

"Aw, naw, ain't sayin that. You do what you need an ain't try telling you no, but . . . takin you to bed, want *you* there, not just your body. An want you knowin it's *me*. Love you, Chess. Dig?"

Thunder broke through the silence following his words, low and thick. Her skin still tingled from the storm in the air.

Or maybe it was more than that. Maybe it was finally starting to know what he meant, and being scared of that because—well, shit, of course it scared her. If that was what he wanted, if it was about her, who she was inside and not her body, that meant the entire relationship hung squarely on that, on her. That he thought she was important, and special, and who she was inside mattered, and if that mattered . . .

If that mattered, if that was what he cared about, then she could never, ever let him know the truth, let him know how little she deserved that. "I'm sorry. I'm really, I didn't know. I've never done this before, you know, I'm not very good at this . . ."

He nodded. "I ain't good with the explains, dig, know I fuck it up tryin."

"You don't. I don't listen very well."

"Guessin we all set up for trouble then, aye?" He smiled at her, sending those happy little wings fluttering in her chest again.

"I . . . So you don't want to not be with me anymore, I mean, you still want to?"

"Told you, weren't me ended it. Never wanted that, neither. Never."

She didn't quite trust her voice; it felt clogged with grateful words, with probably way too sappy words, just like the ache in her forehead told her it was furrowing, the sting in her eyes told her she was about to make an ass of herself.

What else was new? She leaned forward, buried her face in his chest to try to hide it, but she was pretty sure he knew anyway. "I didn't want it either. I thought, I thought you were sick of me and you hated me, and it was awful, I felt awful."

He held her for a minute, his hand tight on the back of her head, pressing her closer. "Aye, weren't . . . weren't good for me neither." He cleared his throat. "Mean it, though, on trust. Ain't can do this iffen you don't trust me. So . . . maybe you oughta give that one some thinking, causen if you always waitin for me to do a run-off, hidin shit from me . . . ain't good, aye?"

And there was the terror again. This time she did understand what he meant. He wanted all of her, wanted her to stop being scared and nervous all the time, to stop doing things like assuming his lack of desire for sex one night meant he didn't trust her and was done with her completely. Or that it didn't matter if she was practically passing out in the middle of it. Wanted her to believe he really loved her.

She wanted that, too. She really, really did. But if telling him she loved him the first time had been like jumping off a cliff, giving him that kind of trust . . . that was like jumping out of an airplane, and it was a demand she honestly didn't know if she could meet.

Her silence sure wasn't making him feel more secure, she knew, but she didn't know what else to do, aside from squeezing him harder and hoping he knew that meant she was trying.

"Well. Just . . . just have you a think on that one, aye?" He gave her a final squeeze before shifting her so he could take the wheel. "C'mon, Chessiebomb. Let's us get ourselves outta this rain."

She'd thought—she'd hoped—that "getting out of the rain" would mean heading back to his place, or to hers, and spending the rest of the afternoon in bed.

No such luck. She sat next to Terrible on Bump's hideous scarlet couch, the cacophony of reds in the room throbbing at her.

He'd rearranged some of his awful "art" as well. Directly opposite Chess hung a stylized, luridly colored painting of several naked women bent over a sawhorse. Chess pressed her forehead into Terrible's upper arm rather than look at it, let her right hand rest on his thigh. She had to admit, Bump's place did have that advantage. She could touch him there, kiss him, hold his hand.

And she could look at him all she wanted, and he could look back at her so their eyes met and heat raced through her body. It kept racing even after he turned away; she watched his craggy profile sharp against the red walls, reached up with her left hand to stroke the line of tiny bruises on the side of his neck, from her teeth. She liked seeing it almost as much as she liked the ones he'd left on her, the little marks and bruises she ended up with when he got carried away—which was often—as though he'd branded her. As though he'd written his name on her skin. Maybe Bump could leave the room for a bit? They still had so much catching up to do, after all, it had—

"Ladybird, you fuckin got the hearing on? Gots the fuckin askin for you, wanna tell up?"

"What? Um, sorry. My mind wandered for a second there."

"Oh, yay? Ain't even woulda fuckin guessed up on there." He glared at her with his pale eyes narrowed. Impatient. Well, if he was so damn impatient he could start talking then, instead of just staring at her like she'd suddenly grown horns.

Or he could do what he was doing, which was stand up—he'd been in his customary lazy lean against his desk, the better to display the loud red, pink, and purple Nehru shirt—fucking *Nehru shirt*—he wore with bright orange pants. What the hell was the deal with badly dressed people and her current case? For a second she contemplated the idea of getting Bump and Monica into the same room. They'd either blind everyone or make them all ill.

His gold toe ring flashed as he oozed around the desk, then back to her. In his hand sat a small wooden box.

Chess's heart gave a cheery skip. That box was Bump's private stash, the stuff he didn't sell to anybody. Hey, there had to be some fucking benefit to being his personal witch, right? Aside from the obvious one sitting beside her.

He set the box down on the coffee table in front of her. "Now mayhap you quit givin Terrible the fuckin slurpy-eyes an give Bump the listening, yay? Thinkin you can? Gots some fuckin chattering wants doin, needs you fuckin head on straight up."

The words should have embarrassed her. Probably would have, if he hadn't given her that box. That dealer-junkie dynamic again; he could say what he wanted and she would take it, because he held the keys to the king-dom and she needed them.

But then, too, she *had* been giving Terrible the slurpy-eye, and she didn't give a shit if Bump saw it or what he thought of it, either.

She would have paid attention anyway once the dis-cussion actually started, but this was even better. So she opened the box, slid out the little bag and blade and got started chopping herself a couple of lines. Not easy to do, because Bump's stash was so pure it clumped. Awe-some. "Go ahead."

"Aw, I fuckin allowed to? Givin you the fuckin mighty thanks."

Whatever.

"What knowledge you fuckin givin Bump on the now-time? New shit, fuckin hopin so, yay? Something on the fuckin use-type side, get that fuckin scum Slobag down."

Slobag hadn't looked at all like he recognized the *hafuran,* the magic that Jia Zhang had been killed for. She'd believed he didn't know anything about it. Hell, she'd told Terrible he didn't.

"Are you sure it's Slobag's witch? I mean, really sure?"

Bump looked at her like she'd just suggested they all paint themselves pink and perform ballet in the Market. "Ain't no fuckin chance-game. Slobag's witch. Bump got the fuckin knowing, yay, no fuckin maybe-nots. Got we the fuckin proof on."

Hold on. If Bump had proof it was Slobag's witch doing the murders . . . holy fuck. Looked like she wasn't

the only Churchwitch who'd found demand for her ser-
vices with Downside's drug lords.

She opened another drawer in the box, both to give
her a second to process that and to pull out the short
gold straw. Just like Bump; tacky and pretentious, but
necessary.

"The witch's name is Aros," she said, holding the
straw. "Aros Burnett. He used to be Church, but he went
kind of insane and quit, and I guess now he's working
for Slobag."

"Ain't got the know you can fuckin quit that Church,
yay, how that one fuckin possible." Calculation flashed
in his eyes. Dream on, Bump. She'd never quit the
Church to become his personal witch.

No point bringing that up, though. "Of course you
can. Usually they do a ritual when you leave, a pretty
major one that . . . sort of makes you forget your Church
education. They laser off tattoos, too, the most powerful ones. And then they keep tabs on you the rest of your
life, they check up on you."

"That happen to that dude Riley pussed out on you
th'other night? He getting him mind erased out?" Terrible asked.

"If he decides to leave the Church, yeah, instead of
just taking a job in a different branch." He even remembered Riley's name. Amazing. "But Aros didn't
leave the usual way. He just took off. I guess—I mean, I
assume—he met Slobag somehow while he was working
on the case at Mercy Lewis. The case I'm working now."

"An that fuckin scum set he onto workin, yay, burn
up Bump's buildings. Leavin fuckin dead pieces in em.
Motherfucker."

"I'm not sure." She leaned forward, sucked up one
of the lines. Oh, that was so fucking nice. That bitter
numbness—so soothing—in her nose and sinuses, the

back of her throat . . . like parts of her didn't exist anymore. Especially when her heart jumped and happiness blossomed in her chest, in her mind. Definitely like parts of her didn't exist anymore. All the bad parts.

Or at least most of them, because if she got rid of all of her bad parts there'd be nothing left.

"The sigil the murder was committed on is a *hafuran*, and it's a basic power builder, so the spell is designed to build and change power. And in this case— Okay. Back in 2001 there was a girl at the Mercy Lewis Second School named Lucy McShane, and she killed herself."

Bump folded his arms, recrossed his ankles in the other direction. Yeah, yeah, boredom, whatever. This was important information, and she felt so damn good she didn't care if he fell asleep.

In fact she wished he would, and she could be alone there with Terrible. Sure, all that speed meant it would take her forever to finish if she managed to at all—which was unlikely—but she could still watch him . . . her insides did a flip.

Bump's eyebrows rose so high they looked like arrowheads.

"Oh, chill out, this is important. Lucy had a cousin named Chelsea Mueller, and Chelsea was almost powerful enough to enter Church training, but she didn't quite make it."

Terrible had given her thigh a quick squeeze when she told Bump to chill, but said nothing, and Bump actually looked almost interested and didn't mention it himself. "What on the dead dame, Lucy, yay? She holding up the fuckin juice do you fuckin magic shit?"

"Her Church-test scores weren't as good as Chelsea's."

"That why they doin the murders? Tryin bring Lucy back for real, dig, not like when we seen her on the other night."

"Right." Chess grinned at him before she bent to the mirror again. Just this one, and she'd let at least ten minutes or so pass before she did the last one, because speed this good should be savored. Empty the lungs with an exhale, pinch the nostril . . . there were better things in life, yeah, but not that many.

"That's what I think, anyway," she continued a second later. "Chelsea wants Lucy back, but she's not powerful enough to summon a ghost on her own. So she gets Aros to do it, and to do these murders to steal power and give it to her. I guess she figures that way she can be strong enough to summon Lucy for good. Like permanently."

Terrible shook his head. "Seem like a dumb fuckin plan, aye?"

"Yeah, but if they want Lucy back it's kind of the only option. Unless Chelsea wants Aros to do the summoning and powering all the time, which . . . she'd really be dependent on him then, she'll have nothing when he leaves her, right? So really she's doing the smart thing not letting him have all the control, making sure she doesn't have to need him so much so she isn't left in the lurch when he ends things . . ."

Even through the speed's cheerful jig in her bloodstream she knew that was the wrong thing to say. Terrible's face hadn't changed, or rather it hadn't changed a lot, but she still saw the tiny downtwist of his mouth, the darkening in his eyes and the faint flush blossoming on his throat. Fuck.

"So why's Slobag fuckin giving the yay to that fuckin plan? Ain't making no fuckin sense, not even on that fuckin scum."

She never thought she'd be grateful for Bump's interruptions, but she was. She took her gaze from Terrible's, took a long drink from her water bottle to help ease her speed dryness. The third line she'd cut sat there on the mirror, waiting. Fuck ten or fifteen minutes, she needed it now. She picked up the straw again. "I don't think he cares. I mean, he might not know, but as long as the stuff he wants done gets done, he might not care."

"Aye, had the thought on that." Terrible didn't quite look her in the eyes again, but he did look at her, and he hadn't taken his hand from her leg. At least that was some reassurance. "Like if Slobag gets heself an address, an he witch—Aros—heads heself over to it afore, does he spell, an the building burns up from it? Like that?"

"Right."

He picked up the map he'd set beside him when they first arrived. "So's we thinkin all them addresses picked by Slobag, or maybe not?"

"What the fuck you got the thinkin you fuckin see?"

The third line hit the back of her throat. Much better. "We think there might be some kind of pattern. In the addresses, I mean."

"Aye." Terrible pulled a thick black marker from somewhere, uncapped it, and started scrawling big Xs on the map. "First one here, dig, Sixtieth an Mercer. Then that school, Twentieth an Foster, aye? An Sixty-fifth an Foster here."

Bump snorted. "Got the fuckin look like a seven, yay. Ain't no fuckin truefacts in that one, what fuckin knowledge we gonna get offen that one?"

"It doesn't look like a seven, it's—you see it upside down."

"Yay, so fuckin what? So Bump's got the lookin—"

"Holy shit." She glanced from Terrible to Bump—who seemed taken aback at being interrupted—to Terrible again. "He's looking at it upside down. And it looks right side up to him, right? But it's upside down."

"Ain't gettin it, Chess."

"Right, I know, sorry, it's—Here, give me the marker."
He did.

"Look." She placed the point where he'd finished his line, at the body they'd found that afternoon. From there she drew another line, ending it at Twenty-fifth and Mercer, then drawing it down to Forty-third and Wayne.

A moment of silence, and Bump spoke. "Be a fuckin star, yay?"

She shook her head. Terrible watched her; she saw the knowledge in his eyes, had another flash of pride. "It's not just a star. It's a pentacle. It's an upside-down pentacle."

Chapter Thirty-two

Vigilance and awareness are two qualities a Church employee must possess.
—*The Example Is You*, the guidebook for Church employees

"So thinking he give another one the try tonight?"

The wet gray streets flew past the Chevelle's windows, almost as fast as her mind whirred and spun. Another two lines from Bump's private stash had her feeling absolutely no pain, despite Terrible's telling her he and Bump had plans for the night that he couldn't break, that he didn't know when he'd be done.

"I don't know. Probably, yeah. But we know where he'll be, that's good, right?"

He didn't reply.

"Can't we set somebody up to watch there, or— I could tell Lex, you know, they could have somebody—"

"Slobag gots he a storeroom there."

Even with her blood dancing through her veins she felt his discomfort. "Where, at Twenty-fifth and Mercer?"

He nodded.

"Well, so there'll already be—oh. Oh, shit, seriously? That's what your plans are for tonight, that's why you can't—"

"Maybe best you ain't ask on it, aye? An won't be all empty there, gots—"

"I have to be there."

The Chevelle slowed enough for him to turn it, passing a few bodies huddled in a doorway. "What?"

"I have to be there. If Aros is going to be there—the kind of power he's generating so far, and where he's getting it from? He's destroying the balance of energy, that could be—"

"Naw, ain't wantin you nowhere nearby, dig? Ain't be safe there, don't even—"

"What am I supposed to do, let him kill someone else?"

"Be plenty people around, he—"

"And if he casts some sort of hiding glamour—which he could do, with that kind of power—nobody but me would be able to see him. Not to mention—" She shut her mouth. Fuck.

"What? Not mentioning what?"

They'd almost reached the warehouse and her car, damn it, and he wouldn't let her go until she told him; she knew him well enough to know that.

"Not mentioning what, Chess?"

Fine. "The sigil. The sigil on your chest. You—"

"Aw, shit. Ain't on this one again, aye? The fuck am I sposed to do, hide—"

"I just think I should be—"

"Maybe you oughta be figurin on makin it stop, aye, 'stead of makin me some fuckin pussy sit on the outside."

He hadn't said that before; their discussions on the subject hadn't gone that far before, though, either. He'd always found some way to distract her, to change the subject.

Now she knew why, and it was so fucking obvious she couldn't believe she hadn't seen it.

"It's not like that." She touched his neck, played her fingers in the hair at his nape, but he wouldn't look at her. "It's not like you can't handle it or something, it's just—this is stuff I can do, you know? So I want to be there to do it, is all."

He still didn't reply.

"You're the one who said that between you and me we could handle anything, right? And this is my part."

The warehouse appeared on her left; her car sat a few lengths down on the street. He stopped the Chevelle next to it, sat there in silence for another minute.

"Aye," he said finally. "Guessin you should be there, handle the magic. Only—only you give me the wait, aye? Ain't come on till I say. Causen if he don't show up . . . rather you ain't be there, dig."

"Yeah. Yeah, okay." She swallowed the sigh of relief that wanted to burst from her, the sigh of something else, too. She'd known how to handle it. Something had bothered him—something big, she knew, how fucking hard must that have been for him to say that, to admit to her how much his reaction to magic since the sigil scared him—and she'd been able to talk to him about it, to make him feel better.

Maybe she wasn't a complete failure at this after all.

"Send you a text then, aye?"

She nodded.

He glanced at the streets around them, then leaned over to kiss her, faster than she would have liked; the rain had slowed, after all, they were visible through the windows. "An Chess . . . ain't want shit bein off with you. But ain't can have you pickin fights and shit, neither, givin me tests."

What the hell could she say in reply to that? Nothing came to mind, not a thing. So she nodded, swallowed, squeezed his hand. And got out of the car as fast as she could.

Her mood didn't improve when, three hours later, she pulled into the parking lot at the Mercy Lewis school and saw Beulah and Lex standing outside.

"You can't come in with me," she said as soon as

she'd parked and gotten within speaking distance. "I'm doing a ritual."

"Aw, Tulip, that any way to give us a hello?"

"You'll be in my way."

If it had just been him standing there she would have been, well, nicer. But it wasn't just him. Beulah was there, too, and Chess had a report in her bag that said Beulah had given her a plate of food with a one-way ticket to the City mixed into it, in the form of several thousand milligrams of psychotropic medication. She also had the memory of the tea, and that Beulah may have introduced Aros to Slobag, that Beulah may have known more about Jia Zhang than she let on.

And she had the knowledge that Beulah not only hated the Church—or at least seemed to, all those snippy comments—but had been suspiciously pally almost since the moment they'd met, with her fucking jokes and smiles and "I won't tell Terrible about the kiss" and "Do you want to talk about it" bullshit.

Chess wasn't sure what pissed her off more: Beulah's attitude toward the Church, or that she'd actually almost started to . . . well, to like Beulah. She'd never had a female friend before; looked like she wasn't going to start. She should have known better.

Sure, it might not have been Beulah who tried to kill her. It might have been some completely random stranger. But the odds of that being the case were awfully slim.

Lex shrugged. "Only sayin, ain't gotta be mean."

"What are you guys doing here, anyway?"

"You said you were coming to do that Banishing thing, so we thought we should be here. Keep watch and everything."

"Aye. We oughta get ourselves inside, we ought. Ain't no telling how long we stay on our alones out here, 'swhat thought I got. Could get us company on the any-time."

"Right." Chess lifted her hands, indicated the empty parking lot around them. "Clearly this is a hub of activity at night."

"There's no need to be a bitch," Beulah said. "What do you care if we want to be here?"

Do not tell her to fuck off, do not tell her to fuck off. "Sorry. I guess I'm just on edge. If you guys want to stand around out here, you go ahead."

"Ain't standin out here, nay. Going inside, along with you. Keepin watch, we are."

The rain had stopped by the time she'd set out, but the breeze still smelled of it, felt cool and heavy with it as it brushed her skin. "Why are you doing this, any-way? Why are you so fucking set on helping me?"

"The fuck problem you got this night, Tulip? You wanna get on down the City, you go straight ahead. Guessin I had the thought you ain't wanted that, figured on givin you the help."

So much for pretending everything was fine. She sighed. "Sorry. I'm sorry, guys. I just want to get this over with, is all."

That was true. The sooner she Banished that fucking ghost the sooner she could get over to Twenty-fifth and Mercer and hide, waiting for Terrible's text.

"Gots other places I could be, I do, too," Lex said, with that air of noble suffering he was so good at. "But figured I ain't have me so much fun iffen you dead, so here I am. Maybe you ain't give me the junters for it, aye?"

"I said I was sorry."

"Let's not stand out here and talk about it, okay?" Beulah glanced around the still-empty parking lot as if she expected a lynch mob to appear any second. "Let's just get in, and you can argue with us then."

Chess shrugged. "Whatever."

None of them spoke again until they got inside the atrium; Chess felt them watching her as she picked the lock and wondered if Beulah had a key and just wasn't telling her. Probably.

Didn't matter, though. As with everything else Beulah-related, she didn't care. "Okay. I'm going to set up in the cafeteria, I think, so you guys can wait here."

"I think we should go with you."

"Well . . . I don't."

"Gots me an ask, I do. What happens them ghost shows up here, an you in there?"

Shit. She hadn't thought of that. Stupid of her, yeah, but then she hadn't actually wanted to think of it, had she? No. Because that meant she had to let them come along if she wanted to not turn them into some kind of sacrificial ghost-bait, and she didn't want to do that. Or at least she didn't want to do that to Lex.

She closed her eyes, wished this was already done and she was out of the building. Too bad it wasn't, and she wasn't. "Fine. Come on. But no talking, and you do exactly what I tell you to. Okay?"

She ended up being kind of glad they'd tagged along after all. The tables in the cafeteria weren't heavy, but they were numerous, and rather awkward to move. It would have taken her a lot longer to clear the floor herself.

The ghost probably wouldn't be outside the building, so she could mark those walls and the windows looking out onto the sad field of scrub grass and rusty goalposts that Mercy Lewis students were supposed to play sports on or whatever. She marked the floor to solidify it on the astral plane while she was at it, had Lex help her get the ceiling just in case.

One set of stairs didn't have a door; she sketched a

quick Bindrune over it to act as a barrier. She'd leave the other doors open until Lucy showed up, so the herb smoke and the sounds would spread through the building more easily.

"Okay. That's as much as I can do until she gets here. When she does, if it's possible for you to close the other doors, do. If she's carrying a weapon or coming after you, just get away. Lex, I know you know the rules, you don't look her in the eyes, you try not to engage her or attract her attention. She might not notice you with me here. Questions? Good. Go sit over there."

Another few minutes to set up her stang in its iron holder, the firedish at its base and the Church-grown blue and black roses wreathed over the top. She poured water into her cauldron, added wolfsbane, and lit the flame under it. A few minutes for that to heat up and she could light the mullein and benzoin to call Lucy's ghost; wasn't always necessary—usually wasn't, actually—but given how large the building was, and given what Terrible and Bump were doing and that Lex would undoubtedly hear about it when it happened . . . she figured the faster she called Lucy, the faster she could get rid of her.

She'd topped up her salt canister, and she set up the bag of graveyard dirt taken from Lucy's drawer in the Church's Grave Supplies department on the right side of the stang. Her black chalk—shit, she should probably do that, too.

"Here," she said, crossing the room. "Let me mark you guys, just to be safe, okay?"

Lex shrugged. He'd sat on one of the long benches at the far end of the room, where the lights were especially dim. "Know it ain't bother me none."

"Yeah." She smiled, went ahead and let him see the fondness in it. "I know."

Beulah didn't say anything. Fine with Chess.

It felt weird to be so close to Lex again, weirder even

than it had felt to be in his room, almost weirder even than it had been to kiss him. Sitting on the couch across from his bed hadn't involved touching. The kiss . . . well, that hadn't lasted long, hadn't meant anything, and had ended almost before she realized it was happening.

But standing with her hand on his cheek . . . his own came to rest on her hip, and she didn't know how to tell him to take it off. It would be kind of prissy of her to say that, wouldn't it? Wasn't that big a deal when he set the other one on her other hip, either. Right?

She could say Terrible wouldn't like it, and that if she knew he wouldn't like it, she shouldn't let Lex do it. The problem with that method was that Terrible wouldn't like anything Lex did to her, up to and including smiling from across a crowded room. So that really wasn't the best guideline.

And it didn't matter anyway, because she had a responsibility to mark him. She focused on putting as much power as she could into the protection sigils she drew across his forehead and down his cheeks. Only protection; he wouldn't be doing anything but sitting, so he should be safe anyway. The marks were just a little insurance.

"Here, look up." This was harder than she'd thought it would be. Not because she still wanted him; she didn't. It was just that . . . well, she still kind of wanted him. How did that make sense?

She wasn't in love with him. The difference between how she felt about Terrible and how she felt about Lex couldn't have been deeper or more obvious. And given the choice between sleeping with him and sleeping with Terrible . . . that wasn't a question, either. Hell, that was a decision she'd already made.

But she couldn't lie and say she didn't still enjoy touching him, looking at him. Couldn't say that when she did, when she stood there with him so close, with his faint smoke-and-spice smell in her nose and his hands on her, her body didn't react, even though it wasn't as intense. Or that she didn't remember other times, didn't recall those hands in other places and how skilled they were. Didn't remember how they'd made her gasp. Or how he'd made her laugh.

Not like Terrible did. And the thought of regretting that choice didn't even cross her mind; how could it? Terrible was who she wanted, he was the part of her that had been missing, and she was terrified she'd lose him, and she'd never worried about losing Lex or felt like Lex understood her. He didn't.

But her fingers curled around the back of his neck anyway, sliding into the hair at his nape, and she rested her knee on the bench just outside his thigh and leaned into him without fully realizing what she was doing. Leaned in probably closer than she should have, while she marked the back of his neck.

"Tulip." His voice, low and a little husky, slid under her clothes, slipped into all those spots where she'd just been remembering his hands; those hands tightened their grip when her eyes met his. "Lessin it were someone I ain't know gave you them neck bites, maybe you oughta be all finished on me now, aye?"

The words were as effective as a bucket of ice water thrown over her head. Shit. In his eyes was a Truth, one she hadn't wanted to see before, one that made her feel guilty. No, he wasn't in love with her, either, at least she didn't think so.

But he wanted her. He still wanted her, and she'd hurt him when she'd ended their—well, she'd told herself it wasn't a relationship, but it had been, the first one she'd ever had. All those memories playing in her head were playing in his, too, and if that familiar tingle of arousal stirred low in her belly, it definitely did in his. He wasn't telling her to stop, he was asking her to. Asking her to give him a break.

She should have known that the minute she started getting involved with other people they started hurting. Bad enough when it had only been herself she was trying to destroy. Now she was taking other people down with her.

All of this flashed through her head in one confused second; all it took for her to remember the last time she'd heard that tone in his voice, and for guilt to crash down on her like a wave, carried on that tide of shameful pain she expected to drown her any day.

She stepped back so fast she almost stumbled. "Sorry, I— Sorry."

He gave her a shrug, a half nod, casual as if he'd practiced it in a mirror. Which knowing Lex wasn't completely outside the realm of possibility.

But he didn't look her in the eyes again.

Well, she wouldn't have to worry about that with Beulah. Not that Beulah didn't present her own set of problems. She did. Not least of which was fighting the temptation to fake some scribbles on her and let the ghost have fun.

Which she wouldn't do. Of course she wouldn't; she wouldn't do that to someone she hated, and no matter what she felt about Beulah at that moment, the fact remained that even if Chess could be so callous, that girl was Lex's sister, someone he cared about. And Chess had hurt him enough, hadn't she.

So she gritted her teeth and set the chalk to Beulah's forehead, pushing her hair back out of the way. Beulah wasn't quite as magic-dead as Lex; her eyes widened a little. "What is that?"

"They're just protective sigils. They won't keep you from dying or anything, but they make it harder for ghosts to hurt you, like they won't be able to solidify around you."

"And you put power into them, or whatever? That's why they feel kind of itchy?"

"Yep."

"Do you have to do that on purpose, or is that just something that happens when you touch people, or when you draw things on them?"

Chess hesitated. But really, what could Beulah do with that information? How magic worked wasn't some big secret. Just some of the individual spells. "I have to channel it. I mean, if I'm not paying attention sometimes it projects anyway, most people have energy around them. But yeah, when I'm doing something like this I'm pushing it, because it gives the sigil strength. It makes it work. Without that, it's just a scribbly line."

"Hmm." The sigil she'd just drawn on Beulah's forehead wrinkled. "So, how does that work, like, if you have to do that for Terrible? Would he pass out the way he does with other magic, or is—"

"Blue!"

"What?" The chalk dropped from Chess's numb fingers; she saw it fall in slow motion, bounce on the tile, tumbling end over end like it would never stop falling. "What did you say?"

But the look on their faces let her know she'd heard right, and that if she'd thought her situation couldn't get any worse, she'd been—as always—totally fucking wrong.

Chapter Thirty-three

Ugly silence shrouded them all, filled the room until
Chess felt herself choking on it. Her voice sawed through
it hard like a rough serrated blade. "I don't know what
you're talking about."

Too late. It was too late for that; it had been the minute Beulah said it. Because she knew. She hadn't been
fishing, looking for some kind of confirmation with that
question. It had been genuine. Honest curiosity. What
the fuck?

Lex didn't know about that. Nobody knew about
that, no one had been told about that. The last thing
Chess wanted, the last thing anyone needed, was for it
to be common knowledge that the most feared enforcer
in Downside had a fatal weakness, one that any two-bit
piece of shit could pay any halfway-talented witch fifty
bucks to exploit.

She looked from Beulah to Lex and back again, at
the matching expressions of dismay. How she'd managed to miss the family resemblance when she met
Beulah she didn't know, except that she'd expected
Lex's sister to look Downside, not to be a tidy, glamor-
ous community organizer. Whatever, it had been stupid

of her to miss it, because they looked so much alike it scared her.

But not as much as Beulah's words had. "How— Who told you that?"

More silence. Her head buzzed loud in it, thoughts and images fighting for dominance. Terrible in the car earlier, his words to her outside the warehouse—

The warehouse where he'd collapsed. In front of several other people she didn't know.

Including one who'd said he'd been out scouting more buildings for Bump. One who'd presumably done it before. One of the few people who probably knew about the Sixtieth Street pipe room being empty that night. The guy with the green hair, what was his name?

"Bernam. That's his name, right?"

Their expressions didn't change; she didn't expect them to. "That's him, isn't it, your spy. Isn't it?"

She couldn't take her eyes off them. Couldn't—both of them. Both of them pretending to want to help her, to want to be—pretending to fucking care about her, and all the while they weren't just trying to fuck up Bump's business, they were trying to kill Terrible, to exploit his lone weakness. They were trying to take away the one and only good thing she'd ever had outside work. If she'd had a gun at that moment she would have plugged them both in the head without blinking and walked away clean.

As it was, she settled for letting her absolute rage ride in her eyes while she glared at them, for pulling out her phone and holding it up so she could hit Terrible's number without having to look away from them.

The light on it blinked; a text waiting. From Church, from the lab. Elder Lyle had come through for her. The rush of gratitude she felt didn't come close to chasing away her anger, but hey, she'd take what she could fucking get.

He'd found a match for the DNA on Bill Pritchard's body, the female DNA, when he checked it against Lucy McShane's.

Not a perfect match. The female DNA was too damaged, or too old. But enough of a match that he could say with high probability that Bill Pritchard's sex partner had either been Lucy McShane or been related to her. Chelsea Mueller again. Not a surprise, but confirmation.

Another angry glance at Lex and Beulah, who both continued to look chastened, although she suspected the impact of her anger was beginning to wear off.

Time to call Terrible, and say . . . what? That she knew who the snitch was, sure. But to tell him Lex knew about his—well, his problem? His problem that she'd caused. His problem that was evidence of her crime. His problem that she felt proud of and guilty for every time it came up, every time she thought of it.

With a shock she realized that wasn't all she felt. Her tattoos tingled. Her tattoos tingled, and the hair on the back of her neck stood on end, and her mouth felt dry, and that wasn't anger or drugs. That was a ghost.

Before she finished the thought Lucy McShane appeared, gliding across the cafeteria floor, the thick steel bars she held catching the dim light and reflecting it back so sharp it hurt Chess's eyes.

Fuck. Terrible would have to wait. She started backing up, moving casually, unafraid—showing fear to a ghost was the sort of mistake people didn't live to regret—and glanced at Lex and Beulah. "You guys go find someplace to sit, and don't— Well, you know, Lex."

He nodded. Good. He'd tell Beulah not to make eye contact, to keep her movements slow and calm. It might not make a difference; ghosts picked victims the way Chess picked Cepts, just grabbing whichever ones were within reach. But sometimes it helped.

In this case it certainly appeared to. Lucy didn't even glance in Lex and Beulah's direction. She headed straight for Chess, gliding slowly on legs almost fully formed. So much more powerful than she'd been, cranked by ritual sacrifice. She looked bizarrely like a bride on her way down the aisle, stepping slow and dignified, pale against the darkness behind, anticipating killing Chess like it was her wedding night. Something she'd waited years for.

Either she didn't see the altar set up behind Chess, didn't understand what it was, or just didn't care, because she didn't seem to be in any hurry. Ghosts rarely were. She kept her slow pace, kept watching Chess with rigid intensity; she had all the time in the world, at least so she thought.

She was definitely stronger than she'd been. Her ethereal form still wavered, revealing the underlying decay, the bones, the gruesome Truth behind the moonglow beauty of death, but Chess suspected that had to do with the power's source—murder always carried a stain—rather than weakness. Lucy glowed too brightly, was too well formed everywhere else, looked too cunning.

Chess reached her stang, the bag of Lucy's graveyard dirt, the salt right nearby with her psychopomp. Just seeing it all gave her strength, made her heartbeat slow as her fear fell away. This was what she did, what she did well. The one thing in the world she knew without a doubt she was good at—hell, she was *very* good, and that made her proud, and that pride gave her confidence, and she knelt quickly to fill her hands, to feel the familiar tingle of power that came only from graveyard dirt.

One more breath, slow and even. Lucy's bars kept swinging, like metronomes marking her invisible steps as she drew closer, watching her.

Another breath. She had to pick the exact right moment, when Lucy was close enough to hit with thrown dirt but not so close that Chess was within range of those steel bars.

Another breath. Get ready, deep inhalation, fill her lungs with air so she could cast her words of power clear and strong—

"Dallirium espirantia!"

The words—designed to intensify the power of the dirt to freeze ghosts, to keep them stiff and controlled for longer than the dirt alone—flew from her mouth, smooth and clean. Her power flew with them, erupting from her in a wave, and the dirt went with it all. She was a vortex; she was the source, something bigger than herself, and the rush overwhelmed her. A perfect cast. Perfect.

Until it went horribly, horribly wrong.

The power that had flowed so smoothly from her flew back, knocked her down, tore through her like a chain of rusty nails and spikes. She fell into her stang, landed on it and on her cauldron and thankfully unlit firedish. Scalding water soaked through her jeans; three fingers on her left hand caught the sharp end of her stang base and were sliced open. What the fuck, what the fuck had just happened, that wasn't supposed to happen—

Lucy was grinning, and she raised her cold bone-bright hands so the steel she held caught the light in a quick flash like shooting stars in the darkness. Not frozen. The spell hadn't caught, she was triumphant, she looked at Chess with unholy glee, making terrified rage boil in her chest.

The dirt wasn't from Lucy's grave.

It hadn't been her dirt, which meant it had no power over her at all, not even the power generic graveyard dirt carried. Hadn't been hers, so it had a different signature or whatever the hell Elder Payne had called it, a signature that actually gave Lucy a jolt of power. Using the wrong dirt was bad news, a bad idea, a very, very bad thing to do, and she'd done it, and she'd done it in front of two other people—two living people—who were counting on her to save them.

She'd failed. Again.

It wasn't just the wrong dirt, though; she knew it, felt it when the energy backlashed at her. Lucy's was mixed with another, the energy of the living. The energy of a witch. Lucy had been bound down; magically held to the surface of the earth by the power of her summoner— her summoners—and by whatever item they'd used to summon her. Whatever personal items Aros and Chelsea held and controlled. Chess couldn't Banish Lucy, not without that object, and she had no idea what it was or where in Downside—hell, where in Triumph City, where in the District, where in the country—it might be. Sure they might have it with them when—and if—they headed to Mercer and Twenty-fifth, but there was no guarantee, and to find out, Chess first had to get past Lucy with her weapon and her cruel triumph.

Fuck, that was bad.

While these thoughts screamed through her head in a blast of pain and horror she scrambled away from Lucy, trying to regain her footing, trying to grab her bag and keep from having her bones turned into dust at the same time.

The steel bars whistled down. She managed to avoid one of them, rolling to her left, but that only put her closer to the path of Lucy's other bar. A glancing blow, and fucking lucky for that because had it not been, it would probably have broken her hip. As it was her vision went white for a second, the pain too intense to feel; for the space of a breath she hung suspended, waiting for it to hit.

It did, with a crash that knocked the air from her lungs and every bit of strength from her muscles. She managed to gasp, harsh and loud in the near-silence, before the bar fell again.

She didn't know how she managed to get away. Somehow she convinced her body to move, to roll farther to her left. Lucy's swing hit so close it caught her shirt with its jagged metal tip, pegged her there to the floor for a hideous moment before she tore the fabric to get away.

A further roll, until she hit her knees. Push off with her hands and toes, try to stand, stand so she could run, stand so she could dig into her bag and get her generic dirt and asafetida. No, she couldn't Banish Lucy, not while Lucy was bound like that, but she could sure as fuck lock her down, and she would.

She glanced back to see Lucy struggling to pull one of her bars away from the combined efforts of Lex and Beulah, while the other one rolled away from them. A second of warm gratitude and something like pride before it occurred to her that fucking right they should help; not only was it their lives, too, but they'd been sneaking behind her back, spying to hurt Terrible, and Beulah might have tried to kill her. They owed her.

Still, it was an enormous help. The generic dirt should be in her bag, where was it? Where the fuck—

A scream from Beulah, but Chess didn't have time to look. She was too busy grabbing her asafetida, digging her hand into the bag of graveyard dirt, which was—of course—empty. Could her night go any fucking worse?

Not a good idea to have that thought. Fate hated her enough as it was.

Her salt had rolled a few feet away. She snatched it up, popped the lid, and stumbled over to where the others still struggled. Well, Lex and Lucy struggled; Beulah crouched on the floor, clutching her head. Shit! Shit, what had happened to her, what had happened that was Chess's fault—

She'd find out soon enough. At that moment she

needed to get Lucy circled, locked in place without first freezing her with dirt.

She might as well try. She raised her left fist with its three sliced fingers, let her blood pool in her palm and run down toward her elbow to soak into her sleeve. Better than dropping it on the floor—or rather, letting more of it drop on the floor—but not great; ghosts could smell blood, sense it, especially powerful blood like hers.

All the more reason to hurry. She ran around Lucy and Lex, staying low, her injured hip screaming at the movement even louder than it had when she walked upright.

A jog in the line as she dipped in to avoid enclosing Beulah in the circle—if Beulah had to be moved she could break the line—and she was done. She lowered her left hand and watched the drops fall, black in the darkness, black against the pure white salt, a Rorschach blot in her own blood that looked like the image of death.

She ignored the superstitious shiver slithering up her spine. At least she didn't need to ready herself to summon power; she had it, pain and anger flowing through her like her body had become a hydroelectric plant. "With blood I Bind!"

The circle snapped into place, clean and strong. Her breath left her chest in a relieved sigh; she'd been holding it, afraid the circle wouldn't cast. The way things were going for her, that seemed a pretty reasonable fear.

But it had.

"Lex," she said. "Go ahead and step out of the circle, but try not to break it, okay?"

Lex and Lucy looked down at the same time. Luckily Lex's reflexes were faster. With a speed and agility that surprised even her—and she'd seen both before—he jumped back, cleared the salt line, and almost fell when the bar swung at him, missing him by less than an inch.

Chess grabbed for it on the backswing and barely

managed to avoid being knocked into the circle. Her blood-slick left hand was too wet to get a good grip; Lucy's eyes widened, and Chess saw she might have a chance to get the bar away more easily. Weapons were good but power was better, power was what ghosts hungered for, killed for. They'd almost always go for it if they had the chance, and that power sang thick in Chess's blood.

"Take the bar," she gasped. Lucy was trying to swing that bar with every bit of strength she possessed, and that was considerable, even without Chess being disadvantaged by her wounded left hand.

Lex had started moving before she spoke. His hands closed around the pole, his arms around her, his chest warm against her back. She ducked, already missing that warmth, and stepped far enough away to give him some room.

Shit, she hoped this worked.

Drops of her blood flew through the air when she swung her hand; drops falling into the circle, into Lucy, who wavered for a second. She'd felt it. Oh, awesome, she'd felt it.

Chess stepped closer, let her hand lead the way. Let it lure the ghost, taunted her with it. Closer and closer until her fingertips turned ice cold where they came in contact with Lucy, like dipping them in a freezing mist.

The rotting skull lurking behind Lucy's face glowed, its mouth wide open in a silent roar, becoming even brighter when Chess's blood touched Lucy's ethereal body, that skull like the embodiment of her unholy hunger, her furious, inhuman greed.

Chess chanced a quick peek at Lex, found his eyes focused on her, on Lucy, his pose tense and expectant. Waiting. There was one good thing, at least, one thing going her fucking way. He knew what she was doing, she didn't have to say it or explain it, and he was ready.

She pulled her hand back, yanked it about six inches away from Lucy, and in the opposite direction from Lex.

And it worked. Thank her Church education and the single-minded lust of the dead, Lucy turned toward Chess's hand, took one of hers off the pole to make a grab for it, and Lex snatched the steel away.

Lucy realized what had happened, reached for it, reached for Chess as she backed away. No more beauty in front of the skull; her features twisted, her expression turned feral, her form wavered with her rage.

All in vain. The circle held and Lucy was trapped inside it. It wasn't the first thing that had gone right, no, but it still felt good. Would have felt better if Chess was able to properly Banish Lucy, but she couldn't have everything. Of course.

What the hell to do next? Her circle would hold, at least unless and until someone deliberately broke it. And unfortunately, Chess knew someone who'd be glad to do just that. Two someones: Aros Burnett and Chelsea Mueller. They had to be stopped, and fast.

She turned to ask Lex to help her pick everything up—damn, she wished she could ask him to hit the streets with her—but the words died on her lips. Beulah still huddled on the floor. Not moaning any longer, sitting up with Lex's arm around her, but tears ran down her face and her left eye was already swelling, turning a dark mottled color Chess could see even in the darkness.

Shit like that made it kind of hard to remember what Beulah had done to her—what Beulah had *probably* done to her. Lucky for Chess she had a pretty good memory, but still . . . She also had little doubt that Beulah wasn't used to that sort of thing, that Beulah felt the shock of having violence committed against her as well as the pain of it. Chess hadn't felt that kind of shock in a long, long time.

But she remembered it. For that split second she re-

membered it, how the first few times—the first dozen or
so times, even—it was a surprise, it felt like a betrayal;
that disbelief that it was being done, that she was being
hurt like that and by the person who was hurting her.
The shock and disbelief that the person she'd trusted,
the world she'd trusted, weren't what she thought they
were, weren't welcoming and caring, wouldn't take care
of her the way she'd dreamed they would.

But it only happened the first few times. After that . . .
after that it was expected. Then it was anticipated. And
after that . . . it was what she deserved.

Beulah didn't know any of that, hadn't dealt with
that. Chess saw that surprise, that almost childlike hurt,
lurking behind the physical pain, hiding so thoroughly
she doubted Beulah even realized it was there.

Just the thought of it made her hand shake as she dug
her pillbox from her bag and grabbed four of them. Shit,
she'd forgotten to ask Lex if he could bring her more.
Maybe she should just take two, hang on to the others . . . she had a dozen left, maybe she should ration
them.

Fuck that. She didn't need them in a few hours, she
needed them now, and she could get more before she
went home anyway. Four it was.

Time to move, too. She started gathering things up,
her hip still aching, her left hand stinging. The blood
flow was slowing but not— Fuck. Fuck fuck shit. The
blood.

She pulled her sleeve down and folded her pinky over
it, wrapped it up. Yes, it meant she lost the use of the
hand completely for cleanup, but her blood already
soaked the area like urine in a Downside alley and she
couldn't let any more fall. Not when all anyone—all
Aros—needed was to get some of that. Not just witch's
blood, *her* blood, and all the uses it had as a weapon
against her: Binding her power down, Binding herself to

him, shielding against her, some horrific curses—almost every bit of nasty magic she knew required blood, and the victim's blood was always preferred.

Fuck again.

In her bag were tissues, bandages, and gauze. Should she ask Lex to help her? He seemed focused on Beulah—which she couldn't blame him for, but which made her feel guilty for pulling him away.

Then again, maybe she'd feel less guilty if she actually behaved the way a normal human being would. "Beulah, are you okay?"

Beulah's voice drifted out of her mouth, thin and reedy like it had been poured through a sieve. "I'm okay. She just, she got me in the eye, and it . . . it just really hurts."

Pause. "Do you want to take something for that?"

A silent nod.

Chess dug out her pillbox, started talking to cover her discomfort. "So, Aros summoned Lucy. Aros is the one who's committing the murders, the sacrifices. It's him, and his magic is connected to the ghost, too."

"How'd you get that?"

"Long story. Just trust me, it's him, and he's committing the murders to bring her back, because her cousin wants him to. I think she's been drugging him. And that was the wrong dirt, Aros must have switched it in the Grave Supplies building, so it didn't catch, it blew back at me."

Lex nodded. "Had the wonder on that one, me. You got the right dirt, then? Get her sent on back the City, aye, we get the fuck outta here. Ain't likin the feel of this, I ain't. Not at all."

"I'm not either," she said, handing Beulah two Cepts and her water bottle. Six left. As soon as they walked out of the building she was going to ask Lex for more. "But . . . no, I don't have the right dirt. I can't Banish her. I mean, any other time I could Banish her with generic dirt, but it wouldn't be as strong and there would be a greater chance she could come back. The dirt isn't to Banish so much as it is to seal the Banishing, you know?"

"Nay, I ain't, but 'slong as you do I ain't bothered neither."

"Right. Anyway, the real problem is that when Aros summoned her he— Remember the ghost house? Kemp and Vanita and all that, how the building was turned into a safe house and the ghosts couldn't be Banished from it?"

Lex looked around. "Shit, we gotta find us some dead cat or whatany? Why you witchy shit always so nasty, Tulip, dead hands and maggots and all like that?"

Her smile felt strange, there in the middle of the wreckage of her ritual, with an angry ghost pacing her circle and her blood drying all over the floor. "It isn't always. It's just you seem to get stuck dealing with black magic, and a lot of that is pretty intense. But this isn't quite like that, no. That was the house holding them, making a spirit home. This is a totem Binding, at least I think so."

He just looked at her, his eyes expectant. Right.

"Kemp and Vanita turned the house into, like, a safe house. The psychopomps couldn't get into it. So it didn't Bind the individual ghosts to something on earth, it just kept them safe as long as they were in the house, you know what I mean? If one of them had gone outside they could have been taken. But this is specific, this locks that specific ghost here, and I can't break that without having whatever totem it is that Binds her."

"Damn. Ain't stupid, that witch ain't."

"No. Especially since I don't think the totem is here. She'd be stronger if it was."

He glanced at Beulah, who still looked dazed. Her tears had dried, though. Chess hoped that meant she was feeling better. "Seems to me she plenty strong on the already."

The skull beneath Lucy's skin grinned its unfeeling smile as Lucy glared at them and paced around inside the salt circle.

"So you just gotta find them totem, get she sent all back, aye? And then we finished up."

Just like Lex. Was there anything that didn't seem perfectly simple to him? "Sure, except it could be anywhere in the city and we have no idea what it is."

He shrugged. "So we get a look-on for Mr. Witch, make him give us the tell. Easy. You always seein the hard side, ain't you? Sad, that is. Oughta be more along with the optimism."

"Yeah. Thanks for that, Lex, I'll work on it." She rolled her eyes. But she smiled, too.

"Come on. I need to get this stuff packed up and get my blood off the floor, and we need to figure out what to do next. I need to make—" Right. "I need to make a couple of calls. But why don't I have a little talk with Beulah first."

Chapter Thirty-four

Funny how eyes wet with tears almost always looked innocent, how people were hardwired somehow to feel sympathy at the sight of them. Funny too how that look of surprise Chess had noticed earlier, that wounded-soul look, wouldn't quite leave her memory, even though she knew it shouldn't make a difference.

At least she thought she did, and that was the problem. Her initial certainty that Beulah had been trying to kill her, that Beulah had been somehow involved with Aros, had faded. Not completely, but enough to make her question a little less . . . blunt than she'd originally intended.

"Beulah, is there something you want to tell me?"

Oh, for fuck's sake. She sounded like she suspected Beulah of having a crush on her or of borrowing her pen and forgetting to give it back. Worse, it alerted Beulah that something funny was happening.

"What? Like what? Oh. No, you know already. You were right."

"What?" Shit, she hadn't expected it to be that easy.

"Bernam. That's his name. But I don't think my father knows yet, about—Terrible, and the magic thing. I don't think—"

She cut Beulah off. Shit again. She'd actually managed to forget that for half a minute, which was incredibly stupid and pretty much just proved that she shouldn't be taking care of anyone, anywhere, ever. "No, not that. About— Fuck. What did you have for lunch today?"

"Huh?"

This was completely not working. "You brought me lunch today. Why didn't you have the same thing I did? Where did you get the food?"

Beulah's brow wrinkled. "I, um, I didn't have the same thing because I just didn't, that's all. There wasn't a lot left. And I got it from the table in the lounge where the rest of the food was, I got yours and then decided I was hungry so I got myself something. Why? Isn't this kind of a weird time to ask about food? I don't know the recipe or anything."

"I do." Chess reached into her bag, keeping one eye on Beulah while she dug around for the report Elder Lyle had given her. "I don't know about anything else, but the main ingredient in my lunch was Vapezine. Enough to kill me. Enough to kill just about anyone."

Beulah's mouth fell open. Surprised, or surprised she got caught?

"Blue?" Confusion spread all over Lex's face, and Chess was more relieved than she thought she'd be. She'd never honestly thought he would know about an attempt to kill her, much less approve, but it was still nice to see his genuine shock at the idea.

It was even nicer—way, way nicer—to feel her pills start to hit, like light spreading lazily through her entire body, like time slowing just a little. She managed not to smile, but only just.

Beulah looked as shocked as her brother. Too bad Chess couldn't quite believe her, not even as she climbed higher every minute. Nor could she believe the surprise, the near-panic, in Beulah's voice, no matter how much she wanted to, and she kind of did. "I didn't. I didn't do any of that. Lex, I didn't, I wouldn't, you know I wouldn't— Chess, I was trying to, I thought maybe— Fuck, I swear I didn't do that."

"Then who did? And why were you really here the night Jia was killed? Your father is working with Aros, and you could be, too. You were here that night, you could have set that up, come inside to keep me from going out to see what he was doing."

Beulah didn't argue. That more than anything made Chess think she might actually be innocent. People who had something to hide almost always denied it. "Someone thought they saw something and called me."

So much for not lying or denying. "That night you said they *heard* something, not *saw* something."

"What's the difference?"

Chess stared at her.

Big sigh. "Fine. No, you're right, nobody called me. Not about that, anyway. I was here because . . . Shit."

Her gaze flicked to Lex, back at Chess. Why did she look so guilty? "I was supposed to meet someone here and he didn't come, okay? He couldn't make it at the last minute."

"This is kind of a weird place for a date, isn't it?"

Another glance at Lex, who hadn't moved, watching the discussion with great interest. The color on Beulah's other cheek began to match that of her injured one. "It wasn't exactly a date. It was . . . we were just meeting here, that's all."

"Why would you meet here?" Chess thought she had some idea already, a small suspicion, but one growing every minute. Why would two people meet in an empty building at night for a not-date? Why would at least one of those people blush and apparently feel somewhat guilty for having that meeting?

Well, why had she usually met Lex at his place, and why had she felt guilty about it?

Sure enough, Beulah looked away from her, down at her hands folded in her lap. "He's married."

"Aw, Blue. Ain't that fucking smell-smock again, that Theo, aye? After what he done on the last time? Shit."

"That won't happen again, it's—it's a different—"

Lex rolled his eyes. "Aye, got a certain it is. Just like on the last time, him keeping you backbenched near two fuckin years, an you cryin all over everywhere. And you ain't even gave me the tell you was seeing him again, you ain't, tryin to gimme the sneak."

"For some stupid reason I thought you might not be pleased," Beulah snapped. "I can't imagine why I might have been worried about that."

"Maybe you oughta get youself some worry on Theo, dig, quit letting him put he feet all over—"

"Guys!" Fascinating as the discussion was—who would have guessed gorgeous Beulah would have trouble with men?—her sense of urgency hadn't gone away; clocks ticked in her head. "I'm sorry, but we really need to get going here, you know? This kind of isn't— You can talk about this later, right?"

They shrugged. Neither of them looked at the other. Great, just what she needed: to work with two people not speaking to each other.

And she would need to work with them. At least, if she decided she could trust Beulah after all.

Another beep from her phone. Terrible?

No. Elder Griffin. The tech guys had retrieved Chelsea Mueller's file.

Looked like it was time to make that Beulah decision. "Beulah. Can I use your computer for a minute?"

It seemed to take forever to connect to the Church mainframe. Chess hadn't expected anything else. The

Church's system may have been faster than the general Internet—and of course it wasn't as strictly censored—but that wasn't really saying much.

Should she tell Lex and Beulah about the pentacle, and where the next sacrifice would probably be?

Lex would get a message about it anyway, when the storeroom caught fire or whatever. Telling them would be a betrayal. Yes, Lex was her friend. Yes, she wanted to help him out. But Terrible . . . he wasn't her friend, he was her life.

If she could let him be, anyway.

The cheerful lightness from her pills helped her think about better things. Or at least about other things. She scanned the bookshelves. "Are all these yours?"

Beulah—who hadn't spoken until then, apparently preferring to glare at Lex—shook her head. "They're the school's. I've never even really looked at them."

The mainframe still hadn't booted. Should she disconnect and try again, or . . . ?

Her fingertips drummed on the desk as she checked the titles. A few Church-based books for students: *Teen Truth, You Are Special, Facts and You.* Some classic novels: Dickens and Austen, Steinbeck and Hemingway. An entire shelf of yearbooks. A bunch of college guides, and another shelf of career— Wait.

"Fuck." The word slipped out before she'd even finished thinking it. Not that she cared; it wasn't like she had to watch her language in front of Lex and Beulah.

"What?"

"Yearbooks." 2020, 2019 . . . 2000 and 2001 were the ones she needed. She found them at the end, yanked them off the shelf. "Fucking yearbooks. These have been here the whole time, haven't they?"

"Well, yeah, but—"

"Chelsea Mueller went to school here. She's the missing link, the one I can't identify. But if I can find her picture in here . . ."

Beulah's brow furrowed. "You think she's back here at the school?"

"Somebody poisoned me, right?" Check the index first. She flipped to the back of the 2000 book, that long list of names broken by pictures of Best Dressed, Best Driver, those dumbshit awards schools gave out so the snotty-ass "popular" crowd could pat themselves on the back even more. Whatever. Chelsea Mueller's picture was apparently on page thirty-three, so . . .

Martin, McElroy, McShane—there was Lucy, smiling that fakey smile—Mertel, Miller, Miller, Mueller . . .

Monica.

A much younger Monica, grinning shyly from beneath incredibly thick eyebrows and a mop of white-blond frizz held back with barrettes. Monica with a different nose, a smaller, more receding jaw, but still Monica, if Chess looked closely. Chelsea Mueller was Monica.

"Chess, holy shit, did you know that?"

"What?"

Beulah's face right next to hers, staring at the yearbook. "Did you know—"

"That Monica is Chelsea? No, of course I didn't, I wouldn't have been trying so hard—"

"No." Beulah's finger moved across the page, stopped beneath Lucy McShane's picture. "Did you know about her and Wen Li? That's Wen Li, right?"

Beneath Lucy's picture, a sentence in tiny grayish print: *"Cutest Couple—Lucy McShane and Wen Li."*

Holy shit was right. Lucy and Wen Li? Lucy had been pregnant, Wen had been involved in all of those student groups . . . She'd just started to think of all the implications when the explosion sounded in the distance.

* * *

Lex's car was the fastest, so they all piled into it. Chess's palms were clammy, her forehead hot. This was it, this was it . . . her fingers shook as she texted Terrible. They were coming, whether Aros was there or not, and if he wasn't she'd just hang back somewhere.

The thought of either one made her mouth feel like she'd been sucking on a vacuum hose. She grabbed her water bottle: almost empty. Just like something else that was almost empty. "Shit, I forgot to ask you to hook me up."

"Aye?" Lex glanced up at her, dug into the pocket of his battered jacket. "Good thing I brought for you, then, figured were about time."

"Thanks." She had to thank him, because he deserved it and because, well, yeah, she was grateful. But she couldn't help the discomfort making her skin prickle, making her cast about desperately for some other topic of conversation. How much attention did he pay to her habit, how closely did he keep track?

Bad enough she knew Terrible did; loosely, yes, but she felt his eyes sometimes when she filled her palm, felt him checking how many pills were in it and how often she took them when she was with him.

Just like Terrible's eyes on her pills, it bothered her to know Lex was watching, too, that he kept track of how often she asked him for more and thought about when she might. Why did people feel like they had the right to *know* things about other people, why did they have to observe and pay attention and think about them, why did they have to do that shit?

Her addiction was her own fucking business. It was *hers*. Hers alone. It belonged to her, and she didn't have to share it with anybody and she didn't have to talk to anybody else about it and it was private.

"So if Wen is involved . . . how did Wen get involved?" Beulah's face in the dull streetlight glow looked too pale, older with anxiety. "With Aros and everything? He hates the Church."

"But he loved Lucy." Another memory snapped into place. "His wife told me Lucy was a slut. She, shit, she said something about men writing Lucy letters—it didn't even hit me at the time, I assumed it was just a common knowledge thing or something. But I guess Wen wrote her letters, and that's what Mrs. Li meant."

"He cheats on her all the time," Beulah said. "I never understood how he manages to get all those women—"

"No telling what some dames like, aye?" Lex shot her a look. "Guessing for some ain't matter iffen them married, iffen them treated shitty, dames always fuckin—"

"Shut up, Lex. You don't know anything about Theo, or our—"

"Know he strung you on the lines two years, know you spent so much time on the cry us thought you ain't never find a way off—"

"Guys, can we drop this for the moment?" Yes, it had been interesting at first, but interesting had turned into a waste of time awfully fast, especially given where they were headed and why. "Don't we have more important things to think about?"

"Yes. Let's talk about something important." Beulah shot Lex one last glare. "Wen cheats on his wife all the time. I think he's slept with half the teachers in the school. So I didn't think anything of it when he started up with Monica, but . . . I guess that's different."

This time Chess didn't need any speed to get her mind clicking. But then she did have a hell of a rough night ahead of her, didn't she? Miles to go before she slept, and after the day she'd had she could use a little help, and luckily she had some she could snort.

She started digging in her bag for her hairpin. "Monica first told me the story of Lucy McShane. Monica does all those student groups, she did a few with Wen.

One of the ones Jia Zhang was in, right, one of the ones that met right by Aros's place? And Aros was sleeping with Jia, too, he had nude sketches and photos of her in his cottage."

Lex made a disgusted face. Beulah just looked sad. "That poor girl."

"Yeah, well, shit, she must have—right. She could have arranged the catwalk with Wen and Aros, or one of the students. There were two people working the bolts."

"I thought that seemed weird when it happened," Beulah said. "Even if it was a ghost, how could one ghost handle two things at once like that?"

Chess nodded. "Then any one of them could have locked me in that trunk in the theater, and she has keys to the building, she could have gotten in the night Jia was killed—Jia had a copy of the—of a ghost summoning handbook and I took it from her. It had belonged to Chelsea Mueller, that's probably why they killed her, because I found it. She's the one who tried to poison me, she was in the room, wasn't she, and— Fuck, she followed me into the bathroom, I'm such a fucking idiot!"

"Followed you into the— You mean earlier, before I came in?"

"Yes. She was waiting outside your office to see if I left, and she followed me to the bathroom to see if I knew anything, suspected anything. She tried to blame you, too, she told me you—"

"That bitch!"

Chess turned in her seat. "*That's* what got your attention?"

"No, I just— What a bitch."

"Yeah. Anyway. She must have set this whole thing up, right from the beginning. She seduced Bill Pritchard to get all those prescriptions for Aros, she started drugging him to make him crazy so he'd do what she wanted him to do. That's why Aros didn't have any problems before. I mean, that's just a guess, but I think it's right."

Lex spun the car onto Ace, heading for Twenty-fifth to turn north again. The music drifting from the speakers changed to G. G. Allin's "Hell in NYC." How appropriate. Wrong city, but still appropriate.

What exactly were they facing? Aros and Monica, yes, and their magic. But probably Bump and Terrible, too, and she knew about it and Lex and Beulah didn't, and that made her feel kind of shitty even though she knew she shouldn't. "So, I think they're going to be doing another ritual, another sacrifice, up there by Twenty-fifth."

Lex's eyes caught hers in the rearview. "Ain't that what's already on the happening? They done they murder, building caught up fire?"

"Oh, right. Yeah, of course." Not telling him was one thing. Lying was another.

"So she's doing all of this to bring Lucy back, then? Her and Wen," Beulah said. Yes! A change of subject, that was just what was needed.

A change of subject, and her speed. She dug a bump from the little bag, braced her wrist to suck it back. And another. And a third for good luck.

"She's not very strong, remember? The ghost. I bet Monica thinks this is just going to be enough power to make Lucy solid, maybe even let her talk. She thinks she can bring her back. She's going to destroy the balance in the world just so she can play with her cousin again and Wen can fuck her or something."

"Damn, that's some sick— Fuck."

"Yeah, I— Oh."

He wasn't calling Wen a sick fuck. He was looking ahead, at the flames scorching the sky, engulfing a building several blocks down. At the corner of Twenty-fifth and Mercer, she guessed, and just as the thought crossed her mind, another explosion, a louder one, rocked the street and sent debris and fire flying into the air.

Not just the building on the corner. The building across the street, too. Bump and Terrible weren't fucking around. She hadn't expected them to.

And apparently neither did Slobag's men. Or Bump's, because plenty of both filled the street, fighting, gargantuan and mad in the bright, changing orange firelight.

Where was Terrible? Was he in there? She checked her phone: any message yet?

No.

Suspicion lurked in Lex's eyes, in the set of his shoulders, when he parked the car and turned to her. "Why Bump got he people here?"

She shrugged, didn't reply as they got out of the car.

"Tulip?"

Fuck. "Bump and Terrible both know we expected another murder here tonight. Maybe they sent some guys to look for Aros or something."

It sounded so lame she half expected him to pull his gun on her. But what was she supposed to do, admit she knew an attack was planned on that storeroom and hadn't told him?

No. Yes, she owed Lex loyalty. But she owed Terrible more, so no matter how shitty it might make her feel . . .

Gunshots sent all three of them racing back behind Lex's car to duck down and hide. "Some fucking fight, aye?"

"What do we do?" Beulah looked from one of them to the other. "Are you coming with us, Lex, or—?"

A wave of magic flew over the street, hard and fast as though driven by hurricane winds. Chess's knees buckled beneath her; she braced herself on Lex's trunk to keep from falling. Shit, that was so strong, so dark . . . so fucking powerful.

"Chess? Are you okay?"

The first effects of the wave passed but the magic remained, beating at her, thickening the air. Where was Terrible, was he feeling that? Her entire body went icy cold. If he was in that crowd, if he was fighting, and energy like that hit him . . . if he fell in the middle of that crowd, he'd be dead. He'd be killed, and the one who did it would be a hero on this side of town.

She swallowed. Swallowed again; too much saliva in her mouth, in spite of the amount of speed she'd done. She was going to be sick, that was the problem. Just thinking about Terrible on the ground, about guns pointing at his head or knives driven into his throat, made her want to be sick. Another swallow, a drink of water, but the energy around her made her feel even worse.

"They're starting," she managed to say in reply. "They've started, I can feel it. The ritual. The sacrifice."

Lex looked around. "Who they sacrificing? You got the knowledge?"

She shook her head. "Could be anybody. They could have grabbed somebody from the streets like they did before. Who knows."

About a block up, at the corner across from the burning warehouse, a parking garage rose from the broken street. Chess bet that was where they were, where they'd do their ritual. Maybe at the top of it? Maybe in the street, yeah, but they might want to be up high if they could; it would be more dramatic, and she had a feeling Monica was into that sort of thing. Anybody who dressed that badly had to be.

She pointed to the garage. "They're in there."

Chapter Thirty-five

As the dead's numbers swelled and swelled the task of defeating them began to look impossible. But still the Church fought on.

—*The Book of Truth*, Origins, Article 96

Her discomfort grew with every step. Which made sense, seeing as how every step took her closer to playing no-you-don't with a pair of homicidal crazies. Every step took her closer to the ritual they were performing, the knowledge that they'd stolen so much power from the earth that beating them would be almost impossible.

Every step carried her closer to the outskirts of the fighting crowd, too. She scanned the heads bobbing and ducking. Terrible's wasn't among them. She didn't know if that made her feel better or worse.

They crept along, hugging the crumbling wall of the apartment building opposite the garage despite the very real possibility it could blow up any second.

Shadows moved in the garage. Shadows? Right. Shadows she could see because candlelight flickered softly behind them. Aros and Monica. Possibly Wen Li. And their sacrifice, of course.

"Lex. Are you coming with me?"

He looked at the fight, then at Chess. "Come along on the start, leastaways, aye."

"Beulah?"

"Yes."

She hadn't expected that. From either of them, but especially not from Beulah; what possible reason would she have to risk her life?

Aside from the fact that if somebody didn't do it, Monica would end up so powerful she could destroy the world.

They trotted across the street onto the bottom level of the parking garage. Rusted trash cans, soggy boxes, rotted wood lined the walls of it, littered the floor, barely visible in the streaks of light from the flames across the street. Heat from them made her already sweaty skin even slicker.

One last look at her phone as they started up the wide ramp to the next level. Nothing. Where was Terrible, shit, where was he? Panic climbed up her spine from her stomach into her chest, making her eyes sting. Fuck, all that magic in the air, all those men fighting, anything could have happened to him . . .

She clamped down on the thought, on the horrifying images of his fallen body—the memories of it—and locked them away. He was fine. He was fine, he was just busy, and she had to make herself believe that because if she didn't she'd be ready to curl into a ball and wait until someone came along and killed her, too.

Beulah and Lex checked their own phones. Lex glanced at his sister. "Father called us up, I give he the ring-back, me." Beulah nodded. Chess wanted to protest, but she wasn't really in a position to do so, was she?

Outside, the fight got closer; bodies pressed against the low wall of the parking garage, barely visible to her as they neared the second level. Soon they'd be over it, in the garage itself. Shit. As if she didn't have enough to deal with, between Monica and Aros and Wen, and who knew how they were armed, or how long Lex would stay.

The ringing phone, just audible over the roar of the flames and the fight, cut through her thoughts. She spun around. Damn it, whose phone was—

Oh. Oh, shit.

Lex and Beulah stood, staring up toward the next level, and the next. Staring into the higher levels of the parking garage, where the phone had started ringing the second Lex had called Slobag; the phone that rang in unison with the sound coming from the earpiece of Lex's phone.

Slobag was in that building, with Monica and Aros, with Wen Li.

"Do you think he's known about this?" Chess broke the silence, hating to ask, but she had to. "I mean, do you think he's in on it, that he's here to watch?"

To their credit, neither Lex nor Beulah seemed shocked or offended by the question. "Ain't thinking he is, nay. Ain't really him kinda action, if you dig."

None of them wanted to state the obvious: if Slobag wasn't up there as part of the plot, chances were good he was the sacrifice. And unless they could stop that ritual fast, he was about to die a very unpleasant death.

Another explosion ripped through the air, another building turning into a shower of cement chunks and sparks. Holy fuck, what the hell were Bump and Terrible doing, destroying the entire block?

Shit, this was not a good position to be in. They had the low ground, their heads would be visible before they had a chance to do anything, and they had less space and less to hide behind than Aros, Monica, and Wen.

But it was their only option.

The light got brighter as more candles were lit. With every one the magic pressed heavier and heavier on her.

She put her hand on the railing and saw it was shaking. Her whole body shook, in fact, struggling against the magic in the air and the anxiety in her stomach. She wanted to be sick. She wanted to run. This didn't feel right, it felt like something awful was about to happen, something awful was happening, and with every step she took, the urge to hide grew stronger.

She gritted her teeth and kept going.

Aros's voice again, harsh in the damp magic-thick air. Calling the energy. Starting the ritual.

Chess took a deep breath, heard the others do the same. Lex raised his gun. Her muscles tightened. Behind her Beulah pulled a long, sharp stiletto from somewhere; a different knife from the one she'd had in Aros's apartment.

They ran the last few steps.

Halfway up she saw them: Wen and Monica. She'd barely registered them in her mind when gunshots echoed off the cement, deafening her so the next few seconds took place in ringing silence.

Monica stood just outside the glowing dark-purple circle Aros had created. Her mouth opened in a scream Chess couldn't hear and she jumped to the side, toward one of the thick cement pillars holding up the next level.

Her leap almost knocked Wen over. Wen, in whose hand a gun caught the light. Wen, on whose white sleeve a spot of blood had begun spreading. One bullet, at least, had hit.

Slobag and Aros were nowhere to be seen; inside the circle, she assumed, and started running for it before she finished the thought.

The closer she got the more it felt like running through soup, cold thick soup that clung to her skin and clogged her lungs. She kept going, pushing herself. It was only ten yards or so, not far at all, but it felt like miles, like the longest distance she'd ever run in her life.

And the fear. The energy that had filled her the night Jia died, that energy without shape or purpose but that found what was inside her and attached to it, became it, found the terror in her heart and created more, found everything else in her head and magnified it to an unbearable level.

Her heartbeat, and the voices. Not real ones. The memory voices. All of them crowded in on her; cruel voices, deceptively cheerful voices, voices cajoling and threatening and yelling. The sound of slamming doors and whimpers, the sound of belts and hands smacking flesh, the taste of hateful strangers in her mouth, the feel of their hands all over her, their laughter and pleasure somehow even more violent than their bodies.

She was nine, and a party was being held, and it was the kind of party where she was the star attraction. They had them once a month, and she counted the days until the next one with growing terror.

She was seven, and her foster brother liked pushing her into things, picking her up and dropping her on purpose. He'd laugh when she cried, kick her if she didn't. Sometimes his mother would take pity on her and give her a pill to take, but usually she didn't, and every day she was afraid to go home from school, afraid he'd be waiting along the way, afraid he'd be waiting just inside the door.

She was eleven, and they locked her in the closet when they weren't home so she wouldn't eat their food or touch their things, and sometimes they'd be gone all day and into the night, and she'd be trapped in the dark alone. There were bugs in the closet, rats in the closet, no toilet in the closet, and every time they left she wondered how badly they'd punish her if she made a mess or if that would be the time they didn't come back and she'd die in there.

Other sounds snapped into place, gave her merciful rest from the memories, even if only for a few seconds. More gunshots, more screams, a woman's screams.

Monica or Beulah? She didn't know, couldn't look. Men's voices, steel against cement.

Fear stiffened her muscles. Her body didn't want to move, didn't want to go farther. Her head didn't want to either. All those images, those feelings, all waiting inside that circle, and the second she broke it they would spill out all over her, drown her in slime, and she'd die the way she should have then.

But scariest of all was the thought of what would happen to the world, to the Church, to Terrible, if Monica and Aros weren't stopped, if they kept going and gathering power, taking it from the earth. Sooner or later the City would fail to hold; sooner or later, with the energy balance so skewed, the veil between the worlds might tear again as it had during Haunted Week, and the world would be invaded by the dead once more.

That's what kept her moving, fighting through all of it: thinking of them, all those people, Elder Griffin, Lex and Beulah, and especially Terrible.

She hit the purple wall of the circle hard. Her already speeding heart cranked up so fast she thought it would explode. Purple like the Binding she'd been placed under before, the spell that wanted to control her, that forced her to bend to its will.

This circle didn't. This circle didn't care if she obeyed or what she said. It was furious and it hated, and it was made of energy so twisted and insane she thought it might drive her crazy too. It burrowed into her head, blinded her, fed off her, hooked cold cruel claws into her brain and heart and soul and yanked.

But it didn't break. How the fuck did it not break, it was a circle, it was energy, she'd stepped through it and that should have broken it, holy shit, this was bad, this was really bad. This was unimaginable power, power that made her shiver.

Through the haze of vicious light she saw them, black

figures against the glow: Slobag tied to the cement pillar, Aros before him with the knife raised. Shit, she was almost too late, just in time—

She lunged for Aros, her arms outstretched. Her vision blurred and spun, terror made her clumsy, but she hit him. Didn't knock him down, but hit him.

He punched her. More lights exploded behind her eyes; hot hollow-feeling pain in her nose and cheeks. She stumbled back, barely managed to keep hold of his robe. Tried to push him again, overwhelmed by the smell of the fabric, dust and slime, rotten old blood and darkness, the penny-biting scent of insanity cloying and musty beneath it all.

Candles lined the circle, and his robe brushed the floor. Maybe if she could push him into the candles it would catch fire. Hell, maybe if she could push him out of the circle it would break. Maybe he could break it.

He pulled his arm back. Against the field of bright purple she saw the knife, the long wicked blade deflecting the light as it rose, hitting her eyes with neon shine as it started to descend. Fuck!

She dove for his legs, trying to knock him off balance. More pain, sharp in her side like her skin was screaming. He'd slashed her. Hot blood began soaking into her shirt.

More screams outside. Another gunshot. Who was shooting, what was going on? Why hadn't anyone come to help her, could they not get through the circle, were they busy? Were they dead? Fuck, what was happening?

Aros's voice cut through her thoughts, cut through her mind like a blade of ice, words of power clouding it further. Agony tore down her spine, throbbed in her head. She fell to the cement, fell on her cut and bleeding side and hardly noticed.

More blood fell on her, spattered hot and thick on her crouched back, in her hair. She knew it was blood, smelled it, felt it, and her heart stopped in her chest as she looked up.

He'd stabbed Slobag.

Slobag writhed against the ropes holding him fast, his jaw working against the gag tied behind his head. She had a split second to look at the wound, to decide it probably wasn't fatal, that in his haste Aros had missed, when she saw him draw back to try again.

Her hand shot out, punching him in the kneecap as hard as she could. It shifted with a satisfying pop. His scream sounded even better.

He tumbled to the ground, landed on his knee and screamed again. Good. Blood dripped from her hair into her eyes, fuck she could hardly see, and Aros lifted the knife once more.

She rose onto her own knees, caught his hand in both of hers. Fuck. No way was she strong enough to beat him at this. She might have the strength of the desperate, the strength of one trying to save her life—trying to save many lives—but he had the preternatural strength of the insane, and he would win.

She raised her knee and slammed it into his balls as hard as she could. Not very hard, unfortunately; she didn't have a lot of room to move. But enough to make him double over, enough to make him drop the knife.

Chess grabbed it, jumped up. Stab him? If she killed him the spell would activate; it needed a death. If he got up too quickly, he could attack her again.

If she and Slobag both got out of the circle, would it break the spell? Did she have time to get him out?

Cement chips flew from the pillar, inches from Slobag's head. Holy shit, they were shooting, they were shooting into the circle, who the hell had the gun and would shoot into the circle?

Slobag's eyes, those eyes that had only been cold and

arrogant every time she'd seen them before, met hers, wide with fear. Begging her to help him.

If he was free he could help her. They could both fight. He could help Lex, help Beulah, while she focused on ending the spell.

She brought the knife down on the ropes holding him. They stuck; the blade looked sharp, but it wasn't sharp enough to cut rope with one blow. Fuck! Aros still moaned on the ground, but he wouldn't be down for long. Any second he'd get up and come after her, probably even more enraged.

She sawed at the ropes as fast as she could. The blade kept scraping the cement with a horrible screech that made her teeth vibrate. She freed his upper arms. Slobag reached for his gag. Chess ducked down to hack at the binding around his legs.

More cement chips flew. Another bullet. How many fucking bullets did they have? Every one of them echoed against the walls and ceiling, echoed in her head, sent more fear through her body. Every one of those shots might have hit Lex or Beulah. Might have killed them.

Aros tackled her. Her arm hit the cement with a painful scrape; the impact jarred her vision.

But she didn't drop the knife. She couldn't. She had that knife in a fucking death grip and no way was she letting go, not until this was over, not until it was safe. The knife was her talisman, her only weapon, everything she had.

She swung it back. From her position on the ground she couldn't see where she was swinging, but she felt it sink into Aros's body. He screamed; not a groan or a grunt, a scream, and she looked over at him and hot wild triumph roared through her head. She'd gotten him good, right in the thigh.

Blood spurted from the wound as she yanked the blade out and started working at Slobag's ropes again.

No time, no time for this, what was going on outside the circle, what the hell was happening—

The ropes gave. Slobag reeled away from the pillar. Aros got to his knees, grabbed Chess from behind, his hand around her throat, his arm locked around her waist.

She slashed at him with the knife but he was crushing her arm to her side just below the elbow so she couldn't reach around. She dipped her head, slammed it back. His teeth hit her scalp, his grip loosened but tightened again. Shit!

Slobag grabbed him, started pulling him backward. Pulling both of them backward, because Aros wouldn't let go of her. His face hit the back of her head again with a jaw-jarring crack. Slobag must have punched him in the head.

Screams outside grew louder. Monica. Monica frantic and hysterical. She thought she heard Lex, thought she heard Beulah. This was it, Slobag was free. Even if he didn't get Aros off her he'd almost reached the wall of the circle, and if they could get out of the circle—especially if they could get Aros out of the circle—it might break, the spell might break, and they could end it all.

She threw herself sideways, hoping to shake Aros off that way, hoping Slobag could get an arm locked around his neck or something as she went.

Another gunshot. Aros's hand tightened at her throat, she was choking, she couldn't breathe—

Not his hand. That wasn't why she was choking. She was choking because of the magic in the air, a thick black fog of it, rolling over everything. She was choking because the purple wall of the circle disappeared, because beyond it was darkness and power rolled out of that darkness, power that hit her hard, that clutched at

her, tried to absorb her. Aros's screams of joy, the feral
sound of his triumph, pierced her ears like spikes.

The power had been accessed, the spell completed,
how the fuck did that happen, how had— Oh no. Oh
fuck, oh no . . .

She turned her head on a neck that creaked and felt
stiff. Turned it just in time to see Slobag fall, to see the
jagged hole in his head. He'd been shot. He was dead.

They had lost.

Chapter Thirty-six

Energy is simply power. It is what the spell caster makes of it that creates magic.
—*Introduction to Church Magic,* by Elder Drew

It seemed to take him hours to fall, his eyes already blank and glazed, already devoid of life. As he fell, so fell Chess's heart, lower and lower; as he fell, so did the power increase until it hurt her, clawed at her, made her head throb. Aros and Monica had all that power now, how the fuck was she going to stop them—

If she didn't manage to get Aros off her, she wouldn't. She leaned forward, her lungs bursting, her entire body screaming for air. Only one chance, if she didn't manage this she'd pass out and that would be it. Explosions of red already popped behind her eyes.

She threw herself back as hard as she could, slamming Aros into the pavement with her on top of him. His hands loosened enough for her to take one breath, one clean sweet breath, and enough for her to move her hand.

She brought the knife down into his thigh again.

This time she didn't let it sit. There was no time to be merciful. She dragged it up, shoved it to the side, the handle slippery with blood, her hand coated with it, hot and disgusting and stinking of copper and crazy.

Aros's screams of triumph became screams of agony.

Chess barely heard them. How could she stop the energy from seeping up from the earth, what did she need to do?

If the spell ended, would it stop?

Aros let go of her, still screaming. She tugged the knife from his flesh and rolled away, pushing herself out of the glowing circle.

Wen Li lay dead on the stained cement floor. His was the only body—oh please let his be the only body—but where were the others, where had they gone?

"Chess!"

She spun around, already throwing herself to the ground, her heart recognizing his voice before her head did. Terrible, it was Terrible, he was there, but this wasn't the time to look up. He wouldn't have shouted like that except in warning.

The bullet flew over her head. Did Monica have a gun? What the fuck?

She did. Monica had a gun, and the metal caught the light and Chess rolled in the other direction, scrambled to run away. Terrible was on the other side of the low wall dividing the parking aisles. She caught a glimpse of him when he jumped up to look for her again—an ugly slash broke the right side of his face, cutting from cheekbone almost to his chin. Even in that quick glimpse she could see the blood soaking into his shirt. Even in that quick glimpse her heart flooded with relief.

She didn't know where Lex and Beulah were. Had no idea if they knew their father was dead.

Didn't matter. She ducked behind a pillar where she could see the wall Terrible crouched behind and as much of the rest of the garage as she could.

The magic didn't lessen, that awful magic that felt like the screams of tortured souls. The energy was taking over. The spell was ending; it didn't need the spell anymore. How was that— Oh. It had to be the fight. All that energy, all that violence and death in the air kept feeding the spell, kept it going, dozens of sacrifices as the circle faded.

And that power, that unimaginable power that was the whole reason for the spell: Was Aros absorbing it, letting it sink into him? What was he doing with it, what was he going to do next? It was so strong, so heavy, it was everywhere. It thrummed against her skin, tantalizing, strong and dark.

Changing. As though it knew her, knew what she wanted. It could be anything she wanted it to be. It could save her or it could kill her; maybe they were the same. It could be the flaming pyre she rode into her own destruction, could take her all the places she tried so hard to go, to that place where it was quiet and peaceful, the place where she didn't exist anymore.

For one long moment desire paralyzed her. She wanted it so bad, so fucking bad, she could erase everything, erase herself, no more pain and shame, no more memories, no more fear and cold and uncertainty. Her fists clenched until her nails dug into her palms. She could have it, she could have all of it, the nothing she craved. The nothing that was everything.

But that nothing didn't have Terrible in it. He wasn't there and she wouldn't have him if she gave in, and when that realization slipped into her head the bonds holding her snapped open like worn-out buttons and she could think again, move again, see through her eyes flooded with tears. The power was still there, still deep, still clutching her, but she could breathe. She was herself. She didn't belong to it.

Her gaze flew over the garage floor. The rain had started falling hard again, slanting through the open spaces. Water streamed across the cement, formed puddles that reflected the blackness. The circle faded, and Slobag's body appeared, crumpled on the floor.

Beulah started screaming. She screamed, and screamed, and her voice sliced through Chess and stung her already burning eyes. That was Beulah's father. That was Lex's father. She couldn't imagine how they felt, she'd failed them, she was supposed to save his life and she'd failed.

Monica ran across the empty space to Aros's side, tried to help him stand. The water on the floor mixed with blood where he lay, where Slobag's body lay, red streaks of it in the dark water.

More noise behind her, more men making their way up the ramp, a few of Slobag's men with rifles who apparently planned to start shooting the crowd below. They caught sight of Terrible, and she practically saw lightbulbs go off over their heads.

Even as she turned to say something, do something—she didn't know what—she saw the pale shape rise from Slobag's body. His spirit. His ghost. It had been trapped by the circle, his psychopomp hadn't been able to come for him, and now he was trapped.

"Daddy!" Beulah's voice shrieked across the empty space. Chess turned and saw her struggling to run, to reach her father, with Lex holding her back. His lips formed words Chess couldn't hear, words she thought were probably not her business to hear.

Then gunshots. Shot after shot after shot, again and again, and Chess looked up from her place on the floor and saw Beulah shooting, over and over, Lex's gun flashing in her hands. Lex just stood and watched, unmoving; he made no attempt to stop his sister.

Chess understood that very well. She saw the look on Beulah's face as clearly as he did. If he tried to take that gun back he'd get blasted in the head, and he knew it.

Bullets flying everywhere, chipping the cement on the poles and the ceiling and the floor; it rained down on her, caught her skin in tiny, painful cuts.

She didn't know how long it went on. Ten seconds,

ten minutes. An endless eyeblink of a moment while Beulah screamed and shot the world. Chess knew exactly how that felt. She did that deep inside herself every minute of every day.

Finally it stopped. Complete silence. Dead silence. Whether it was because they all stood still, barely breathing, waiting for something to happen, or because her eardrums were completely fucked and she couldn't hear anything—maybe never would again—she didn't know.

Then Beulah's sob broke it, and she knew. With that sound came a sort of exhale, as though they'd all been waiting, and the world snapped back, everything snapped back. Lex had his arms around Beulah again, pulling her away down the ramp, and she was going with him. Terrible had jumped Slobag's men. She couldn't see their guns anymore but they all had knives. That fight would not end soon. Fuck!

She couldn't leave Slobag like that. For the moment he simply stood watching, but he wouldn't stay like that for long. Not all ghosts wanted to kill, just almost all. Ninety-nine point nine percent. And sometimes they managed to hold on to their humanity right after death. Some of them even managed to hold on for several minutes, but not usually any longer than that. She couldn't leave him there, couldn't condemn him to that, not with Lex and Beulah so close. She couldn't let them see him like that if he turned—when he turned.

Chess didn't see any weapons lying around, either. Her fingers still curled around the knife, so tightly it hurt. Everything hurt anyway, her heart hurt, every inch of skin hurt from power and fighting and worry. Monica had a gun and Chess didn't, and she had to find a way to beat Monica and stop the spell while heavy magic confused her thoughts and made her sick.

No time to salt a circle, not to mention that trying to

do so would probably get her ass shot. She'd just have to hope her lousy luck changed and her psychopomp didn't go rogue.

When the psychopomp came it opened a passage to the City. A metaphysical passage, one that made a small, weak vacuum. One weak enough that the psychopomp could easily carry the spirit through it, but if she could jack it up, if she could feed extra power into it . . .

She knew how to do it, too.

Her bag was still in the circle. She'd need to get it, fuck, it was about three feet away from where Monica and Aros hid behind the pole.

How many bullets did Monica have left?

Did it matter? Chess didn't have a choice, right? Right. Breathe. Breathe. Breathe. Go! *GoGoGoGOGO!*

She flipped herself around the pole and ran toward her bag. The power from the earth emanated icy gray death-breath toward the remains of the circle that made her gag. She wouldn't make it without them seeing her, she knew she wouldn't—

She was right. Just as she ducked to reach for the strap of her bag, someone grabbed her hair. Grabbed it and yanked it, hard.

She hit the cement. Didn't even have time to feel the scrape on her elbows, the pain of impact; wouldn't have felt it anyway because the pain in her head canceled it out. Canceled out everything. The hand kept pulling, dragging her by the hair, fuck, pulling it out of her head, and there was nothing she could do without making it worse.

Except twist enough to see their legs. Monica's legs. Maybe Aros was too injured, maybe he was bleeding out behind the post. Maybe someone would shoot Monica. Maybe both of those things would happen. She could only hope.

Hope—and grab Monica's legs just below the knee and tug as hard as she could.

The knees buckled. Monica went down. Chess went with her, lunged on top of her. Yes!

Punching Monica in the face felt better than anything that had happened to her since she'd climbed out of the Chevelle that afternoon. The pain of it shot up her arm and vibrated deep in her bones; glorious pain, almost a sexual thrill from getting to do what she'd wanted so badly to do.

But Monica was too powered up. Just touching her skin was like sticking her hand into the blades of a fan. When Monica slapped her and knocked her onto the floor, that power vibrated around her, through her soul, hurting far more than the physical pain.

Aros reached for her but she managed to duck away. When he moved, more blood flowed from his leg. He really was bleeding out. When he died, would the hole close, what would happen to it when he died, if he died?

The strap in her hand. Her feet hitting the cement, awkward and unsteady, trying to get her balance and move fast, fast enough to get away from both of them.

Another shot. Where had it gone?

More yells, more sounds in the background as the fight moved farther into the garage. Those men weren't going to stop, the flames ate the air so all she could see on that side, through the open spaces between the floors, was fire. Smoke drifted into her eyes and nose, making them sting.

Monica followed her, stumbling but gaining. The grin on her face was awful, terrifying. Chess waited for her, wrapping her bag's strap around her wrist, her muscles tense. Then Monica was upon her. Chess pulled back her fist, threw it out, and caught Monica solidly in the chest, just below the neck. Damn it, she'd wanted to hit her in the throat.

Monica stumbled back, gasping. She wheeled around, hands crossed over her chest as if she was trying to pull away an imaginary cord. Aros grabbed her, held her.

Time to work fast.

Chess pulled her psychopomp from her bag, untangled it from its silk shroud, and set it on the floor.

Chapter Thirty-seven

These spells take energy from outside sources. Any spell that requires too much from you is best left to Church employees. Putting yourself into a spell can be dangerous.
—*You Can Do This! A Guide for Beginners,*
by Molly Brooks-Cahill

She didn't bother with her stang or anything else. What was the point? She didn't have a circle. Didn't have anything but hope to keep her psychopomp from killing them all, which meant their chances of getting through this alive—especially her own chances—were about as good as her chances of discovering she was the long-lost daughter of some millionaire who couldn't wait to have her back. Hope wasn't something she'd ever had much of.

But that part way down deep inside her, the part that had been buried, the part she thought might have grown, even a tiny bit, over the last month . . . it was there, and she took what she could from it.

And she hoped.

Hoped Terrible would finish with Slobag's men soon and take care of Monica and Aros. Hoped the tingling and burning of her tattoos, the itching, stronger than anything she'd ever felt, so strong she thought she might go crazy from it and wanted to shed her skin like a snake, didn't mean the earth's power was fading to the point that ghosts were starting to appear.

Hoped that she could do what needed to be done, that

she could be good enough to do it, even for just that one moment.

The cement cold beneath her knees. Pain in her nose, her left eye swollen. Pain in her scalp, her arms, her legs—hell, pain everywhere. She pushed it all aside, cleared her head as much as she could.

One second of listening to her heartbeat, her breath in her chest. Concentrate. Silence.

The power around her still battered at her, that dark promise she'd refused before. Now she accepted it. Opened herself to it, let it wash through her.

She'd been right. Oh, fuck, she'd been right, it was everything, it felt like everything, every drug she'd ever taken and then some, every high, every orgasm, every rush of power wiping her clean.

It swept through her, taking the fear still clenching her chest. It took the memories—they disappeared, they were gone. It took the shame, the sadness, the pain, the blame, all of those things, every bad thing she'd ever felt. It took her deepest and most horrible Truth, the one she'd had all of her life, her knowledge that she was nothing, deserved nothing, meant nothing. That all disappeared, gone in the space of a single breath.

She wasn't Chess anymore, not entirely. She was someone else, someone with all of her power, all of her skills, someone whose life began the day she stepped into Church for her first day of training and for whom the cold hellish years before didn't exist.

A Chess who didn't need pills to get through the day. A Chess who lived on-grounds with everyone else, who could be part of that life because she didn't sweat and shake at the idea of letting others know her, the thought of not having space of her own, or of not having privacy and distance because she needed it so bad. A Chess who was confident, happy, strong, who had lifelong friends and made new ones easily. A Chess who let herself be loved.

That Chess opened herself more, let more of that power into herself—hell, she didn't let it in, she sucked it in, she pulled on it the way the old Chess inhaled Dream in the pipe room—until she blazed with it. She was a live wire humming there in the gloom, a shining golden light so bright it would blind them all, proud before the black hole opening between her world and the other side, before the endless sea of ghosts moving across the shore.

And she wasn't even worried. Wasn't even scared.

Instead of Aros's knife she grabbed her own from her pocket—she'd been given it, hadn't she? Who gave that to her? That had been the other life, the one she didn't know anymore—and sliced the point, deadly sharp, across her left pinky, where earlier wounds had barely closed.

Droplets of blood fell on the skull. "I call on the escorts of the land of the dead. By my blood and by my power I call you. By my blood and by my power I command you. Take these spirits back to their place of silence, take them back to their place of rest."

The skull began to vibrate. Somewhere behind her, noises, grunts and scrapes and yelps. A fight. She didn't—couldn't—care.

"I offer a sacrifice to the escorts for their aid." More blood, faster now. The air before her rippled like heat rising off pavement. Wider and wider, taller and taller. The gateway opening.

"Let my power be pure," she cried, and took the energy inside her, that immense incredible energy, and threw it into the gate. Fed it into the skull.

The gate exploded into being. The dog did the same, leaping off the floor, bones and skin and fur growing from it to form a body. Its eyes glowed green just like they were supposed to; it was silent just like it was supposed to be. Everything was working; everything would always work for this new Chess, who smiled with confidence as magic rolled from her fingertips, who kept smiling as she stepped back from the gateway.

The immensely powerful gateway. She was a conduit, and the power ran from the hole through her into the gate.

The dog bounded ahead, exactly where she wanted it to go. Too much life in her, too much power in her, and as it moved she realized she could control it. That psychopomp was *her* psychopomp; her blood and power had created it and she could make it do anything she wanted to.

It wasn't even hard. It was like bending her fingers, so simple a child could do it.

She sent the dog after Slobag, considered sending it after Aros and Monica as well. No, it would be too hard to keep hold of one ghost while pulling a soul from a still-living body. The psychopomp might get confused.

So how to end that spell?

Monica and Aros had created a totem to hold their ghosts to the earth. But they'd used that totem in their ritual, had had it there because they were trying to direct the energy to it, and to Lucy as well as themselves. It was still there.

Where was it, what was it? What would they have that belonged to a young girl, a girl who dated lots of boys, who maybe even dated a teacher, what could be personal enough?

Jia and Maia had been holding a book that day when Old Chess had found them outside the school. A used-looking book with a cracked cover. A diary, a school notebook, whatever it was. That was it. That was the totem.

She turned her head, scanned the floor for it. Aros and Monica were digging around in a backpack; that could not be good.

But it was too late for them. They were going to lose, they'd already lost, because when people went up against New Chess that's what happened to them. She ran toward them.

"Where's the totem?" Her voice sounded so light and confident and cheerful. Almost not even like hers. Happy. It was weird, but only for a second. Then it was awesome, the voice she was meant to have.

Monica lunged for her. This time her skin didn't burn, this time it didn't hurt to touch her. This time Chess was the stronger one, the more powerful one, and she ducked Monica's swing with slow calm ease, her voice still cheerful. "Where is it?"

Monica, in contrast, sounded like something about to be run over for the tenth time as she swung again. "I don't know what you mean."

Chess caught her hand. All the power in her body, all that energy . . . she could sting Monica with it, let it hit her, and she did. Monica's face paled in a way that would have pleased the old Chess. The new Chess didn't want to hurt anyone.

"Yes, you do. Look, it's over. Give me the totem, and I can end this, and you get to live." For a while, anyway. But she didn't say that. Monica didn't need to know she'd be executed. "It's that book, right? The flowered one, the journal, the diary? Where is it?"

"You can't have it."

"Where is it, Monica?"

Monica didn't answer, but Chess didn't need her to. While she'd been talking, Aros had started slinking off to her right, back to the remains of his circle where the book clearly sat beneath his firedish. How Chess had missed it when she was in that circle she didn't know, but she hadn't been herself then, had she? She'd been that old Chess. The losery junkie one.

A bark from behind her. The psychopomp had Slobag. It sat at the gate, looking at her. Of course. He was probably bound by the totem as well, since he'd been created in the circle. In fact, the spell might be bound to the totem, she might be able to end that spell by destroying it.

She was almost done. She practically flew over to where the circle had been; the book lay just around the corner of the post.

Monica shrieked. Yes! Heck yeah, that was it, she had it, time to clean up this mess.

Over to the gate, that glowing strong gate so wide and ready like a starving mouth about to be fed a gourmet meal. It was ready, the dog was ready.

Slobag was ready. She saw his face, saw him looking at the two people, the man and the woman, standing on the ramp watching him. Funny, she didn't see hatred in his eyes, or the violence she'd normally see from a ghost. Perhaps because of the talisman, the spell's power, maybe it had helped him hold onto some vestige of humanity. Chess didn't know.

But she did know that when she threw that talisman into the gate, he would follow it. He had to, because he was bound to it.

The old Chess might have worried or wondered if it would work. Now she knew it would.

With one confident stroke she flung the book through the gate.

Monica's scream hurt her ears. Monica's body slammed hers into the cement. Monica's fingers curled in her hair, yanked her head up. Oh no, Chess braced herself, stiffened her neck to keep Monica from driving her face into the cement. She needed to flip over. She'd still be beneath Monica, but if she could flip over she could at least hit back.

Slobag and the psychopomp disappeared through the gate. The skull fell to the ground before it. Chess felt the gate shiver, felt it react. The gate had her power and was connected to her, and she felt it do its job. Some of the earth energy from the spell started seeping into it, going back to where it came from, so slowly.

Too slowly for her. She felt so . . . good. So great, and she didn't want to waste a second. Once she got this finished she could leave, leave this stinky place and head back to Church, where she belonged. Where she could be happy—could keep being happy, of course she was happy, why wouldn't she be?

Monica's palms slapping her, the back of her head, her back. "You fucking asshole, let me go, I'll kill you—"

Chess ignored those hands, and those uncouth words. With one mighty shove she flipped herself over, catching Monica's face with her open palm and knocking her to the floor.

That spell had to stop, that energy had to stop cycling. Chess felt the gate again, reached for it in her head, reached for it with her power, and pushed more into it. It was strong, it was big, but it needed to be stronger. It needed to pull. She twisted it a little, tweaked it somehow, and the vacuum increased. Yes!

Stronger and stronger. The energy followed the book. The hole was strong, the gate was strong, and all of that was connected to Chess. She was the strongest.

Monica jumped up. Her scream pierced Chess's ears. "Lucy!"

She started running, running toward the gate, and Chess reached for her even though she knew she was too far away. "Monica! No, don't—"

Monica ran through the gate.

Light. Blinding, searing light, brighter than the fire outside. Chess bent over, shielded her eyes. The heat of it warmed her chilled skin.

But it wasn't a good light. It was an impact, a backdraft, and the heat faded and she opened her eyes and saw blood everywhere, blood and hair and bits of things she didn't even want to know what they were, scraps of horrible fabric.

Monica had exploded. She'd crossed the line into the gate, and she'd exploded.

The thought barely had time to skip through Chess's mind before it happened. The power. The power of the hole, the magic of it. The hole wasn't closing, hadn't closed yet. Instead it was feeding from the gate, they were feeding off each other, forming a circuit of magic. A circuit that ran right through her.

The power wasn't leaving anymore. She assumed that meant the spell's connection to the talisman had disappeared, which was a reasonable assumption to make. And probably correct. She knew how magic worked, after all. She'd been doing this job a long time.

But being right didn't always mean being glad about it, and in this case she didn't think she was. The power was equal, running through her, and the energy didn't have to go anywhere as long as both were open, and the spell wasn't ending.

It needed to end, and she needed to end it.

She reversed the circuit through herself. Took from the hole to give back to the gate, more and more. Watched it shrink.

A disturbance in the power behind her. Aros. Aros limp-shuffling like the Hunchback of Notre Dame, his bloody knife—the one he'd used to stab Slobag—dangling from his hand. Hatred blazed in his eyes, hatred aimed at her. Darn it, she didn't want to have to fight with him, too.

She didn't. Instead a man leaped from the shadows, a huge man with black hair. He knocked Aros down with a horrible splatty *thud*. She knew him, didn't she? Her heart somersaulted, but her mind . . . couldn't quite seem to grasp it.

Terrible. That was his name. What kind of name was that?

Whatever. What mattered was ending the spell.

She could close the gate now, end the spell herself. And she knew in that strong part of herself, that big well of hope and joy and confidence and magic, that big well that looked forward to the next day and the next and the next because only good things would happen to her from then on, that she could close them easily. They wanted something in order to close, and she had something to give them.

But she could keep whatever of the power she wanted.

And she would. She'd keep it. She'd hold on to it. That old Chess, the addict Chess, the one who hated herself and whose life was one long story of pain and horror? She was gone, just a vague memory like a movie Chess had seen once and hadn't enjoyed. She could be gone for good, she didn't need to come back. She wouldn't come back unless Chess agreed to bring her back. Eventually she'd forget it had ever existed, ever happened. She'd forget all of it, and by forgetting, she'd make it so it didn't happen.

She'd needed to sacrifice something to open the gate, needed to let go of something. It still waited for another sacrifice. To close the gate, to close the hole, she had to give it some power, some piece of her. Something.

She could get rid of all the pain. She could throw Old Chess onto the fire and rise like a phoenix fresh and new, start the rest of her life—the life she should have had—that very minute.

One simple movement, and nothing but happiness from then on. All of her hopes and dreams coming true. What the heck was she waiting for?

Chapter Thirty-eight

There are sacrifices and there are sacrifices. Only the Church knows the difference. Only the Church can decide.
—*The Book of Truth*, Laws, Article 508

The pieces of that old Chess—not pieces, more like images, quick flashing images that didn't make a lot of sense, at least not to her—raced through her head. All so miserable, so painful. This was hardly even a sacrifice, it was a mercy killing.

She stood there staring as those images flashed in front of her. The last memories, the last vestiges of that other girl who'd been in her body. She owed it to her to watch them, didn't she?

"Chess?" Not a familiar voice, not really. Not to her. But it should have been. It meant something.

The images in her head slowed, and she turned to see that big guy standing there, an uncertain look on his craggy, bleeding face. "You right, baby? Be a problem?"

Terrible.

He never called her *baby*, though. Did he? That didn't seem quite right, *baby*.

Movement to her right. The man and the woman—Lex and Beulah were their names, right?—and they looked so sad and shocked and pale, and she remembered them, too. Slobag was their father. Lex . . . she'd slept with Lex, hadn't she? Gee, she'd really been kind of a slut.

But then, she could see the attraction. He was a handsome guy, even though he looked awful at that particular moment. But the old Chess still had those memories, saw him at his best. Saw him laughing. Saw him naked—well, that was interesting—saw him sleeping and smiling and smoking and being her friend, saw him fighting at her side, being fond of her. Liking her.

And Beulah. A new person but one who actually seemed to like her, too, who she actually sort of seemed to understand, didn't she?

What difference did it make? She could get new friends. She didn't need these people, who were they? They certainly weren't good people by any normal standard. Not by the standards of decent, proper people. Lex sold drugs or something, didn't he? And she thought she remembered him killing people. And Beulah was kind of a bitch, right, and—she was an adulteress, if Chess remembered correctly. She was sleeping with a married man, in violation of the law. Shameful.

And Terrible . . . he was just a thug. A violent thug at that. And he had something to do with drugs, too, and prostitution and all manner of other things. He was not a good person. What redeeming qualities could a person like that have?

No. She didn't need those people. None of them were worth her time. She could move on, she could find new friends, have a new life, the one she'd always dreamed of. It would be so good, so darn good, fun and happy and easy, and she could leave all the bad behind once and for all and really live.

Decision made. She gathered it all up, all of the memories and thoughts and tics and habits and everything else that made up Old Chess. Gathered it in her head like a bundle in her arms and got ready to throw it, to cast it into the hole and close it for good. And when it closed and the power left, the gate would close on its own.

"Chess? What's troubling?"

He loved her.

It came to her in a flood then, one huge hot rush of jumbled memories and images. But not like last time. Not painful ones, not rough ones. These were . . . they were security and warmth and happiness, and they were even brighter because of the contrast. They were safety and kindness. They were feeling cared about and special and protected, caring about someone and protecting him and feeling that together they were unbeatable, and its being all so amazing because it was new. And— Whoa, some of those memories were pretty intense, too, intensity that made heat rush to various parts of her body that kind of embarrassed her.

All of the bad stuff came with it. All of the horrible memories and pain, the insecurities, the hatred of herself and the rest of the world, the exhaustion and the drugs and everything else.

But Lex came with it, and Beulah came with it. Elder Griffin—she remembered him, he cared about her, too— came with it.

And Terrible came with it, and those long nights lying in bed barely able to breathe because she thought her happiness would choke her as his chest rose and fell beneath her head. Or the mornings when she woke up and he was looking at her, watching her sleep, and there was something in his eyes that she knew was hers, just hers, that nobody else in the world had ever seen before.

With that came the uncertainty, the fear. She'd been terrified, hadn't she? Somewhere inside her she'd been terrified every minute of every day that she'd lose him and go back to being alone, only worse because she'd know what she'd missed.

But somehow the knowledge that if she threw it away now, threw it into the hole, she wouldn't actually remember, wouldn't know what she'd missed, didn't help. She didn't want to forget it. She didn't want to lose it. Even if it ended, even if she ended up with her heart broken into thousands of pieces, she couldn't bear the thought of forgetting it. She'd fought for it, she'd fought so hard, she'd earned it. It was hers and hers alone, the only thing in the world that really and truly was.

Her power was hers, yes, but she wasn't the only witch in the world. She wasn't the only Churchwitch in the world, or the only Debunker. Not the only addict, not the only one with pain, not the only one who hated and feared and felt sick and wanted to die but didn't have the guts to do something about it. Not the only one who listened to the music she listened to, drove a car like hers, wore her hair in that dyed-black Bettie Page cut. Not the only woman in the world who dressed like her, ate the same foods, drank the same things, read the same books. She wasn't the only one of any of those things; yes, she was unique, but only in the mundane way that everyone was unique.

But she was the only woman—the only one in the entire world—Terrible loved. And he did love her; the new Chess could see it so clearly, how obvious it was, how obvious it had been for so long.

If she lost that, she'd lose what made her special. She'd be happy, yes. She'd find some other man eventually, probably, and maybe he'd be good enough. She'd look different, act different. Be different.

She would never again feel that, though, that feeling of being the most special woman in the entire world, of knowing no one else could possibly be as happy as she was because they honestly didn't know how lucky they were, how truly and amazingly lucky. Because they didn't feel like they'd been lost their entire lives and they'd finally found home.

If she gave up the memories, she'd lose that. She wouldn't remember it, it would fade like tissue paper in the sun.

She wouldn't quit. She wouldn't give up. She'd never done it before and she wouldn't now, she'd fought all her life to be someone and something and she'd done it, and maybe she wasn't the greatest person in the world but she was a person and that was enough. She was a person who'd achieved something, and if other people thought it wasn't good enough, that she wasn't good enough, that her weaknesses were all that mattered? That was their right, but she was still a person, and she still deserved to be proud of her achievements.

She wanted those back. She wanted that love back. Wanted her friends. Wanted it all, because it was who she was, and if she gave it up she wouldn't be herself and she truly would be dead.

Before she could stop herself, before she could double-think it, she ripped the power out of her chest and mind and soul, ripped it out and threw it at the hole as hard as she could.

For a second nothing happened. Oh no, what if it didn't work, what if she'd lost anyway, what if it wanted her first sacrifice, her original sacrifice, what if she had to give up the old Chess because she didn't have a choice?

Then the old Chess would have died saving them all, and that would have to be enough.

The screaming grew louder so slowly, so steadily, that she didn't realize at first she heard it. The second she became aware of it she couldn't hear anything else. It was there, and it was everything, so loud it hurt her head, hurt her all the way down.

It was her scream. Not an audible scream; her mouth wasn't even open. It was the scream of her soul, the screams inside her, all of those memories and pain and horror and shame and everything else. All of it coming back, hitting her so hard it knocked her over. She barely felt the ground beneath her, it was so loud, she cringed on the floor, curled up and wrapped her arms around herself, her hands over her head, trying to hide. So awful, it was so awful . . .

Arms around her. Hard, strong arms, the kind that could keep her from flying apart at the seams. Terrible's arms. Shit, he was holding her, making her safe, and the screaming quieted enough for her to grab hold of him and bury her face in his neck. Tears poured from her eyes, tears because of what she'd lost and what she'd gained, what she'd almost given up and what she *had* given up. Tears because she knew she'd forget it soon, that she'd never remember making that decision and how it felt.

"I chose you," she managed, choking out the words in a strangled, warbly sounding whisper. "I chose you, I chose you all but I chose *you*, I love you so much and I chose you—"

His lips brushed her forehead. "Hush now, Chessie, I know, ain't nothin—"

"No, no, it is. I could have given it all up and been different." Her long, shuddering breath burned in her chest, but she couldn't stop. Had to get it out before she forgot. "I could have been not me, some other girl who didn't—but I didn't do it, I stayed, I stayed because I love you, and I want to be with you and if you weren't there I wouldn't want to be. I chose you."

He always smelled good. Even before, even when they'd first met—well, not when they first met but when they first spoke, really spoke, the night he took her to Chester Airport. The night her entire life changed. She'd noticed it even then, that it felt kind of nice to be close to him.

Now she knew what it was. He smelled like home.

"Love you, too, Chess." He held her tighter, almost as tightly as she held him. If she'd had fingernails to dig into him she would have, hooks to catch him with and never let go. "You got that, aye? Ain't you know it? Love you right, till it hurts. Ain't goin nowhere, don't need to cry, 'sall right up—"

She kissed him. Kissed him as hard as she could, as deep as she could. She'd never be able to explain what had happened. Hell, he'd be hurt if he knew she'd even considered leaving him behind.

And it was already fading anyway, disappearing from her head, sinking below the surface of the blood-red memory ocean. Almost gone. No one would ever know that other Chess or know she'd existed, not even her.

But she'd remember this, this moment, this suspended moment outside of everything else. This moment alone in his arms, with his mouth passionate and fierce on hers.

His hands touched her cheeks, slid into her hair. He always touched her like she was special, like she was precious to him, and for the first time she thought maybe she could believe that she was. His body under her palms, her fingers—his hair, his face, the breadth of his shoulders, the hard muscles of his back and arms and chest—she didn't ever want to stop touching them. It felt like if she stopped, her hands themselves would start to cry.

But she had to, and she knew it. Because the rest of the world was still there. They weren't done yet, damn it, as much as she wanted to be done they weren't, and even as she thought it, she heard a discreet cough and looked up to see Beulah and Lex, their pale faces and pink-rimmed eyes aimed carefully toward the ceiling.

Chapter Thirty-nine

The eyes of the Church are always on you, for you belong to it. Take comfort in that.

—*The Book of Truth*, Laws, Article 1145

Her first instinct was to jump away, but what was the point? They'd seen what they'd seen, and fuck it, it wasn't like they didn't know anyway. Obviously they did.

Besides, she had something more important to say, didn't she? It was still there, something in her head that felt important even though she wasn't sure why. She kept her hand tight in Terrible's and cleared her throat. "I chose you guys. I didn't have to stay but I chose to, because I didn't want to leave you. Any of you."

Lex's brow furrowed. "You right, Tulip? What got you, what was on the happening?"

What did happen? Something about memories, and she'd seen something different, or felt different? She'd had a fuckload of power, she remembered that, she'd felt like she could actually create a whole new life or a huge change or something, but for herself. A new life for herself.

But she couldn't explain that. So she just said, "I had—I could've—I can't explain. But I thought about you guys, all of you, and I chose you."

Even through the thick unhappiness coating their

faces, she thought they looked pleased, and that felt good. At least she could—

Yeah. The good feeling disappeared, replaced by something else she'd almost forgotten. Slobag. Slobag was dead and it was her fault. She was supposed to save him but she hadn't. She'd failed, failed hard-fucking-core, and he was dead.

Another death on her head, on her hands. He could join Brain and Randy, Jia Zhang, the hookers she'd failed to help in time, Bruce Wickman who'd died in the City—along with some of Lex and Terrible's men, also her fault—because she hadn't figured out the Lamaru's plan soon enough to stop the battle from starting.

Now Slobag stood with them, another solemn disapproving face sneering at her from the murkiest depths of her mind.

Another disapproving face she deserved. "I'm sorry. I'm— Shit, I'm so sorry, I had him untied, he was helping me, he was dragging Aros off me and then . . ."

If she were lucky, if she lived in the kind of world where things went smoothly, one of them would interrupt her to fill in the blanks: "Monica shot him," or whatever. But this wasn't that kind of world, not one little bit. They didn't say a word.

She swallowed. Where was her bag? She'd kill for a drink right about then. Oooh, a drink and her Cepts. It sounded like the heaven people used to believe in.

But she had to get the words out first. "Aros was choking me, inside the circle. Really choking me, I couldn't breathe."

Terrible's hand twitched in hers.

"Slobag did something—knocked him on the head or something—and he started to let go. So I could take a breath. He saved me, really." That wasn't entirely true, necessarily, but that didn't matter. He'd certainly helped her, and that mattered and they deserved to know it;

he deserved to have them know it, because they hadn't been able to see anything beyond that glowing purple wall.

"He'd almost pulled Aros off me and I heard the gunshots, and Aros grabbed me again and I saw him fall . . . It was really fast, he didn't feel it. I know he didn't feel it, he was gone before he hit the ground, he wasn't there anymore. He didn't suffer or anything."

Somewhere in the middle of her story Beulah's face had crumpled again. Seeing it, feeling the sadness and pain from across the wide cement floor, felt horrible, made her ill. She didn't want to feel it. She had enough of that already, enough for a lifetime, for two or three—

The screaming in her head—

But she couldn't help it. Well, she could have, but she couldn't. She couldn't because it was her fault Beulah felt it, she was responsible for it. She deserved to feel that pain, too, and she owed it to Beulah—to Beulah and Lex—to feel it along with them.

It was really the least she could do.

The silence felt even better than she'd expected. Almost as good as her pills felt—would feel, when they kicked in. They'd do that any minute, and she couldn't wait.

Meanwhile, she busied herself scooping up the last of the salt ring, dumping the salt along with the herbs into an inert plastic bag to dispose of later. No way was she throwing that stuff into the school's trash. Not when Monica or Aros—or Wen Li—might have taught those kids anything.

"Hello."

She jumped. So much for silence.

Martha Li stood by the hall entry. A respectable distance away, a deferential one. Maybe losing her husband had knocked some of the snot out of her.

That was shitty. The woman *had* just lost her husband. Lost her husband, and probably learned he'd been cheating on her, too. No matter how big a bitch she was—probably was, had seemed to be—she didn't deserve that. Maybe it would be good to give her a break.

"Can I help you with something, Mrs. Li?"

Mrs. Li made a face, one Chess couldn't quite interpret. Anger, sadness, disgust? Maybe a bit of all three.

Whatever it was, her walk was still the stride of an officious woman, one who was used to being obeyed. It wasn't until she got close enough for Chess to see her eyes, see into them, that she slowed, that her steps became uncertain. "I'm wondering how my husband died."

Shit. She'd been afraid of this. Best to just stick to the facts, she guessed. "He was shot."

"Can I—can I see him?"

"I'm sorry, no. Church law." The body had to be buried behind the Church grounds immediately so his grave supplies could be created, then sent to the Crematorium three days later. She didn't think Mrs. Li needed to have the process explained, though.

Mrs. Li nodded. Kept nodding. Like one of those baby dolls with its head on a hinge or something. Or like she was having some sort of spasm. Or maybe she didn't know what else to do, which seemed the most likely.

Wasn't like Chess knew what to do either, but she didn't have the other woman's discomfort. She probably would have, but she had Cepts and the thick velvety rise of them in her stomach up to her chest, that feeling that was both exciting and soothing at the same time.

So she could stand and wait for Mrs. Li to decide what she wanted to say.

"He cheated on me for years. Almost since we got married. I always pretended I didn't know, because . . . it would be so embarrassing to admit I did. To have him punished. To divorce him. Everyone would know then, they would see how I'd failed . . ."

That was not at all what Chess had expected to hear. Wasn't anything she was prepared to answer, either. What was she supposed to say? Sure, that makes sense? I can totally understand why what a bunch of strangers think of you matters more than the fact that your husband treats you like shit? People could be so fucked up sometimes—most of the time—and their priorities even more so.

But Mrs. Li apparently didn't want an answer, or need one. "This time was different, though, with her, with Monica. He was—obsessed with her, I think. Hardly ever home. And when he was, he started . . . He'd get out his old books, notebooks and things, love letters, all of that stuff. From when he was in school. With her."

"With Monica? Chelsea, I mean?"

"With Lucy. I expect you know about that, about him and Lucy, when they were in school. They— I always thought maybe he cheated on me because I wasn't her. And when I couldn't have children, well, that made it even worse. He'd lost the only one he'd ever had."

"What?" Oh, damn, of course. Wen Li was the father of Lucy's baby. Had his obsession with Lucy created the situation? Or had it been Monica—Chelsea? Which had the idea first, when they met up again after all those years?

Did it matter?

Chess had turned in Monica's gun. The labs would be able to determine if her bullet had been the one that killed Wen. Whether it had happened because Monica wanted to be rid of him or because she'd seen the plan was going to fail or, hell, because he'd asked her to, or it had been an accident, she'd never know.

Slobag's body had gone with Lex and Beulah, not that

it mattered. Chess didn't need a lab to tell her which gun took his life.

Better that one was never analyzed.

Mrs. Li's face took on that I-know-something-you-don't-know look Chess hated so much, and found so typical of women like her, women who lived for public opinion. Even in her grief it made her happy to feel like she was in the know or some shit, like she was the important one who had the information. "Lucy was pregnant when she died. You knew that, didn't you?"

"Yes, of course. I just—" What the hell. The case was done, the ghosts were gone, and it didn't matter anyway. It was a side issue. "I thought someone else was the father at first. The teacher."

The ha-ha look disappeared. "Yes. So did I. And then I found this. After Beulah called me, told me he and Monica had both been killed, I—anyway, I found this."

Chess's heart jumped. It couldn't be the— No, of course it wasn't. That notebook, the talisman, had been destroyed. Probably exploded the way Monica had.

But the one Mrs. Li held out to her, in stubby hands with rounded fingernails painted the sickly pink of unhealthy gums, looked just like it. Identical. Wen and Lucy had probably bought them together, wrote notes to each other, or . . .

No. Or not exactly. It was a journal. Wen's journal; but as Chess flipped through it she saw notes in a different hand, a girlish hand. Lucy's, she imagined, and when she read the notes she saw she was right. It wasn't a regular journal, it was notes back and forth. Love letters.

In the beginning, anyway. As it continued, references to other people started slipping in. Other men—well, boys. Boys Wen thought Lucy was too close to. Jealousy and anger dripped off the pages, rose from them like noxious fumes. Bill Pritchard, the drama teacher . . . other names.

The entries got angrier and angrier. Chilling, really. That kind of possessiveness, that kind of need to control . . . Chess had known people like that, grown up with them. They hadn't seen her as a person, just a plaything, something they owned.

"Read the end. The last pages." Mrs. Li's voice barely carried over the sound of shuffling paper.

The last entry was dated April 3, 2001. *Dear Lucy,* blah blah blah . . . Holy shit.

Mrs. Li met her disbelieving stare with a nod, her face sagging more with each one. "I didn't know. I never knew, I never had any idea . . . I never thought he could kill someone. Kill someone he was supposed to love, and let that . . . how can you ever really know someone, if my husband could do that? How can you ever trust someone, commit to them, when they can hide something like that?"

The words chilled Chess even more than the knowledge that Lucy's death hadn't been a suicide. She was murdered. Murdered by Wen Li. Murdered when she suggested they take some time apart, that they think about whether they wanted to keep their baby or give it up for adoption.

He'd killed her, and then he'd written her a letter— several letters—telling her what he'd done and why, blaming her.

Pretty fucking chilling, yeah. But not a surprise. No horrid little bit of madness and evil people cooked up in their sick twisted heads could really surprise her. So Wen Li had killed a girl in a fit of jealous rage, a girl he was supposed to love—probably did love? So how did that make him different from any other person, any other sick fuck pretending to be normal? It didn't.

But that was the scary part. He'd fooled lots of people. He'd fooled his own wife; she'd been a good cover,

Chess figured, to make it look as though he'd gotten over Lucy.

His wife had believed he was a certain person, and he wasn't. She'd believed that he loved her, and he hadn't. He'd hidden all of that from her so completely and fully that even after reading the words in his own handwriting she looked at Chess with a plea in her eyes, begging to hear it wasn't true, that it was some kind of mistake.

But Chess couldn't tell her that.

"I don't know," was what she said. "I'm sorry, Mrs. Li, but I don't know."

Love was full of secrets. Love masked so many evils. Love controlled people, it lied to them, it made them believe things that weren't true and it hid the truth from them. People said love was blind, but what they meant was that love blinded them. It made them more vulnerable than anything else could.

And it felt so fucking good.

Almost like her Cepts, really. Except those didn't lie to her. She'd always known what they were, what they would do to her. Most important, she'd chosen them. She'd gone to them, she'd sought them out. No matter which sack-of-shit "parent" had given them to her in the beginning as a reward, or to keep her quiet, or to stop it hurting so much after they were through with her, she'd still gone to them in the end. She'd made the decision.

She hadn't chosen to fall in love. She hadn't gone looking for it. Hadn't even wanted it. It had just—happened to her, and there it was. That was the worst thing about it. It just happened, and there was nothing she could do about it, and she would never be, could never be, entirely sure it wouldn't go horribly wrong.

All of those thoughts wandered through her head as she bumped up in her car, ducking low so no one could see. They stayed with her as she put away the vial of powder, as she wiped at her numb nose and pulled air hard through her sinuses until it hit the back of her throat with a bitter white rush, as her eyes closed for a second with relief.

The thoughts stayed with her even after the world started to sparkle and shine, as she walked across the Church parking lot and wished she had her sunglasses to protect her eyes from the already-too-bright morning sun. With the rain and storms of the previous night had come a change in the weather; spring wasn't coming anymore, it had come.

It was never spring in her head, in her soul. The contrast between what happened outside and what happened inside was almost a physical ache.

But the Church building comforted her, at least a little, when she entered the huge pale-blue hall with its frieze of ghostly faces and forms done in dark wood near the ceiling. Her skin tingled faintly from the energy, a nice complement to the rush already in her system. Part of her wanted to sit down on one of the long, low benches by the door and just *be,* just sit and feel the way her cheeks tightened and created a smile, the way her blood zipped through her veins like it was on its way to a party.

But she couldn't. Especially not since more of her fellow employees, more Elders and Goodys, would be arriving any second and they'd probably wonder what the hell she was doing if she just sat there by the door grinning. She'd look—well, she'd look fucking high, was how she'd look, and that wouldn't be a good idea at all.

So instead she entered Elder Griffin's office when he responded to her knock, exchanged the usual greetings, and sat down in the cushy chair opposite his desk. The cool herb-scented air caressing her skin felt wonderful. The room, always her favorite in the building, looked even more charming on that particular morning, with its globe and shelves of skulls.

"So." Elder Griffin sat down, folded his hands on his desk. "It was indeed a haunting. But a summoned one."

She nodded. In her bag sat the report she'd completed in the school library before she left. She pulled it out and handed it to him, along with Wen Li's high school diary. "Lucy's murder wasn't a suicide, either. Wen Li murdered her. It's in there—he wrote about it."

Elder Griffin's brows drew together, a subtle expression of distaste. "And he brought her back as well? You said on the phone he'd died when you went to retrieve that talisman?"

"Yeah, I mean yes, he died, but I don't know whose idea it was originally, to bring Lucy back. Monica—Chelsea—was her cousin, she would have been helpful in the summoning, since she had some power and the same blood and everything, and Lucy's possessions. I don't know which one of them came up with the idea, though. Maybe Aros will, if he . . . if he survives."

He nodded, took a piece of paper from his desk and handed it to her. "You were correct about the drugs, as well. Elder Lyle said the amount of Vapezine in his blood was three or four times what would be found with normal dosages. We're fairly certain that it started after he was assigned the case. Of course, we know Bill Pritchard was intimate with Monica, and that he prescribed the medication, so . . ."

"She seduced him into giving Aros the drugs. And after he'd served his purpose and made Aros insane, she killed him."

Elder Griffin nodded.

"Will Aros recover?" she asked.

"That we do not know. He may. But he may pass on."

Her turn to nod. That made her realize she'd been tapping her heel on the carpet, bouncing her knee, since she'd sat down; speed-fidgets in full swing. She could kill for a cigarette, too. And a— Oh, at least she had some water. She tugged the bottle from her bag, took a hopefully normal-looking drink. So much better.

"Wen's wife didn't know," she said. The words popped out of her mouth so fast, so unplanned, that it took her a second to realize she'd said them. "They'd been married for almost twenty years and she didn't know he was a murderer, she never even guessed. He cheated on her all the time and he wasn't very nice to her, but she stayed with him, and she didn't even know him really. And all she got out of it was—was being hurt."

He was silent for a minute, while she forced herself not to get up and run. Yeah, speed made her talky, but for fuck's sake. What the hell was the point of even bringing that up? Who the fuck cared?

"If I may ask, Cesaria, has there been a resolution to your . . . situation?"

Shit. She'd hoped he wouldn't ask about that. A stupid hope, sure—weren't most?—but a hope nonetheless. "Oh, um . . . we talked. We ran into each other yesterday, and we talked."

"A good talk?"

Her fingernails had never interested her so much. "I guess so, yeah."

"And you feel better?"

She nodded. Might as well tell him; he'd ask anyway. She watched her toes wiggle inside her shoes. "We're, he still wants to be with me, so . . ."

The light filtering through the sheer curtains on the window behind his head was too bright; it made it hard to see his face, turned him into a gold-edged silhouette. But she thought he was smiling.

Well, of course he was. He wasn't the one sitting there being sliced open and inspected.

Or maybe normal people—people not like her—

didn't mind talking about this stuff. Even liked it. Normal people actually wanted to talk about themselves, to toss their guts on the table before them and invite others to pick through the mess. It made them feel important.

It made her queasy.

He leaned forward. "Perhaps an act like murder causes people to make mistakes. Perhaps they feel that mistake in themselves constantly, and replay it, seeking to correct it somehow by doing to others what was done to them, or by accepting behavior they themselves performed in the past."

Where was he going with this? She tried to arrange her features into an "of course I totally understand" sort of expression, but if he had a point, if he planned to actually tell her anything, he was picking a very strange and convoluted way of doing so.

Unless of course she was just speeding half out of her mind and wouldn't have understood a kiddie story at that particular moment. Which was far more likely.

"I also believe that any action can . . . leave a scar on the soul, the sort of scar that always causes discomfort. Perhaps Wen Li had such a scar, and perhaps it covered the parts of himself that would have permitted him to be a faithful husband."

Oh, fuck. If that was the case, she was fucking doomed. She had nothing but scars; she *was* a scar.

"And perhaps there are people out there who sense those scars in others and want to heal them. That's why they're there. Or perhaps there are other people with similar scars, and they understand each other. Perhaps they aren't even scars, but traits. Perhaps people don't understand what they feel, or lie to themselves."

This was just getting cheerier by the second, wasn't it? What the hell was he trying to do to her?

"I'm digressing a bit, and I apologize. My point, my dear, is that there is no guarantee in the world. But I believe 'tis better to take the chance, even if we later fail, than to never try. I believe the joy is worth it. That is my feeling."

That sounded familiar, didn't it? Rang a bell somewhere in the back of her head. Not the Tennyson quote about loving and losing, but something else. Something . . . She didn't know. The memory slipped away from her even as she tried to grasp it.

He seemed to be waiting for her to say something, hoping she would. What was she supposed to say, though? She'd already bugged him enough. She knew he liked her, sure, but liking her didn't mean he'd want to sit there while she whined.

Finally he cleared his throat, sat up straighter in his chair, changing the atmosphere. "Do you, by any chance, have the recommendation for me?"

"I do." She dug into her bag to get it, finished just that morning at a desk in the school office. "Let me know if it's not okay. I didn't really know what I was supposed to say."

"I'm certain it's very good." He skimmed it, but thankfully didn't stop to read the whole thing. Instead he just set it down. "Thank you."

She nodded, and with relief and sadness mingling in her chest, stood up. Relief because she could go. Sadness because . . . well, she didn't really know, but it was there just the same.

He watched her, his blue eyes kind as always. "I expect you'll be taking the rest of the day off?"

"I'd like to, yes."

"Good. See you tomorrow, then. Facts are Truth."

"Facts are Truth." She curtsied without really paying attention to what she was doing, headed for the door.

"Cesaria."

Her hand rested on the doorknob, cool beneath her palm. It felt great. "Yes?"

His mouth opened, closed again. She braced herself for another question.

But it didn't come. Instead he just sort of nodded and tilted his head to the side, like he was making some kind of decision. "Get some rest."

Beulah waited for her, leaning against her car, smoking and staring. Sadness radiated from her still form, came to Chess on the soft warm breeze, stronger with every step she took.

"Hey," she said finally. Black smudges hung below her eyes; she looked almost as if she'd lost weight in the few hours since she'd left the parking garage, her skin somehow tighter on her bones.

Chess's heart sank all the way down into the empty pit that had once been her stomach. Even her high couldn't keep her from feeling it; even her high couldn't protect her from the question she knew Beulah was there to ask. The question Chess would give almost anything to not have to answer.

Especially not after her discussion with Elder Griffin in there. She already felt raw. Not bad—she had too many drugs in her to feel bad, though she could definitely use a bump—but like she'd talked too much. Or rather talked about herself too much.

At least she could smoke, though.

"You look tired," she said. Where was Lex? She figured he would have come along, figured he'd want to know, too. "Why aren't you sleeping?"

Beulah must have seen her curiosity. "Lex has a lot of stuff to do."

"Oh?"

"Well, he's in charge now, I mean, there were . . ."

Beulah kept talking. Chess knew she was talking because she saw her lips move, but she didn't hear what Beulah said. She just heard "He's in charge now" over and over, like an echo chamber made by someone with a really sick sense of humor.

If she hadn't been so distracted she would have figured it out herself, would have realized. But she hadn't really had a second to think about Slobag and his death. Or, more accurately, she hadn't wanted to think about it, so she hadn't.

But Lex was in charge now. It wasn't Slobag's side of town anymore, it was Lex's. They weren't Slobag's men anymore, they were Lex's.

Which meant Terrible and Lex weren't just enemies anymore. They were at war. And they probably wouldn't stop fighting until one of them was dead—Lex would probably go after Bump first, of course, but without Terrible, Bump's power would be considerably less. Nobody else scared people as much as he did, had the kind of reputation he did.

Lex wasn't going to sit back and be half-assed about it either, not like his father had been. She knew him well enough to know that. Just like she knew—had always known, really—that the fires were his idea, not his father's.

Fuck. She'd failed to save Slobag's life, and in doing so she'd brought her own life that much closer to utter destruction. And she hadn't had that far to go in the first place.

"Chess? Are you okay?"

"What? Oh, yeah, sorry, I kind of drifted. What were you saying?"

Hurt flashed across Beulah's face, so fast Chess couldn't be certain she'd seen it. "I— Are you going home now?"

"Yeah. And so should you. You need some sleep."

"I will, I just . . . what do I tell them, at the school? They're going to want to know what happened, and I don't know what it's okay to tell them."

That was totally not the question Chess thought she was going to ask. Not at all. It wasn't a bad question, either. "You can tell them it was Monica and Wen, sure. It'd be good if you didn't mention that Aros summoned the ghosts, I mean, I'd really appreciate—"

"I had the gun." The words came out fast, in a flat monotone. "I had the gun because I was standing farther to the right, I could see around the circle. And I was shooting. He got hit on the left side, which way was he facing? I don't know—you didn't say, and I thought, you would have said if it had been her, but you didn't say, and I need to know, I— I want to know the truth, so could you tell me please? I really need to know."

There it was.

Chess looked at Beulah, at her puffy bloodshot eyes and pale skin, at the grayish T-shirt and jeans she wore, the flip-flops on her feet. She wanted the truth, she said. And Chess's duty was to tell it. Truth mattered, Truth was Fact and Facts were solid and concrete. The world was built on them. They were necessary.

But the other Truth she knew was the sound of Beulah's screams echoing off the cement, the bullets wasted on her grief. That too was a Truth. And that one felt more important.

So she gave Beulah her eyes, put as much warmth into them as she could, as much honesty, as much . . . as much of herself as she could. "It was Monica. He was facing the outside of the garage, she hit him in the left side. Her side of the circle. You didn't shoot him."

Beulah's eyes closed; her entire body sagged with relief. "I was so . . . I thought maybe . . . fuck."

Should she touch her arm or something? Or just leave her be? If it was her, she'd want herself to leave; if it was her, she'd feel sick and horrible about talking even as much as Beulah had.

So she reached out an awkward hand, patted Beulah on the shoulder once, twice. "It wasn't you. It wasn't."

Another thought came to her then, too. "You know, if you ever want—and Lex, if he wants to come—I can get you in to meet with a Liaiser, you could talk to him again. If you want to. It's usually pretty expensive but . . . I can get you in if you want. Just let me know."

Beulah sniffled. "Thanks. I don't know if . . . Thanks, though."

Chess didn't know what to say next; there didn't seem to be anything to say. It was always strange when a case ended, when suddenly people who'd been among the main focuses of her life became unimportant again, people she didn't know and wouldn't see again.

But Beulah was different. How big a part she might continue to play remained to be seen, but she was Lex's sister, and if Lex stayed in Chess's life, so would Beulah.

"I have to go," she said finally. "I need to get some rest, and so do you, so . . ."

"Right. Okay, well—"

Before Chess could stop her, before she even knew what was happening, Beulah leaned forward and wrapped her arms around her. Hugged her. Tight.

Chess's hands were in her pockets; she pulled them out, rested them on Beulah's back. When was the last time someone had hugged her, someone other than Lex or Terrible? She couldn't remember.

She let it go on longer than she was comfortable with, longer than she would have any other time—Beulah had just lost her father, she could have an extra minute of hug—before she finally pulled away. "Hey, um, I've really got to go, I'm sorry. And you should get some sleep."

Why did people say that? Like it made anything better. Chess couldn't remember a single situation in her life that had ever been improved by sleep. Sure, maybe it made her feel better physically, but so did her pills. Too bad all of her problems were still there when she woke up.

But it seemed like the thing to say, so she said it, and thankfully Beulah nodded. "Yeah, you too. And thanks for telling me, about Monica being the one. And for . . . Thanks."

"Sure."

They both stood there for an awkward minute, not talking. Like something wasn't finished, but Chess didn't know what it could be.

She pulled her keys out of her bag to give her an excuse to look away. "Okay, well, tell Lex hi for me, and I guess I'll talk to him soon, I mean, I assume I will, I don't know . . ."

Holy fuck. She didn't know. She had no idea at that moment if she'd ever talk to Lex again. He knew everything; no more suspicions, he *knew*.

She didn't think he'd cut her out entirely. But their . . . their friendship, their relationship . . . it would be different now, wouldn't it? More different than it had become when she'd stopped sleeping with him, the kind of different they could never go back from.

"I'm sure you will," Beulah replied. "Hear from him. You know Lex."

"Yeah." She smiled. "I guess I do."

Terrible was asleep when she got to his place. That was a disappointment; she'd hoped he'd wait up for her. But then, if she hadn't been snorting speed all morning she probably would have gone to sleep, too. Especially since she'd left the parking garage to fill out reports, whereas he'd gone out to find Bernam and show him what happened to spies and snitches in Downside.

Which she guessed he had. Even in the faint light seeping in from under the blackout curtains on his windows, she could see new scrapes and cuts on his hands and forearms, new bruises that hadn't been there when he'd left her that morning. When she went into the bathroom to splash clean water on her face, she saw his shirts soaking in cold water dark red with blood.

She guessed she'd find out later. Later he could tell her the story, if he wanted to; she didn't always ask about that stuff, but maybe she should. Maybe he wanted her to ask. Just like he always asked what happened in her work.

Lex had given her a dozen Oozers with the rest of her pills. Excellent. She grabbed two of them, washed them down with the last of her water, and slipped off her clothes.

He stirred when she climbed between the sheets. "Hey. You right?"

She nodded, lifted her head so he could get his arm under it, rested her cheek on his chest so she could hear the slow steady beat of his heart. "Right up, yeah, just . . . a hell of a day."

"Aye, it were."

She ran her hand over his chest, enjoying the feel of his skin against hers. Laid her leg over his so she could feel that too. "I'm glad it's over."

Pause. "Aye, me too. Ain't . . . ain't so much like thinkin of you goin over there, if you dig, not now. Gonna be some shit changing."

"Lex."

"Ain't got the thought he planning a hang-back, get heself some time. Come out right, aye."

Her fingers curled into the hair on his chest. "Yeah. I know."

"I dig iffen you're wanting to stay out, Chessie. I ain't gonna ask you put yourself inside. But . . . shit."

She swallowed. She knew what he was really asking, what he was really saying. That he was trying to trust her, that he did trust her, but that he needed reassurance. And fuck, who didn't? Not her. How much of the pain she'd been through in the last week had been because of her own need to be reassured, and the fact that she wasn't as brave as he was, hadn't been able to make herself ask?

Which was especially stupid because he would tell her. He would tell her anytime she asked.

The Oozers were starting to hit; good thing, too, because fear dried her mouth and made the words stick a little in her throat. She didn't think she'd be able to say them without the high; didn't think she could ever say anything without it, if she were honest.

"I'm not . . . I don't know if . . ." Shit. She was fucking it up. "The thing is, you were right. I didn't trust you, I mean, I wanted to but I didn't. It's really—it's just kind of hard to believe that you actually do want . . ."

How much worse could she make all of this? "But I'm trying, I want to try, because I want to be with you. I really, really do. And I don't know if it's what you want or, I'm not very good at this, but I'm yours. I mean . . . that's it. If you want me to be. There's, um, there's nothing, no other people or anything, that really matter. Just you. And I do trust you. I do."

He watched her, his dark eyes focused on hers, his face completely immobile. She wasn't doing it right, obviously. The sound of her own voice was starting to panic her, making her face feel hot and damp, making her legs yearn to jump out of the bed and run away.

"Shit, Terrible, I don't know how to do this, I'm sorry I'm fucking it up, I wish I could do it right. But if you were wondering, you know, like if you weren't sure or whatever . . . I belong to you. If you want me. I do. And I never did before, to anybody else."

Something in his eyes then, something she wanted to believe was a good thing but her own were so blurry and wet at that point she couldn't tell. Her face slid from uncomfortably warm to hot; she couldn't look him in the eyes anymore.

"Please say something. I'm sorry, I'm, never mind, we can just forget I said anything, okay? Just forget it, don't worry about it—"

"Ain't thinkin I wanna forget." He shifted to face her and pulled her closer with his left arm so she was tucked into his chest, half-under him. "Maybe you oughta gimme that again."

More panic. He had something now, he had something to use against her, something he could— No.

No, she would not let herself think that. She trusted him with her life; had trusted him with it more than once. She'd just told him she belonged to him.

But she wouldn't, really, not if she couldn't trust him with all of her. If she wanted to say she was his and mean it—and she did—she needed to trust him like that. She owed him that.

So she took a deep breath, glad she wasn't speeding so much anymore, glad she could look him in the eyes and really feel it. "Even if it's not what you want, I'm yours."

Now she did see the change in him, saw the slow smile start, the one that always made her feel so good because she could make it appear. "Always want you, Chessiebomb. Always."

He kissed her, slow and tender, like she mattered. Because she did, at least to him. And she thought she might even be able to believe it.

No, nothing was guaranteed in life. She'd always known that. She'd always had to fight, always had to struggle. She'd always had to be alone.

The fighting and struggling wouldn't stop. Would never stop. Thinking of the coming weeks and months, of what an all-out war between Bump and Lex might mean, sent a cold chill from her head all the way to her toes.

Having a fight with Terrible, having him decide he didn't love her anymore . . . she'd always known those weren't the only ways she could lose him—not after she'd seen him shot on the pavement--but the threat seemed more real than ever. She couldn't bear to think of it. Didn't want to think of anyone dying, either of the men she cared about. That she loved one and simply liked the other didn't change that.

But she could worry about it later, think about it later. Because at that moment Terrible's hands were caressing her, caressing her body that belonged to him, and just thinking it made her heart pound. She belonged to someone. She belonged to him and he belonged to her the same way, and she'd never had that before, and her last real thought before she gave herself over completely was that she would do whatever she had to do to keep it.

She just hoped it wouldn't come to that.

CHASING MAGIC

All of the documents were in place: The Affidavit of Spectral Fraud, the Statement of Truth, two Orders of Imprisonment and two Orders of Relinquishment, and, of course, the list of Church-approved attorneys. The Darnells would want that—well, they'd need it, because they were about to be arrested for faking a haunting.

At least, they would be when the Black Squad got there to back Chess up. She didn't always want the Squad to come along; police presence tipped people off, made things more difficult, and most people came pretty quietly once they realized they were busted, anyway. The Darnells didn't seem like the come-quietly type, though. Something told Chess they weren't going to take this well.

But she'd told them she'd be there at six, and it was five past already and their curtains kept twitching. They knew she was there.

Right. She'd taken a couple of Cepts before leaving her apartment in Downside, so they were just starting to hit—smooth, thick, narcotic warmth spreading from her stomach out through the rest of her body, a pleasant softness settling over her mind.

That was the best thing about the drugs, really; she could still think, still be coherent, still use her brain. She just didn't have to if she didn't want to, and it was so much easier to keep that brain from wandering into all those places she didn't want it to go.

And she had so fucking many of those places.

She grabbed the Darnell file from her bag, locked her car, and started walking along the cobblestone path to the front door, weaving around the flowers and plants scattered like islands across the impossibly green sea of grass. Bees made their way from bloom to bloom, doing whatever the hell it was bees did. Oh, sure, she knew it was something to do with pollen or whatever. She just didn't give a shit.

By the time she reached the porch, sweat beaded along her forehead and her body felt damp. Summer sucked. Only the middle of June and already it was scorching.

Brandon Darnell opened the door before she'd finished raising her hand to knock. "Miss Putnam. You're late."

Asshole. She faked a smile. "Sorry. Traffic."

At least they had air-conditioning.

The entire Darnell family sat in the pretentious high-ceilinged living room, slouching on the ridiculously overpriced suede couch and chairs that were partly responsible for the enormous debt they were in. Debt they'd planned to clear by faking a haunting and getting a nice fat settlement from the Church of Real Truth.

Too bad for them, the Church wasn't stupid—being in charge of everyone and everything on earth for twenty-four years proved that—and had contingency plans for such things. Chess was one of them.

Brandon Darnell indicated an empty chair along the back wall. "Have a seat."

Alarms started ringing in Chess's head. He seemed a little too calm, a little too . . . cheerful.

But all the other chairs were full, so she sat, shooting another glance out the window to see if the Squad had arrived yet. Nope. Damn it!

The Darnells sat there, unmoving. Just watching her. Because that wasn't creepy at all.

Mrs. Darnell—frowsy, bad perm, blue eyeshadow up to her brows—showed her perfect white teeth in what passed for a smile. "Do you have any news for us? When will you Banish the ghost?"

Chess's phone beeped—a text. A text from the Black Squad, thank fuck; they were almost there. Good. She didn't have to sit around wasting time with these people.

"I do have news." She pulled the forms from the file. "This is my Statement of Truth, copies of which I've already filed with the Church. This one is for you to sign. It's the Affidavit of Spectral Fraud, which is basically your confession, and this one—"

"What the hell are you talking about? We haven't committed any fraud, there's no—"

"Mr. Darnell." Normally she'd stand up for this part, but what the hell. The chair was pretty comfortable. "I found, and photographed, the projectors set up in the attic. I won't bother to point out to you where the holes in the ceiling are, since you already know. The 'ectoplasm' on your walls has been analyzed—twice, for confirmation—as a mixture of cornstarch, gelatin, iridescent paint, and water."

She waited for a response, and didn't get one. Good. "I also have pictures of the portable air conditioner you set up beneath the house—that's another crime, by the way, putting anything underground, but I imagine you know that—to fake sudden changes in temperature. One of my hidden cameras caught you breaking the mirrors yourself, and another one caught very clearly you and Mrs. Darnell discussing your crimes."

Mr. and Mrs. Darnell looked guilty. Their children—Cassie and Curtis, how cute—looked confused. Chess directed her next comments to them.

"I have two Orders of Relinquishment here. You two are going to be taken to the Church with your parents, but when they go into prison, you'll be moving in with another family member or, failing that, a home will be found for you. You'll be safe there."

She could only hope that last line was true. It hadn't been for her. None of those "homes" she'd been sent to had been safe—or at least no more than a couple of them.

But that had been a long time ago. That had been before the Church was really settled. That had been a mistake; she was an anomaly—or something—and it only mattered in her memories.

Because the Church had saved her. They'd taken her out of that life and given her a new one. The Church had found her and made her into something real.

The two children looked at each other, looked at Chess, looked at their parents. What was the expression on their faces? Shocked, curious? Chess couldn't quite seem to read it.

She squeezed her eyes shut, opened them again. Shit, she didn't usually have problems like this from her pills. And no way had she gotten a bad batch; Lex had given her those, and Lex might be in charge of the Downside gang in direct opposition to the one Chess's . . . Chess's *everything* worked for, but Lex wouldn't try to do her any harm. She knew that. Lex was her friend.

So what the fuck?

Her eyes itched, too; she raised her hand to rub at them. Struggled to raise it, actually. In fact, she'd been sitting still for a few minutes, hadn't she? Without moving.

The room started to rock around her, as if she and the Darnells sat on the deck of a ship in stormy waters. Nausea slithered through her stomach, up her throat.

Her skin tingled. Not her skin, actually. Her tattoos—runes and sigils inscribed into her skin with magic-imbued ink by the Church—tingled. The way they always did in the presence of ghosts . . . or in the presence of magic.

It took forever to turn her head to the left, on a neck that felt like it was being squeezed by strong, hard hands she couldn't see. Who was . . . fuck, someone was casting some kind of spell on her; who was it, what was it?

She couldn't tell. Couldn't see well enough to tell—just a shape, a spot of darker shadow in the long hallway. But whatever it was—it felt like a man, she had enough presence of mind to know that—it was powerful, it was strong, and it was about to beat her.

Something inside her struggled. The noise of the Darnells shouting faded, faded like a stiff wind had come up and was blowing them all away. The adult Darnells yelling, cackling; the young Darnells panicked and confused.

And over it all the words of power were beginning to seep into her consciousness, spoken in a deep smooth voice like smoked glass. Smoked glass with jagged edges; she'd cut herself on them, they'd slice into her skin and her blood would spill out onto the floor, staining the carpet the Darnells couldn't pay for. Staining everything except her soul; that was filthy enough already, covered with grime and pain that would never go away no matter how many pills she took or lines she snorted.

But she didn't want to go. Not just because she was afraid of the City of Eternity, either. Everyone else thought the enormous cavern below the earth where the spirits of the dead lived on forever was peaceful, beautiful. Only Chess knew what it really was: cold and horrible and terrifying.

That wasn't the point, though. As her breath came shorter and shallower, as the black edge around her vision thickened until she could see only tiny spots of the room around her, all she could really think about was Terrible. The only man in the world who made her feel . . . like she was okay, like she could be happy. The only one who understood her. The only one who loved her.

The only one, period.

She would not leave him. She refused to leave him.